LOVEBOAT FOREVER

LOVEBOAT FOREVER

ABIGAIL HING WEN

An Imprint of HarperCollinsPublishers

HarperTeen is an imprint of HarperCollins Publishers.

Library of Congress Control Number: 2023933505
ISBN 978-0-06-329799-9

Typography by Corina Lupp
23 24 25 26 27 LBC 5 4 3 2 1
First Edition

For my parents

1

CHAGRIN FALLS, OHIO

The white envelope that drops through our mail slot is the size and heft of a magazine. Or a music book of piano sonatas, which have often found their way through that same slot. But I know it's not either this time. I swoop down on it as the metal flap slaps shut. A bass drum has replaced my chest, pounding out my heartbeats to a metronome on overdrive.

"Mom! It's here!" I yell.

At this weight, it can't be a rejection letter, can it? No. No, it can't. But months of anticipating, dreading its arrival . . . and I can't muster the courage to open the package just yet. I run my thumb over the gold embossed monogram that stands for Apollo Summer Youth Symphony.

Old-fashioned, elegant. You can practically smell the generations of excellence—centuries of tradition—wafting off the heavy paper stock.

Okay, go time. "Please, please, please, please, please!" I whisper a fervent prayer—and rip it open.

Mom hurries into the foyer from the kitchen, drying her hands on her blue-apple-print apron.

"*Dear Ms. Wong, we are delighted—*Oh my God! I'm in!" I fling my arms around Mom's frail neck, almost knocking her over—and sending her bifocals clattering to the floor. "I got in! I got in!"

I recover her glasses, which she returns to the tip of her nose. She reads, "*We are delighted to admit you to this year's class.* Oh, honey. You worked so hard for this!" Her brown eyes shine as she wraps her arms around me, then pulls back to look me in the eyes. "You deserve this, Pearl. I'm so proud of you."

I can barely believe it. Two months ago, nine judges listened to me play my heart out on a Steinway piano in the Hunter College auditorium, and at least six of them decided my music was good enough to make the cut. At least six of them were pleased.

"They only take a hundred kids from the *entire country*." I scan the roster of names that form a pair of elegant columns on their own page. With a thrill, I recognize a few heavy hitters from performances I've played in over the years.

"I'm the only pianist, which means . . ." I page through to my repertoire, the songs I'm assigned to play for the concert series at the summer's end. "I'm playing the Mozart Concerto in D Minor!" His darker concerto, written later in his tragically short life. It's incredible—the contrast of light, sweet notes with the darker raging ones, bound together into three movements, thirty minutes in length. And I'll play it accompanied by the full symphonic orchestra, before an auditorium of 2,738 seats at Lincoln Center in New York!

My head is fogging over. Pink clouds of happiness obscure

any rational thought. There are too many words on the pages I'm gripping. Big ones that in this moment I'm too ecstatic to comprehend. I shove the papers into Mom's hands.

"Read the rest," I beg. "Tell me if this is real."

She scans the pages while I storm up and down the living room. I can't focus on anything. *Calm down. Take notice of the things around you. Breathe.*

I inhale, then a looooong exhale. Okay. Blue curtains, blue couches, blue carpet. God, everything is blue. How did I not notice that before? I pause before Mom's collection of brass miniatures—a piano, a grandfather clock, an iron. I pick up a tiny park bench, with three words engraved on its backrest: *thankful grateful blessed.*

Yes. I squeeze it in my hand. *Yes.*

"I peeled you a grapefruit!" Mom says, her eyes still on the papers. "Eat some."

Food always comes first in our family. Feeding me semi-non-stop is her equivalent of *love you, kiddo.* I set down the miniature and head for the kitchen, where Mom's big blue bowl of citrus sits on the counter. But I can't eat. A *concerto.* Most piano pieces are written for solo performance, which is one of the reasons it can be such a lonely instrument to dedicate your life to. But a *concerto.* It's a piano solo *with the entire symphonic orchestra in a semicircle behind you, playing along*—a hundred strings, woodwinds, brass, and percussion. It's the opportunity of a lifetime! One my dad helped me work toward and cheered me on to so faithfully, until he passed away two years ago.

Mom is opening a small box left on our doorstep as I return. She removes a glass globe on a velvet stand. Inside it floats a tiny grand piano and golden words Apollo Summer Youth Symphony. I weigh it in my hands.

"It's beautiful," I breathe. "And, oh my gosh, I'll be in New York! I'll get to spend time with Ever!" My older sister, who works as a choreographer for the New York City Ballet. She's twenty-four to my seventeen. We're super close, but since she left home for college, we haven't had nearly as much time together as I wish we did. And now, we'll have the whole summer!

Mom waves the papers. "Everyone is performing three times during the festival week in August. You're playing a solo, a piano-violin duo, and . . ." She starts to sob uncontrollably.

"Mom, what's wrong?" I grip her arm and hand her a tissue from the box. "You're not doing that thing where you get over-invested and my successes become yours, *are you*?" I tease her gently.

She dashes her hand over her eyes. "Your dad would be so proud of you."

My throat aches. Yes. He was the one who discovered Apollo online a few years ago: *What a fantastic program. If you can get in, Pearl. It will change your life!* I wish he were here to celebrate with us, pushing his thick glasses closer to his face and squeezing my hand in his worn ones. We've had happy moments since we lost him, but the happy is always constricted by the vacuum he left behind.

Mom sniffs noisily. "I was remembering, just this morning, that time we were detained at the Canadian border trying to come back home here. You were only a baby. The way they looked at us. So suspicious. I remember your father and I saying then, 'My God, this country will never accept us.'" She clasps the Apollo papers to her heart. "And now, I know we were wrong.

4

They *have* accepted us. Thanks to you, and your sister, and all your hard work. I just wish he *knew*."

"Oh, Mom." I hug her tight, tucking her graying head under my chin. She and Dad moved to the United States over twenty-five years ago. All these years later, I didn't know she felt this way about my music performances. Maybe Dad did, too. In this moment, I feel the same, looking at the official gold emblem on the page. Apollo Summer Youth Symphony. This is *legitimacy*.

After so many years of standing on the outside, gazing longingly in, I've been invited to the club.

"Congratulations, Pearl," my manager, Julie Winslow, says on FaceTime later that day. Her dark-blond hair is twisted into her usual chignon, and her ice-blue eyes, framed by long mascaraed lashes, crinkle with her broad smile. "You earned this. I'm so proud of you."

"Thank you," I say. Julie signed me a few years ago and walks on water; praise from her is hard-won. "I have one solo song to decide on. I thought, maybe—"

I chew on my bottom lip, unsure whether to continue. I recently ran into a beautiful and complex modern piece on YouTube by a composer no one's ever heard of. Chaotic but organized rhythms that didn't restrict themselves to the eighty-eight keys but also came from drumming on the piano cover and even plucking the strings inside. But would Julie go for it?

"Play the Rachmaninoff," Julie says. "Incredibly technically difficult. It shows off your abilities to the fullest. The reviewers will take note. I'll arrange for the accompanying pianist."

I exhale. It's the composer's hardest piece, going from a trickle of notes to a finger-twisting torrent that plumbs the depths of human emotion. One of Dad's favorites, and I do love it, too. I push down the whisper of disappointment—drumming on a piano would be gimmicky anyway. I'm grateful for her guidance in a world I'm learning to navigate.

"Sounds perfect, Julie." I set Apollo's glass globe on my piano where I can see it as I play. "I'll get to work."

I've been hooked on music since I was four and Dad played me Leonard Bernstein's recording of *Peter and the Wolf* by Prokofiev, with all the ways animals could be imitated by strings and woodwinds. Then there was Mozart's opera *The Magic Flute*; the very idea was delicious. Songs are how I experience the world: they lure me into secret gardens and stormy rivers. Piano was also my bonding time with Dad, who sat with me, first to help me with my dyslexia, which made it hard to read the music, and later, to keep me company. He was always positive, even when my fingers wouldn't cooperate with my ears. Even now, every time I sit down at the piano, I still imagine his gentle, encouraging presence beside me. *You can do this, Pearl.* Piano doubles as my way of staying close to him, and I'm so thankful I have it.

Mom and I make the half-hour trip to Cleveland to splurge on an updated headshot with a professional photographer. We're used to spending hours in the car together driving to my music events.

Probably why she and I have a closer relationship than she and Ever do.

Ever had it rough—she was the one who broke the mold. She paved the way for me by choosing dance as a profession. At the time, my parents thought the only viable career path was medical school, until she showed them the trail she was blazing for herself.

And after Dad passed away, for better or worse, Mom lost a lot of her will to fight us.

Pierre, our photographer, has a head full of wild brown curls and a studio bursting with Renaissance paintings. I feel the Apollo aura shining on me as he positions me standing and seated. He tugs my purple beret over my left brow for a dramatic effect and smooths my long black hair down my back.

"*Magnifique!*" he says. "*Vous êtes très belle.* Very beautiful."

"Take one of my mom," I say, tugging at her arm.

"Oh no." Mom blushes, something I've never seen her do, and runs a hand through the graying leaves of her hair. "I'm too old for photos."

"No you're not." I guide her to the backdrop. "The red background is perfect with your skin tone. And it's just for us anyway."

She protests, but when Pierre lifts his camera, she smiles.

Afterward, we sip sparkling water and pore over our glossy images on his screen. "You look so pretty," I say to Mom.

"It turned out okay, didn't it?" she says, embarrassed but obviously pleased. She flips to the next image of me: gazing over my shoulder and backdropped by plum blossoms at night. "I like your smile."

My beret is like a cloud floating over my head. I fell in love with berets in middle school French class, and they've sort of become my signature piece on social media. Beneath its soft fabric, my black hair tumbles down my shoulders, framing glowing cheeks and mysterious dark eyes. My body, which has always been heavier than I'd like, looks surprisingly good in my black concert dress.

"I look like a movie star," I say, dazed.

"Maybe you will be one someday. A star!" Mom says, and I just laugh.

A few days later, I email my glammed-up photo to Maude Tanner, the Apollo administrator, who I envision as a grandmotherly white-haired woman.

"Thank you, Pearl!" she responds immediately. "We look forward to seeing you soon."

I feel a thrill deep inside me.

Mom contacts the *World Journal*, the largest Chinese language newspaper in North America. They profiled my debut at Carnegie Hall when I was thirteen, all of which sounds more impressive than it actually is these days. They tell Mom they're interested in doing a piece on me attending Apollo, so she arranges for an interview the day before I leave.

Two weeks before the program kicks off, Apollo sends me an update: their website for the summer program is live.

"Mom, it's up!" I rush into the living room, and Mom joins me on the couch. We scroll through on my laptop: The daily rehearsal schedule is packed but exciting. The final performances, including solos and ensembles in smaller halls, are all day Saturday, August 11. Mom will fly in from Ohio, and it will be a chance for her to see Ever, which is always at the forefront of her thoughts.

Last but not least, we scroll through the musicians, savoring them. It's a virtual hall of fame, with classes from the 1980s to present day: eighty musicians between the ages of fifteen and eighteen, hailing from Hawaii to Maine and Seattle to Boston. Marie Smit draws her bow across her violin strings. Geoff Pavloski plays a marimba, two mallets gripped in each hand.

At the end of the alphabet, I come to my airbrushed headshot: Pearl Wong, concert pianist.

"I'm not dreaming," I say. I scan the bio. Words leap out at me. Beautiful ones: *Known for her effortlessly expressive playing, Pearl Wong has a command of the piano well beyond her youthful years. She plays with her entire body and soul, bringing audiences with her.* Um, wow. Are they talking about me?"

"He's very nice-looking. Good hair." Mom points to a Korean American flutist. "There are only three Asians," she notes.

"I'm Asian *American*," I correct her. "They might be, too." But she's right about the numbers. Besides the cute flutist, there's an Indian American cellist . . . and me. I click on my name and arrive at a page with my repertoire:

| **L. van Beethoven** | Piano and Violin Sonata no. 9, op. 14, |
| 1770–1827 | no. 1 |

| **W. A. Mozart** | Piano Concerto no. 20 in D Minor, K. 466 |
| 1756–1791 | (with orchestra) |

| **S. Rachmaninoff** | Piano Concerto no. 3 in D Minor, op. 30 |
| 1873–1943 | (with piano orchestral reduction) |

I close my laptop. It's real. *Dad, I'm really in.* My throat swells. I can barely choke out the big truth in all of this: "I'm so lucky they took me."

I learn everyone's names, faces, and instruments by heart. Not because Julie is constantly telling me it's important to network, but because they're about to be my new friends. The rest of the time, I practice. All our individual prep is to be completed before we arrive, so our days can be spent practicing together for our performances.

For hours at my piano, I run my fingers over the ivory keys, mastering the concerto page by page. Ever once asked me if I'd rather have an exquisite, emotive painting with a scratch down its middle or a flawless painting that meant nothing to me. The answer was clear: focus on the beauty of the sound instead of on perfection. Of course, I still do have to get the notes right. I execute the cascading runs, pushing the tempo but also the emotion. Again. Again. *Again, again, again* until I've brought my hands in line with what my ear tells me the music should sound like.

Most professional musicians play eight-plus hours a day, but I usually cap out at six. It's not as impossible to fit the time in as it sounds: I wake up with the sun and play two hours before breakfast. After school, I get a snack, then sit down for another two hours before dinner with Mom. I dash off my homework, then play another couple of hours before bedtime.

I know it's not a normal teenager's life. It doesn't leave much time for friends and *definitely* not romantic relationships. Friday nights are for practicing. Saturday's are at the Cleveland Institute of Music: private piano lessons, theory classes, and choir, which teaches me to be a part of an ensemble and overall musicality. I travel six times a year for performances—most recently, Philadelphia, Atlanta, Denver, Chicago, San Jose, and London.

Sometimes, when the kids at school are talking about weekend plans—movie theater, road trip, shopping, dates—a part of me wishes I could join them. But the music demands to be what it deserves to be. And so my fingers keep tackling the keys. I imagine Dad's encouragements. "That phrase! I felt it right here," he'd say, closing his eyes and touching his fingertips to his heart. I wish he could hear my debut concerto performance in Manhattan. I wish I could see his gently lined face light up with pride.

Thank you for keeping faith, Dad. I miss you. So much.

My phone chimes with a text from Julie, a blue bubble with white type: **How's your Apollo TikTok coming?**

I groan and slip off my piano bench. Julie has me post twice a week to "keep the algorithms fresh," all part of the overall plan to build my profile as a public artist and be relevant to my generation. Julie's biggest clients have huge followings on TikTok, and I know I'm lucky to have her advising me.

But there's nothing more discouraging than spending hours making one of those short silly videos, only to have it viewed by, like, five people. Still, I've posted faithfully for the past year, and my posts have steadily climbed to about two thousand to ten thousand views, depending on the whims of some secret programming I haven't cracked yet.

Now, fortunately, I've got something good to post about.

Haven't made it yet, I confess. But it's coming.

Post a selfie of you at the piano. You're excited to be joining the crew. Your classmates are already posting.

Nudge, nudge. That's Julie.

You can see their samples online.

I'm on it, I promise.

The cool thing about the TikTok icon is it's actually an eighth note. Endearing. I open my app and search for posts tagging @Apollo: a violinist from Los Angeles with her hair in a long blond ponytail. An oboe player from upstate New York.

I get up to change my clothes for a selfie, and an envelope falls from the overstuffed storage compartment of my piano bench. It's labeled with the Chien Tan logo—an invitation to a six-week summer program in Taipei to learn language and culture. I get one every year, offering an all-expenses paid scholarship. They like me for my musical accomplishments, and of course, my sister attended six years ago, when she was a year older than I am now. She was popular there, despite the early gray hair some of her (ahem) *adventures* gave Mom and Dad.

I touch the logo. The scholarship is flattering, and I've always secretly wanted to go. Not for the cultural part—but the *transformation*. Chien Tan has a secret identity: Loveboat. That's what the students call it. Parents don't know it's a huge party with hookups galore.

Ever came back with the incomparable Rick Woo as a boyfriend and a boatload of courage. That's when she dropped out of her premed program to pursue dancing and changed our whole family. Without Ever—without Loveboat—who knows what kind of path my parents might have pushed me toward. A business degree? A career in law? Nothing wrong with either—they're just not for me. I'd much rather fly—the clear, crisp notes swirling around me, and my hands soaring over the keys.

"What's that?" Mom asks. She's come in with a broom and black trash bag to clean out the hallway closet for the first time in ten years.

"Mom, Ever's not going to look in there." I smile. Ever's coming home from New York tonight for a weekend visit, and Mom's gone into extreme nesting mode. I show her the creased letter, dated a few months ago. "It's a Chien Tan invitation. All expenses paid, plane ticket and everything."

Just as I expected, she frowns. "Again? Every year they hound you. Don't they know by now the answer is no? I should call them and tell them to stop sending you those ridiculous invitations."

I smile. "They're not so bad, Mom."

Mom just *harumphs* and opens the closet door.

In my bedroom, I pull on my slim brown dress with the cowl neckline. I prefer bright colors, but Julie is adamant that my outfit should never draw attention, only my music. But she's okay with me wearing my berets for social media, so I adjust my orange one over my black hair.

When I return to the living room, Mom is tossing old winter coats from the closet to the floor. I adjust the Apollo glass globe on the piano, then sit on the bench at an angle that lets my face catch sunlight from the window. I pop my iPhone into the phone stand Julie had me invest in for just this purpose and snap photos of me looking down at my keys, and a few looking straight into the camera.

"Almost done!" Mom says triumphantly. She dashes her arm over her sweaty hairline and plops a wide, conical straw hat onto the coffee table, beside a pile of gloves and scarves I haven't worn since middle school.

"Where did we get this?" I ask, picking up the hat. I've seen it on the closet shelf for years. It looks Chinese, old school, with a cool woven pattern that makes me think of the rhythms of a song. It's lightweight, with a circumference like a very large plate. Perfect for keeping off the rain.

"I don't remember," she says, tugging at a stubborn scarf.

"It's cute." I don't usually wear anything ethnic, not since I was a little girl taking Chinese dance classes. But this one's fun. I swap my beret out for it and snap a few more selfies, seated and standing. I like the way it frames my face, and its roundness complements the rectangular piano background.

"Mom, what do you think?" I show her the best four photos, though I'm not sure she knows what TikTok is, or how multiple photos can be turned into a video collage.

She laughs. "*So* cute. East meets West."

I assemble the photos for a video collage that makes me pop up in different poses around my piano, ending with my hands coyly tilting the hat's brim over my face. Pierre would approve. I text the finished video to Julie, who reviews all my posts before they go live. She usually has comments—make it more personal, show more of me instead of inanimate objects. Things like that. I draft a sample caption: *Can't wait to join the cohort @Apollo in just a few weeks.*

Add "of amazing musicians" after "cohort," Julie writes back. **Thanks for getting this done.**

I upload the video onto TikTok, add a pop song, then shut off my phone and head back to my piano.

Morning sunlight pierces my eyes. Mozart's *Magic Flute* fades with a blurred dream, punctuated by a rap on my door.

"Come in?" I mumble.

Ever pops in, holding her phone out toward me. Her sleek black hair frames that oval face tapering gently to her chin. That face I know better than my own, that makes everything here feel complete.

"Pearl—"

"You're home!" I fly at her and squeeze her in a hug, swinging sideways with a rush of lightheadedness. She flew in last night after I was already asleep, and now she's in her old high school pajamas with fluffy blue bunnies hopping everywhere. Just like old times.

But she looks terrible, with dark circles under her eyes and a distressed expression.

"Is everything okay?" I ask. "Is it Rick? I know the breakup's been hard. Do you want to—"

"It's not that. It's your TikTok. It's blowing up."

"Well, that's great! I'm really bad at getting any engagement there. It's so tricky, and I—"

"Pearl! Listen to me!" Ever's delicate brows furrow over her eyes. Her voice is clipped and urgent, and she thrusts my phone into my hand. "This is bad. You need to delete your post *right now.*"

2

"What happened?" Fully awake now, I tap open TikTok on my phone. My photos at the piano leap out at me. Overnight, I've gone viral, with over 560,000 views and thousands of comments . . . but not the kind Julie was after.

> This is exactly the sort of racist caricature we are trying to stamp out.
> A farmer at a piano? How many Asian stereotypes can they fit into one video?

"What?" My chest tightens with the sort of panic I feel in nightmares when I get onstage and don't remember what to play. "I didn't do anything racist." I'd never want to inflict that pain on anyone, not after what I've experienced growing up. Like the kid slanting his eyes at me. Or the woman shouting at Mom that she didn't belong here. Or, just like this, being horribly, terribly misunderstood. It isn't everyone. But you never forget those moments.

17

"We just had that hat lying around. Mom pulled it out of the closet."

"I know. I bought it in Taiwan years ago," Ever says.

"This is ridiculous. I am Asian. The hat is from Asia. How can this be racist?"

Ever groans. "This is all my fault."

"It's *not* your fault," I say. "And since when did *piano* become an Asian stereotype? Um, Mozart? Beethoven? And I'm the only Asian American pianist who's attended Apollo in like, ten years."

Hi all, I AM Asian! I write back. I took these photos just for fun.

I may as well be writing in invisible ink. Or maybe my app has frozen because of all the notifications. The comments keep coming, not just from followers, most of whom I don't know personally, but from random people and even fake accounts.

This post is incredibly irresponsible.
THIS is what they're serving us? Not the role model I want for future generations.

"What the heck? Who is 'they'?"

I type back: No one is serving anyone anything!

"This is ridiculous," I say. "How many posts have I uploaded of me in *berets*? So when I post a photo of Asian American me wearing a *French beret*, that's okay—and this isn't?"

"Damn. There's a thread on the berets, too," Ever says.

I spot it, kicked off by an @AvrilDurand:

She's not even French. Why not wear a Chinese hat?

I groan. I can't win, clearly. Another comment catches my eye.

Why are none of your backup singers Asian?

They must have looked at my YouTube videos. Of course no one in the choirs I've performed with is Asian. This is *Ohio*. I'm the only Asian musician in my high school. But it's like open season.

I did the recordings at school, with friends from choir, I write. **I don't have any Asian friends at school.**

Which is exactly the wrong thing to say.

No Asian friends? What are you, self-hating?
Jeez, have some pride.
Unfollow Pearl Wong.
Unfollow!

"Pearl, maybe you shouldn't keep responding—" Ever begins.

"I don't even *want* to be anyone's role model!" **I don't have any Asian friends at school BECAUSE THERE ARE NONE except me,** I type like my fingers are on fire. I have Asian friends outside of school. Like the kids at the Chinese Church in Orange that we drive miles to every week. But I'm shouting into a vacuum. My TikTok has just become a platform for people to poke spears at me.

My follower count, built up painfully to ninety thousand over three years, has tanked by half. The comments keep coming. A lot of the people aren't even Asian or Asian American; one middle-aged guy named @TrumpNeverDies comments:

BET YOU $10 THE OP BOWS TO THE MOB.

"OP?"

"Original Poster. You," Ever says.

Before my eyes, a whole new nightmare thread unfolds commenting on *that* comment. I moan. I must have hit the algorithm just right and triggered this attack of orcs, hell-bent on marching over my face.

"Delete it!" Ever urges, and with a tap and a tap, I delete the entire post.

I heave a steadying breath. "It wasn't important anyways," I say. "Nothing I post on TikTok is." I scroll through the posts that have tagged *me, me, me, me, me,* smiling under that stupid hat. My heart sinks. "It's been reshared thousands of times." Each repost has its own viral thread. They're not even about me, they're about what people think my photos stand for and everything wrong with the world.

"It'll . . . blow over." Ever sounds doubtful.

"This is so silly. No one will care by tomorrow," I say. But I don't really believe that. I can feel the heat of anger radiating off my phone.

Another call buzzes in. "Oh no, it's Julie." I moan. Julie never calls this early, which can only mean one thing. She's seen TikTok.

"I'm so sorry, Pearl. I'm here when you need me." With a quick kiss to my head, Ever slips away.

I hit accept on my phone. Julie blooms on my screen, already in full attire.

"Hi, Julie," I say nervously. "If this is about TikTok, I can explain—"

"Pete Taverner, the director of the Apollo Summer Youth

Symphony, just called. They're concerned about getting caught in the crossfire."

Apollo? Oh no. Of course they've seen it. They're tagged in all the posts, too.

"I'm so sorry. I never expected it to blow up like this."

"Well, between you and me, they're already facing accusations of reverse discrimination. So any hint of racism is triggering for them."

Racism? Apollo is supposed to be about music. Not this.

"We have lots of random Asian things in our house. I didn't think I was doing anything wrong. I'm so sorry if I made them look bad. I really didn't mean—" I'm babbling. Begging Julie and the powers that be at Apollo to understand.

Julie cuts in. "The director made it clear this is not the kind of attention they want."

"Yes, I *completely* understand. I already deleted the post. I can post an apology? Maybe we can ask TikTok for help taking the reposts down? Please tell them I'll be extra careful about what I post from now on, and I won't tag them—"

"Pearl. *Pearl!*"

I fall silent. She's been saying my name for a while.

"Pearl, there's no way to remove those posts." Her kindness only makes her next words detonate harder on impact. "Apollo has rescinded your invitation. They've asked you not to participate this summer."

3

"They're . . . they're kicking me out?"

"I'm sorry, Pearl."

Julie says other things, but I can't process her voice. I open my laptop and the Apollo website is already open to their schedule: 9:00 a.m. Introductions. 11:00 a.m. Kick-Off Concert. Noon Lunch in the Park.

I click on the tab of summer participants and scroll all the way down the alphabet of headshots.

Pearl Wong, concert pianist, is no longer among the virtuosos.

"I'm not on their website anymore!"

"Well. Those bastards move fast," Julie says.

"They can't do that! I got in!" What just happened? I can't make sense of anything. "I wore a *straw hat*."

"I'm sorry, Pearl. It isn't fair." Julie sighs. More tags keep popping up on my phone.

Her NAME is an Asian cliché.

22

"The big pile-on made Apollo very nervous," she continues. "They don't want any negative publicity."

"I don't either! Can you please help?"

"Believe me, I tried. They'd rather hold off on you attending until after things die down."

It's the nail in my coffin. Julie Winslow is one of the heavies in the music industry. I won the lottery when she agreed to represent me—and I know how easily that could change. She has no shortage of talented musicians making six figures per performance begging her to represent them. She's had to drop clients because her stars take up so much time.

So if Apollo is still insisting—even on her watch—then what I've done must really be unforgivable. A shaky sob comes from my throat, and I press my hand to my mouth and walk toward my window.

Once when my family was visiting Ever in Manhattan, I heard music coming from the park. It called to me like a siren. I found myself crossing the street to listen.

Under a birch tree, a man in a shabby leather suit was playing an upright piano balanced on wheels. His face was hidden under a mass of tangled gray and brown hair. But his music was heavenly.

"Why is he playing here?" I asked Ever, who came to stand beside me. "He's so good. And no one's listening but the birds."

"I don't know," she said. "He's here almost every day."

That image stuck with me for weeks. I wish I'd had the courage to speak to the man myself and ask him why. I asked Julie about him. Not because I expected answers, but because his music had moved me so much.

"It's very hard to make it as a musician," Julie said. It was a subtle reminder of the truth that underlies our business relationship: the only way I can make a living as a performing musician is if I get into the upper echelon of players. Julie's with me because she expects I *will* make it there one day. But I need to put in a 200 percent effort if I'm going to break out, especially as an Asian American girl. I've seen the ceilings my parents hit, and even Ever, who is the most talented dancer I know, has run into biases in the dancing world. I have to be twice as good and play the game twice as well.

With Apollo, the establishment had finally opened the door to my years of knocking. I thought they believed in me. That they'd listened to my audition and seen promise in my music, just like Dad did. The promise of a future.

"I was so close," I say hoarsely. I lean my forehead against the cool glass of my window. "My dad wanted me to do this program. He knew it was important. I can't let this door get slammed back in my face because of a stupid *hat*."

"We won't let that happen." Julie's voice sharpens. "I've arranged for an interview between you and Pete for the last week of August. With some effort on our part, this will have died down by then, and I've asked him to reconsider you for next summer's lineup. You'll still take this next big step—just a bit later than planned. But between now and then, we need for you to lay low."

"Lay low." I grasp at her words like a lifeline. "Yes, anything. What does that mean?"

"Stay off social media. No more Pearl Wong news."

"I'll tell my mom to cancel the *World Journal* interview."

"Yes, absolutely. Nothing that draws attention to you or gives anyone new reasons to criticize you online. That's the thing about a little notoriety. You need it to succeed, but it can also put a target on your back."

I shiver. Thank God I'll still have a chance to get in front of the director and explain. *I never meant any harm. I'm sorry I caused trouble for your program.*

She continues. "So lay low this summer, and let people forget about the controversy. Then you can reemerge fresh and new. *And* if we can lock in that *Teen Vogue* piece I've been chasing, that would be the perfect reentry."

A feature in *Teen Vogue* is another moonshot I'd never have considered without Julie. Julie has been maneuvering to get the nine letters of my name onto one of their glossy pages since we started working together. We had talked about doing a piece in August around the Apollo Mozart concerto performance.

"Why would they feature me now?" I ask.

"For the same reason Apollo will take you back in the fall. They'll have the opportunity to discover you, a rising star. And we'll reemphasize your *real* image: sweet, hardworking, uber-talented young Asian American pianist."

Ugh. That description has never sat well with me. But it's PR. Presenting myself in a "way," with a specific "image." I have to trust Julie. She definitely knows her stuff.

"But what will I do this summer?"

"Yes, this is a critical one, isn't it?" she muses. "It's the summer before your applications to college and conservatories."

All the music camps are long filled up and applications closed. My weeks are suddenly gapingly, pathetically empty.

I cast about my room, looking for a solution. My eyes fall

25

on a pink sky lantern swaying from my ceiling, a souvenir Ever brought me from Taipei, years ago.

An idea strikes.

"There is one possibility," I say. "Hold on."

Do I even still have it? I rifle through the papers on my desk. It's a long shot. It's not nearly as good as Apollo would have been. But it's my only hope . . .

Where is it, where is it? Did I throw it out? Dear God, I hope not . . .

I head out my bedroom and down the stairs to my piano.

The Apollo glass globe catches my eye first. I feel a fresh stab of pain. Is it even mine anymore? I tear my eyes away and search through the loose sheet music stashed in the piano bench box until I find it, with a corner torn off. I smooth it out with shaky hands.

"Julie, I've been invited to a, uh, cultural program in Taipei. The Overseas Chinese Youth Language and Cultural Training Program. *Highly* respected. Ever heard of it?"

"No, but it's in Taipei?" she says. "Far out of the limelight. A good start. Tell me more."

4

Ever is lying on her bed in her darkened room. The shades are still pulled low. She shifts over to make room for me, and I stretch out beside her over her lilac comforter. My whole life, Ever's been my role model. Every major decision I've ever made, I talk to her about it. Even though she's rarely home these days.

"Apollo pulled the plug on me," I say.

"No! They didn't. Oh, Pearl." She sits up and opens her arms, and I fall into them, feeling about ten years old again. "Just because of a few photos?"

"Apparently."

She strokes my hair while I cling to her. "Social media's not the whole world. They should know better."

"I don't know. I feel like a pile of manure was dumped all over me. The stench might never wash away." I voice the doubt that has been building inside me since my call with Julie. "I mean, what if the only reason I got in was because Julie rammed me through, and this was their excuse to get rid of me?"

"You're underestimating yourself. Julie couldn't have gotten you in if you didn't have the talent to begin with."

I want to believe her, but it's hard. I swing my legs off the bed and walk to her window and look down on the street. We live in a neatly kept neighborhood. Solidly middle class. I've always felt safe here, but my home can't protect me from the harsh reality of the world.

"I heard a line in a Victorian movie once," I say finally. "'The girl has no dowry, no manners, no connections.' It meant she wasn't suitable to marry the heir to the family fortune. The words *no connections* used to go right over my head. It sounded like a period thing. But as I get deeper into the music world, I'm realizing, that's me. So different from like, say the son of the conductor of the San Francisco Symphony, who's my age, and already performing in the biggest concert halls in Boston and London. I have no connections. Dad knew Apollo could be my opportunity, my breakout. I worked so hard to get it, and now . . ."

Ever joins me at the window and rubs my arm gently. "It'll be okay." Her warmth is a small comfort. But my heart is racing painfully in my chest. I set my hand to it, willing it to still. "I wish there was something I could do for you. But dance is a whole different space."

"Honestly, part of me was like, I'm barely Asian! I don't wear qipaos or jade necklaces like our aunts. I don't even *think* about being Asian, and now, all of a sudden, I have to." I scowl. TikTok has made damn sure of that. I slump onto the edge of her bed. "I bet none of Julie's other clients have to deal with things like this." And therefore, Julie doesn't have to deal with them either.

I expect her to scold me, but she just sighs. "Oh, Pearl." She frowns. "I want to say everyone has their issues . . . but the truth is, it's harder for some of us than others."

I finger the taped-together letter in my hands. Some people are really into their ethnic identities. But music is *my* identity. I'm a concert pianist. So I can't help feeling like a hypocrite as I hand the letter to her. "I want to go on Loveboat."

"Loveboat? You?" She frowns, opening it.

"I need to lay low for the summer. Julie thinks Taipei is a good move. It's totally separate from my music world. I can just . . . recharge. And in the fall, she says I can talk about my cultural immersion." I cringe. I can already imagine the talking points Julie will write for me. *I spent a lovely summer in Taipei. I love my Asian heritage!* I hate how I'm being forced into a trip I'd much rather take for the fun of it. "Honestly, it's not like I have a burning desire to get in touch with my cultural roots. But it's what I'll need to combat all this . . . nonsense."

"Loveboat." She shakes her head, still having trouble processing it. "It turned out I needed to go to figure myself out, but you've always known who you are."

"I thought I knew." My whole life, I've been a performer with a future. Now I'm not so sure.

She scans the letter. "Julie thinks *this* is the answer." She smiles wryly. "All these years later, and still no one understands what Loveboat really is."

"It's true. The program has an, um, *reputation*. But it's not like it has to be a hedonistic free-for-all. You always said Loveboat is what you make of it. And jetting off to Taipei is way more interesting than moping around here all summer."

"Mom won't let you. Which is my fault."

Yeah. Even Ever doesn't know how bad it got at home when she was there. I remember hearing our parents argue after the program head called. After *the photographs* were discovered. Should they pay the thousand-dollar airline change fee to bring her home earlier? Should Dad and Mom both fly out to get her? What if she refused? Did they even know her anymore?

In the end, what seemed like the worst thing ever turned out to be the best thing. Dad flew out and found out not only that Ever loved to dance, she was super talented at it. The rest is history, and I've benefited from my parents' new openness. Even if Mom would rather forget the scandalous pictures of Ever *totally naked*. Which, of course, I won't be taking.

"I'm pretty sure I can get her on board once she understands what's at stake. I just need to make sure I can still get in. It starts next week."

Ever looks at the second page included with my invitation and whistles. "All expenses paid. Fancy. They didn't offer me that."

"I'm riding on your coattails. They want more Ever Wong."

"The up-and-coming classical music star is who they want. Smart of them, too." She purses her lips, then pulls her cell phone from her purse. "My friend Marc is the director this summer," she says. "Let me try to reach him. He should be awake over there."

She thumb-types, and her phone chimes with a returning text. "He's up! Do you mind if I explain your situation?"

I frown. "What if he rescinds the invitation, too?"

"He'll need to know why you're deciding to come just a week before the program starts . . . well, I'll just tell him you changed your mind."

I exhale sharply through my nose. "Okay."

They text back and forth while I pace the carpet. Finally, she looks up. "He'd be thrilled to have you. He says to call the front desk and see if they have dorm rooms left."

"Really?" I didn't realize I was clasping my fingers so tightly until the blood starts to flow again.

"Give him an hour, then call with your information. You still have the full ride. The flight, tuition, everything."

Ever was right. They *really* want me. But would they still, if they knew what just went down on TikTok?

I bury the worry. A lifeline is in sight. I just need to swim toward it with everything I have left.

Exactly one hour later, I dial the number on the letter. A woman's voice answers in Mandarin, then switches to softly accented English. "How may I help you?"

"This is Pearl Wong. I got an invitation to Love—I mean, Chien Tan. The director said I should call with my information?"

"Just a minute," says the woman.

"Sure," I say calmly, but my insides quiver like a bowl of cold jellyfish. Chinese music begins to play on the phone. I recognize the instrument—one of those two-stringed violins. I forget the name of it, but I've heard one played in an exhibit at the Cleveland Art Museum. It's a good sign. I give Ever a thumbs-up, but then a dagger of regret stabs through me. "I was excited to spend the summer with you in New York," I say wistfully.

"Me too." She gives me a hug. "You'll have a different experience is all. I won't tell you not to do anything I wouldn't have done, but you should definitely go out on the town. Make friends from other countries. Date some people." She smiles. "Kiss a few frogs."

I snort. "I'm like, going into exile. I don't intend to have the time of my life."

"Well, you might be surprised. Loveboat has a magic of its own."

Magic. Who *wouldn't* want a summer of transformation? But the sad truth is, I'm in a totally different situation. I shake my head no. "You know I don't have time for boys." Not to mention Ever is the beauty in the family.

"If you don't mind some flawed big sisterly advice? I've dated *one* guy. Hooked up with one other. Now six years later, Rick wants to propose. But I can't say yes because I don't know what I don't know. You know?"

"Wait, you hooked up with someone besides Rick?" I ask, scandalized. It's always just been Ever-and-Rick. Forever and ever. "Who?"

She shakes her head. "It was on Loveboat. Way in the past."

"Maybe you're having the seven-year itch," I muse. Their biggest problem has always been geography, not love. Rick's in Taipei at a hot start-up. But Ever's job—and Mom and me—keep her in the States. Since Dad passed away, she hasn't wanted to leave us alone for long, but she's also adamant that Rick can't quit his job for her, especially since she's always carried the weight of Dad sacrificing his career for us to have a better life in the States. They've been doing this dance of how to end up in the same city for years now, and they finally decided to take a break for a few months to figure things out independently.

"That's not it." She chews on her lower lip. She rarely comes to me with her issues. She probably figures I'm too young to relate. But I can.

"I kissed Bobby Aquila at a spin the bottle party in eighth grade," I offer. "It was very wet, and it's been awkward ever since."

She laughs. "Yeah. Well, maybe remember that on Loveboat when you're surrounded by five hundred cute boys."

"Ha!" I say, but then we're both distracted by a blue Audi pulling up to our curb outside. A guy in a brown leather jacket steps out. I catch Ever smoothing her black hair back and realize she's wearing lipstick. She's changed to go out, in her blue satin jumpsuit with a long golden sash knotted above her hip. Ballerina-themed. At her vanity, she picks up her makeup brush and applies blush across the arc of her cheekbones.

"Um. Ever. Why is Stanley Yee coming up our driveway?"

She runs her hands through her hair, combing out the ends and smoothing them under in a way that makes me seriously want to smack her. "Rick and I agreed to date other people."

"YOU DID WHAT?" I follow her into the hallway, phone still pressed to my ear. This whole time we've been talking about my problems, and here she is, *dating new people*?

She laughs, but her eyes are a bit strained. "Were you not listening to a word I was saying?"

"I thought you were just taking, like, a time-out before you got engaged. For perspective—not this! You hate Stanley Yee! My entire childhood you pretended to barf every time you saw him!"

"We were little kids. And Stanley's been texting me for weeks," Ever says. "He was always the Other Asian Kid at school. Everyone thought we should be together, so I ran the other way. But he's no joke. He went to MIT. Now he's at Goldman Sachs in

33

Cleveland to get some experience before business school."

"Bo-ring!"

"Not everyone is cut out for a glamorous life in the arts," she teases.

Nothing she can say can make this right. "At least Rick's at a *start-up*. Working abroad. Taking risks." I'll get to see him in Taipei, another silver lining of this exile. And maybe Ever can visit and figure out how right they are for each other . . .

"Look, if Rick or I connect more deeply with someone else, someone who actually lives on the same continent," she swallows hard, "it's better we find out *before* we torture ourselves for another seven years, right?"

I open my mouth to argue. If Dad were here, he'd have a lot to say. He *adored* Rick. The two of them would go fishing whenever Rick visited, never catch anything, and be so pumped to try again the next time. Dad would have provided perspective. But I'm just the little sister, and all I can do is scowl as she heads for the door/disaster.

"What's this?" From the foyer table, Ever picks up an exquisite rosewood box, swirling with an intricate floral pattern of inlaid mother-of-pearl. In her other hand is a simple note card with "Ever" printed in Rick's clean handwriting. "How did this get in here?"

"Looks like Rick Woo strikes again." I smirk. Mom must have unwrapped it when it arrived. "I knew I could count on my future brother-in-law to not let me down."

"Don't call him that!" She shakes her head, exasperated. She slides her fingernails along the edge of the box, trying to open it. It doesn't budge. "We're supposed to be taking a *break*." But she runs her hands over its polished surface, already intrigued. Ever loves a good mystery. Rick knows her too well, and he's not getting pushed out just because my sister's having a quarter-life crisis.

"It's a puzzle box." I wiggle my hips in a little happy dance. There is hope in the world. "See? This is why I'm Team Rick!"

Ever growls. "You're supposed to be Team Me!"

"That's the thing. I can be both!"

The bell rings. We stare at the door.

"It's not too late to pretend we're not home," I whisper.

"Don't be ridiculous." Ever's hand is already on the brass handle. "It's just lunch." She tucks her purse under her arm and, a second later, she's gone.

The Chinese music ceases on my call. "Hello, Pearl?" The receptionist is back.

"Yes?" I cling to the phone.

"We look forward to welcoming you to campus next week."

5

TAIPEI

My brother-in-law-to-be meets me outside the Taoyuan International Airport. He removes his shades and waves as I approach him through the muggy air. The wind makes his thick black hair wave in every direction and tugs at his untucked Cleveland Browns shirt—an old present from my dad.

"Here's our jet-setter." He snags my blue felt beret from my head and plops it onto his own. Then he folds me into his warm bear hug. "I can't believe your mom actually let you come." I love Rick's voice, which is low and soothing, like a cello.

"She understood I don't have any other options." It hurt to have to tell Mom what had happened. That as proud as Dad would have been, as much as Mom hoped we were finally accepted, it turned out we weren't there yet. I couldn't even go into all the details around the farmer's hat and TikTok. I just said that there was a blowup, Apollo wanted me to lay low for the summer, and Julie and I came up with an alternative plan. If there's one person who Mom listens to, fears even, it's Julie.

"How's Ever?" Rick asks, taking my bag and heading toward the lot.

His tone is casual, but his brown eyes are hungry and vulnerable. I need to cheer him up. I fold my arms over my chest and give him a mock glare. "If I didn't know better, I'd say you're picking me up just to grill me about my boring old sister."

"Yes, after you tell me everything you know, I'll drop you off on the side of the road to walk the rest of the way to campus. It's just a few hours."

I grin as Rick loads my suitcase into the trunk of his electric car. Rick and I actually have a similar sense of humor. Maybe that's why we get along so well. But to be honest, Rick looks like he hasn't slept since Ever broke up with him. His eyes are underscored by dark circles, and his jaw is stubbled. He's lost about ten pounds.

I mean, he's working at a start-up, so who knows what his hours are. But this is not the put together and self-assured Boy Wonder I've known all these years.

"She's okay . . . ," I say. Should I tell him about Stanley Yawn? I decide against it. "She's intrigued by your puzzle box."

"Good," he says. "You'll help her if she can't figure it out, right?"

"Pearl's on the job. How are *you* feeling?"

He's quiet a moment. A battle is raging inside him. He takes the driver's seat, and then, as I buckle in, he reaches into his pocket and pulls out a blue velvet jewel box, opening it to a beautiful diamond set between two sapphires.

"Oh my God, Rick. It's *gorgeous*. Has she seen this yet?"

"Yes."

What is wrong with that girl?

"I never once doubted we were headed for the altar," he admits.

"That makes two of us." I squeeze his meaty hand as he falls silent again. "Are you going to do what she asked you to do? Stay put here?" *Let her date lame guys?* I add silently.

"I can't go against her wishes. And I don't want to pressure her by asking her to come here. That's not what any of this is supposed to be about."

I was young when Dad was working as an orderly. He couldn't practice as a doctor in the States. But I know he went through years of frustration, and even depression, to be kept from the job he truly loved.

"Maybe this space and time apart is the only way she can know what she really wants for our relationship," Rick concludes. He's thought about this a lot, clearly.

The car rumbles to life and music begins to play. Pachelbel's Canon in D. Baroque Germany, early 1700s.

Rick quickly shuts it off.

"Um," I say.

"Sorry. I'm such a cheese ball."

"Well, it's THE classic bride-marches-down-the-aisle song." And the poor guy is obviously heartbroken. I smile, trying to cheer him up. Yes, classical musicians find Canon in D cliché, but it says something about the piece's staying power that it's so overplayed. And—"To be honest, Canon in D rip-offs happen to be my guilty pleasure."

"Rip-offs? What are those?"

"Like that old pop song from the 1990s, Pet Shop Boys' 'Go

West.'" I play the YouTube video on my phone, starting with the dramatic cymbals clanging. The song makes me want to get up and dance on the roof, though doing it gracefully is Ever's gift.

Rick nods along, slightly offbeat. "Catchy. I think my Aunty Claire listens to it."

I hum the melody to Pachelbel's cadence on top of it: D → A → Bm → F#m → G → D → G → A.

"Wow, no way," he says. "It's Canon in D!"

"Fun, right? Most people don't realize how many songs over history have been lifted right from it. Like 'Memories' by Maroon 5 that came out in 2019. Lady Gaga's 'The Greatest Thing.' Green Day, Aerosmith. Bon Dia. Some church hymns—"

"Pearl Wong! You are blowing my mind."

I laugh. Rick Woo—Mr. Yale-football-player-Boy-Wonder—should be totally intimidating. He's got it all. The grades, the looks. An awesome career at maybe the next Google or Amazon. But he's so sweet and enthusiastic and comfortable in his own skin that everyone, me included, ends up feeling at ease around him. Yet another reason he's such a keeper.

The song ends, but the music is still racing through my veins. I sigh. "I'd write my own lift if I had a single composer's bone in my body."

"Your manager wouldn't approve, I take it."

"Ha! Any whiff of pop and I'd get sent to the guillotine."

Out my window, the city of Taipei comes into view, and I crane my neck to see better. Taipei is exactly as it appears in all of Ever's photos. Green mountains. Red pagoda rooftops peeping through. The huge glassy skyscraper, made of blue-green segments, pierces the sky. Taipei 101, the most modern pagoda in the world. I've heard so many of Ever's stories over the years that I feel like I've been here before, in a dream without the humidity. Now everything is REAL.

"You could ping your fingernails against Taipei 101 and see if it reverberates," Rick says. "That's musical, right?"

"And random!" I smile, but then my smile fades. I wish I could just enjoy being here. But in Manhattan, all the Apollo kids are touring the Empire State Building now, talking about their favorite songs and getting ready to make incredible music together.

Rick seems to sense I've gone quiet now. He takes over as tour guide, pointing out a huge red building on a cliff the size of a city block, with two tiers of bright yellow roofs floating over rows and rows of arched balconies, quite possibly the biggest, reddest, most gorgeous building I've ever seen.

"The Grand Hotel. It's one of the best views in Taipei, and you get it right from campus," Rick says as we pass a brick and white stone sign with two characters. "And here's Chien Tan. Your home away from home."

"Cool," I say, trying to muster up enthusiasm. We take a long winding road into campus, passing a guard's booth to my right and then circling, on our left, a pond floating with lily pads.

I recognize everything Ever described to me. The rock with the red characters inscribed in its surface, where couples pose to commemorate meeting here years ago. The grassy lawn with a group of kids playing volleyball, yelling, *"Shì wǒ de!"* and *"Qù tuánduì!"* Their jeans shorts and T-shirts mark them as Americans, but they speak Mandarin almost as well as my parents. And beyond the lawn, I get a glimpse of the blue pipe the brave ones shimmy across to escape campus and dance all night in the city.

Loveboat.

For the first time, I feel a glimmer of hope. This is where the metamorphosis happened for Ever. Duckling to swan. Doctor to dancer. And meeting Rick. My ending doesn't have to be hers, but maybe there's some magic in store for me here, too.

As we pull to a stop before the main entrance, a familiar-looking guy steps out. A navy sweatband holds back his long milk-chocolate hair. He's wearing athletic shorts and a gray shirt. I recognize him from my sister's Loveboat photos. Marc Bell-Leong.

"Hey, man! Déjà vu!" Rick hops from the car and they exchange ginormous bear hugs.

"Can't believe you're the head honcho now," Rick says.

"It's a whole new Loveboat," Marc says. "Renovations. New Night Markets popping up around town. All the clubs we went to are closed. Man, I feel old." He turns to me as I nervously join them. I've met Marc through Ever at various gatherings, but I don't know him well, and it's been a few years. Plus he's in charge. "*You* look exactly like your sister when I first met her."

"Doesn't she?" Rick says wistfully.

"The students won't believe the famous Pearl Wong is in their program this summer."

"I'm not that famous," I say quickly. In fact, Julie told me to keep my name on the down low, too. The fewer people who know about my life in the music world, the fewer who will actually look me up and see all the controversy, and the sooner my blowup can die down.

Rick claps a hand on Marc's shoulder and winks. "Should we get her registered?"

"All done! Everything's digital now. No more paper folders."

"Nice," Rick says.

"Have you downloaded the app?" Marc asks.

"Soon as the plane landed." I hold up my phone.

"Excellent." Marc pulls out a tablet. "Let's see, Mandarin Level One."

"I'm remedial," I groan, embarrassed. Ever fought my parents so hard over Chinese school that when it came time for me, they didn't bother, not that I'd have had time. Music is my second language. I've picked up some Italian from my music lessons, but for Mandarin, I can sing the pinyin alphabet to the tune of "Twinkle, Twinkle," and that's it. It's always made me feel like a lesser Chinese.

A lesser Chinese who doesn't know enough not to take pictures in a straw hat, I scold myself.

"My Mandarin *is* really terrible," I admit.

"We all start somewhere. And that's what Chien Tan is for! Immersion!" Marc says. Rick tries to cover a snort, unsuccessfully. Marc isn't deterred. He looks proud as a peacock over his program. "Pearl, you're registered for your own electives, right?"

"Traditional Chinese Music," I say. A double elective. I'm pretty excited about it, actually. I know my way around a symphony orchestra, but I don't know anything about Chinese music.

"A perfect choice!" Marc says.

"When Ever was here, your mom picked all her electives," Rick says. "Times *have* changed, I see."

"The benefit of being the second child," I say. "The eye of

Sauron is trained on the oldest." They laugh.

"Poor Ever," Marc says. "She paved the way for you. Be grateful."

"Oh, I am!"

Marc steers us toward a group of students taking selfies before the entrance.

"Let me introduce you to a few new friends," he says.

"Oh, um . . . sure . . ."

"Hey, gang. This is Pearl. Her sister was on Loveboat my year."

"I'm Iris," says a tiny girl with a beat-up volleyball under her arm. "Your face looks familiar."

Oh no. TikTok? "Um, I, uh—"

"She's your resident Girl Wonder," Rick says.

I give him a not-so-discreet side kick in the leg as Marc waves another small crowd of kids over. My heart sinks. How many of *them* might know about the TikTok fiasco and mention it in front of Marc? "Meet the famous—"

"Normal girl," I cut him off in a low voice. I stick my hand out for a shake. "I'm Pearl," I say, omitting my last name. I hope Marc gets the hint.

"Pearl just arrived," he finishes without a hitch.

I thank him with my eyes as I shake hands and smile at a blur of friendly faces. Five hundred cute boys is about right, but I'm worried. Iris might have recognized me. Maybe it's just a matter of time before she or someone else puts two and two together.

I'm grateful when Rick finally takes my elbow and announces, "All right, you have her all summer. Let me get her settled and you can all bond at dinner later."

43

"Bye, Pearl!" they chorus.

We head up the broad entrance stairs toward the sliding glass doors.

"I'm just trying to have a normal summer," I say.

"You're a celebrity. Own it!" Marc says. "You might be the most well-known student here since Rick!"

Rick turns his eyes on me, all soulful now. "You know, Ever hated me on sight just because I was all over the *World Journal.* Boy Wonder, she used to say."

"Exactly. You put people up on a pedestal, and there's only one thing for them to do—fall." My throat swells to aching.

"But sometimes," Marc says, "the pedestal is just a boost up to something higher. Greater."

Rick squeezes my shoulder. "This is your time, Pearl. Climb. Soar."

My heart twists. *Thanks for the thoughts, but I've already crashed and burned.*

"Speaking of infamy, I was wondering, could I go by my mom's name?" I say. "Honestly, it's the best way for me to just have a low-key summer, which my manager says is really important." With everything else spun out of control, it's the one thing I *can* do to work myself back in to Apollo. "Can we change it in the directory? Pearl Lim."

Marc's eyes are sympathetic. "Of course." He hops on his phone. "I'll have it changed right away."

It's a small win. I breathe a sigh of relief as he leads the way up the stairs to the wide glass double doors. I'll be cocooned in anonymity instead of on display for target practice.

Inside the lobby, ancient Chinese artifacts are on display

under glass boxes, one collection each to a pedestal sculpted from driftwood. There are coins carved from shells. A string of bronze chime bells etched with sweeping Chinese characters. There are so many artifacts, the pedestals meander down the hallway out of sight.

I pause by a white jade dragon textured with veins of minerals, followed by a bronze snake, followed by a rosewood horse.

"These are the Chinese zodiac," I say, impressed.

"Fancy," Rick whistles. "They didn't have all this while we were here."

"In addition to the famous Pearl Wong—Lim, I mean—we have an art history major among the students this year," Marc says. "He coordinated with the National Palace Museum to bring some of their inventory here on loan. I'm a fan, too."

I pause before a zither, an instrument with a dozen silk strings stretched horizontally over a thin, flat body made of a lacquered wood. It's beautiful, and my fingers itch to pluck its strings and let the notes ring in my ears. The person who created this exhibit clearly knows his or her musical instruments. Those are the best pieces here.

"Pearl?" Marc asks.

I glance up, startled from the song in my head. "Sorry, got distracted."

"Amazing, aren't they?" Marc smiles and takes us up the elevators to the third floor, past a cute student lounge of blue couches and a furry sheepskin rug. Two girls are making a TikTok dance video, and I duck to avoid ending up as their background.

"And here we are." Marc unlocks a door down a short hallway.

"Isn't this . . . ?" Rick trails off. His expression is pained.

"Ever and Sophie's room," Marc finishes. "Gave it to you for old times' sake." He grins at me, oblivious to the pain that crosses Rick's face.

"Thank you," I say. On the wall is a faded scroll painting. In a grove of knobby trees and gnarly rocks, a Chinese maiden in a white robe and blue scarf plays a pear-shaped lute.

"My great-grandmother on my mom's side played an instrument like that," I say. I don't have many memories of my grandparents on either side, and none of the ancestors beyond them. Everyone had passed away before I turned four. But at home, we have one faded brown-and-white photo of my great-grandmother cradling a lute in her arms, and my great-grandfather with an affectionate hand on her shoulder. The face of her lute was painted with cherry blossoms.

I study the painting before me. Like my great-grandmother, the maiden is resting the instrument upright on her knee. Her delicate fingers are plucking the strings. I'd never had the occasion to mention this to Dad, but if I had a second life, I'd be a guitarist. Something about its twang in my ears makes me feel like a cat needing to purr. This isn't a guitar, but its gracefulness calls to me.

"I've seen paintings like this at museums." Rick whistles.

"Only the best for Ever Wong's sister." Marc smiles. "I've got to take care of some admin stuff, but Pearl, there's a Steinway in the new auditorium. You're free to use it anytime."

"Thanks, Marc," I say gratefully. I brought all my music books, and having a piano nearby, especially such a nice one, is like having an oxygen tank in outer space. Necessary for survival.

Marc heads out and a moment later, a knock sounds on the

open door. Beautiful Sophie Ha swoops in, stylish in a green and purple vertical-striped dress that swishes as she walks. Her long black hair tumbles nearly to her waist, and a fat rattan basket fills her arms.

"You're here!" she sings.

"Sophie!" I squeal, and run to fling my arms around her.

"I brought sustenance!" Her dark-brown eyes glow as she unpacks paper-wrapped mooncakes, fresh guavas, and yellow mangoes. Gifts are her love language, and I've benefited from them over the years. "I got you a sampling of the best of everything in town. Let me know if you need anything anytime. I'm so happy you're here! I'm launching my first fashion show in August—you're invited!"

I smile. "Congrats! I'd love to come!" Sophie is a fashion designer, Rick's cousin, and Ever's best friend—and the most energetic person I've ever met. She and her boyfriend, Xavier Yeh, have been together almost as long as Rick and Ever.

"I'm your aunty this summer." Sophie gathers me into another enormous hug. "Can Xavier and I take you out to dinner tonight? We need to give you the unofficial Loveboat orientation."

I laugh. "It's, like, physically impossible to say no to you. Thanks, Sophie."

"Fabulous. I'll book us a table at Cé La Vi."

"Do you want me to take a photo of you two?" Rick asks. "We can send it to Ever."

He's thinking of her. Of course he is. "Sure. Let's do it." I hand my phone over, and he snaps a photo to be shared via private text only.

"Parting words of wisdom," Rick says. He pretends to check

whether Marc's still around. "I don't recommend the escape route over the blue pipe. Super Mission Impossible, but also, super unnecessary. Sneak out the service door like the other students."

"Or just walk out the front!" Sophie adds.

"Thanks." I laugh. "I'll keep that in mind."

"If you need a ride home from a club anytime, just call me," Rick says. "I'll have my phone on for you."

"And don't worry about that whole TikTok New York program thing." Sophie gives me a squeeze. "We can talk more about it at dinner, but I know you'll be a meteor this summer all on your own."

"I'll be a stone under water. Quiet. Undercover," I say. But my throat is tight as I squeeze her back, and then give Rick a squeeze, too, trying to convey what they both mean to me.

But no hug can possibly do it justice.

6

It feels good to settle in, setting everything in its place in this tiny microcosm. I hang up a blue duster dress Ever lent me, although, since I'm bigger in the chest than she is, we sadly can't share that many clothes.

I'm on my knees, trying to shove my empty suitcase under my bed, when a knock sounds.

"Come,"—*shove*—"in!"—*shove*—I call.

The door opens and the volleyball player from out front pops her head in. What was her name again? Iris. Her deep-black, wavy hair is damp from a recent shower and flowing over a blue T-shirt that reads: I Wear Bubble Tees, along with an iconic picture of a cup and straw. She's fit. Leggy. Must be all the sports.

"Hey, Pearl," she says, her eyes falling on my face, which is probably red from my effort. "Need a hand?"

She darts forward. Despite her tiny frame, she lifts the entire corner of my bed, frame and all. I shove my suitcase under the railing, and she drops the bed back into place.

"Thanks," I say, rising gratefully.

She smiles. "We're wrapping Spam musubis. Want some?"

She gestures toward the room across the hallway, from which a delicious smell is wafting, reminding me I haven't eaten in almost twenty-four hours. Apparently, we're neighbors. *Make some friends*, Ever said. Besides the fact that my all-encompassing music career has made a social life nonviable, I've always sort of suspected music kids and sports kids wouldn't have much in common. But now we've got Loveboat, and an entire summer to be fish out of water together.

I return her smile. "I can't resist anything with Spam in it."

"I knew you were a kindred spirit!"

I laugh as she bounces toward her door, and I follow her across the hallway. Her room is a mirror image of mine, with a different painting—a craggy mountain landscape—on the wall. The closet is jammed with so many clothes and boxes that the doors can't shut.

Near the window, which is propped open, a very tall person with short green hair is frying fat pink slices of meat in a pan over an illegal burner.

"Hey, I'm Hollis," the person calls over a shoulder. "Hungry?"

"It's a Hawaiian snack," Iris explains. "We're from Honolulu. We'll be seniors at Punahou High."

"I'll be a senior, too. I've never met anyone from Hawaii."

"We brought the Spam from home. This is Hollis. We're fraternal, obviously."

"Twins." I smile.

"Hollis uses they/them pronouns," Iris says. "I use she/her."

"You don't need to speak for me," Hollis chides gently.

"Sorry!" Iris flutters a hand good-naturedly. "I'm too protective. Might be a twin thing. I'm working on that with our therapist," she tells me, and heads for a tiny rice cooker steaming on her desk.

"All good." Hollis shakes my hand. Their face is a near-exact copy of Iris's, from the high cheekbones to their button noses and perfectly pointed chins. They're both tanned and outdoorsy, the opposite of me in a way that's appealing.

"I'm Pearl," I say. "She/her. I need to find out what conditioner you use. Your hair is like glass!"

Hollis smiles, running their fingers through it. "Thanks."

"I'm still trying to place you," Iris says. "I know we haven't met." She sets a plastic rectangular mold horizontally over a strip of dark-green seaweed, then fills its bottom with a scoop of brown rice.

"Pearl's a common name, sort of," I hedge. "And I've been mistaken for other Asian American girls before." True, actually.

"Oh my gosh," Iris says. "I didn't mean it that way! I mean, it's not like I think all Asian girls look alike!"

"Oh, uh, no. I mean, no worries." Dang, didn't mean to make her feel guilty. I only meant that I have a face that's not distinctive. But Iris has moved on already.

"I'm almost done with this one. Have a pineapple cake while you're waiting." Iris points to a yellow package on her desk. "I found those in Taipei 101 this afternoon. My favorite so far."

I tear the foil wrapper on the pineapple cake and bite into the delicious sweetness as Iris's hands fly over her musubi. She dashes a sprinkling of Japanese sesame and seaweed seasoning on a small pad of rice, then sets a perfectly fried slice of Spam on top. She pushes the sandwich out of the mold, wraps the strip of seaweed around it, and hands it over to me.

51

I hold the warm, pink-white-green heft of it in my palm. "It's like a Christmas present."

"Never heard it described that way, but yes!" Iris says.

"I heard you already know the program director," Hollis says.

"He's an old friend of my sister's. They met here, believe it or not."

"That should come in handy." Iris laughs.

"Or maybe the opposite," I point out ruefully. "He's *looking out for me*. Sounds like babysitting, when you think about it." I take a bite of the musubi and let out an involuntary groan. "Oh my gosh. This is so good. My mom used to make Spam and eggs for me. This tastes like home."

"Glad you like it. Our dream is to open a gourmet snack line one day. Asian-themed."

"If you need a guinea pig this summer," I say. "I'm it."

"Problem is, we can't agree on the menu," Iris tells me. "Too many choices." Iris moves her backpack off her bed. "Here, have a seat."

"Our parents met on Loveboat, years ago," Hollis says, flipping meat in the sizzling pan. "Our mom didn't want us to come. She knows firsthand what Loveboat *really* is."

"She's not exactly a party animal," Iris explains. "She actually *improved* in her Chinese while she was here."

"But our dad said I need to learn to put myself out there more," Hollis says. "Be more assertive. Make new friends."

"You're fine," Iris says.

Honestly, I need to learn to make friends, too. I've benefited from growing up in the same school district, with the same school friends since kindergarten. But when was the last time I made a

52

new one? I take a seat on Iris's bed. "Are your parents American-born then?" I ask. I've never met Chinese American kids whose parents were born in the States. How different that must be, to not have to explain school and friendships and relationships— all the parts that are so different from their upbringing. To have them just *know*.

"Yep," Hollis says. "We did bilingual immersion school since preschool, so we speak Chinese better than they do!" They lift the last of the Spam slices onto a plate.

"I can't speak at all," I say ruefully.

"But you can still learn!" Iris says.

"Like our parents," Hollis says. "They're always taking some class or other."

I smile. Iris and Hollis seem cool. Friendly. Open. I like how Hollis could speak their mind with Iris and it was all good. Not everyone's like that.

"You know, I've got a basket of snacks in my room. Let me bring some over," I say.

I pop back into my room for Sophie's gift and bring back a lotus mooncake and a mango to share.

"It's delicious," Hollis says, spearing a piece of mango.

"Mmm-hmm." I bite into a sweet lotus mooncake. I have a sense of calm, just sitting here with them in this coziness. There's no point to what we're doing. No goal. It just . . . is.

I feel oddly satisfied.

Hollis's phone chimes with a text at the same time as Iris's.

"Your parents?" I ask.

"No, they're asleep," Iris opens her phone. "It's from someone named WOLF. A US number." She reads, PARTY IN THE DARK.

Come one, come all to a Loveboat-exclusive event! TOMORROW NIGHT 1 a.m. after FRANK Taipei.

Wear masks or pick one up here, Hollis finishes reading. And remember, anything can happen in the dark.

Iris laughs. "What *is* this?"

"Do you think it went out to all the Loveboat students?" Hollis asks.

"I didn't get one," I say. "But I just joined. Maybe my info isn't in the directory yet." In fact, I should ask Marc to just keep it out altogether.

"Who's Wolf?" Hollis asks.

"A student, probably. Using an alias." Iris considers the message. "Should we go?"

"It'll be fun," Hollis says. "And this *is* Loveboat. We're *supposed* to sneak out clubbing, right? Pearl, you in?"

"Oh!" I say. This is all happening faster than I expected.

Hollis claps me on the shoulder. "If we're here, we owe it to ourselves to have the full experience. Don't you think?"

I have to admit I'm curious what this is all about. But I know what Julie would say. Sneaking out is a risk I can't afford. And she'd be right.

"I don't want to get . . . into trouble." I hate how that makes me sound like a prude.

"It's a party *in the dark*," Hollis says. "No one will know who we are. Or that we're even there." Hollis is already rummaging in their closet, piling silky black clothing onto their bed.

"I'll think about it," I hedge. I glance at my watch. "I've got a dinner tonight with my sister's friends. Maybe if I'm not wiped

54

out, I could go after." Although I've already decided. It's a risk I can't afford.

"Well, let's have a toast, at least." Iris passes out another round of warm musubis. "To Loveboat!" she says, and we try for a three-way clink, dropping rice everywhere.

Back in my room, I change for my dinner with Sophie and Xavier. I pull on a charcoal dress with spaghetti straps, which I wore to a reception in Chicago. I'm no fashionista like Sophie, but I like how the soft fabric caresses my skin and the lace hem skims my knees.

An image pops up on my phone. It's an official mass text from Apollo, featuring a photo of eighty students in front of Lincoln Center, captioned: *Today we welcomed our newest class to Manhattan. We can't wait for a summer of merry music making.*

Ugh. Guess I'm still on their mailing list. I should ignore it, but I can't help clicking the link to Instagram. Their post has over ten thousand likes already. Famous musicians are congratulating them. I spot the cute flutist, then I shut it off. Right about now, I would have been workshopping Dad's favorite piece with my fellow Apollo classmates. Are any of them wondering about the girl in the straw hat who hasn't shown her face? Would Apollo's staff say anything to them, bringing the online stain into the real world?

My heart aches. I realize I still have a whole hour before Sophie and Xavier pick me up. I need to settle. With more than twenty-four hours of overseas flights here, my fingers are itching for a keyboard.

I head downstairs in search of the Steinway that Marc offered. In the brightly lit lobby, a counselor is passing out open cups of bubble tea. I swirl my straw through the ice and boba and take a pull of the sweet milk tea. It's a bit weak, but hey, it's free.

I pass a lounge whose large glass window overlooks the green Keelung River. The space is deserted except for a guy in a blue-striped shirt on the couch, sitting with his laptop on his lap. His head bobs under a nice pair of Sennheiser headphones, to a beat only he can hear. His jet-black hair is overgrown like a weedy garden, making my fingers itch to set it right. From under his poppy-red shorts, his legs stretch out so far he must get tangled up if he stands up too fast.

And the sounds he's making! From his mouth, perfectly in time:

UM-chica-*UM*-chica-*UM*-chica-*UM*.

Then his feet join in. His sneakers thump an intricate counterpoint: an entire percussion section from one guy. His hand swings in time like a conductor's baton, then accidentally tugs the cord of his headphone free of his laptop. An amazing song floods the room. Plucked strings twang—not from a guitar but some other instrument I don't recognize—like a glorious firework display. Their vibrations hum at just the right frequency in my ears. I'm like a cat getting rubbed in all the right spots.

"What's that amazing instrument?" I finally blurt.

The beat ends abruptly as he jumps a foot into the air. The song cuts off mid-note, leaving its unresolved melody hanging. He yanks his headphones off and turns to fix me with dark eyes in a tan face full of angles.

"Sorry, didn't mean to scare you," I apologize.

"How long have you been standing there?" he demands. His lips pull down in a frown, making his bladelike cheekbones stand out even more.

Nearly ten minutes, but I'm afraid to admit it. His hands are shaking. His knuckles are white. Maybe he's private about his music. I can understand that. I silently curse myself for interrupting the way I did.

"Sorry, I couldn't help listening," I say, wanting to put him at ease. "I mean, those fifths against eighths. I felt it all right here." I tap my breastbone, Dad-style.

He exhales. Then recovers his laptop. His jaw is clenched and a vein pulsing in his temple. I should leave him alone, but that rhythm is still ticking inside me.

"I'm Pearl," I say. He doesn't answer, so I say, "What's your name?"

He's plugging his earphones back into his laptop, dismissing me. "Kai."

I should just leave him alone. "Do you play an instrument, or—"

"Look, if you're hitting on me, I suggest you try someone else." He scowls. "I'm not here for the Loveboat meat market."

My face burns. I pull back, straightening my shoulders.

"*If* I were here for a meat market, which *I am not*," I retort. "I wouldn't be hitting on *you*."

"Could've fooled me." He puts his headphones back on his ears.

What an ass! My eyes suddenly sting. This jerk is just like all those trolls on TikTok. He doesn't understand and won't let me explain. Well, screw that. He doesn't get to have the last word.

I don't know what comes over me next. But I snatch off his headphones and dump the rest of my bubble tea on his head. He yelps as the liquid streams down his hair all over his shirt. I step out of harm's way as the ice pings on the floor. Then I toss his headphones onto the couch beside him.

"Convinced now?" I ask, acid dripping from my voice.

And then I'm out of there.

The *sheer nerve.* Just because I'm on Loveboat? Or because he knows he's cute? My blood boils as I stomp down the hallway.

Then I breathe out. What have I done? This is not what laying low looks like.

I need to get a grip. I need to recenter myself, seriously.

The new auditorium is empty when I arrive. Thankfully, there's no one to witness my jaw fall to the floor as I open the door. It's a modern stage with glass panels and delicate mics hanging at intervals from the high ceiling. The chairs are red plush. The stage is flanked by man-sized vases covered with artsy Chinese calligraphy in blue ink, and in the center sits a black grand piano, top opened to the widest angle. In the silence, I can already hear the inflections of its voice.

I move toward it. Steinway in gold letters. My face and bare shoulders reflect back at me in the polished surface. I'd forgotten I was wearing my fancy dress. Was this dress why Kai thought I was hitting on him? Whatever. I wore this for Sophie, not a guy on Loveboat.

I lift the keyboard cover to reveal the familiar rows of ivory and black keys and play a delicious A. I only get to play Steinways at performances. Having one to play all summer is a treat, and judging from the fingerprints I've left in the dust on its cover, I won't have much competition.

I play a C, dipping my toe in a pool, letting the note hang in the air until it fades. Now that the need to perfect my pieces for Apollo is gone, I can spend my time however I want. I could even choose not to practice, which feels enormously rebellious. But who am I kidding. I need this too much.

I take a seat on the bench and run a few scales to warm up. Then I let the notes fade, and let the music of my first song fill my head in preparation.

There is a magic in this hush before I begin. When the audience is silent with anticipation of the opening notes and I myself am hearing them.

And then I lift my fingers onto the keys, and the music in my head becomes music in the world. Debussy's Arabesque no. 1, another favorite of Dad's and mine. All thoughts of Mr. Grouch dissolve. I'm thousands of miles from Julie—from anyone in the music world. I'm anonymous. There's just me and the music, and the memories.

Every negative feeling fades away.

I play Rachmaninoff's Piano Concerto no. 1. The powerful, moody song I would have played with the Apollo orchestra on Lincoln Center stage, I now play for the empty chairs and for Dad. The clean notes ring in the room. With the finale, someone usually brings out a bouquet of flowers. But of course there are none now.

Intrusive thought, they would say in meditation. Acknowledge it, and let it pass. As my fingers fly across the keys, what might have been at Apollo is a weight in my chest. So I transition away from their repertoire and improvise a chord progression to fool around with. I match them to some demanding rhythms in my head. My foot taps along.

I stop abruptly, but the notes hang maddeningly in the air.

That was Grouchy's beat. Why did it have to be so catchy?

I return to the keys and pour out Stravinsky's Sonata in F-sharp Minor. The reflections of my hands in the polished black surface glide from right to left, passing the Steinway logo. The acoustics in this room are *soul*-bending—

"Hey," says a voice behind me.

My bench scrapes the floor as I turn to find someone vaguely, dismayingly familiar.

He's holding a violin case with one hand. And his face . . . is beautiful. A perfectly proportioned nose in a squarish face with earnest thick-lashed brown eyes. Medium build, black hair as glossy as the sharps and flats on this piano, trimmed in a tidy haircut that he probably schedules every other week into his calendar. Even in jeans and a black short-sleeved shirt, he somehow looks ready to step onstage.

"I heard the music," he says. "I had to see if there was a fairy in here. And there is!"

"A fairy? Oh, you mean me?" I laugh self-consciously. Why do I know him? Then a memory swims up out of the depths of my brain. "Carnegie Hall." He was another of the young musicians there to perform. He was handsome even then. But in the time since, he's gotten a major glow up. His face is vampire-level perfection. Born to seduce. My hands immediately go to smooth my hair. Then I remember that I'm actually wearing something nice.

His warm smile crinkles his dark-brown eyes, like maybe he's also a mind-reader. "That's right. Carnegie Hall. You played Beethoven. Op. 110, no. 31, A-flat Major."

"Good memory." I think for a second. "You played . . . oh my gosh, *the Bach*, right? Chaconne from Partita 2."

I was awed by how effortlessly he'd played one of the most difficult pieces ever written for violin.

His name clicks. That's how my memory works. Music, images, then some lucky details.

"Ethan Kang, right?" I ask.

His smile is adorably bashful. "I remember your music, but I'm terrible with names."

"Oh, um. Me too." I should tell him my name, but Loveboat is supposed to be my hiding place and sanctuary. Ethan Kang is huge in classical music. He attended the prestigious Tanglewood Institute when he was just a freshman, playing for people like Yo-Yo Ma. I admire him—but I'm also intimidated, capital I.

Ethan Kang is exactly who Julie didn't want me intersecting with this summer.

"Uh, I was just . . . I didn't think anyone would hear me." I rise from my bench. I need to go. Anywhere else but here.

"Pearl Wong." He snaps his fingers. "Now I remember. Nice Stravinsky just now. What are the odds we'd both be here?"

I feel a dig of panic. Not so low, apparently. I should have expected *someone* to be here. Ever's constantly running into other alumni out in the world.

To my alarm, he flips a chair around and sits backward in it, facing me with his arms casually draped over its back. "So, how long have you been playing?"

My fingers skim over the keys. The faint scent of his cologne is unsettlingly masculine. I have to get out of this conversation. But there's no graceful way to leave.

"Almost my whole life," I say. "You?"

"Violin since I was two. My father is a cellist with the Boston Symphony Orchestra."

"Right, I read that somewhere." I sigh enviously. "Music is in your blood." I wish I had such reassurance—that I'm on the right track. That I'm doing the thing I'm destined for. Dad deeply loved music, but his performances were limited to singing in the shower.

"I was lucky enough to study under Itzhak Perlman," Ethan says.

"He's only like the greatest violinist alive! Didn't he play at the White House?"

"For Obama's inauguration, and even for Queen Elizabeth, years ago."

"Wow." I can't even imagine keeping that kind of company. "So what brought you to Loveboat?"

He smiles and runs both meaty hands—a musician's hands—through his black hair. "I did twenty performances last year. I decided I'd earned a break."

I know how he feels. So much hard work goes into hitting that bar for playing on a stage. And my whole TikTok debacle shows just how quickly a career can get decimated.

Ethan opens his violin case and draws the horsehair of his bow smoothly over a velvet-wrapped cake of rosin, prepping it for action.

"I came by to play, too," he says. "Maybe we can try something together?"

"Um, what? You mean, right now?" Ethan Kang wants to play . . . with me? In normal situations, I'd jump at the chance. But Julie's word is law.

"I'm laying low this summer," I say apologetically. "I need to, actually."

"Burned out?" He's sympathetic.

"No . . . but in some ways?" Getting blown up makes you burned in its own way.

"I'm taking a break this summer myself. But I still play every day." He smiles. "I don't need an audience. Sometimes, it's better when there isn't one."

My shoulders relax a fraction. "It's like air."

"Can't go long without it," he agrees.

He lifts his orange-red violin from his case and plucks a string, tuning it.

"Can you give me an A?"

OMG twist my arm. It's not like there's anyone around. I hit the A key on the piano, letting the note hang in the air as he tunes the strings on his red-orange violin to match. I stare at his instrument.

"That's no ordinary violin," I say.

He holds it out for closer inspection, pleased. "1925 Johann Kuljk. It's Czech."

"Oh my gosh, it must cost like, ten thousand dollars!"

"It's insured. At Carnegie Hall, I played a 1703 Stradivarius. *That* was pure magic."

He played an Excalibur for violinists. They're considered one of the finest instruments ever made, which is saying a lot. "Wow, can I touch you?" I ask.

He laughs and holds out his bare arm, which I run my fingers down. He smiles mischievously.

Wait, what is happening right now? I pull away, surprised by my own boldness.

He rests his foot on his chair as he tucks his violin under his chin and draws a low, quavery note. A row of blue birds tattooed on his bowing arm seem to flutter.

"Cool birds," I say, and he smiles and makes them dance with a syncopated measure.

"My manager almost killed me. *A little too badass for a classical musician,* he said. They're usually hidden under my sleeve. Something easy to warm up? 'Ode to Joy'?" He laughs, teasing. "We must have both played that lovely one ad nauseum in second grade."

"Don't diss on the masters," I say. "'Ode to Joy' can be improved."

"How do you improve on perfection?"

I strike the opening notes on the piano. I make them as grounded and familiar as we learned them. Ethan plays along, perfectly plodding, wearing an exaggerated resigned expression.

But then I jazz it up. Ethan follows my lead. He does a mock tap dance with his feet while his bowing arm keeps playing. We move seamlessly into the other classics of our training years: "Amazing Grace," Bach's Minuet in G, Schubert's "Ave Maria."

On a piano, there are many ways to play a single key that, inside the box, taps its corresponding string with a velvet hammer. But on the violin, the possibilities are infinite. Ethan pulls them all from his. Not a note is a straightforward sound. Each one is textured, growing and diminishing in intensity. His bow teases all sorts of feelings from his strings—a laugh, a caress, then a shout, then a wail of sorrow. The birds dance along.

Together we caper up and down the octaves. When a clock strikes outside, I run my fingers down the length of the piano keys in a dramatic glissando finale. Ethan tucks his violin under his arm in rest position. His eyes shine. We're both a little damp with sweat. Having him play with me is a little like having Dad keep me company. It feels fuller, in a stuffed Christmas stocking kind of way.

"You're so *good*," I say. "Such a powerful sound out of such a tiny box."

"It's rude to talk about the size of someone's instrument," he jokes.

What?! *Not* what I expected of Mr. Ethan Kang. A warm blush spreads across my cheeks as I lower the piano cover over the keys.

"I-I have to go meet some friends for dinner," I sputter.

"We should play again," he says. "I've been lusting after piano-violin duos for a while now." *Lusting?* I swallow. Is he *trying* to plant ideas in my already addled mind? "Do you know Beethoven's Sonata no. 9?" he continues, seemingly oblivious to his own vibe, setting his violin back into its case. "How about Sarasate's *Zigeunerweisen* op. 20, *Gypsy Airs*?"

"Actually, I know the first one cold." I was supposed to perform it with the Apollo violinists. "The *Gypsy Airs*, I've heard. Would be fun to learn it."

"There's always an end-of-summer performance on Loveboat," he says. "Maybe we could play one. Or all of them. Why not?"

"Perform—with you?" I ask dumbly. "I thought you wanted a break."

He smirks, one eyebrow raised. Gestures with his bow to take in the room around us. "It's not exactly the Musikverein."

The Musikverein—the world-famous concert hall in Vienna. Okay. I get it. For him, this *is* a break. Loveboat would be a no-stakes performance, just for the fun of it. And a duo with Ethan Kang? It's a huge opportunity. Especially if it happens at the end of summer, when things will have hopefully blown over.

Still, Julie's face swims before me.

"There's just one thing, though. I'm sort of undercover this summer."

"What do you mean?"

He's from my world. To be honest, if he just Googles me he'll find it, and I'm desperate to talk to someone about it.

"I recently had a . . . well, a kind of blowup on social media."

"Oh?"

"There was a misunderstanding," I say. "I wore a straw hat in a photo collage, and I guess some people thought it was a caricature of Chinese culture, and then I got trampled by all of TikTok." I explain the whole flaming debacle, including Apollo rescinding my spot. It sounds as ridiculous as it is—a hat in the online world, not even the real world—became my downfall. "That's why I'm laying low. Until it blows over."

He's quiet, listening with his whole body. I wait for his reaction, holding my breath. Is the fairy a toad after all?

Ethan shakes his head. "I'm sorry. I learned the hard way: never engage with trolls. They can't be reasoned with. Not in an online forum."

I breathe out. He gets it. "Part of my laying low is I'm going by my mom's maiden name. Lim. Pearl Lim."

"Smart decision. For people like us, always in the spotlight, it's good to be anonymous. I'd have done that, too, if I'd thought of it sooner." He cocks his head. "But laying low all summer doesn't mean you can't still play. The end of summer can be your reentry into the music world."

It's like the stars are aligning. He's walked these paths before me and probably has had to deal with a whole lot more in his career. But I don't want to get my hopes up just yet. Apollo deleted me from their web page so fast. Ethan's rep might not want him associating in public with me either—even at a summer program.

"I can ask my manager," I say. "Maybe you should ask yours, too?"

"This is just an informal show. He won't fuss about it," he says with a confidence I can't help envying. Ethan latches his case closed, his expression suddenly stern. "But I do need to interview you beforehand. Part of my own screening process."

I finger the hem of my shirt nervously. "Go ahead."

"Coffee or tea?"

"What? Uh, tea?"

"Early riser or night owl?"

"Early riser. But I can stay up late. I just still wake up early."

"Favorite color?"

I pause. "Iridescent."

"Iridescent?"

I give a tiny shrug and a mischievous smile. "You know, like *pearls*?"

"Hmm. Not strictly a color, but I'll allow it." He pulls out a small box of candy. "Sour Patch Kid?" With his thumb and forefinger, he aims a red one like a torpedo at my mouth. I open up and he pops it in, the pad of his thumb brushing my upper lip.

I suck on peach flavor, wincing. "Oh, it's sour."

He laughs and pops one into his own mouth. "Can't wait to make more music with ya, Pearl."

Whistling the "Bacchanale" from Saint-Saën's *Samson and Delilah*, he hops off the stage, not bothering with the stairs, and heads out the doors, leaving me staring after him. I rise from my bench. Jam sessions with the rising star Ethan Kang, who didn't care that Apollo booted me out. A new, smoking-hot friend, who gets my need to go incognito . . . gets how music makes me feel . . . what would Dad have thought of him?

A shiver runs through me. Did I just meet my own Boy Wonder? Am I going to have Ever's summer after all? I don't know, but my skin tingles as I head off myself. Like maybe the Loveboat magic is already at work.

7

"Ethan Kang?" Julie exults when I call her from the courtyard. "Violin prodigy from Chicago? That's fantastic!"

"We hit it off," I admit. "He suggested we perform together at the end of summer. There's always a talent show then." A car pulls into the lot, but it's not Sophie and Xavier, who are coming to pick me up for dinner.

"What date?"

I pull up the Chien Tan calendar on the app on my phone. "The last day of the program is August twelfth, so probably August eleventh. It's usually the night before." I pause. August eleventh is the day I was supposed to play my concerto at Lincoln Center. How ironic.

"Well, this is exactly what we need. Good work, Pearl. We can stage your comeback from Taipei. I'll reach out to Ethan's manager."

"Wait, what?" I ask, alarmed. "He said he won't mind. It's just a talent show. For the students. Low stakes. We don't need to involve his manager. I just wanted to make sure you were okay with it because I'm supposed to be laying low."

"Yes, lay low for the summer, and then a *smashing* comeback."

She smacks her hands together. "Ethan's just what I need to nail down the *Teen Vogue* story. We'll run a spotlight piece on you two getting in touch with your cultural roots. 'Music Prodigies' Summer of Cultural Exploration Takes Them to Taipei.'"

My stomach dips. At least *exploring cultural roots* sounds much better than *fleeing from destroyed reputation*. But for a moment, it felt like things could just *happen* this summer. That everything didn't have to be part of a plan. A freedom I didn't even realize I'd tasted is suddenly bottled back up.

"By the time you interview with Apollo's executive director, this social media situation won't even be in the rearview mirror," Julie says. "This comeback performance with a fellow rising star will really drive that home."

"Um, yeah. I just don't want to make it that big a deal—"

"Great! I knew I had his manager's contact. We were in touch about another mutual project."

She's not listening. She's doing what she excels at. Networking among the heavy hitters to build my career. The machinery is already rolling under my feet. This is how it's been since Dad signed me with Julie. She makes the earth move in the right direction. I just have to run fast enough to keep up.

A black BMW van glides into the driveway, the twin beams of its headlights sweeping over the quiet lawn. Sophie's head and a fluttering orange scarf emerge from the back window. Her warm brown eyes catch the light of the streetlamps as she waves.

"Hey, Pearl! Hope you're hungry!"

"I gotta go," I say to Julie. "Thank you, as always."

A driver in a navy cap opens the door for me.

"Um, hi," I say. "I'm Pearl."

He smiles. "Minha." He holds out a helping hand. I touch it briefly, ducking as I climb awkwardly inside.

"Minha's been with the Yeh family for years," Sophie says from deep inside the van. Ever has described Sophie's and Xavier's lives. Their families, their wealth, but this is my first time actually experiencing it. Minha touches his cap and softly shuts the door behind me.

In the back, Sophie and Xavier are adorably nestled together. Her chic orange chiffon dress skims her white ankle boots, and he's in all complementary black, with soft curls spilling into his eyes. He's holding Sophie's hand in a way that tugs at my heart.

"I can't believe you're here," she gushes, squeezing my arm. "This is Xavier. You've met before, right?"

"Once, in Manhattan," I say, bumping the fist he offers with my own. I only know him in the context of Sophie: Sophie visiting us on Xavier's jet. Sophie working with Xavier's family, which apparently controls a Taiwanese empire. "We were all visiting Ever then."

"Xavier just finished his tour of duty in the military," Sophie says. "Every guy over eighteen has to do it here."

I wince. "The army? That seems tough."

"I didn't mind it," Xavier says. "I got to see a different side of Taiwan. Plus, I got pretty buff, see?" He crooks his arm and makes Sophie a muscle with exaggerated effort. He's joking, but the truth is, he's pretty jacked.

Sophie just laughs and swats him arm playfully. "Now he's working at his family's company."

Xavier's lip tugs in a half smile. He seems content with having Sophie do much of the talking for him.

Sophie points out the sights on our way to the restaurant. We pull closer to the enormous pagoda that is Taipei 101, alighting just before it, outside a spectacular black-tiled entrance glowing with purple lights and flanked by stone tigers. An attendant checks our names against a list before admitting us through a security check. Then a sleek glass elevator shoots us up toward the thirty-fourth floor. I gaze out at the city as we rise above it.

"Cé La Vi has a spectacular view of Taipei 101," Sophie says. "Especially on New Year's Eve for fireworks. Ironically it's better to be outside looking at it than inside. That's Xavier's apartment, just across the way." She points out a building with rows of balconies dripping with lush green plants.

I soak it all in. All the photos and stories didn't do any of this justice. Everything is so glamorous. I step out the elevator to face an enormous wall of glass windows and steel beams. A waiter leads us in a wide semicircle around rectangular pillars. The entire floor is one big restaurant, with tables for big family gatherings sunk into the floor and surrounded by benches, spaced evenly in a large ring.

A few people stop Sophie and Xavier to say hello. One guy—a Loveboat alum from the 2000s, apparently—asks Xavier about a film he's making. The two of them are seriously like royalty. Sophie introduces me as "practically her little sister," which is so sweet. I feel a pang of missing Ever. I am so lucky to have her as my *actual* big sister, because it means that all her wonderful friends are my friends, too.

At last, we come to a corner table with the best view of Taipei

101. Lit up against the night, it's even more incredible than Sophie promised: a sleek blue-green tower stabbing upward at the starry night, with every square window blazing.

The waiter hands us menus labeled Contemporary Asian Cuisine. Sophie opens hers wide while Xavier orders a bottle of wine. I stare at the choices on my menu. Oysters on shells. Avocado sushi rolls. Half a lobster with sweet chili and a mango salsa. One dish costs the price of an entire trip to the grocery for Mom and me.

"We invited Marc to join us, but he's got 'staff meetings.'" Sophie laughs. "We never realized all that was going on behind the scenes while we were on Loveboat."

Xavier smiles. "We thought *we* were the action."

"Well we were." Sophie bats her eyelashes playfully. They both turn to me.

"What about *you*?" Sophie asks mischievously. "You've been there an entire day already, which is like a week in the real world. Have you met anyone you connect with? New friends? Romantic prospects?"

"There are twins across the hall from me. Iris and Hollis. I like them. And um, I met a really talented violinist. He reminds me of Rick, actually." Although that's not exactly right. Only in the sense that he's like a Boy Wonder, but otherwise, their personalities seem pretty different. And that flirty moment with the Sour Patch Kid—did it mean anything?

"Sounds promising," Sophie says.

Then Kai jumps to mind, and I smile ruefully. "I met a grumpy beatboxer, too, but he doesn't count."

"A grumpy . . . beatboxer? Can't say I've ever met one of them

73

before," Sophie laughs. "I suppose I should be grateful. Sounds like the kind of people you'd want to avoid."

"Maybe the beatboxer's going through a rough spot. You never know what's happening in people's lives." Xavier winks at me. "Don't count him out, Pearl. Not yet."

"Fair point." Sophie moves her cloth napkin into her lap, and I discreetly copy her. "Loveboat is great for a whole lot of reasons, but mostly because it changes people—helps them evolve. I went on Loveboat totally boy crazy. But it turned out, the *real* love story of that summer was meeting your sister." She smiles at Xavier. "We came later. We had to grow up a little."

He brushes his fingertips along her forearm. "I knew a guy who had to go through a lot of heartache before he found the love of his life."

"Oh, was that you?" she asks, mock innocent. I smile, a bit wistfully this time. They're so, *so* obviously crazy for each other. Will Ever and Rick, will *I*, ever get to a happy ending like theirs?

A well-dressed man approaches our table. "Jonathan, wassup?" Xavier greets him with another fist bump.

"Very busy these days. It's a good problem to have. What can I get for you tonight?"

"Do you have the crispy shrimp burger appetizers?" Sophie asks. She smiles at me. "They're not on the menu, but it's one of their chef's specialties."

"Yes, of course. For you, always," Jonathan makes a note.

I didn't know you could order things not on the menu. It's like access to a secret club. I tuck the information away in case it comes in handy later.

"And for the rest of your meal?" Jonathan asks.

I order the beef noodle soup, a little embarrassed that, with this entire menu of sophisticated entrées, that's the one that calls to me most.

But Xavier gives me a thumbs-up. "It's the national dish," he reassures me.

"I'm happy to try new things, too," I say bashfully.

Sophie laughs. "For sure, that's what this summer's all about!"

"Although you won't necessarily like everything you try," Xavier points out.

"Or every*one*," Sophie says slyly. "Back to the prior Loveboat topic."

I smile. Even their advice together is so complementary. "Honestly, I'm mostly here to hide out," I admit. "My life in music has been . . . exhausting lately."

"Ever told me about the whole Apollo thing," Sophie says. "Totally unfair. It makes me so angry."

"Honestly, I still feel like I got hit by a train," I confess.

Sophie looks thoughtful. "You know, Chanel came under fire years back for posting an ad with a Chinese girl in a straw hat with a bamboo pole. They're a multi-billion-dollar French fashion company, so it really is a different situation and they probably deserved to have come under fire. But my point is, these things are complicated to navigate. Don't beat yourself up." She puts her hand over mine. I tuck myself into her steady warmth, grateful for her support.

"I'm waiting for it all to blow over. I hope it will," I say fervently. But my stomach knots with worry. Chanel deserved to come under fire . . . so maybe I did, too. What if my "comeback" isn't enough? What if I return from my summer here . . . to nothing?

The waiter interrupts to pour a ruby-colored wine into three glasses for us. The bottle is wrapped in gold foil imprinted with a large Chinese character inscribed in a circle.

"Try it," Sophie says, picking up her glass. "It's from Xavier's aunt's vineyard."

She offers a toast. I try a sip, but it's bitter, like other wines I've tried on my music trips, much prettier to look at than it tastes. Maybe it will grow on me over time. But it's cool enough that it came from Xavier's family.

"Well, since you're laying low, you'll have plenty of time to have the time of your life on Loveboat," Sophie says with conspiratorial smile. "Let loose! Within reason, of course. You're younger than we were by a year."

"Which, translated to Loveboat time, is seven years," Xavier points out, straight-faced.

Sophie nudges him affectionately.

I take a drink from my glass of water. That's why I'm here, right? I don't want to waste this summer fretting about my future. "Well, there's a party later tonight," I say slowly. "Some exclusive Loveboat thing."

Sophie's brows go up, and she exchanges a look with Xavier. "What kind of party?"

"The text said it was a 'party in the dark.' That's all I know about it." I shrug. I wasn't technically invited either, although Iris didn't seem to think that mattered.

"Are your friends going?" Xavier asks.

"I think so. But I'm not sure—"

"Go, Pearl," Sophie says. "Just make sure you stick together. Do you have something to wear? I can help with that."

The dress I'm wearing is too delicate for a night on the town, and I mostly brought shorts and T-shirts and a few of my simpler skirts. I wasn't expecting to need my fancier stage dresses, and none of them are right for clubs anyway. "I'll make do for tonight." If I go. "But um, I'm actually doing an end-of-summer performance. I could use your advice for that."

"Excellent! I have a gown in my debut line that will totally complement your figure. Would you wear it for me?"

Would I? Wear a gown from glamorous Sophie's brand-new fashion line?

"I couldn't," I protest. "I mean, you're building your business. I would want to pay, just like any other customer."

"You can't pay me. I haven't had the chance to spoil my little sister yet." Her dimple flashes at me. "I've just had little monsters around. I mean brothers."

I can feel myself weakening. "My manager's trying to get me into *Teen Vogue*. If it works out, can we like, highlight your fashion company?"

She shakes her head. "You're just like Ever, always thinking of other people. It's okay to let the folks who care about you take care of you once in a while. I'd be honored to lend you the gown."

Our waiter sets our crispy shrimp burgers on a chic black square plate before us. They smell heavenly. As my first savory bite melts in my mouth, I peek out the window at the dizzying view and twinkling lights of Taipei. Up here, it's hard to remember the trolls ever came after me. Because it can only be uphill from that point. And watching Xavier brush his lips softly against Sophie's temple while she laughs into her wineglass fills my heart with so much hope. After all, this is Loveboat.

Sophie and Xavier drop me off at campus right before curfew, and I head upstairs, still dazed. My summer is already unfolding so fast in ways I couldn't have imagined. But now the more pressing question is, do I go to this party?

I hear Iris and Hollis arguing as I reach our rooms.

"It's not safe," Iris says.

"It's in the dark!" Hollis answers. "No one will see me."

I poke my head inside. The twins are both in black: Iris has her hair twined in a braided crown and clad in a form-fitting catsuit. Hollis's wearing flowy printed pants and a lightweight black shirt with long sleeves flaring at the wrists. Their green hair glows like a lava lamp.

"Everything okay?" I ask.

Iris's face is flushed red. "I don't think Hollis should go clubbing tonight, that's all." They've obviously been arguing for a while.

"This is such a double standard," Hollis says. "I'm even dressed more modestly than you."

"We're in a foreign country. I don't know if it's safe out there at night, when people can misunderstand." Iris waves a hand at the window.

Hollis gives me a pleading look. "Pearl, you tell her."

"I'm missing a whole subtext," I admit.

"The world hasn't exactly been the safest place for nonbinary people," Iris says. "They—"

"*They* can speak for themself," Hollis says, dignified.

Iris's shoulders slump. Their dynamic reminds me a little of

Mom and Ever. Iris loves Hollis so much, and is trying so hard, but Hollis clearly doesn't want that kind of protection. But I'm not that familiar with what they're struggling with.

"I get how sometimes we need to lay low," I say, choosing my words carefully. Although my experience laying low is really different from Hollis's. "But well, you guys did say your parents want you to have the full Loveboat experience. They trusted you *both* to come."

"*Exactly,*" Hollis says.

Iris frowns. "Hollis is . . . more vulnerable. A lot of people still misunderstand them."

"A lot of people misunderstand a lot of things," Hollis says. "At home, some people hate anyone with our Asian faces. Doesn't mean we don't go out." The twins stare at each other a beat, with expressions identically set and stubborn.

"Pearl, help!" Iris says. "Do you get what I'm trying to say?"

I'm glad they both consider me a safe person to talk to, and I want to do right by them both. "My sister's boyfriend's sister complains he gets a lot more freedom from their mom because he's a boy. Their mom worries about her being more vulnerable as a girl, because of the Big Bad World, which is sadly real. And that's like what you're saying, Iris, right? Hollis might be more vulnerable."

"Yes, that's it!" Iris nods vigorously.

"But . . . I also think the point of Loveboat is we're supposed to make our own decisions, right?"

"Right!" Hollis says. "And my decision is, I'm going. I just want to be a normal person."

I can relate to that.

"I don't like it!" Iris heaves a breath, trying to steady herself. "But Pearl's right." She rummages through a plastic bag on her bed, changing the subject. "All right. We bought masks, in case we don't like any of the ones there. We got you one, too, Pearl. It's pretty comfortable."

She passes me a glittery purple one with a curl of ribbons over the left brow. "Wow. Thank you," I say. I hold it uncertainly, letting it catch the light. It's so sweet and considerate of them to have gotten me one, and such a pretty one, even when I was on the fence about going. But I've never gone to a masked party before. I set it to my face and look through the eye holes at my transformed reflection in the mirror. It covers the entire upper half of my face, leaving only my chin and the curve of my mouth exposed. I look like a wild thing, and even though I can feel my heart beating nervously in my chest, I like it.

A knock sounds on the open door. It's a bunch of the kids I met in the courtyard, dressed in everything from a full-on red leather cat suit to a bikini top paired with a black skirt so tiny it's practically a Band-Aid. Plump, bare arms swing, glossy hair gets shaken back, a girl applies deep-red lipstick.

Whoa. This group is *hot*.

"Ready to roll?" asks a guy.

And I make my choice. It's a party in the *dark*, masked to the hilt, and this will probably be the only time I go out all summer. So I may as well make it a night.

"We have to look out for each other," I say, looking from Iris to Hollis. "We have to be smart about staying safe and out of the spotlight."

"Definitely," Iris says.

The spotlight . . . reminds me of Ethan Kang. He's here to take a break, too, and if his tattoo is any indication, it seems he'd be down for cutting loose for a bit.

"I'm going to invite my new friend Ethan," I say. I find his number in the student directory and text him: **It's Pearl. We're going out. Want to join? Meet in my hallway.**

I cross to my room and rummage through my closet, finally settling on a sleeveless white eyelet top with pearly buttons over a black skater's skirt. I frown at my reflection. Iris and Hollis crowd into my doorway.

"Is this okay?" I ask anxiously.

"You look *fab*," Hollis reassures me.

But I tilt my head. Do I look . . . stiff? I undo the top three buttons of my shirt, letting the cool air hit skin that doesn't usually see the light of day.

"You have such a great body. I wish I had your boobs," Iris says, and I laugh self-consciously. "And don't forget this!" She hands me a cloth bag to stash my mask.

I tuck it away. The night air feels charged. I may not be hobnobbing in Manhattan, but tonight, just for one night, I get to be someone I've never been before.

Ethan's reply chimes: **Sure, thanks! I'll bring the Sour Patch Kids.**

I can still feel the ghost of his thumb against my lip. An overlarge smile spreads over my face.

"He's in," I say.

Iris smirks knowingly. "And so it begins."

8

We have one major problem: counselors are stationed *everywhere*. A group in blue shirts are gathered in the art gallery in the main lobby, so the front doors are out. Another group is playing Mahjong in the kitchen, shutting off a second escape route. The fire escape windows are barred with an emergency sign in Chinese and English for good measure: Alarm Will Sound.

On our way down the hallway that leads outside to the blue pipe, we run into five girls in matching mini dresses.

"Everywhere's guarded," says one girl. "We've been trying for an hour, but they aren't going anywhere. We're crashing upstairs. Join us when you give up." They slip up the back stairwell.

"Maybe we should join them?" Ethan says, raising a brow. He's wearing a sleeveless black shirt that shows off surprisingly cut biceps. A gold chain hangs around his neck. Flirty Sour Patch Kid aside, I'm glad he accepted my invitation, and I don't want to let him down.

"Do you think the admins heard about the party?" Iris asks. We've already filled Ethan in on it, although he didn't get an invite either.

"Maybe, but this is all just Marc's fault," I say. "*He* snuck out when he was a student here, so he knows all the routes."

"Should we just give up?" Hollis looks crestfallen. They finger a fold of their silk top.

"No way," I say. "This is Loveboat."

"That's right!" Iris says. "Our dad and his friends climbed over the wall to get out!"

"Which is exactly what we need to do," I tell them. "But we'll need a distraction."

Ethan's brow rises even higher. "What do you have in mind?"

I smile. "I'll take care of it. I did it for my sister my whole life. You guys go out the back."

Iris frowns. "What about you?"

"Just tell me where you're going and I'll meet you there."

Ten minutes later, I carry Sophie's cornucopia into the kitchen. The counselors look up in surprise. Four of them are sitting around a shiny stainless steel counter with creamy Mahjong tiles laid out in a partial square.

"Hi, I'm Pearl," I say.

"Marc's little friend. Come join us," says the lone girl.

A thin guy shrugs off his jacket, frowning. "It's past curfew."

"Oh, it's just the first night," says the girl, spinning a woven friendship bracelet on her wrist. "I'm Zao. This is Hao-Yu," the naysayer, "Mike, and Jayden."

"I brought snacks to share. There are too many for me." I set the basket on a counter far from the back door . . . and it tips over. Oranges, guavas, and mooncakes spill onto the table and a few carefully selected unripe mangoes bounce on the floor. "Oh no!"

The counselors set down their game tiles and join me in a scramble after the rolling fruits. Out of the corner of my eye, I see Iris and Ethan slipping toward the back door. I tear open a box of mooncakes, making as much noise as I can, and thrust them into everyone's hands. It's chaos for a few minutes, and when the fruit is all packed and the crumbly cakes opened, we're friends.

"My favorite brand!" Mike says, sitting down with a golden square stamped with a floral pattern. "Very fancy. Very generous of you."

I don't know a lot about the culture here, but thanks to Sophie's gift baskets over the years, I know something about gourmet mooncakes.

"These are red bean, lotus paste is my favorite. This one's more savory. Does anyone have a nut allergy?"

The counselors are pretty cool. They're all college students here in town. They joined this program to practice English and meet students from all over the world. They tell me stories about previous years of counselors. Someone is a member of the local congress. Another is a famous singer.

"Amazing," I say. "This program is pretty special."

"It's because it chooses future leaders. Like you, Pearl. I hear you're a musician like up to here." Zao holds her hand at a level high over our heads.

I cringe inwardly. "I play some. What about you guys? Anyone else play an instrument?"

"Zao plays a mean French horn," Jayden says.

"I love the horn. Would love to hear you sometime," I say.

Zao dips her head, bashful, but a smile lights her face.

Not a sound from the corridor beyond the kitchen. The others must be long gone by now. Mission accomplished. I stand and nudge the basket toward them.

"I've gotta go, but please, help yourselves and I'll just pick up the rest tomorrow."

Zao winks at me. "We saw nothing. Not even your friends."

Dang. So she clocked everything after all. I smile ruefully. "Sharp eyes."

"It's Loveboat," Zao says. "And that was quite an effort. Seriously standing ovation." She mimes giving me one, and I have to laugh.

"You'll still need to get past the guard booth at the driveway's end," says Mike.

Hao-Yu opens his mouth, pulled low in a frown, but I'm already rushing for the door.

"I'll figure it out, thank you!" I say, and disappear before they can change their minds.

A full moon illuminates the courtyard almost as bright as day. The night air is still muggy. The others are stuck next to an enormous dumpster by the stone wall. Hollis and Iris are arguing with two guys, but when they see me, they fold me into a three-way hug.

"I can't believe you got out!" Hollis says.

"It was, uh, easier than I thought," I say. Now if only we can make it the rest of the way. "Where's Ethan?"

"He's scoping out the main walk," Iris begins, but Ethan appears from the shadows.

"Bad news, kids. There are guards *everywhere*. Even under the blue pipe."

Hollis scowls. "We *have* to go over the wall. It's the only way."

I tip my head back to study it, experimentally fingering the brush that covers the bricks. Too soft to provide any kind of climbing leverage.

"It's really high," I say. "At least a story?"

"I don't know how our dad got over it. Maybe they've built it up since?"

"There are probably guards on the other side," Iris says. "Marc has our playbook, right?"

"Yeah, but he won't expect us to go over *this*. And he doesn't have enough counselors to man every foot of it. If we can get over it, we have a fighting chance at making a run for it."

"Someone's coming," hisses one of the girls. Iris tugs me into a space in the dumpster's shadow. My head bumps a metal beam overhead, and I see stars. Everyone is cramming into me. My heart pounds in my throat as a counselor passes by, close enough that I could reach out and grab his arm. If he catches me, my mom will get a phone call for sure.

But back home it's midmorning, and in Manhattan everyone is rosining their bows and tuning up their instruments. Me? I'm wide awake from jet lag. And Taipei is calling to me.

"Come on." I retrace our steps. "We'll need to find a ladder. Or build one."

The dumpster is promising. It's surprisingly not totally disgusting. I grasp a metal edge, find a toe hold, and boost myself on top. My heart pounds as my head clears the stone wall. I've

86

never done anything like this before. The street on the other side is rushing with cars.

"Someone may see you," Ethan whispers. "Duck down."

I crouch low in the shadow of the wall. "We need cushions," I say. "Lots of them."

"There are cushions on the lounge chairs," Hollis says.

They disappear with a few others, and return five minutes later, arms loaded with fat bolsters and couch cushions.

"Perfect, hand them up to me," I say. Plush velvet presses into my hands, and I rise up and drop the cushions over the wall until a small mountain has risen on the other side.

"If I make it, follow me," I say.

"Be careful!" Hollis says. "People have broken arms falling off this wall."

"Now you tell me!" I ease myself onto the rough stones on top, then lower myself off the other side until I'm hanging by my hands, stretched out like an elongated cord. Breathing a quick prayer, I drop the last few feet into the pile. My feet plunge between the cushions, but I land softly on my rear. The cushions slip under me, and I twist around to face the road. Cars rush by without a care in the world.

"Tell me you're not dead," Ethan calls softly.

A laugh bubbles from my lips. "Alive and over!" I roll off and reposition the cushions. A few minutes later, Iris drops down beside me. The rest follow.

"Ugh, I made out with a pile of bird shit," says a guy.

A bottle of hand sanitizer gets passed around.

"How will we get back in?" Iris asks.

We look back up at the wall. There's no going back, that's for sure.

"Who knows?" I ask. Then we all laugh.

We take the metro toward the heart of the Xinyi District, the same part of town I had dinner in. Even at midnight, the streets are packed with people eating fluffy golden bread out of brown paper bags. Hollis buys us all a round of boba tea, and we saunter down the streets with a rainbow of cups. On the corner just outside, a man in a stained coat and shabby pants is preaching in Mandarin, but the fire and brimstone still comes through.

"This is awesome!" Hollis crows. "I feel like such a badass."

"A badass with boba!" Iris laughs. Hollis looks crestfallen.

"Boba *is* badass," I say, and clink cups with Hollis, who gives me a grateful smile.

Iris leads the way to a high-rise fronted by glass doors. She compares the building's number to the address on her phone.

"Is this it?" she asks. "We're on the right street."

Music is spilling from an upper-floor window. I point to a sign: Frank Taipei. Two bouncers dressed in black turtlenecks and black pants are checking IDs at the door.

"Isn't that it?" I ask.

She studies the text from Wolf. "It says *after* Frank. I don't get it."

"There's no address in his text," I say. "Or . . . hers?"

Iris texts back: **Hey Wolf, we're not sure if we're here**. There's no answer.

Ethan cranes his neck to see around the bouncers. "I don't

think this is it," he says.

"Come on in," says the bouncer. "No cover before midnight."

"They always want more cuties like us." Iris elbows me in the ribs. "Party in the Dark doesn't start until one anyways. Let's try it." Iris is already handing her ID to the bouncer. She leads the way up the elevators to the tenth floor. Asian paintings of craggy mountains hang on the walls and leafy vines hang from a trellis, all bathed in soft lantern light.

"This is *definitely* not the Party in the Dark," I say. A part of me wonders if I should even be here, so exposed. But the music is solid, and after being on my own for so many years, it feels good to be with people. And it's only for tonight. Tonight no one knows me yet.

Iris glances anxiously at Hollis, who lifts their chin bravely and smooths their green hair. "Let's try it."

We link arms and move into the club. Hip-hop music blares. Guys with cigarettes lounge around tables, eyeing the dance floor.

"Oh no," Hollis moans. "Don't look now."

Across the dance floor, Marc is dancing with a tall guy his age, slow and intimate. He's dressed for the night out—a slim black button-down over black jeans. I try to duck behind a pillar, but he spots me. Recognition crosses his face.

"Damn," I say, spinning around. I need to get out of here, but the space is packed. There's nowhere to go.

Marc says something to his date and makes his way toward us.

"I'm so busted," I moan.

"Hello, Pearl. I should have guessed you'd make it past my extra security." Marc stops at the bar and orders a drink from the bartender. "A milk for you?" He smirks.

"On the rocks," I say.

He laughs. "Do you even know what that means?"

"Definitely not."

A guy has sidled up to Hollis and Iris, and the three of them are chatting. Ethan is holding court with two girls hugging designer purses.

"Are you here to bounce us?" I ask Marc.

"Not yet." He winks and pours two glasses of lemon-flavored water. "Actually, I convinced my staff that I'd be able to keep a better eye on you guys out here rather than chasing you with them from inside. And you know what? I was right. Here you all are on Day Zero—even better than your sister. She and Sophie waited till we were here at least a week."

He puts a glass of water into my hand and we toast. I smile. I'm reminded of something Ever told me just before I left. "Ever said she dated someone on Loveboat besides Rick. Do you know who?"

"I wouldn't call it dating." He reaches for his oncoming margarita. "You should ask Ever yourself."

"She won't tell me."

He shrugs. "Curiosity killed the cat." He takes a sip.

"I could ask around, but I'd rather hear it from a friendly source."

He smiles and chews on an ice cube. "It was Xavier Yeh. He's the son of—"

"*Xavier?*" I yelp. "But he's with Sophie."

"So you know him."

"My sister dated Sophie's Xavier?!" My head is spinning. No,

90

no, no, that can't be right. Ever has never once mentioned this to me. He's basically like an extended member of the family. "Wow, I can't believe it. I mean, they're friends *because of Sophie*. And they're always so formal around each other."

"That's probably why." Marc leans against the bar. "Sometimes romantic entanglements can wreck a friendship. But that's life. We figure it out through trial and error. Hopefully less error and more trial, and lots of forgiveness at the end."

He tips his drink at me, then toward the guy he was dancing with earlier. "I'll watch you all from across the room. And now that I'm chaperoning, you all better have a good time."

The guy is chatting with an elderly couple. He seems friendly. Respectful, which always scores points with me.

"So you and he . . ." My voice trails off.

"It's kind of an open secret. My counselors know, and my family of course, but that's about it. I prefer it that way."

"I get it," I say. It's nobody's business but his.

"Well, cheers, Pearl." With a smile, he heads back to his date on the floor.

9

We dance for hours. A bunch of other Loveboaters arrive, equally confused by the address, and we overrun the place. One kid takes over the DJ's stand, spinning all the songs of the moment. Ethan busts out a few killer dance moves, surrounded by a cheering ring. He takes two giant steps onto a chair, then a large wooden table, and the kids go wild cheering as he grabs his knee and pumps it up and down.

"Ethan Kang! Ethan Kang! Ethan Kang!" they chant.

Eyes sparkling, he tugs me up with him for a few spins under his arm that end with my back pressed against him, his arm around my waist, and my body giddy and warm all over. I have a view over everyone's bobbing heads. But then I catch sight of Iris aiming her phone camera in our direction. Exactly what I need to avoid.

"Pumpkin time," I say to Ethan, who looks confused. I untangle myself and hop off the table. "It's from Cinderella," I call up to him. "Means it's time to disappear."

"Oh, okay," he laughs, still a bit confused. "Not for long, I hope."

I smile and join Iris, who shouts over the music, "It's like they opened the club just for us!"

I whip my hair out of my face and let it shake down my back. Another girl is climbing onto the table with Ethan. Phone cameras are out, memorializing this night, all of which will end up hashtag-Loveboat on social media. I head outside to the patio, glad I've managed to dodge them all. Although my photo getting posted doesn't seem like a huge risk anymore. There's no Pearl Lim to tag, and as long as I don't reshare anything myself, the trolls aren't likely to run across me.

Besides, this place is nice, with glass lanterns, an outdoor patio with a slanted view of Taipei 101, and people chilling eating shrimp tempura. Marc has settled into a couch with his date, just talking.

"Ethan is *so hot*," says a girl setting aside her large coconut cocktail.

"He's a great dancer!" I report.

"I heard he used to be super shy and nerdy. Never talked to girls. Now he's the life of the party."

"That's so sweet," I say. I envision an awkward teen Ethan finally realizing he was a swan. Now he's a natural ham. I look in his direction and am surprised to find him looking right at me. The girl winks. "Wish me luck, I'm going in!" She raises her arms and undulates her body, then sidles in his direction.

I watch her reach his table, but then I'm distracted by Hollis. A middle-aged man with a bristled mud-colored beard is dancing too close, trying to put his hands on their waist while Hollis tries to escape. I nudge Iris, pointing, and her eyes narrow dangerously.

93

We both push through the crowd toward them until I'm close enough to grab Hollis by their arm. I stomp on the guy's foot for good measure, getting a rewarding yelp of pain. As soon as we're back with the Loveboat crowd, Hollis rubs their cheek, relieved.

"I couldn't get away," they say.

"This is why I didn't want you coming out," Iris scolds. "People have all sorts of ridiculous misconceptions."

"Hollis's not the problem," I say. "That gross guy was."

"Seriously. Tell her, Pearl," Hollis says.

Iris huffs. "Well, should we find that other party?"

"Maybe we don't need to go anymore," I say.

But a text chimes on everyone's phones. Mine included this time.

PARTY IN THE DARK. COME ONE, COME ALL.

My details must have been loaded onto the directory after all. And this time, the mysterious Wolf has provided an address. My insides twang with nerves as we meet each other's eyes.

"It's right across the street," Iris says.

"Guess it's one o'clock," Hollis's eyes are wide, as nervous as I am.

"Are we really doing it?" I ask.

"Are you kidding? Of course we are," Iris says.

Our skin is glistening with sweat, and it's later than I've ever been out before. I should call it a night. But the club is right there, and I'm dying to know what this is about.

"All right, let's go then." I catch Ethan's eye, where he's downing a glass of amber beer at the bar. I smile and signal that we're headed out. Then I wave to Marc, who gives me a small two-fingered salute.

"Think Marc knows about the party?" Iris whispers as we crowd into the elevator.

"I doubt it," I say. "Although a bunch of us just left all at once, so maybe he'll wonder what's going on."

We're deceiving him, and I feel guilty. He put up a good fight tonight, stationing his counselors everywhere, and even showing up himself. But . . . we put up a better one. I link arms with Ethan and Hollis as we head outside and spill onto the streets. Iris lights a cigarette, blowing a cloud of smoke away from us.

She catches my gaze and waves at the smoke. "Sorry. I need to stop. Bad for sports."

I dig in my purse for a stick of gum and pass it to her. "And maybe you've got an undiscovered talent as a tuba player. You'll need all your lung capacity."

She laughs. "Ouch, you know how to hit it where it hurts." She takes another drag, then puts out the cigarette on a public ashtray and pops the gum into her mouth. "I played piano for five years until I realized I'm tone-deaf! Tragic, right? If only I'd realized it sooner, I'd have tortured myself less and played volleyball more."

We both laugh. The crowd of Loveboaters is making their way into a line. Iris squints at the name on the door. The Dark Club. It looks like a new sign.

Iris's face grows sly. "I have a feeling this is the *real* program kickoff." She tugs us toward it. "Come on."

"I'm pretty wiped out," Ethan says. "Guess it's *my* pumpkin time." He grins.

"It's one in the afternoon back home," I point out, surprising myself. I've become the Loveboat party evangelist. Who knew?

But time has frozen tonight, and nothing we've done and will do before the sun rises counts toward our existence on earth.

"Tempting, but I need my beauty rest," he drawls. "You girls will be okay? Do you need a bodyguard?"

"Oh, *please*," Iris rolls her eyes.

"Pearl's taking care of all of us," Hollis adds.

"I know." He smiles at me. "I'll see you tomorrow? We're"—he lifts his arms, pretending to play his violin, keeping mum, mostly—"right?"

I can't help smiling, even though I'm disappointed he's leaving. I was looking forward to dancing with him more, and in the dark . . . who knows what might have been? But dancing in the dark can still happen at this party, with or without him.

"Meet you in the auditorium after classes," I say, and he touches my arm with what feels like a promise, then heads for the metro.

"All right, let's do this!" Iris says.

We all slip on our masks: Iris dances in her white Peking opera mask, Hollis smooths the whiskers on their soft cat mask, and I tighten the glittery purple one over my cheeks.

"How do I look?" Hollis asks. Under their sweet feline mask, their voice is anxious.

"Very mysterious," I say, and they smile.

"At least mine covers the zit on my nose," Iris says, leading us to the door. Loud guitars and bone-deep bass vibrations are pouring out, but two large bouncers in black turtlenecks jam shoulder to shoulder and block our way.

"Loveboat only," says the heavier of the two. A weight of silver chains hangs around his neck. By the looks of his powerful hands, no one who doesn't belong is slipping by without a throat choke.

"We're Loveboat," Iris says airily. We pull out our Chien Tan IDs, and after a close inspection against a list of names on their phones they let us through.

Inside, the space is dark and swirling with a cold smoky mist, like liquid nitrogen. We pause at a table loaded with face masks of every kind, along with hats and accessories. I wrap a gold feather boa around my neck. Iris hides her thick hair in a duchess's conical cap. Hollis trades their top hat for reindeer antlers and strikes a pose.

"We look totally amazing," Iris gloats.

Hollis moves further down the table, peering into little white cups. "Hey, look. Mouthwash." Hollis laughs.

"Only in Taipei! But it's a nice touch." Iris hands little cups around. I swish the minty liquid around in my mouth, and we take turns spitting into a metal bucket.

I run my tongue over my clean teeth as we follow the crowd into another darkened room pulsing with music. Shades are pulled tight over a row of windows, which admit just enough ambient light for me to make out the silhouettes of people dancing to a beat loud enough to thump my rib cage. Heads are distorted by long paper noses and feathery plumes on wide-brimmed hats.

"This Wolf is quite the party-thrower," Iris says. "There must be over a hundred Loveboaters in here!"

"Do you think Wolf's here?" Hollis asks.

"Of course, but we'll never find them!" Iris answers. "They're anonymous for a reason."

A cold bottle is thrust into my hands by someone manning a

drinks table. Beer by the scent of it. I twist off the top and take a swallow. The clinking of bottles is everywhere. I turn back to Hollis and Iris—but they're gone! I turn, searching for antlers above the head of the crowd. Nothing. I panic. There's no way to find them again in here.

Then Hollis grabs my hand, and Iris my other. Cold beer sloshes onto my leg.

"Oh, thank God," I gasp.

"Sorry. I can't see anything!" Hollis yells.

"You're not supposed to!" Iris sways against me, laughing.

"This DJ is great!" I say. I set my beer on a table my hip found, and the three of us move into the center of the floor.

It's dizzying to dance in the darkness. Both forbidden and freeing. We aren't here to impress, and for the first time in my life, I don't have to worry about protecting my reputation.

And so I throw my arms up and let loose with an abandon I would never let my own mirror see. Bodies bump me from all sides, out of sync with the music. A warm pelvis shimmies against my backside, some jerk showing off a boner, and I yell and leap out of reach, gathering Iris and Hollis closer, tightening our circle protectively.

My eyes have adjusted enough that I can see silhouettes kissing on the dance floor. Shadows and black lights play over their bodies. A hand tugs a spaghetti strap off a thin, bare back. A guy in a shiny gold outfit materializes beside me and before I know what's happening, he plants a mouthwash-flavored kiss on the corner of my mouth.

He moves on to Iris, then melts into the crowd.

"Oh my God!" Iris laughs. "*That's* what the gargle was for."

I touch my fingers to where the kiss is still burning on my lips. The adrenaline of dancing in the dark gives way to another surge. The darkness and booze and anonymity has turned everyone from mice into lions.

Ever went clubbing here in Taipei, but I doubt she attended something like this. She would not approve. And now she's regressing. She and Stan Yee are probably sitting in a starkly lit coffee shop talking about stocks or whatever.

Well, I'm not ending up like that. I'm halfway around the world, and no one except Ethan, Iris, and Hollis knows I'm even here.

Iris has draped her arms around the neck of a tall guy, who goes in for a kiss. She lets him, and the embrace is deep and passionate. I feel my face warm under my mask. Another guy is dancing just to my right. I turn to him, and our masks bump as his cold lips brush my cheek. A nervous laugh slips from me and I slide away. I grab Hollis's hand, only to find it's not Hollis, but a stranger's, who takes hold of my arm and presses his mouth to mine.

He tastes like the mouthwash. I shiver, torn between liking it and not. A warm hand gropes at a random height on my midriff. I smack it away, feeling powerful and invincible. How many of these people will I pass on campus tomorrow and not know that we've shared a moment in the dark? I reach the shaded windows where the glow of light makes the colors of people's masks more visible, although not much else.

From one of the windows, a guy is moving to the Adele song toward me. His black mask and devil horns cover the upper three-quarters of his face. He grabs my hand and dances with me, pulling my body firmly against him.

I sway with him. He smells like soap, like he just took a shower. His hand goes on my hip, tentative at first, asking permission, and I give it, moving closer into his orbit. I slide my hand down the soft skin of his bare arm. Our bodies meld together, moving and grinding in time to the music.

The crowd surges, sandwiching us more tightly together. Something hard presses against my lower abdomen, and I know what it is and what it means. A thrill of adrenaline courses through me. Do I dare take the initiative for once in my life? He'll never know who I am, and the fact that we're both here is an open invitation the curious part of me can't resist. I slide my hand up to cup his jaw. My fingers graze a scar at its base.

And then I rise on tiptoes and his mouth meets mine.

His lips are full and soft and taste like lemonade. They nibble along my upper lip, taking hold of it teasingly. Wherever he learned to kiss, it was a very good school. His hand braces the small of my back. His lips glide lightly over my cheek and find my earlobe. My body hums, and I let out my own moan of pleasure as his hand slowly caresses my jaw.

The song ends and a new one begins. An indie pop hit that was big last year. Our dancing adjusts to match the syncopated beat, and this time, his tongue parts my lips and sweeps my mouth, tasting me. My skin flushes with heat. My first kiss in spin the bottle, and a few from summer camp a few years ago, were all clumsy bumpings of noses and lips. This is *completely* different. I grasp him tighter, pressing him even closer. There's a kind of hunger building, driving me to keep going and never stop.

Another surge of the crowd knocks us sideways. My head

bumps his chin, bending my mask. Its strap tightens around my head, then snaps. The whole thing falls to the ground.

"Oh no!" I drop to a crouch, groping along the sticky floor until my fingers find its glittery surface between his blue sneakers. Pressing it to my face, I rise again, but he's already turned away, slipping into the crowd. Gold filigree on his horns flashes in the moonlight.

"Hey, wait!" I dart after him, but dancing bodies are everywhere.

And just like that, he's gone.

Hours later, the club begins to thin out. I keep searching for the devil's horns, but I can't find him in the crowds. I saw the texture of his mask, so did he see my face? Would he recognize me if he spots me in class? I swear under my breath. I was supposed to *lay low*. What if somehow it gets out that I was here?

I touch my lips with my fingertip. They feel tender and slightly swollen. I'm not normally a random hookup person, but that whole encounter sort of rocked my world. I need to find that guy to be sure this night stays a secret. But I also *want* to find him.

I spot Hollis and Iris dancing in an almost empty room. Both of them are giddy with the late hour.

"There you are! Let's go," I urge, and they both loop their arms around my waist.

Hollis lays their head on my shoulder, still rocking to the music.

"Oh, what a night," they sing off-key. And I can't help but smile.

The three of us spill outside into the gentler night air. My sweat-dampened blouse clings to my skin. I yank it loose and shake it to create a breeze. Ethan texted me a while ago: **let me know when you guys get home so I don't worry.** I text him back, smiling a bit: **Okay, DAD.** Purple glitter on my fingers catches the light.

"I'm in love!" Iris wails. "I'm in love with a total stranger with clammy hands that I'll never kiss or see again. There must have been a few hundred Loveboaters in there. And look—lucky them!" Iris points out a couple making out in a dimly lit doorway, black masks dangling at their sides. "Guess they decided to leave together."

I feel my own dig of disappointment. I have no idea who my Devil was. And now he's gone forever.

We round a corner and pull off our masks. Light from a dress shop's window display shines on our glitter-dusted faces.

"Do you think they'll hold another one?" Hollis asks dreamily. "I danced with someone. They were so sweet and warm. They kissed my hand. I wouldn't mind finding them again."

"We can try Wolf," Iris says, her fingers already flying over her cell phone screen. "When he knows how good a time we had, maybe he'll want to have another party! **We had a blast**," she speaks aloud as she types. "**Let's do it again!** Should I put a heart at the end? Three? Is that too much?"

"Maybe leave them all off?" I suggest.

"Yes. Good call. Keep this simple. I need to stop overanalyzing." Iris shoots the text off and pockets her phone. The metro has long since shut down, so we cram into the back of a cab and head back to campus.

"How'd it go for you, Pearl?" Iris asks.

"I kissed someone, too," I admit, "but he vanished."

"That was the point." Iris's arms slump miserably to her side. "No strings."

"He was about this tall, wearing blue sneakers." I grasp at the memory. The white V logo along the side. "Veja's brand."

"Oh, that's cool," Iris says. "Aren't they the company that are big into sustainable practices? Regenerative cotton and all?"

"You're right." The choice says something good about my mystery kisser, doesn't it? I trace my fingertips along the underside of my jaw. "Also he had a scar here. Probably not visible."

"So you actually have things to go on. Like the glass slipper— that's how the prince found Cinderella. Pearl! You could make a Loveboat fairytale come true!"

My heart does a little lurch, and I try to quash it. I didn't come on this trip to meet a guy. But I also haven't ever had an encounter like that before. "It's not much to go on."

"Better than me. The only way I'll find my guy again is if I kiss everyone on the program." She pauses as our cab reaches the Chien Tan campus and pulls past the darkened guard booth. We're so late that even the night watch has gone to bed. "Maybe that's not such a bad plan. If you can't find your loafers, Pearl, you can always resort to that."

I laugh. "I have to say, this Wolf guy is pretty impressive getting so many people to come out. I wonder who he is."

"All we know is he's a Loveboat student," Iris says. She releases the latch on her seat belt and, since we're jammed in, considerately unbuckles mine, too. We pour from the cab and head inside on tiptoes.

"Was everyone on Loveboat invited?" I whisper as we finally reach the safety of our doors.

"No. The girls down the hallway didn't get an invite. Not sure why."

"So it's a smaller pool of people. I wonder why I got added?"

"Maybe Wolf just kept adding people throughout the night. If we could find him, we could get that invite list we were checked against," Iris muses.

That would be a starting point for Veja-wearing kissers. And if my name is on it, it's a list I definitely don't want out there.

"Let's check the directory for his number." Iris opens their door, drops her mask on her dresser, and opens her laptop. "It isn't here," she concludes after a minute. "He's probably using a burner phone or Google number. Maybe someone can trace him. Someone here has to be a hacker."

"Well, we've got all summer to find our missing princes, right?" Hollis sits on their bed and kicks off their shoes.

Ethan pops to mind. My maybe Boy Wonder and the maybe possibilities between us. As opposed to this mystery guy. But Hollis's right. We've got all summer.

Why can't I figure out both?

A smile spreads over my face, mirrored on Iris's. "So let's go find them," I say. "Game on."

10

When I wake up, the sun is blazing through my room's blinds, beaming right into my eyes. The scent of smoke has soaked into my skin. I sniff at a sweat-crusted lock of hair and wrinkle my nose, then haul myself over to the showers. It's past noon. All is quiet. My first Mandarin class has fallen by the wayside, which is not really a loss, but if I hurry, I should still make Traditional Chinese Music. That one I definitely don't want to miss.

There's no answer to my knock on Hollis and Iris's door. Downstairs in the dining hall, though, I spot them behind the serving counter with the chef. Hollis's hands are wrist deep in a vat of flour, and Iris is pouring a frosted jug of cream into it. Must be the food elective. Or maybe they're just adding a personal touch to dinner on their own.

I wave and Iris waves back, and I grab a *bāozi* from a steamer on the buffet and take a bite. Hot! Too hot. The sweet pork filling scalds my tongue, and I ruefully fan my burning mouth.

Other students are lingering at the round tables, sorted by style—casual, grungy, swanky, prim. Maybe that's how they found each other? I find myself scanning the shoes of every guy of medium height that I pass, all the way to the music room. Sneakers, Crocs, sandals, even terrycloth slippers, but no Vejas. And I don't recognize anyone . . . but does anyone recognize *me*? I hope not, and I hope so, and I'm not sure which is stronger at the moment.

My phone chimes with a text from Julie: **All set with Ethan's manager. Everything's working out great. Just keep your nose clean. Come fall, you'll be back in the game.**

Keep your nose clean. Too late for that. Guiltily, I pocket my phone. All the more reason I need to find my mystery kisser and convince him to keep that party strictly under wraps.

Traditional Chinese Music is in a smaller auditorium in the east wing. About a dozen students are gathered around a collection of instruments onstage. A gong reverberates as I enter, struck by a padded mallet held by a mischievously smiling woman. Her mane of rich, dark-red curls tumbles over a green plaid dress tied at the waist with a gold chiffon sash.

As I move toward the stage, I recognize the zither from the lobby display. The rest I study eagerly: the two-stringed violin called an erhu. A reed instrument made of three bamboo pipes and a gourd. And at the end, a pear-shaped lute, like my great-grandmother's. I've only ever seen it in photos and paintings, never a real one. It's larger than I expected, with a cheerful, open face like a paddleball paddle.

"*Huānyíng lái dào guó yuè xuǎnxiū kè.*" The teacher greets us in flawless Mandarin. Her eyes twinkle as she translates. "Welcome to the Traditional Chinese Music elective. I'm Maya

Davis-Lin and I'm excited to introduce you all to these wonderful instruments. Please find a seat."

I feel a jolt of excitement as I approach a crowded circle of chairs. I may not be able to be Pearl Wong, semi-famous musician, but I do get to make music! I take a video of the whole set of awesome instruments, just for myself.

The circle has filled up, with only one chair left, next to a lanky guy in sick royal-blue pants and a matching striped shirt, arms folded over his chest. His fingers tap a subtle rhythm at his rib cage. His messy black hair hides his face, but as I pull out the seat, his eyes rise to meet mine and open wide with surprise.

Damn. It's Mr. Grumpy Beatboxer. Kai. Last I saw him, his hair was gloriously streaming with pearl milk tea. A definite improvement.

"Kindly take your seat," Maya says. I'm the only one still standing. I drop into the open chair, and Maya smiles. "This is an introductory course in which I'll give you an overview of the major instruments and a lesson for each one. But before I begin, since we'll be spending the summer together, let's get to know each other."

She lifts a conductor's baton, holding it delicately by its bulbous cork bottom. "I was born in Ireland, came here as a missionary kid when I was ten and have stayed ever since! I married a Taiwanese man, and we have two kids at Taipei American School."

I lean in, intrigued. So *she's* an immigrant *here*, the opposite of my family. And she speaks Mandarin way better than I ever will. I glance sideways and find Kai gazing at me with a furrowed brow. I recoil slightly, and he scowls and turns back to Maya.

I blow an impatient puff of air at my forehead. What's his

107

problem anyway? And *why* did I have to get stuck in the same class as him?

"I've been playing the pipa professionally for almost twenty years," Maya says. "The pipa is the lute over there." She points to the paddle-faced stringed instrument. A pipa—so that's what it's called. The name suits it. Light and cheerful. Maya continues, "I'm especially glad to have one of my longtime students, Kai Ai, in this class. Why don't you go next?" She crosses the circle and extends the baton to him.

Ugh, he's her student? For the pipa, or another instrument? And his name *rhymes*. Isn't that a little on the nose for a beat-boxer?

He glances sideways at me, almost as if he can hear my annoyance, then slides upright in his seat. "I'm Kai. Born in Boston, moved here when I was eight, grew up in Taipei like Maya. I'm taking a gap year before college."

He passes the baton to me. Our fingers accidentally brush, and he snatches back his hand. Like we're in third grade and I have cooties. I grit my teeth. "*That* was an accident," I grate in a whisper. But fine. If this is how we're rolling, I'll just keep my distance. And he *really* needs to comb his hair.

"Kai is the most talented pipa player I've ever taught," Maya adds. Ugh, so he really does play my great-grandma's instrument. "I asked him to join us here this summer. His Mandarin is impeccable. Hit him up for tutoring if you need it."

So she's like his number one fan. But she seems so great and he . . . I don't get it.

"Kai is also responsible for the wonderful art display in our lobby. He's studied art history extensively and I believe plans to major in it in college."

A murmur rises around the room. "It's amazing," says a girl.

It *is* amazing. And he put it together? I feel a grudging respect wanting to rise in me. If it wasn't for our first interaction, I'd have a really different impression of him.

But talent doesn't change the fact that he was a jerk.

Maya's eyes have turned expectantly to me. It's my turn.

"Hi, I'm Pearl." I follow their lead. "Born and raised in the States." Keeping it vague. *I'm a pianist*, I'd usually continue, then give the recitation Julie wrote up for me, ending in my most recent performance. Just the thought of it makes me cringe.

Normal student, Pearl. Just. Normal.

"I, um, like music. And I'm excited to learn more here." I pass the baton to the girl on my right. The rest introduce themselves. Many play instruments—cello, drums, oboe. One guy with a lucky square jaw dabbles with an erhu, and others have never had any music training. I don't recognize anyone from the music world, which is a relief, although does the erhu player have the same build as my devil in the dark?

"I'm hoping this class will be interactive, so please interrupt as we move along." Maya pens a quote on the whiteboard, "'Music in the soul can be heard by the universe.' Lao-tzu, one of my favorite Chinese philosophers."

"'Music is the universal language of mankind,'" says the erhu player. "Longfellow said that."

Plato said almost the same thing. *Music gives a soul to the universe.* These are my people. And this class is such a gem. Who knew? Ethan would have loved this class, too. Maybe he didn't know about it.

Maya gives us an overview of all the instruments. They're classified by materials into eight groups: *jin* (metal), *shi* (stone), *tu* (clay), *ge* (hide), *si* (silk), *mu* (wood), *bao* (gourd), and *zhu* (bamboo). She moves from instrument to instrument, narrating.

"The zither belongs to a family of instruments with many strings." Her hand runs down them, emitting a delicate waterfall of notes. "It's in the same family as the hammered dulcimer and piano. The earliest known surviving variation is a Chinese guqin, a seven-string instrument found in the tomb of Marquis Yi of Zeng dating from 433 BC."

Maya next picks up the erhu, the two-string violin-like instrument played with a horsehair bow. "The most famous song played on it is 'Two Springs Reflect the Moon' (二泉映月), composed by a blind, streetside musician called Ah Bing, to express his sense of bitterness at the unjust society he lived in." She balances the instrument on her knee. A lively tune leaps free as her arm deftly draws the bow with quick, fluttery movements.

Next is a flute made of bamboo, called the dizi. Finally, she cradles the pear-shaped lute reverentially in her arms, holding it horizontally. "The pipa is a *mu* instrument, also a plucked one. Sometimes called a Chinese lute. It's a descendant from Central Asian instruments played over people's laps like so, and which gradually came to be played upright."

She rotates the pipa ninety degrees until the frets tower over her head. "Around 100 BC, the Princess Liu Xijun was sent to marry a Wusun king during the Han dynasty. The pipa, according to legend, was invented so she could play on horseback to ease the loneliness of her journey." She smiles. "There are many stories about this instrument, but I just love that one."

I love it, too. So much is made in piano playing about having the right posture, hand positions, finger positions. I get why it's important for any instrument, pipa included. But the princess on horseback could just enjoy the chance to make music. The part that matters when all else is stripped away. And it's *ancient*. The piano was only invented in 1700, as an improvement on the harpsichord, which itself was invented in the sixteenth century. This pipa—people were playing it in China while Christ walked the earth!

"This song is the 'Dance of the Yi People.'" Maya's curly hair moves in time as her fingers dance a jig on the strings. The harmonies and timbre pull a shudder of pleasure from me, like that cat getting petted in all the right places. "We'll play all these instruments this summer," Maya concludes. "Kai, give me a hand with the pipas?"

I feel a dip of excitement as Kai heads out to a side room and returns with an electronic cart loaded with leather cases. He operates a remote control to navigate the cart, more of Marc's tech improvements, slowly circling the chairs for each person to take one.

I avoid his gaze and choose a simple wooden case. My pipa is new, not a scratch. Its clean round face is a pale wood. Four long tuning pegs remind me of ears, and a cascade of deliberately uneven frets flows halfway down its face. I swivel the instrument on my knee to admire the varnished back, which is shaped like the back of a Chinese soup spoon.

Then I rest it firmly against my torso, encircling it with my arms like a lover. Plucking its strings, I soak in their cadence: A, D, E, A. It's different from a guitar, but the timbre is familiar. Where have I heard it before? My fingers settle into a comfortable position on the fret and I pick out the first notes of a lullaby. The sound is fresh and bright like a spritz of lemon.

I smile. How many ways are there to string strings over a wooden box, like a piano, guitar, or zither? Somehow, over time, people on different continents created the same kind of instrument. Stringed ones were just meant to be.

Wait. This is why I've heard the pipa in recent memory. Kai. The song he was playing on his laptop when I met him, the instrument that made me want to purr—he was playing a pipa song. Ugh.

"Set the pipa upright on your thighs," Maya begins. "Like this."

I shift my focus to her voice, which guides my hands, which guide my pipa, which towers over my head by a foot. We learn the basic fingering for chords. Just enough to give everyone a good first experience. We work through a right-handed technique called *tan* and *tiao*. The students with trained fingers master it quickly, but most stumble painfully through.

I've never tried to learn a new instrument before, and it's wild to learn the same basics that I've always just known for piano, transposed onto a different medium. Like opening another box in my mind.

Kai slouches, sullenly listening, arms folded and legs jiggling in his blue pants. He rotates one wrist, and then the other. He seems annoyed—because everyone's an amateur? He makes no effort to pick up a pipa of his own. I don't understand why he's even here, or what value he's adding to the class, or why Maya seems to favor him so much.

I put him out of my mind and bend over my pipa, playing until my fingers ache, trying to compress what must take years of practice into a half-hour lesson. I want to know all the ways to make this instrument produce sound. The thousand ways to pluck the string. How the box magnifies their notes. All the chaos and rhythm and emotions inside me, I channel through my fingers.

When I open my eyes, everyone is watching me. Mouths hanging open.

"*Wow,*" Maya gushes. "Looks like we have another accomplished musician in the group!"

And I realize I've made a mistake. I hadn't meant to play so well and draw attention to myself. I'd thought only of how to make this magical box sing as beautifully as it deserves to be played.

Even Kai is watching me with startled eyes. Like he's just noticed I'm here and wondering where I came from. Heat creeps up my neck. Maybe this is how he felt when I caught him beat-boxing.

"Pearl, surely you've played the pipa before?" Maya says, approaching me.

"Oh, um, no. I didn't even know instruments like this are still played," I say. Wrong answer. I've only made everyone more curious.

"Then another instrument?" Maya suggests.

"I've had musical training," I hedge. "Some piano." I open my pipa's felt-lined case to put it away and end this conversation that I shouldn't be having, but I can't quite part with it yet. "I've always wanted to learn guitar, actually," I add. Which is true.

"Well, it's not as big a stretch to take up another instrument as you'd think."

I gulp. My wanting outweighs the need to hide, and I blurt out, "Will you show me how you do that cool trill?"

"My pleasure." She tugs a chair beside me and models her fingers dancing over her strings, producing a cascade of notes. "Try it." A few awkward attempts later, I get to a strong sound, though not nearly as distinctive as hers.

"You'll have it down in no time," she says. The rest of the students are gathering around the other instruments, trying them out. Kai drives the cart up next to me to take back my instrument. His expression is less hostile. I hold it out toward him. An olive branch. Sort of.

"Can I hear you play?" I ask. "I promise I won't baptize you this time."

His lips twitch. They have a natural heart shape, with a softer lower lip. Sexy lips, to be honest. Maybe that's why he's so jumpy about people hitting on him. But if he's about to smile, the expression peters out.

"I don't play," he says.

"Not at the moment," Maya adds.

Kai just scuffs a shoe on the floor. I'm clearly missing something.

"Nice playing," Kai says grudgingly.

I smile. There's something refreshing about talking to people who don't have any preconceptions of me as a musician.

I turn back to Maya. "Is there any way I could borrow this?"

"These pipas are rentals for today." She catches my disappointment and adds, "But you're welcome to borrow mine for a few days."

"Oh!" I say. "That's so generous." Her pipa seems incredibly valuable. "Are you sure?"

"You're a pro." She runs a thumb lovingly down faded nicks along her fret. "A well-made pipa can be played for two to three hundred years. This one's about twenty-five years old. Still a baby."

"I'll take good care of it," I promise.

She smiles. "Kai can give you pointers. He's an excellent teacher."

He scowls at the floor. Jesus, he really does hate me.

"It's okay," I say stiffly. "I can just noodle around on my own."

"It will do wonders for him and you both," Maya says, surprisingly firm. "Accelerate your learning as well as giving Kai a chance to make a meaningful contribution to class."

His face flushes. She got him with that one. We exchange uncertain glances.

Kai shrugs. "I'm free Friday afternoon."

I *do* want to learn the pipa. But can I really stomach learning from Mr. Grump?

I cast about for a way to gracefully decline. My gaze falls onto his shoes, below the cuffs of his blue pants, and then all the air is sucked from the room.

Blue sneakers, with a bold white V.

No. *No.* He can't be him.

11

I pound frantically on Hollis and Iris's door. When Iris opens it, I fall into her arms.

"Shoes," I gasp out. "A guy in my music class. Has. The shoes."

Her lashes widen around her eyes as she rights me. "Wait, what? Slow down. Are you saying you got a lead?"

I nod, catching my breath. "Kai Ai."

"He's in our Mandarin film class!" Iris says. It's the highest-level language class for the native speakers. Which makes sense.

"Wow! Do you really think it's him?" On their bed, Hollis sets their laptop aside.

Iris yanks me inside, shoving me to a seat on her bed. "Talk," she orders.

"He was wearing the same shoes. But are they THE shoes? I don't know!" I wail, setting Maya's pipa beside me. And his mouth? Is that heart-shaped pout what I was kissing in the dark? I slump back against Iris's pillow. "I need to find out. I'm meeting him Friday for a private lesson. But he was the jerk who thought I was hitting on him! He told me he didn't want to be in the

Loveboat meat market." I've already filled the twins in on that lovely encounter.

"No way. If it's him, that's pretty hypocritical," Iris says.

"*So* hypocritical!" Still, people can be that way, can't they? Claiming by day that they're one thing and being something else when no one's looking? And if Mr. Surly is one and the same as Mr. Kisser, does he know I'm me? If he does, it hasn't made much of a difference in how much he dislikes me.

"He's from here, right?" Iris asks. "He's tight with these two other local guys."

"They got in trouble for breaking into Marc's office," Hollis says.

"Why would they do that?" I ask.

"I don't know?"

How is it even possible that prince in the dark who rocked my world . . . could be him?

"Well, my mask slipped at the club. So if he saw me, I need to make sure he keeps his mouth shut."

"You could straight up ask him," Iris says.

"No way. What if it's *not* him? Can you imagine? 'Hey, Kai, did we happen to passionately make out at a party the first night? And no, I'm not hitting on you, absolutely not.'"

Hollis laughs. "Okay, maybe not."

"I need to get the truth without tipping my hand. Like 'so . . . did you happen to attend that party we all got spammed about?' But if he says no, then what?"

"He might not tell you the truth," Iris agrees.

I realize my fists are clenched, and I force them open. But

seriously. If it's him? What. A. Waste. Who cares that he's environmental enough to buy Veja's shoes?

"Well, *we've* got a small lead on Wolf." Hollis points to a photo of a guy in the directory on their laptop. "Randolph Azan's in our cooking class. He's a sophomore from Duke. He's Jamaican-Chinese and his Chinese name is Langdun." A lot of us have Chinese names in addition to our names on our birth certificates, although only my grandparents ever actually used mine.

"It means 'shield of the wolf,' apparently," Iris says. "So he could be him!"

"Did you see him at the club—Frank?" I ask.

"We don't remember but we'll ask. See if he blinks." Hollis smiles.

"Even if he admits it, we still have to convince him to give up his guest list," I say.

"Exposure is always on the table," Iris says.

"We're not *threatening* him," Hollis says witheringly.

"Of course not! Not if he gives us the list."

"That is the *definition* of threatening!"

I laugh. These two are definitely making this summer more interesting.

"And if he's *not* Wolf," Iris continues, "Gloria Beldin down the hall is an actual hacker. She's looking for a girl she met at the party, so she's just as motivated as we are. She can't reverse engineer Wolf's texts to find him, but she's working on a tracker."

"I'm not good with code, but what about some IRL detective work? I can call the club and ask if they ever saw Wolf in person," I offer.

Iris throws her arm around my shoulder. "You know what?

We *are* good at this. We should open a detective agency!"

We laugh, then Hollis asks gently, "Do you like Kai, Pearl?"

"Oh God, no!" I groan, surprised they're even asking. "He's, like, allergic to me. So if he's my guy in the dark—ugh. Just ugh. He can't be that good of a kisser when he is the absolute bane of my existence!"

"Who's the bane of your existence? Not me, I hope."

A cherub-like face appears in the doorway. Ethan is holding a stack of music books under his arm and his violin case by its handle. He waves at me. "I just tried your door."

The sight of him sends a little thrill into me. "Don't worry. It's not you."

"Phew." He pretends to wipe his brow. "I see you three survived last night," he adds.

"I see you got your beauty sleep," I tease back. Seriously. He literally glows, unlike Kai, whose mere presence sucks all light away."

"But you missed out," Iris adds.

He kneads the back of his neck, modestly sheepish. "Maybe I'll brave the next one."

"I hope there is one!" Iris says. "We're on the hunt for our potential soul mates."

Ethan's brow goes up. "Wow. That's . . . intense."

His tone is the slightest bit mocking. But good-natured. He didn't attend, though, so we can't expect him to understand why we'd be obsessing over nameless, faceless people we met in the dark.

"What's that?" Ethan points to the leather case beside me.

"A pipa. I'm borrowing it for a few days." I open it to show off

119

Maya's beautiful instrument. "I got corralled into taking lessons from this grump, Kai Ai." Safe enough to mention him in this context.

"Oh yeah, he's in a single on my floor," Ethan says. "Doesn't talk much, does he?"

"He's so full of himself," I say. "When I first met him, he thought I was after him."

"Well, maybe he wished you were?" Ethan suggests.

"Definitely not. He was very clear about that."

"Is he hot?" Hollis asks.

"If you like the brooding bad-boy type," I say at the same time Ethan makes a "meh" sound.

"He's probably used to getting hit on," Iris muses.

I grate my teeth together. "Except I was *not* hitting on him."

"I know his type." Ethan smirks. "Guy gets vibes from a beautiful girl. He feels exposed and vulnerable, so he shouts 'no, no, I don't like *you*!'" Ethan puts his hand over his eyes, pretending to hide from the sight of me. "Keeps him from hoping too much. From feeling foolish later on."

I blush, stuck on a few sentences earlier. Ethan . . . thinks I'm beautiful. "I didn't realize you were such a ham," I say. "Must be all those hours onstage."

"*I* didn't realize you were such an expert on love," Iris adds.

He shrugs. "Lots of unrequited crushes."

"Ha! You?"

"Always the confidant, never the love interest. That's me." He spreads his hands, charmingly wrecked. Our eyes meet and heat creeps up my neck. He smiles at the three of us. "*But* hearing who

120

everyone else is pining after makes me a very good matchmaker. So if you'd like to engage my services . . ."

Iris taps her lip thoughtfully. "I might take you up on that."

Ethan furtively lifts his violin case and pretends to check the hallways. Then he comes toward me and puts his mouth to my ear.

"Ready for our top-secret mission?" he whispers.

12

Ethan locks the auditorium doors behind us as we enter, "to make sure no one accidentally walks in on us and blows your cover." Technically against the rules if we were in a dorm room, but no one said anything about auditoriums. Still, I shiver as we move down the aisle. He sets a steadying hand on my back. The woody scent of his cologne wafts over me.

"You okay?" he asks.

I think I answer. But I'm not sure. *Is* something happening between us? And if it is, what?

I keep my cool as I take my seat at the piano and he tunes up. I'm a pro as we settle on Beethoven's Sonata no. 9 and Sarasate's *Zigeunerweisen (Gypsy Airs), op. 20.*

"So I have one old song and one new one to master," I declare.

"And me in reverse," he says.

We play through Sonata no. 9 first. It's grounding. Ethan's violin sings over the piano parts that I know so well now, his notes like liquid magic hanging in the air. I lean into the finish, the tips of my fingers race over the keys and sail high over my head with the ringing of the final chord, and he mimics me with a flourish of his bow.

We share a smile. Neither of us would go all out like that before an audience, but we're just hamming it up for the fun of it.

"That was like . . . flying, wasn't it?" he says.

"To the moon and back," I joke, quoting one of my favorite picture books.

"Should we critique?" he asks.

"Yes, for sure. Measure fifteen, we should rebalance our dynamics," I begin. "Measure thirty-six, after hearing you play it, I realized my pacing's been off . . ."

We break the song down to its studs, analyzing the hardest sections together. Where to tighten our rhythm. How to build the crescendo more organically. *Gypsy Airs* is next, same exercise. It feels cathartic. This was exactly the intensity and rigor I'd have had at Apollo. And like playing soccer with a great player, it's guaranteed to make you better.

"You've got an amazing head for music," Ethan says when we've finished parsing the songs.

"What do you mean?"

"You kept track of everything in a ten-page score without writing anything down."

"Oh. I've always just done this." Never asked how or why. "I just remember what parts deviated from the music in my head," I say. "They're like . . . points of dissonance, so until they get resolved, they're just there, ringing at me."

"That's amazing," he says. "If I don't write it down, it's just gone."

A compliment, a real, insightful one, from Ethan Kang. I can't help glowing.

I close the lid over the keys. "What's the worst performance you've ever given?"

He frowns, considering. "You mean besides the nightmare when you raise your violin onstage and can't remember what you're supposed to play?"

I laugh. "Yes, I've had that nightmare, too. You wake up in a cold sweat."

"You go first."

"Two years ago, the back of my dress came unzipped as I was playing at a recital in Cleveland. My sister could see it, but she couldn't do anything without drawing attention." I shudder, remembering the moment, mid-song, bent over the keys, when I realized the back of my bra had emerged into plain view for the audience.

"Wish I'd made that concert," he says.

"Hey." I fake-frown at him, and he cocks a flirty brow, before getting serious again.

"That's the thing, isn't it?" he says wistfully. "When you're on a stage, you can't escape all the eyes on you."

"And now that we're on social media, we sort of are always onstage." For all I know, my name is still getting mud slung at it on TikTok. My stomach tightens with the reminder. "Anyone can post anything about you at any time."

"We live in a fishbowl," he says.

"Right?"

We're both quiet, reflecting. It's the ugly side of what Julie calls *notoriety*. Things about us are more likely to go viral, whether we want it to or not. Dumb, unimportant things. Ethan was smart enough not to go to the Party in the Dark. Unlike some present company.

"Your turn," I say. "What are the embarrassing Ethan Kang stories?"

He smirks. "I've never had anything bad happen at a concert."

"You're holding out on me." I throw a foam eraser at him and he ducks, chuckling.

"Okay. Since you asked. When I was ten, I played background music for a fundraiser at a local high school. It was during a football game. Totally the wrong vibe. The audience was rowdy, and before I even finished, two drunk guys gave me a standing ovation, yelling, 'Too bad your face isn't as pretty as your music!'"

"Ugh, you're joking."

"I sadly kid you not."

I make a face. The girl at the club said Ethan used to be shy and awkward. How traumatizing that moment must have been. "Well, the joke was on them. I mean, look at you now."

He smirks, and a dimple appears. "That's what my sister said. Older sister. She's in college studying psychology."

"Cool. I have an older sister, too," I say. "She's a choreographer."

"So we're both youngers. Spoiled, less intelligent, undisciplined?"

I laugh. "How about creative, independent, and risk taking?" He laughs, too. As he sets his violin back in its velvet-lined case, I'm reminded of my class. "Hey, why aren't *you* in the music elective? There are a bunch of musicians in it."

"Didn't really think of joining when I signed up. I figured

another instrument might be a distraction. Though seeing how much you love it, it might have been nice to blow off some steam and play an instrument that doesn't matter, right?"

"Yeah," I say, but that's not quite it. The pipa matters. Maybe not in the way piano does, but . . . I need to call Mom and find out more about my great-grandma and her playing. Maybe that's partly why it matters. It's tied to family, when all I have left in the world are Mom and Ever.

"We make a good team, Pearl." Ethan comes around behind me, brushing against the back of my shoulder. I inhale his warm scent with a flutter of nervousness. "Take a selfie with me?" He holds out his phone, framing the two of us together.

"Oh, we shouldn't." I try to duck, but his arm is in my way. "The last thing I want is for you to get trolled on TikTok, too."

He laughs. "It's just for me," he says. "Promise."

I allow myself to study our image as he adjusts the framing. My hair is darker than his, but our faces have a similar shape, our eyes a similar glow. A musician's glow, maybe. Ever has a theory that people are attracted to people who look good in relation to them. I have to say, Ethan and I seem to enhance each other's images.

I turn to face him at the same time he turns to face me, and our lips brush. His lashes widen around his eyes. My own gaze is locked on his and neither of us move. Or breathe.

Then he gently touches his lips to mine again.

I kissed Ethan Kang.

I kissed Ethan Kang! I move in a daze into the dining hall,

bumping into people by mistake. It happened so quickly. And was it different from kissing a guy in the dark? Not really, except that I knew who I was kissing this time. I shiver. Things are moving so fast with Ethan. But then again, isn't that Loveboat? A day is a year, or something like that? And Ever and Rick met on the first day themselves. I need her advice but she's not awake yet in New York.

In the dining hall, Iris and Hollis wave me over and I join their table. Ten dishes, covered in earthenware lids, are spread out on the lazy Susan. Hollis is carefully crushing a block of instant dried ramen noodles over their steamed vegetables.

"So, uh. I kissed Ethan," I tell them.

"You did? OMG!" Hollis says. The block bursts, drowning their plate in noodle bits. "Whoops," they say cheerfully, popping a stray bite into their mouth. "Good thing I like these."

"How was it?" Iris demands. "What does it mean? Are you dating now?"

"I-I don't know." I'm at a loss for words, and suddenly famished. I lift one of the covers, freeing a puff of steam and revealing a whole fish covered with greens. "We just parted ways after. But it was a good parting. And we're practicing every day. Oh, except tomorrow, because I'm doing pipa with Kai." I grimace.

"Kai of the hot Veja shoes," Iris says. "What if he *does* turn out to be your prince, and he changes his attitude, does that change anything?"

"Would you date *both of them*?" Hollis's eyes open wide.

I glance around for Kai, spotting him across the dining room at a table with two guys. One has a blue birthmark on the back of his neck that reminds me of Dad. The other is stout, built like a pro wrestler. "Those the guys who broke into Marc's office with Kai?" I ask.

"Yes, Jon and Basel," Iris confirms. They look local, like him, judging by their haircuts and the style of their clothes. Maybe fellow students from his school here.

"Although I heard Kai wasn't actually with them," Hollis says.

I turn back to the twins. "He's not my prince," I say firmly. "I just . . . need to rule him out."

"At least you have a lead," Iris says. "My kisser was *so good—* after you mentioned the tuba, it made me wonder if he played a wind instrument. Trumpet, maybe."

I choke on tea. "Did he try to play you?"

"Not exactly," Iris says dreamily. "His mouth was just . . . very strong."

I'm still laughing, but it plants an unwanted idea. If I *kiss* Kai, I'll be able to tell for sure if it was him or not, won't I? Which would almost definitely backfire on me somehow.

"If we find Wolf, then you two only need to kiss-test, like, a quarter of the guys here," Hollis says, straight-faced. Or in my case, expose-me-to-the-world-test.

"Wolf is definitely the shortcut," I say. "Let me call the club. He had to pay them, right?" I dial the club, but I get a voice mail and leave a message to call me back.

"Maybe we're going about this from the wrong angle," Hollis says. "What's Wolf's motivation? Why throw a party like that and not get any credit for it?"

"Maybe he's not cute?" Iris suggests. "I mean, there's something nice about not picking someone based on how they look, right? In the dark, it's all about how they touch you. How you move together. How considerate they are. The vibe . . ."

"Maybe he's afraid to be himself in the light," Hollis says.

It occurs to me that I, Pearl Wong, am not being myself either. "Aren't we all?" I say.

"Maybe he doesn't want credit," Iris guesses. "Maybe he likes the satisfaction of just making it happen. Standing there all night with a beer and watching his brainchild come to life."

We polish off dinner and head upstairs to the lounge. On our way, my phone rings—it's the club owner, but he only speaks in Mandarin, so I hand the phone to Hollis, who speaks with an American accent at length while I listen enviously. I wish I could speak it, too. So much more here would be open to me.

Hollis hangs up. "Wolf paid in cash. The club owner never met him face-to-face, but the bouncer remembers a handsome young American man."

"Which *could* rule out Kai," I say. I grimace. "Although someone might consider him handsome. And he's American, even though he grew up here."

"He's in my martial arts elective," Hollis says. "I think he's handsome. Those dark eyes . . . he's really cut, too." Hollis mimes pulling open a tunic. "Everyone noticed when he was changing out of his—"

"*Stop.* Please," I groan. But I can't *unsee* the flash of chest that's already entered my imagination.

"I don't think we can rule anyone out," Iris says. "They're *all* handsome."

I smile. "So Iris."

I stop by my room to drop off my backpack. Night has fallen, so I turn off the lights, hold my glitter-shedding mask to my face, and gaze into my mirror. In the dark, I can't make out much of my mask or face at all. I wait for my eyes to adjust, then let the mask slip.

If I tip my face to catch a sliver of moonlight, my nose becomes more distinctive. One medium-brown iris. I just can't know how much light hit my face last night. And it's weird to imagine Kai's eyes looking at me in this getup. Maybe it wasn't him. But I'm not going to get any answers spinning wheels on my own.

Leaving the mask behind, I rejoin Iris and Hollis in the lounge and we play Chinese chess for the rest of the night. Close to bed-time, our phones chime simultaneously with a text. We all share a *look*.

"That can only be one person," Hollis says.

Iris reads it aloud. **Loveboaters: I knew you would surpass all my expectations and you did not disappoint. Thanks for coming out. Cheers, Wolf.** He's included a photo of the table of masks, taken before the night began, and another of the deserted space after-ward, littered with beer bottles.

"Now's our chance," Iris says gleefully. She uploads a few pho-tos from the club. **"We had a blast! Sharing some fun pictures of the scene of the crime."** She sends it, explaining, "Grace embedded a tracer code in them. If he opens one, we'll know exactly where he is, down to his dorm room."

I shiver. "Remind me never to open random pictures from strangers."

"It's a big, bad cyberworld out there," Iris says cheerfully.

"Wolf won't open it either," Hollis says doubtfully. "Not if he's careful."

"We'll see!" Iris says. "Remember. We're doing this in the name of love."

Counselor Zao pops in, twirling a whistle hung around her neck.

"Random bed check tonight," she says. "I'll be by again later. Sleep well!" She scampers off to deliver the message to people down the hallway.

"What, are we ten years old?" Iris grumbles.

"Mom and Dad had bed checks here, too," Hollis points out. "Didn't stop them."

"Well, if our lights are off, the counselors can't know that we're not already sleeping like the dead." Iris tosses her head. "We're actually headed out tonight on blind dates," she tells me.

"What? You could've told me sooner!"

Iris smiles. "Ethan set us up."

"Ethan of the many talents," I say.

"Did he set you up, too, Pearl?" Hollis asks.

I feel a pang of insecurity. "No," I begin, but Iris interrupts.

"Of course not. He wants Pearl to himself."

I scoff, but are they right? "I'm okay staying in," I say truthfully. Is it possible that only one night has passed? "I mean, how can we possibly beat that party?"

In my room, I try to sleep, but my sheets feel hot and I'm still too jet-lagged, so I snap the lights back on. My eyes fall on Maya's leather pipa case sitting on Sophie's old bed. Taking out the pipa, I softly strum its strings. They're louder in this small room, and beautiful. Still giving me a shiver. I have to admit that despite Kai being a curmudgeon, I'm excited to learn the pipa from him. Maya said he was one of her best. I just wish he wasn't also possibly the devil in the dark.

I play through the rest of the student book, learning open-string crossing, left-handed and right-handed techniques. The primer contains the usual suspects—"Hot Cross Buns," "Jingle Bells," but also a song that's new to me, a simplified, haunting "Whisper of Pipa."

The instrument feels so natural in my arms. The piano will always be my first love, but there's something exciting about the challenge of mastering twenty-six frets, six ledges, and four strings. I make the notes bend and slide, then I search the internet for more pipa songs, but there are disappointingly few out there. At least in English.

My sister pings me: **How's Loveboat going?**

My legs are as stiff as chopsticks from sitting too long. I unfold them and hit the call button. Ever blooms on my screen, back in her apartment in New York with daylight showing in the window behind her. Her hair is in a ponytail, and her face is freshly washed.

"Ever! I was going to call you."

"Hey, Pearl." She laughs. "Jet lag keeping you up?"

I wanted to get her advice, but the thought that pops into my mind when I see her face is, "You hooked up with Xavier Yeh?"

Her brow goes up. "Oh my God. Who told you that?"

"I figured it out on my own."

"Sophie." She sighs and scrubs a hand over her face. "It was years ago." She squints at my background. "Hey! Are you in my old room?"

"Yep, Marc did it." I spin the phone around to give her a view. "Fun, isn't it?"

"It's so much nicer than when I was there!"

I lie back against my pillow. "Why did you choose Rick over Xavier?" I press.

"Oh my gosh. You're not suddenly Team Xavier, are you?"

"Wait, what?" I sputter. "*Team Xavier?* Was that a thing?"

"Sort of," Ever admits.

"Wow. This goes deeper than I thought! My sister was in a love triangle with Xavier Yeh and Rick Woo!"

"Not for long, because he and Sophie got together right after," Ever cuts through.

"Obviously! Look, I'm Team Rick forever, you should know that by now. But I'm making a point. *Why did you choose Rick over Xavier?*"

She frowns. "On the surface, Xavier and I might seem more similar, especially when we first met. Both closet artists. Both trying to escape our parents' expectations. And of course, he's considered, like, the biggest catch of our generation."

"I can see that," I say.

"But if we'd ended up together, we'd have turned . . . inward? We'd have been all about our art and less about the world. Sophie keeps him grounded. And she knows how to navigate his family. She's done so much good for them. I would just be lost. And that's Rick for me, too. He'll do anything to support my dreams." A smile touches her lips. "On Loveboat, he literally ran his shoes off

133

to get to my dance performance." Her smile fades. "That's why I can't take advantage of him and make him give up his career to come to New York for me."

"He'd do it in a heartbeat," I agree. "So even if you haven't figured out this geography question with Rick yet, you *have* considered other options. Great ones, right? And Rick won out. So why even waste your time with Mr. Yawn?"

"Who?" Her brow wrinkles.

"*Mr. Yee,* I meant. Stan *Yee.* Freudian slip."

"*What* did you call him?" She tries to scowl, but a smile tugs at her lips. "He's not that bad!"

"How was the date?" I prod.

"Fine," she snaps. "We went on like, two."

"That's already too many."

She laughs. "That's what Mom said."

"She's not always wrong."

She shakes her head. "I'm changing the subject. How's Loveboat? Is it everything you dreamed and more?"

Do I tell her about the Party in the Dark? Or Ethan, my own Boy Wonder? Kai? I open my mouth, but it all feels too complicated to convey over the phone. Maybe once I have more clarity.

"So far so good," I hedge. "Rick picked me up from the airport."

Her expression tightens. I let that one slip on purpose. Keeping him in the picture. "Sophie told me." She fiddles with a box in her hand.

"Ooh! The puzzle box. How's it coming?"

Her frown deepens. "He shouldn't have sent it to me."

"Are you even working on it?" I demand.

"Yes," she admits reluctantly.

"Good," I say before we trade "love yous" and sign off.

I ring Mom next. She's in our sunlit kitchen, her blue-apple apron over her blouse. Her worn hands are kneading dough for dumplings that she'll freeze by the dozen for the rest of the year.

"Hi, Pearl! I've been wondering how you were. How is . . . that place?" she frowns, like it's a bad word. Definitely not her dream summer for me. And now I get why.

"Oh, it's good," I say vaguely. "I'm taking a Chinese instruments class."

"That's nice."

"It's why I'm calling, actually. I played a pipa today and loved it. I'm trying to pick it up this summer."

"Pipa? Did you say pipa?" She's pronouncing it correctly, *pee-pu*, unlike me.

"Yes. Pipa," I try again, but learning a new tongue is even harder than learning a new instrument. "Didn't Great-Grandma play it?"

"Yes, my father's mother. How interesting you're taking to it."

"We never really talked about that part of her life."

"I'm sure I mentioned it. Maybe you were too little. She was a professional musician for a time. She wore a beautiful blue hairpiece and played on stages in Shanghai. That's what my aunty shared—my father's sister. Your grand-aunty, whom you've never met."

"Wait, so Great-Grandma was a *performer*? Like me?"

Mom laughs. "Yes!"

I swing myself upright into the space between the twin beds. I have a musician ancestor. My own musical talent didn't just spontaneously appear like a genetic mutation. It came from somewhere. It's in my roots, my soul.

"Do you have any pictures of her performing?" I ask. "How long did she play? Was she part of an orchestra?"

"I don't know. She died when I was young. So much information was lost when people moved. They left their lives behind and never looked back. But I'll ask my big sister. She'll know more."

I'm dazed when I hang up. I came here to lay low. But unexpected things keep happening. And now this—discovering the pipa.

I shiver as I rub my tingling arms. All the Apollo kids are awake on the other side of the world, practicing concertos and duos for the Lincoln Center—having the summer I should have had. And yet, I feel like I'm on the verge of something new and different and wonderful. Loveboat's working its magic. Changing my life already in ways I never thought of before.

I can feel it, just like Sophie promised.

13

"Wolf hasn't opened any of the photos," Iris fumes the next morning as we hustle ourselves across campus. It's early, so the air is still balmy rather than heavy with sticky humidity.

"He's smart," I say. "Plus, he's probably getting bombarded with texts."

"Well, I'm talking to Randolph after cooking class," Iris says. "I have a feeling he's hiding something."

"Wait. Didn't we get a Wolf text while we were all wrapping zongzi?" Hollis is lathering a cream onto their face. "Randolph couldn't have sent it without someone seeing him."

"He could have sent up a mass message in advance and put it on a timer," Iris says.

"Hmm. Pretty devious. Sunscreen, Pearl?"

"No thanks. I need the vitamin D." Too much time indoors practicing. I lift my face sunward and shove a warm pork bāozi from the cafeteria—mmm, *so good*—into my mouth. Meanwhile, Iris goes through all of Randolph's possible reactions and her possible responses.

"How were your blind dates?" I ask when she finishes.

137

"Zero chemistry." Iris holds her thumb and forefinger in a circle. "Ethan was SO SURE he could fix me up, but it's the story of my life. If I meet someone I like, he doesn't like me. If he likes me, I don't like him. How can two people ever find each other in this world? Juliet's dad got it right in *Romeo and Juliet*. It's easier to be a nun."

I smile. Shakespeare. So dramatic. Iris has a knack for it. Maybe that's why we get along. "Well, maybe it's not you, it's Ethan. Maybe he was overconfident. He's got other talents besides matchmaking. How about you, Hollis?"

"I'm in love again!" they answer.

"You're *always* in love!" Iris rolls her eyes, good-naturedly.

I wave to a few kids from my Chinese instruments elective. Iris waves to the volleyball kids. A cute guy bursts into hysterical laughter, turning bright red and hiding his face in a neighbor's shirt.

"Someone has a crush," I say slyly.

Iris smirks and brushes her hair back over her shoulders. "Everyone's still trying to figure out who they met at the Party in the Dark without giving away that they were there."

"Right," Hollis says. "They're all *asking for a friend*."

"The phrase of the day!" Iris says.

A bundle of nerves knots in my middle. I'll be *asking for a friend* soon enough myself—when I meet Kai after Mandarin.

All the language classes are held in the eastern wing. The twins head off to their advanced class, and I head to my beginner class and settle into a bright orange chair. It's surprisingly interesting. Every syllable has a tone: even, rising, dipping, falling, stopping short. We sing through them: *mā má mǎ mà*. And that doesn't just make the language sound good, the tones change the meaning of the words. The language is literal music to my ears. I could have used it with Dad, and I feel a pang that I'm only now beginning to learn it.

The lessons are all immediately useful, too. Especially the ones on how to order at a restaurant, get a taxi, and even ask for and turn down a date. Asking is done indirectly, and saying *no thanks* can come across as rude in the culture, so we learn alternative phrases.

Ethan and I partner up for the exercises, facing each other across our table. His lips turn up in a shy smile and I blush, remembering our kiss.

"*Míng tiān wǎn shang nǐ yǒu shí jiān ma?*" Ethan puts on a pleading expression. Are you free tomorrow night?

"*Wǒ men xià yī cì zài qù ba,*" I answer. Let's go next time. "*Wǒ yǒu diǎn shì.*" I've got something to do.

We laugh. "Those both still feel like overpromising to me," I say. "But also explains why my mom's feelings get so hurt when people turn down her invitations. I always just thought she was being oversensitive."

"Maybe it's about staying hopeful," Ethan suggests. "We can always hope, right?"

His fingertips brush my fingers, and matching smiles spread over our faces. How is he so insanely perfect?

When I walk into the music room, Kai's there alone, tapping out a soft rhythm on the window ledge overlooking the Keelung

River. A red bandanna holds back his heavy hair. It complements his skin tones, and maybe it's because it makes him look hotter, but my determination to ask him about the party only doubles.

But he's wearing sandals today. Chunky and protective, with straps around his ankles and over his toes. Really nice toes, if I'm being honest. Clean, neat.

Pearl, what are you thinking? Focus, dork.

"Hi, Kai," I say, and he knocks over a plastic cup of water. It bounces on the floor and rolls toward my feet. I pick it up.

"Damn," he says, mopping it up. "Hi." His mouth *is* really nice, I can't help noticing. Pink and plump and slightly curved at the corners. But he's not making eye contact, and my heart sinks a bit. Whatever happened in the dark, if it *did* happen with him, truth is, he really doesn't want to be here. If not for Maya twisting his arm, he wouldn't be.

"You don't have to teach me if you don't want to," I say.

He pauses in the act of reaching for a black tote bag labeled Tokyo Philharmonic. A souvenir bag that's seen a lot of use.

"We sort of got off on the wrong foot," he says.

He means our first meet-not-so-cute, clearly.

"Um, yeah?"

"It was kind of my fault," he says.

"Kind of sort of?" I frown. "Try *definitely.* Why were you such a jerk exactly?"

He scratches the back of his head. "You surprised me. And I knew about the Loveboat reputation and I—I'm not getting involved with anyone this summer."

"I get that. But why go on the offensive? Did you go through a bad breakup or something?"

"No." No hesitation there. He exhales noisily. "I didn't even want to come. I'm just . . . not in a good place right now. "

Okay. So no ghost-of-an-ex hanging in his background. For some reason, I feel relieved. And to be honest, I want to probe more, but it's obviously personal.

"Well, I escalated it with the bubble tea. Not my usual style, and I'm sorry, too."

A brief smile flashes over his face. It brightens it, bringing a boyish light to his eyes.

"I'll pay you back when you least expect it," he promises.

"I'll watch my back then." All right. At least we can laugh about it now. "As a truce offering, I'll admit I really love your art display in the lobby."

He smiles. "Had fun putting it together." He reaches into his tote bag for a stack of pipa primer books. They're old, old books. His name is printed on the cover in childish handwriting.

"Did you just happen to have these handy?" I ask, surprised.

His eyebrows are elegant, in contrast to his unruly hair. One quirks upward. "No, I went home to get them."

He did that, just for my lesson. For some reason, it hits me, because this lesson matters to me. And to him, apparently.

"Thank you," I say.

We takes two of the empty chairs and he hands me five clear plastic rings, each with a sharp edge protruding. "Nail picks. These are how we really play, but Maya didn't want to complicate the lesson," he says. "You can't get as good a sound without them."

"I saw them online. They're fun." I slip each ring over the fingernails of my right hand and they act like longer, tougher fingernails. I flick my fingers in the circular motion Maya demonstrated in class.

Kai sets the first primer on a music stand between us and pages through. He moves a lot: leg jiggling, toes tapping, moving constantly to an internal rhythm in a way that reminds me of Ever.

"You're new to the pipa, but you're really musical, so I figured we could accelerate through the early books."

Musical. That I am, obviously, but it somehow means something different when he says it. So much deeper than being called a pianist. It feels right. Not to mention it's the longest sentence he's spoken to me.

"I, uh, I've already gone through that book, actually."

"Perfect." He's not surprised, which is great. I prefer a teacher who's not easily impressed. I learn more that way.

"Second book then." He flips it open. "They simplify the classics. These are some of my old favorites." His eyes are lit up. He flips pages to songs that are all new to me. "'White Snow in Spring.' 'The King Chu Doffs His Armour.'"

"Cool titles," I say, taking Maya's pipa into my arms. "I heard Chinese music is based on a pentatonic scale and Western on an—"

"Eight-note scale," he choruses with me. Then he snorts. "That's SO not accurate."

Back on the offensive again. "Oh?"

"If you Google it, that's what you'll find. But it's an oversimplification," he says. "Chinese music doesn't have the same concept of major and minor, but vertical harmonies are really common. It's more that the palette of chords and notes are different. At least, that's my personal take on it."

It resonates with me. My respect for him grudgingly rises another notch. My own knowledge of Chinese music is so limited . . . but that's why I'm here. He finds and plays a YouTube video of "White Snow in Spring," then has me take a run. The deep downturn to his lip makes me self-conscious, and I fumble on some of the notes.

"Sorry," I say.

"It's more like . . ." He reaches for my hand, then pulls back. "May I?"

Something about the motion feels familiar. "Yes, please."

He adjusts my left hand more securely over the fret. My piano teacher often did that when I was first learning to play, but even with me giving him permission, his touch still startles me. My hand tingles under his, and when he pulls back, I catch the warm scent of his hair. It's surprisingly cozy. Like wrapping my palms around a mug of hot chocolate laced with vanilla.

Cozy was not a sensation I'd have associated with Mr. Grouch. But it's also definitely *not* the same as the devil in the dark.

His cheeks have pinked, as though he read my thoughts.

"Don't worry about speed yet. It can take ten years just to master playing notes well. The cool thing about the pipa is each note can be played in infinite ways. There's more attention on the inflection of each note than with a violin. It gives us a greater range of sounds."

"It's a little like the Chinese language," I say. "All the inflections."

"Maybe." He smiles. "I have a theory about musical instruments reflecting their culture's languages."

His knuckles brush my kneecap, and he pulls back. He was

sitting a little too close. My heart beats faster and I lean into the strings, focusing on pulling as many variations of sound from them as I can.

"Wow. It's like you found your soul mate," Kai says.

"Um, what? No, I haven't!" I lift my head, flustered. He's watching me. Did I just reveal something else? "I'm not even dating anyone!"

"The pipa." He points to my arm. Goose bumps have risen on my flesh. I rub them, embarrassed at how my body can give me away without me even knowing it. And my mouth.

"I like the way it sounds," I say. And why do *I* sound so defensive now?

He flips through his stack of music books, but it's more like he's needing something to do with his hands than searching for another lesson.

"Why don't you pick it up this summer?" he asks finally. "People take up second instruments all the time."

"I want to," I say. "But Maya needs her pipa back, and I can't ask my mom to buy me one. I looked them up, and a wooden sandalwood pipa with bamboo frets cost over a thousand dollars. Even renting is a good chunk of change. And of course, a master-crafted instrument from Beijing costs as much as car."

"Yeah." He shades his eyes, even though it's not sunny in here. "Good ones are an investment."

For the fun of it, I pluck the notes of the song he was listening to when I first met him. I'm teasing him. Showing off a bit, how quickly I can pick up a song I've only heard once.

A smile tugs at the corner of his mouth. "Have you heard that song before?"

"Not before you played it. It actually reminds me, just a little, of Canon in D lifts. The chord progression."

He snorts. "It's *definitely* not based on Canon in D."

"Of course not. But I like the lifts. When I was younger, I made it a personal quest to find all the variations on Canon in D out there."

"I actually happen to know a lot of them myself."

"Oh yeah? How many?"

A smirk creases his lips. "A lot more than you, I bet."

"Ho-ho! I challenge you to a runoff. Canon in D variations. I'll start . . . with 'Go West.'" I strike the opening line on my pipa.

"'Streets of London,'" he says, and plays the first few lines on YouTube.

We go back and forth: I pick out the melodies on the pipa; he plays them on his laptop. Playing the pipa is so different from playing a piano. A piano I only touch by its keys with the tips of my fingers. But with my arms around the pipa, its wooden box vibrates against my whole body. It's a kind of intimacy in itself. Soul mate was not far off.

Kai and I play for over an hour before we finally reach the edges of my memory. Turns out, he really does know his Canon in D's. I've never actually met anyone who did.

I play the church hymn next, which he doesn't know. "I think that's it." Now it's my turn to smirk. "I win. No one is as Canon in D nerdy as me—"

"'Puff the Magic Dragon,'" he says.

"What? No way!" I flop back in my chair, devastated. "I listened to that song a thousand times growing up."

"*Before* you heard Canon in D, right?"

I frown, thinking back. "Yeah . . ."

"That's why you missed it. But at some moment, you should have said to yourself, oh my God, Canon in D is really just PUFF!"

I hum through Puff on fast-forward. "No, those two chords aren't the same."

"The rest of it is!"

"It's *not* the same chord progression." But I smile.

He laughs. It's a nice laugh. Warm and deep.

"Okay. So we tie," I say. "Not a bad outcome to our second fight."

"You're so weird."

"And I misjudged you."

He blinks. "I did the misjudging. I guess I had some preconceptions about Loveboat kids."

"Like what?"

"Bratty. Entitled. That's what some people here think." He slips the books back into his tote bag. "My parents used to own a 7-Eleven around here. Once a group of Loveboat kids came in drunk as old men and started eating food right off the shelves. They made a mess and wouldn't leave, and then when they did, they didn't pay."

"Ugh, I'm sorry." A bunch of kids acting like they literally owned the place. "I can see how that left a bad taste in your mouth."

"It was like that all over town. Every summer since I was a kid, American and overseas kids taking over the city, traveling in big loud packs and throwing their parents' money around."

Definitely not a flattering perception. Ever told me about the program's secret, salacious reputation among students, but not

146

this view from the Taiwanese side. "So that's why you didn't want to come? Because Loveboat's a bunch of spoiled Americans?"

He frowns. "It was like they thought they were better than us because they grew up in the West. Someone even slanted their eyes at my grandparents thirty years ago. Can you believe it? Another Asian person! I couldn't stomach all that disrespect."

"I'm so sorry." It explains, a little, some of his aloofness. "I've experienced things like that in the States. But to get it from someone who shares the culture . . ." I shudder. And maybe this is what the trolls thought I was doing with the straw hat. God, I really hope not.

I run my hand along the pipa's smooth slope. "Why *did* you decide to come then?"

"Maya said it would be good for me to meet some actual American kids and not be so closed-minded anymore." He gives me a lopsided smile. "She's been my pipa teacher for years. Couldn't say no."

"Well, I hope we both live up to her expectations," I say and his smile twitches. "Can we try for a truce then?" I hold out my hand.

"Truce." His hand meets mine, and we solemnly shake. I hang on a beat longer than I mean to. My eyes linger on his soft lips. Are all kisses the same, or would I be able to tell it was him?

His face reddens, and he slips his hand free. My eyes drop to his sandals.

His toes wiggle. "Why are you so fascinated by my feet?"

Ugh. My eyes shoot back to his face. Either I'm really that transparent, or he's that good at reading me. If he *is* the devil in the dark, he doesn't seem to know it's me he kissed. He doesn't say a lot, but he's too honest, too transparent himself to hide something that big. So maybe I don't need to worry about him exposing me, plus now that we're becoming friends, maybe he wouldn't anyway.

"No reason." There's no gracious segue into the party, so I just go for it. "Hey so did you happen to get invited to—"

My phone chimes with a text. Then another. "It's my mom." A black-and-white photo of a pipa appears. The question will have to wait. I open the photo eagerly. An elegant Chinese woman smiles out, her sleek black hair done up with a pearly hairpiece, and her paddle-faced instrument cradled upright in her arms. The pipa's face is decorated with blossoms.

"Who's that?" Kai asks.

"Wow, my great-grandma was a babe! Check her out!" I show him her photo and read my mom's incoming texts impatiently, willing her to type faster.

"*She was with the Shanghai Symphony Orchestra. She played a pipa concerto in Shanghai Symphony Hall before the civil war ended her career.*"

"Shanghai! That's huge!" Kai says. "Amazing you still have a photo. My parents lost almost everything when they moved to the US."

"Ours too," I say. Which makes these photos all the more precious. "I've always been envious of my friends in Ohio with trunks full of poodle skirts and old books in their attics. All that *history*."

Our entire life in the States is only a generation long, and the Wong family have been like four notes floating in the air, unconnected to a full song. With Dad gone, it has often felt like we might just float away. This photo feels like one link that can keep us grounded, even if only for a little while.

Kai's reading Mom's text over my shoulder. "Wait, her last name was Tan? Tan Mei-Li?"

I nearly drop my phone. "You've heard of her?"

He crooks his thumb and points to himself. "Art history major. With a focus on music. I don't know a lot, but I've definitely heard of her."

I grab his arm. "You know my great-grandma! This is amazing!"

Kai blushes, color spreading over his cheeks once again. "Not that amazing."

"I don't get it. You're like, Mr. Pipa Master, but you won't play. Why not?"

Kai gives me a hard look. "Come with me."

I latch up Maya's pipa case. "Where are we going?"

He doesn't answer, but he's not ignoring me. He just waits for me to gather my things. Words aren't really his strong suit, I suspect. Unless maybe when he's talking music. I follow him into the elevators and out on the third floor, past the lounge where I originally baptized him with tea.

Just two doors down the hallway is his room. I duck slightly as I step inside.

Kai's got the usual bed, dresser, and desk setup. A suitcase he hasn't fully unpacked, like he's still undecided on whether to stick around. On his dresser, a bottle of contact lens fluid and a prescription bottle of painkillers. My dad had to use it after an accident and he joked half a pill was enough to knock him out. Why does Kai have them? He seems perfectly fine, other than his mangled temperament.

He removes his sandals at the door, and I imitate him. We all do that. It's part of our culture, leaving the outside dirt outside. His sneakers aren't in sight, which probably means they're in his closet, but it's shut tight.

Then I'm distracted by what's sitting on the empty second bed: an enameled red leather pipa case. I open it to a beautiful lacquered instrument.

"Why did you bring a pipa here if you don't want to play?" I ask.

He yanks off his bandanna, letting his wild hair spill free. "People collect instruments."

I frown. No. No one carries a collector's item around with them. Something isn't adding up. But obviously he's not ready to tell me the truth . . . yet.

"May I?" I gesture toward it.

He frowns. "That's why I showed it to you."

I take it into my arms and sit on the edge of the bed. He takes a seat in his chair on the other side of the second bed, putting as much distance between us as the room will allow. Which is fine by me. It's actually a little hard to breathe when he's closer. I check the pitch, but it only needs a few tweaks to bring it back into perfection. It's been tuned recently. I move it into position on my lap and play one of the new pipa songs he just taught me.

As I play, he stretches out his hand, spreading thumb and little finger as far as they can extend. He rotates one wrist and then the other. It's an exercise I saw him do in class, almost unconsciously.

"Why do you do that?" I ask.

"Do what?"

"Your hands."

He settles them in his lap, furtive. "Nosy," he says, but there's no bite this time. "Just stretching. Keep going."

I bend back over his pipa and pluck out the melody of a bluegrass song I've heard on the radio a few times. When I finish playing, he's looking at me with an oddly haunted expression. He loves this instrument. It's not a collector's item. It's been played. A lot.

"It's a wonderful instrument," I say.

His throat moves with a swallow. "You can borrow it. For now. Since Maya needs hers back."

"Seriously? I can't. It's too valuable."

"I'd rather it be played by someone good than sit around silent," he says forcefully.

It's his. So obviously his instrument that he's loved and played. He knows its voice. Something must have happened.

"Play with me?" I say impulsively.

His eyes fall on Maya's case. "I told you, I don't—"

"Not the pipas. Do like, your beatboxing thing with me."

His eyes narrow, cautious. He's going to refuse. Then he comes around to my side of his bed, flutters his lips to warm up, and begins. *Boom-boom, chaka-chaka-chaka-chaka dadedada. Boom-boom, chaka-chaka-chaka-chaka dadedada.*

His head moves to the beat. His feet tap out a counter rhythm. I give him two bars. He sinks deep into it, taking me with him. A longing and urgency flows out of him, held in check only by the tight form of the rhythm.

151

My toes tap, and I play the Mozart concerto double-time against him. His rhythms interweave with the pipa notes coming from under my fingers. It feels strangely intimate and—even with him across the aisle—more intense than kissing in the dark.

I'm pretty sure now, even if I ask him about that party, he won't tell me if he was really there. He's hiding things. Lots of things.

Maybe I really *do* need to kiss him again to find out if it's him. Surprisingly, that isn't as unpleasant a prospect as it would have been just yesterday.

As we reach the end of the song, I feel a stab of regret. I'm not ready for it to be over yet. I look up at Kai. We've both inched our way deeper into the gap between the beds, so close that we're almost touching. He notices just as I do and sits back, putting a space between us again.

"Wow," he says. "Never thought I'd hear dead white man's music coming out of my instrument."

I suck in a breath. It feels like a slap. Like he's looked into the special place I have for Mozart deep inside me, and flat out laughed in my face. I lower his pipa back into its case. "It's not a 'dead white man's' music. It's my music. *I* played it just now, in case you hadn't noticed."

Kai shrugs, rubbing at his wrists, not looking at me. "A dead white man wrote it. The Hapsburg imperial family made him famous. Just like Queen Elizabeth made Shakespeare famous."

He's so . . . *dismissive*. I seriously want to pull out his hair and leave him bald and bleeding.

"I don't get you," I say again. "You've got this amazing pipa and you're like the god of rhythm—but you won't play. You just

152

scowl and brood, which by the way, as a vibe, really isn't working for you. Like, comb your hair already! So what's the deal?"

A pulse is ticking in his cheek, and the cords in his neck are straining. He closes his pipa case and fastens the latches. He pushes it toward me.

"Take it," he says. "Lesson's over."

I shove it back at him, snagging the comforter. I don't care if he is Mr. Kisser or Mr. Grump or how freaking smart he is or how good he looks in red.

"Know what?" I say. "I don't want anything from you. Never did. The sooner you understand that, the better."

Then I grab Maya's pipa and storm from his room, leaving his behind.

14

"How was the lesson, Pearl?" Hollis notes Maya's pipa case in my hand as I return to our hallway. The twins are sitting comfortably on the floor, barefoot, working on Mandarin homework.

I set the pipa case down by my door, along with Kai's tote bag, which I'd automatically taken and now wish I'd left behind. As usual, the air smells of something freshly baked, likely the product of their cooking class—but the thought of Kai is a sour taste in my mouth.

I take a seat beside Hollis. They glance up. "What ha—"

"Don't want to talk about it," I cut them off. "Did you talk to Randolph?"

"He's not Wolf," Iris says. "I watched him go through his backpack and about a thousand pens and erasers and whatnot slipped out. He couldn't organize his sock drawer, let alone an entire hundred-person party. I'm trying to track down the DJ from the party now. Maybe he's got a better description. Oh, and Hollis got a lead."

"What, really?"

"Grace asked if I remembered a sweetheart kissing my hand and if I'd be willing to meet in the light," Hollis says. "She was

154

'asking for a friend.'" They smile sheepishly.

"Oh my God, do you think that's the one you met? How did they identify you? What did you say?"

"I said yes!"

They squeeze my hand with a nervous laugh. I squeeze back. I'm glad Hollis has movement. But no one's searching for *me*, so either the devil in the dark doesn't know I'm me, or he doesn't care. If he *is* Kai, then at least it's mutual.

"But what if I don't like them in the light?" Hollis asks, growing sober.

I purse my lips, reflecting. "I think how you feel will tell you everything. Like if you're disappointed when you find out their identity, then maybe it means you should be with someone else." I laugh. "What do I know? I've never even been on a blind date."

Hollis's eyes open wide. "No, I think you're right. It's just a tough thing to think about. That appearances matter for so much."

Seriously. Maybe if I saw my mystery kisser I'd be turned off, too. Maybe my lack of experience overall is why I'm obsessing over my devil in the dark.

"What if we just ask Wolf to message the whole guest list for us?" Iris muses.

"As in, '@all anyone kissed a girl in a glittery purple mask and want to be reunited?'" I ask.

Iris makes a face. "Yeah. We need to keep thinking."

A week passes. The jet lag wears off and classes provide a structure to our days. Iris's DJ trail goes cold—the DJ never saw Wolf's face either. Grace is acting as Hollis's go between with their secret admirer, passing notes back and forth, gently gearing up to meet in person. In the auditorium, Ethan and I intertwine the sounds of piano and violin, then we find ourselves entangled in each other's arms, our kisses growing more and more bold.

I'm excited by everything Ethan, but my fight with Kai still weighs on me. I haven't spoken to him since our last meeting. I stay on my side of Traditional Chinese Music and he stays on his. I've returned Maya's pipa, and now all I have left are Kai's books, which I study on my own, but seeing his name printed in his childhood handwriting on the covers is a reminder that he's not a complete ogre. Which I don't really want to admit because his whole "dead white man" comment just goes to show he's still misjudging me.

I'll have to return his books to him eventually. Maybe I'll just leave them by his door.

On Thursday, Rick drops by with another box of snacks from him and Sophie, which I share with Iris, Hollis, the rest of our hallway—and Ethan. Our repertoire is actually no cakewalk. Onstage, our chords crash and thunder. My fingers on the keys chase his bow on the strings. As Ethan finishes with a flourish of his bow, I release my keys and let my hands and head fly back from the keys. He flexes his arm, making the blue birds undulate.

The harmonics in the air slowly fade to silence. Then we both dissolve into laughter.

"*So fun,*" I say, wiping my eyes. This piano is wonderful, although of course, no piano holds my heart as much as my trusty upright back home.

"These weeks have been the best I've played in *years*. And I'm even on break."

"Maybe it's the break that's doing it." I smile back.

"It's nice to just be all in on the musical, instead of anything technical," Ethan says.

"What do you mean?"

"It's a stereotype of Asian musicians. All precision, no passion."

"That's ridiculous," I say.

"Of course, but it's more difficult for us, you know? I have to show conductors and music directors that I have my own phrasing, my own style. Then I have to convince them to let me use it." I frown. Now that he's mentioned it, I have been dinged in competitions with those exact words. Was it because of the stereotype, which I've never heard of, or because I was having an off day? I hate that I'm even asking the question.

"I have to work three hundred percent harder to get to the same place as others around me, because if I don't, they'll hear what they want to hear, instead of hearing me."

"I feel that," I tap my breastbone. "Right. Here."

"We're so alike." Ethan touches my arm. "So many same experiences. I'm glad this summer put us on each other's path."

"Me too," I say. I rise to my feet. "I've been meaning to ask, why did you choose the violin? I mean, how did you know it was *the one* as opposed to, like, cello. The way you play—it's like an extension of you."

He smiles. "A reporter wrote that in a news article about me once."

"I didn't read it." I laugh. "So it must be true!"

"I was drawn to it at first because it sounded like a human voice," he says. "It can laugh and cry and shriek and whisper. Like us. Why did you pick piano?"

"I didn't," I say. "I was musical, so my dad started me on it. My neighbor Liz Manning played, and he was inspired by her."

"It's pretty common to start with piano or violin."

"Yes, and I do love it." I close the cover over the keys. "Have you ever considered another instrument?"

"Yes. If I had bandwidth, I'd become a percussion player."

"I could see you as a drummer. Why don't you pick it up? A second instrument."

"I've never considered it for real. Hmm." He executes a catchy rhythm on the edge of the piano with his two hands.

"Impressive," I say. "Consider it. Why not?"

His eyes are soft. But then he shakes his head.

"Reputation matters. Mine is as a concert violinist. Yours is as a pianist. We've built them, and now they're all we have."

I frown. Is that true? If I weren't a concert pianist, then I would be . . . nothing?

"Having to worry about reputation and brand—all that feels like a box built around the music. Containing it." I illustrate a small space with my hands. "Instead of just letting it out to let it ring like it's supposed to." I open my hands wide.

He plucks a string. "I came on Loveboat to figure some of that stuff out."

"What have you figured out so far?"

"That I hate being a nobody."

"A nobody?" I laugh. "That's like Queen Elizabeth wishing she wasn't so oppressed."

His eyes are a bit haunted. "Maybe we're all nobodies in our own spaces. After this summer, my goal is to really break out in a big way. Taylor Swift level. But as a classical musician. I know

it might sound impossible, but if we don't shoot for the moon—"
He opens his own hands.

"You'll get there." I like that he's so ambitious in music. "For me, I just want to be good enough that I can make an actual living doing what I love. That's already a hard enough bar to reach."

He smiles. "You're so grounding."

"Me?" I smile back. "When you're aiming for Taylor Swift, I might come across that way."

"It's good for me to hear how you think about your music." He gives me a hungry look I recognize. "I have a sort of confession to make."

My skin tingles. "What?"

He sets his violin back into its felt-lined case and slowly closes the lid. Then he turns to me.

"I'm getting a cramp from all our practicing and need a break."

I laugh. "That wasn't your confession."

He stretches. Then puts his hand on the piano and leans toward me. "*Zhōu liù wǎn shang nǐ yǒu shí jiān ma?*" Are you free Saturday night?

Wait, is he asking me on a date? Or is this a game? "*Wǒ men xià yī cì zài qù ba?*" I use the line we learned in class. Let's go next time?

He smiles, but his eyes are serious. "I got backstage passes and tickets to a concert to hear the Danish National Symphony Orchestra at the National Concert Hall. Would you like to come with me? We can get dinner beforehand. Maybe Gustoso. Italian?"

He was working up to this. My skin tingles.

"Do you mean, like, on a date?" I ask.

He smiles. "I like you a lot, Pearl. More than I've liked anyone in a long time."

I've always been the one with the unrequited crushes. I had one, I thought, on the guy in the dark. But now in the light . . . something's happening with Ethan. Is it real? As I wonder, for some reason, my mind flits to Kai. What's his deal? What is he hiding?

Ethan is still waiting, with a sort of terrified expression on his face. I'm making him terrified. Me.

"Yes, thank you!" I squeeze his hand. "I've never been backstage for an orchestra. And they're world class! I'd love to go."

He looks like he wants to say something. Then he leans in and presses his lips to mine. His mouth is soft and hungry. I find myself responding, and he takes hold of my arms at my elbows. His strong fingers tuck into my hair, cradling the back of my head.

We're moving, disappearing off stage behind the black curtains. He cups my cheek as he kisses me, holding me tighter to him. The heel of my right foot connects with something soft, and then his hand goes to the small of my back and he dips me flat onto a couch I hadn't even noticed was here.

Its springs creak as he climbs onto me, his full weight pressing me into the cushions. A button digs into my neck, but I barely notice it. His mouth is everywhere at once, trailing kisses across my cheek and down my neck. His fingers are curious, exploring all the curves of my body through my shirt. Then under it, warm fingers gliding up my bare stomach. I can feel the gap in our experience—I didn't even know I had so many nerve endings—and I want to feel these new things he's making me feel.

Then a knock on the front doors echoes through the space.

We untangle and sit up sharply, straightening out our clothes. I run my hands through my hair.

Ethan grabs my wrist. "Don't answer."

But the knock sounds again. "They know we're in here. Coming!" I call, and jog up the aisle.

When I open the door, Marc is standing just outside. "Why is this locked?" He leans sideways to see Ethan and the rest of the auditorium. "Are you two in here alone?"

My face must be strawberry red. This is like a cross between getting caught by your big brother and the principal of your school. Just awkward vibes all around. I want to say, *C'mon, Marc, this is Loveboat.* But he doesn't look amused like he did at the club that night.

"Must have locked it by mistake," Ethan says, catching up.

He's completely believable, but I feel bad lying to Marc. He deserves better.

"*I* locked it," I say, although it's always been Ethan. "We're practicing music. I didn't want anyone to walk in on us and hear, since I'm laying low this summer."

Marc uses his toe to wedge the doorjamb in place, firmly propping the door open. "This needs to stay like this. Sorry if that makes it a little hard to maintain your cover."

I glance at Ethan. "No, I mean, of course. I totally understand," I force myself to say.

After Marc leaves, there's a pregnant pause.

"What are we doing?" I ask finally. "I mean, are we—what are we?"

"What do you want us to be?" he asks.

"Are we dating?" I ask. "Because honestly, I'm not—"

"Not ready?" he says.

"It's just, things are happening so fast," I say.

"Well, let's slow down then," he says, and I'm relieved.

"Yeah." I smooth back my hair, realizing too late that a heavy lock of hair was hanging in the wrong direction. No wonder Marc was giving me a LOOK.

"So then I, uh, I'll see you here tomorrow?" I say to Ethan.

He smiles, but it doesn't quite reach his eyes. "See you then."

On Friday, Julie calls while I'm studying Kai's pipa books. "Pearl, good news! *Teen Vogue* is in! We've arranged for a professional camera crew to film your performance. Their reporter will interview the two of you afterward. They love the angle I pitched them: *Prodigies' Summer of Cultural Exploration Makes for Beautiful Music.*"

I laugh. *Teen Vogue!* Julie's like a fairy godmother, making all my wishes come true. "Amazing, Julie. *Thank you!* At this rate, this summer will end up even more spectacular than performing at Apollo."

"Yes, we wouldn't have gotten a hit like this. And a spotlight, too!"

"I can't wait to tell Ethan."

"I'm so glad you two have connected," Julie says warmly.

If only she knew just how much. I doubt a romantic entanglement was what she was hoping for. I feel like I'm playing with a beautiful flame—so seductive I have to be careful not to get burned. I hope that everything will be clearer when Ethan and I leave campus for our date tomorrow. Maybe the new setting will help give us both some perspective.

"Get a great outfit," Julie continues. "I'm sure you can find something wonderful."

For my date with Ethan, I hope so. I can ask the twins to go with me. But for the performance—I can almost hear Sophie's excited squeal.

"I'm sure I can, too," I assure her.

After we hang up, I swing downstairs for a quick walk outside to clear my head. On the way back, I pass Kai's display, and spot Kai by the zodiac symbols, deep in conversation with Maya. Maya sets a hand on his shoulder, which is slumped. I can tell they're close, with that teacher-pupil affection and trust I share with my own teacher back home. But it's hard to reconcile that guy over there with the Kai I know.

I head upstairs and knock on Hollis and Iris's door.

"Just in time," Iris says. "Today's special is Korean street snacks."

The smell is heavenly, and my stomach rumbles. I step inside to find Hollis deep-frying something on a stick in a pan over their illegal burner. It looks dangerous. Living on the edge, I guess that's what we're doing this summer.

"How did you guys get so into food?" I ask as Iris hands me what looks like a corn dog. Inside, it's full of gooey hot dog and melted cheese. Dairy gives me a stomachache, but I can't resist. "Um, yum, this is *so good*."

"Korean hot dogs!" Hollis says.

"Our parents traveled a lot. Growing up in multicultural

163

families, they just like sampling everything," Iris explains. "We grew up eating it all—stir-fry, falafel, couscous, mutton. We've even tried alligator and ostrich. Now we're coming up with our own recipes."

"And I'm your very lucky guinea pig." I catch a gooey drip of cheese with my mouth. Hollis hands me a napkin, and I mop myself up ruefully. "Can't take me anywhere." I toss it into their trash. "Your parents seem so supportive. My dad was my biggest supporter. My mom tries, but yours—do they actually *want* you guys sneaking out?"

Iris laughs. "Our dad wants us to have fun, but of course he expects us to be smart about it, too. He trusts us. Just as long as we don't get kicked out!"

"They want us to experience other cultures up close," Hollis says. "You realize people are just people, you know?"

"So true," I say. I pop the last bite of my hot dog into my mouth. "Want to go dress shopping tonight? I need to find an outfit for my, uh, date with Ethan."

"Lucky girl," Iris croons. "I'd bear that hottie's children in a heartbeat."

"Iris!" Hollis scolds.

I laugh a little sheepishly. "We're meeting an orchestra backstage afterward."

"Ooh, fun! We can definitely help," Hollis says.

"And we need outfits for clubbing ourselves," Iris says. "We can go to Wufenpu. It's like the outlet shopping district."

She grabs the pans. The three of us return them to the kitchen, then we head out and take the metro. Night has fallen, but the city glows with the lights of store windows and streetlamps. At

Wufenpu, vendors line the alleys, their racks of shoes and clothes spilling onto the walkway.

"Everything here is pretty affordable," Iris says as we navigate the crowded sidewalk. "It's way better than shopping in the States. Ten times the selection. Great prices."

We lose ourselves among the shopping racks. Iris zips through racks of silks and cottons, the hangers clicking a metallic rhythm. I paw through dresses in every shade and texture.

"I need more *color* in my wardrobe," I say. "Everything I have is black and white."

"What do you think of this?" Hollis holds a green ladybug-printed duster to their body. "Hideous or haute couture?"

Iris and I study them and speak at the same time.

"Hideous," Iris says.

"Haute couture," I say.

We all laugh, and the duster goes back on the rack.

I browse through sexy shirts, fun skirts, and cute overalls. But nothing seems right for my date. Maybe it's because of Kai's annoying comment about my dead white man's music. Everything I pick out—long, flowy, simple—feels like it's screaming *I ♥ Mozart*. But so what if I do?

I set the latest hanger back on the rack with a sigh. Maybe another day I'll be in the right frame of mind. Only Iris finds an outfit she likes: black leather pants with a drapey off-the-shoulder shirt. Hollis turns out to be incredibly picky, down to checking the shades of beige against their skin. They return a white sports jacket to a display. "Nothing really captures the way I feel on the inside."

"How do you translate that to clothes?"

"More pink and more blue, if that makes sense. I don't really want gender neutral." Hollis frowns at their sister. "But Iris wants me to lay low. She doesn't want me to appear obviously non-binary."

"I mean, in some towns, I've worn a baseball cap down low to hide being Asian," Iris says.

"But I don't want to do that," Hollis says. "Not because I'm an activist. I don't want to be one. I just want to *be*. That shouldn't be too much to ask for."

I just wanted to be a musician. Only the world doesn't always just let me be. Not TikTok. Not Apollo. But it's helpful to hear Hollis making the distinction. What they're going through is so much more complicated. And they're absolutely right. It isn't too much for anyone to ask for, to just be.

"I've had my own set of Asian American blowups," I admit. "But if not for them, I'd never have come on Loveboat. I'd never have met you guys. So maybe things have a way of working themselves out. Or we reshape them ourselves."

"What happened?" Iris asks.

I chew on my lower lip, not ready to share just yet, but not wanting to push her away.

"You don't have to tell us if you're not ready," Hollis says. "I'm actually admiring how we're all different shades." They point to us in the mirror, smoothly diverting the conversation. I've diverted enough conversations myself for Ever, and I'm grateful.

And it's true. We line up our three forearms. I'm pink, Iris is tawny, and Hollis is gold. I snap a photo of just our arms and share it among us over text. Just behind Hollis, I spot a familiar blue-striped shirt and swing it out from the rack.

"Hey! Kai has this shirt," I say. "I wonder if he got it here."

"A lot of locals shop here," Iris says.

I sigh, annoyed by the whole reminder of him. To be honest, he dresses really well. His bright-colored pants always complement his tops, and they make a statement. But they don't match the bad-hair-day vibe. It's like he used to care how he looked and doesn't anymore, but is still stuck with his old awesome clothes.

"Why is he so . . . pugnacious?" I ask, using the most fitting word I can come up with.

"He takes up a lot of your headspace," Iris observes. "Just saying."

"Does he?"

"What's his story?"

"I don't really know," I admit.

"Have you looked him up?" Hollis asks.

"No," I admit. I've been avoiding social media and the internet like the plague since I arrived.

Iris pulls out her phone. "Kai Ai, right?"

I nod. Iris is right. Kai is taking up way too much brainspace. He's gotten totally under my skin. Like a splinter, or a bee sting. It's time I do some surgery to get him out.

"Wow, he's huge," Iris says, staring at her screen.

"What?" I shove in beside her to read her phone, but rain suddenly begins to pour, spattering on her screen. She snaps it off.

"Let's get on the metro," she says, and I chafe as we head through the turnstiles and grab the next train thundering in.

Iris takes a seat, and Hollis and I crowd in on either side of her. Her phone search has pulled up a few YouTube videos of Kai in an all-black blazer over a dazzling silver shirt, seated in a chair with his pear-shaped pipa cradled upright in his lap. His hair is still longish, but styled, like an anime character. He looks so different. Happy, cocky, confident.

And then I read the title: "Kai Ai, Pipa Concerto with the Tokyo Philharmonic Orchestra."

The Tokyo Philharmonic? *Really?*

"Click there," I beg, pointing. "The Tokyo Philharmonic is only like one of the greatest professional orchestras on the planet. And a concerto?"

Iris hits play on the video. Kai's hand moves dramatically to poise over the strings of his pipa. The camera view zooms out to showcase the entire symphonic orchestra behind him.

He plucks the first note. The music of the orchestra swells with him. "A *concerto*," I whisper. Just like the one that was supposed to be my big break at Apollo. Kai's played one with a world-renowned orchestra . . . and a pipa!

I watch, mesmerized, as his left hand rotates with a vibrato on the fret. His right fingers dance low on the strings, plucking that circular twang I was working to perfect myself. The mood shifts. The camera zooms in on his face, which is turned toward the pipa's neck, close to his playing hand. His knuckles are bent and his fingers labor down the frets. His curtain of black hair falls in his eyes and whips to one side as he plays with his entire body. My own tingles with the sheer raw pleasure of his rhythms.

"Wow, he's good," Iris says.

"He's a *virtuoso*," I say, mystified. I read the notes. His concerto was played in Suntory Hall in Tokyo almost two years ago. "'The youngest pipa player to perform with the orchestra.' Wow.

So why does he keep insisting he doesn't play?" What turned him from this pipa maestro into the sullen creature who mopes around our class?

"Why don't you just ask him?" Iris asks.

"Oh, I'm going to," I assure her. I scour the internet the rest of the way home. But that concerto was Kai's last performance. Since then, nothing at all, not even a local recital.

We reach campus just a few minutes before curfew. The hall before the elevators is crowded with kids heading to bed, so I make a beeline for the stairs, waving goodbye to Hollis and Iris.

I'm breathless by the time I reach Kai's floor and speed down the darkened hallway. His door is firmly closed, but the light is still on underneath. I knock, softly at first, but there's no answer so I knock harder, until I'm banging on the wood.

"Kai?" I say. "It's me. Pearl. Kai?" I press my ear to the door, listening for the sound of movement, a bed creaking—

"Find him?"

At the disembodied voice behind me, I yell and spin around, smacking my wrist against the doorframe. In the lounge I just passed, by the moonlight, I make out Kai's moody profile seated on a couch. His hair, if possible, is even bushier than usual.

He holds up a bottle of water, toasting me.

"You scared me!"

"Yeah, I could tell."

I put my hands on my hips, trying to bring the trembling in my body under control. "How long were you just *sitting* there watching me?"

"A while."

I come around to his side of the couch and shove my phone displaying his YouTube video at him. He raises his arm, warding me off, and our arms brush.

"This is you!" I say. "You were so—so—"

"Sexy?"

"Incredible!" I heave a breath. "You were incredible." I sink onto the couch beside him. A bottle of prescription medication rolls toward me, pills clattering inside. "I can't believe you gave up your music."

"Yeah, well, not everyone can be a prodigy like you."

"*You* were more than a prodigy," I say. "It was my *dream* to play a piano concerto with a professional orchestra. But you *did*. Why did you stop?"

He mumbles something.

"Sorry, what?" I say.

"Gimme a moment." He checks his phone, where a timer is counting down from fifteen seconds. He takes out a pill from his bottle. As soon as the timer dings, he pops it into his mouth and chases it down with water. "Um," he says, shuttering his eyes briefly. Then he sets his alarm for another six hours.

"Are you okay?" I ask, concerned.

"Yeah. I'm only allowed to take these four times a day." He rises. "That video. It's nothing."

I follow him toward his room, bewildered. A million questions are on my tongue. "It's not nothing!" I say. "No one with a gift like this just gives it up! Why do you keep saying you don't play?"

Just outside his door, he glares at me. "Why do you keep

170

pushing me about none of your business?" His fists clench, the tendons in his arms popping out.

"Because I care," I snap back, surprising the both of us. My tone softens. "Why did you stop?" Because he thought he wasn't good enough? Because he had his own version of a TikTok blowup? "Did something happen?"

He lifts his arms, then lets them fall helplessly. Lines deepen in his cheeks.

"I can't use my hands anymore."

Oh no. What does that mean?

"Why not?" I ask quietly.

He looks like he'd rather slam his door in my face. But instead, he shows me the label on his pills. Meloxicam, an anti-inflammatory. My dad had started to use it for his arthritis.

"It's not even heroic," he says. "Like, I didn't pull someone from a fire or get tortured by a rogue spy. I have repetitive stress injury, RSI. Because I've played so much. Because of the way I'm built. Now when I play, my hands start screaming."

I had no idea. He's built like an athlete, with strong shoulders and powerful-looking hands. That glorious performance on You-Tube. I'd never have suspected.

"When did it start?"

He walks into his room, sets his bottle of pills beside the other bottle of painkillers on his dresser, and flops down on his bed. I kick off my shoes and take a seat on the other bed, instinctively looking at his closed closet door, where his sneakers must be.

Then Kai runs his hands down over his face and begins.

"Leading up to that concert, I was feeling pain in the back of my hands whenever I played. Afterward, it got worse to the point that the doctor said if I didn't stop, I'd have to get surgery and I might not be able to use my hands at all." His mouth twists. "I planned on studying *music* at the Tokyo College of Music. Not art history. My pipa was home, you know?" he says. "Now, it's like I've been kicked out."

"I'm so sorry." It was one thing for me to lose a summer at Lincoln Center. Kai has lost his music forever. His moment of glory was his downfall, and now, to never play again because your hands have rebelled against you? I can't even imagine it. "You— you can't play at all?"

He looks out the window. "Look, I don't want anyone's pity. It's why I didn't want to talk about it. Like I said. It's not like I have a terminal disease."

"No but if I couldn't make music . . ." my voice trails off. Music is like breathing. Like air. Without it, I wouldn't know how to live.

"Can it get better over time?"

"I'm seeing doctors." He studies his bare feet.

"Why didn't you just tell the class the truth? It's not something to be ashamed of."

"Maya wanted me to. But I can't even get myself on board with being in that class. I'd prefer not to have to watch other people dancing when I can't stand, you know?"

"Why are you doing it then?"

"Maya thought this would be good for me, and that anything would be better than moping at home all summer." He shakes his head. "It was a big mistake."

"I'm glad you're there," I say impulsively. I fold his spare pillow into my arms and hug it to my chest. I mean it. Without Kai there, I wouldn't have learned as much as I have already about the pipa.

Kai's mouth twists wryly. "Beethoven had it worse, didn't he? He couldn't even *hear* the music."

"He could feel it," I say, tapping my chest. "Even if his ears no longer worked, he would be able to feel the base in his breastbone and the reverberations in his feet. What about beatboxing? You're already doing it."

He shakes his head. "Beatboxing's fun. I like how it's rooted in a bunch of cultures. But it's just . . . not enough for me."

I get that. Especially when he played the pipa like he did. It would be like getting both arms cut off.

"Well, there must be instruments that can be played without being hard on your hands. What about voice commands? They're everywhere now."

"Voice commands? In the middle of a song?"

"Okay, not that. But something." I set his pillow aside and type on my phone: Electronic musical instruments that don't require hands, I say aloud as I type. Kai doesn't try to stop me. He leans in to see my screen. I pull up an instrument I've never heard of. Theramin. Shaped like a rectangular box with two antennae sticking up. It's the summer of new instruments for me, I guess.

"What about this one?" I ask. "Patented in 1928. You play by moving your hands in the physical proximity of two antennae." I pull up a few YouTube videos, and he watches them with me. His mouth is slightly open. He's more intrigued than I'm sure he wants to let on. In the video, a bunch of people wave their hands with precision, playing songs like "Over the Rainbow."

"They're making specific hand shapes," I point out. "Will that be a problem?"

"Not sure. They're not actually putting any weight or tension

173

on them." Kai has leaned forward, and I've shifted so my leg is pressed against his knee without either of us realizing it. I pull back discreetly. "But where am I going to find a Theramin?" he asks. "Looks like people make their own."

"I bet there's an online app somewhere." I Google that next and voilà! "Theramin.app. LOL, I love it!" I open it to a simple image of a red rectangular shape. "'Turn on your camera for hand-tracked gestures'—this is it!"

"No, don't!" he says, but I've already turned it on. I move my hands before it, producing eerie notes. Real ones. "It works!"

"Cool sound." Kai's expression is cautious. "But this isn't a real instrument. It's just for kicks."

"Says who?" I prop my phone against his desk lamp. "There are no pipas in Western music. Doesn't mean they're not real, so don't be a snob. People can make music out of cardboard boxes, glasses, rocks. Why not an app?" I take out his pipa and strum the strings, tuning it. "It *wasn't* a mistake you joined Maya's class," I say smugly. "Because you met me, and I'm obsessed with good music. So come on."

Unbelievably, he's smiling now, shaking his head.

"Play with me," I say, encouraged. I pluck the opening cadence of a song from his books. I keep to the simplest melody line so that it *demands* accompaniment to complete it, or it's like watching a duet without half the duo. Excruciating.

"Kai," I sing. "My song is lonely."

He exhales sharply. Then he moves his hands before my camera. A random sound emerges, and he immediately lowers them.

"I feel so stupid," he says.

174

But I don't stop playing. I want him to try. I want him to find a path back to releasing that amazing music inside him. He lifts his hands again. The sounds are random at first as he gets the lay of the land. But he can't resist the challenge of making this song work any more than I can.

He establishes the rhythm first, then he finds the notes. Only a few are intuitive, the rest he'll have to figure out later. But we can hear the shell of the song this could be. The eerie electronic wail is a funky contrast to the pipa's discrete, acoustic twangs. And I'm a fan.

I shift into a second song, then a third, then wind us down. "That was so weird, but I got shivers!" I say. "How do your hands feel?"

"They're okay." His eyes are wide. "I've never done anything like that."

"Maybe you can ask your doctor if this is cool."

"Yeah. I will." He's on board.

"How else does it impact you?" I ask. "Your condition. I mean, what are the boundaries?"

"I need to take lots of stretch breaks. Keep everything at right angles. No small, repetitive movements like typing essays. And carrying anything heavy is hard. It cuts off my circulation," he says with embarrassment. "That's why Maya has me using a remote-controlled cart in class."

"I'll remember," I say, and the shy, surprised gratitude on his face strikes a chord in my chest. How lonely must it have been to carry this on his own. No wonder he's been such a curmudgeon. I would be, too. I shouldn't have judged him as harshly as I did.

He pushes my phone at me. "Pipa really does run in your blood. I'd be happy to give you my pipa permanently—"

"No." I cut him off. "You'll get your hands back someday. Then you'll want your baby."

He skims his fingertips over the pipa case. "There *must* be a way to get you your own."

"I wish I could afford one," I say wistfully. "I bet there are really nice ones here. I wish there was some way for me to earn the money to at least rent." I walk over to his window to look out toward Taipei. His room is high enough that I can see over the wall, and on the corner, I can barely make out a man waving a big sign: Jesus Saves.

"I have a sort of crazy idea," he says slowly. He's come up right behind me. He's just the right height for my Mr. Kisser, but I don't want that to distract me now.

"What?"

"We could go out to the Xinyi District and play. For money." He smiles as I raise a brow. "Between you and me, I bet we'd make a killing."

15

Even though it's nearly midnight and the sky is an inky black, Taipei's Xinyi District is still hopping with people. It's possibly the most modern part of the city. A pedestrian mall, two massive buildings built of long red beams, lines a central walkway that runs an entire block. The trees twinkle with artificial lights like it's Christmas all year.

We set up at the far end: amp, speakers, a lightweight chair for me, Kai's laptop on a stone wall open to the Theramin app, and a foot drum below. I carried everything to spare Kai's arms. He read the Theramin user manual on the metro ride over, and we are careful to set up his station in a way that lets him stand upright, elbows bent at right angles and wrists straight.

He's leaning in, ready to jam. But now that we're surrounded by all these people, I almost lose my nerve.

"My manager will *kill* me if she ever finds out about this," I say.

"Because it will taint your little *brand*?"

Obnoxious as usual, but I'm in too good of a mood to mind.

He calls it like he sees it. And he used to have a steaming hot brand himself.

"Yeah, actually," I say, setting out our "can"—an empty boba cup. "*Street performer* is the worst insult Julie can slap onto a player."

"But she's on the other side of the world," Kai says. "She doesn't need to know. It's your time and your life."

"True . . ." Surprisingly, I'm more nervous performing on this street corner, where the audience is a fluid, unpredictable thing, than I am on a stage, when the audience is captive and eager. My hand shakes around his pipa's neck.

But no time to think too hard. Kai's already kicking us off: "A one, two, a one two three!"

His foot drum sets a clipping pace. The meter is contagious, and my fingers dance over the strings. He's a fast study: his hand shapes grow more confident and his music accelerates in pitch and accuracy. We play like the sky is falling. Our song echoes off the skyscrapers surrounding us. We are making music out in the open air, and yet this feels way more forbidden than the Party in the Dark.

Kai starts up "Two Springs Reflect the Moon" (二泉映月), the piece by the blind composer we learned about in class. I close my eyes and lean into the bitterness he felt. The unjustness of society. My heart is on fire. Infinitely more than words, that's music. Pure feelings, unbounded and unleashed.

When I open my eyes, a crowd has gathered, despite the late hour. A group of girls in camp uniforms are literally dancing on the street before us. Slow-moving cars honk and move around them, but they just keep grooving, arms pumping, all in sync. I grin. There's nothing like having a song flow from your fingertips, and having it enter the bodies and souls of other people. I can't remember when I've had this much fun.

And the best part is, no one knows who I am. I'm not here to build my image for Julie or be a personality. I can just be a girl playing a pipa, still a little clumsy at it, but happy enough with her imperfection. This moment is just for me.

Kai pulls back a bit, maybe taking a break for his hands. So I lean more into the pipa. Musicians do this in duos all the time, back and forth, taking turns in the spotlight. He wags his head to the beat. People stuff pink and blue dollars into our boba cup and soon it's overflowing.

"Use your case!" I call, and he dumps the cash into his pipa case and pushes it forward. We both double down and he flashes me a sly smile I've never seen before, like he's stolen cookies from his grandma's jar. I smile back. "Let's do that song you were playing when I met you."

He grins like he's in on a joke. "Sure."

We start it up. The twang of it, the chords, penetrate deep into my bones. He layers on the notes of the Theramin like the rhythm's already in his blood. I close my eyes, savoring it.

As we wind it down, I say, "I haven't been able to get that one out of my head. Who's the composer?"

He smirks. "Me."

"Liar!" My fingers falter over my strings before continuing. "*You* wrote it?"

The smirk deepens.

"You let me play your song and you just sat there listening? How much are you gloating over there?"

He pretends to consider, chewing on the corner of his lower lip. "Not an insignificant amount."

I laugh. And whack him on the shoulder. "What's the song called?"

"Words aren't my forte. It's just 'Pipa Song' for now."

"What about 'Canon by Ai'? 'Ai Aria'?" I grimace. "Never mind. I'll keep brainstorming."

By two in the morning, the crowds have thinned out. The humid night air has cooled a few degrees to a warm, soothing blanket. Kai collects empty cups and paper bags left behind by watchers, dumping them in the trash. It's respectful, and I really like that about him. We count up our coins and pink 100NTs, worth about three dollars each, and even one blue 1000NTs.

"About fifty bucks. Not bad." He smiles. "This will definitely rent you a pipa for a month."

"We're splitting it in half," I say. "Only fair." It means I'm not quite to the rental price. But the experience is one I'm hoping to repeat. "This was . . . so *fun*," I say. "I'm glad you suggested it." He's massaging his hands. "You okay?"

He shakes them out. "That was sick. I've never played anything like this." His eyes are bright under the lamps.

I smile. "Who needs concertos, right? We could make a real living playing out here every night."

He has a great smile, when he's not hiding it under one of his scowls. "I'd consider it," he says. "But I should rest my hands. Lay off."

I reach for his backpack.

"I can get that," he protests, reaching for it, but I just sweep it over my shoulder.

"It's easy for me," I say.

His face twitches. According to the traditional rules, *he* should be carrying *my* backpack. But why do we care so much about traditional rules? Who made them? A bunch of dead people, that's who. Right now, I couldn't care less about how those dead people want me to live, not to mention Kai's the one who brought them up in the first place.

"Seriously, I'm just glad you trusted me enough to let me in," I say. "And the sooner you recover, the sooner you can expand your repertoire again."

He looks a little relieved. "Thanks," he says simply. "I'll ask my doctor about playing the Theremin tomorrow."

We start back down the sidewalk. Neither of us flag one of the passing cabs, though it would be the faster way back to the dorms. I'm not in a hurry for this night to end, and he doesn't seem to be either. I hum our last song, and his palm taps his thigh.

I bump his hip slightly, then again to the beat. He bumps me back in rhythm. A laugh escapes my lips, and then his. We somehow manage to walk and bump every other beat, down the entire block, until we're laughing too hard to keep it up. He touches the small of my back with a quick, furtive gesture, then pulls away, leaving the warmth of his fingertips there.

"You're such an imp," he says.

"Do you always just say whatever's on your mind, no filter?"

"No. In fact, I had a thought while we were playing earlier. And I held it in until now."

"What?" I asked, intrigued.

"Does your family still have your great-grandma's pipa?"

"Her pipa?" I blink.

"Valuable musical instruments don't just get thrown away. Although for immigrants, things get left behind."

"I never even thought of it," I say, but I see where he's going, and I'm getting excited. "Her pipa would be a hundred years old. Maya said that a good pipa could be played for two to three hundred years."

"Exactly. If her pipa's still around, by rights, it could belong to you, couldn't it?"

We're on the same harmonic wave.

I text Mom: whatever happened to Great-Grandma's pipa?

She replies: It was lost during the war. Aunty heard that it ended up in a museum.

"Makes total sense," Kai says when I read him the text. "She was famous. But if it's in a museum, we might be able to trace it."

"Really?" Which museum? I ask Mom.

We don't know. What time is it over there? Shouldn't you be asleep?

I'm ok, I text back.

"Wow, what if I could get her pipa back?" I hug myself. The strings may have to be replaced. It might be old and decrepit and dried out—the blossoms faded or painted over.

But maybe, just maybe, it will be magic in my arms.

Kai is watching my face closely, in a way that makes heat creep up my neck. I'm doing it again. Breaking out into goose bumps right in front of him.

"If it's in a museum, we could find it," he says. "We could make a claim for it."

We. The word warms me as much as the night air. Would he really try to help me? On my phone, I run a Google search for music museums. "How many museums could have century-old instruments from China?" I ask.

Turns out a lot. Wikipedia lists music museums in over sixty countries from Argentina to Uzbekistan, not including thirty-nine states in the USA. Not to mention all the regular public museums—Google search: almost a hundred thousand world-wide, including over five thousand in China. Any one of those could have a random pipa in one of their many collections.

I lower my phone, discouraged. "It's like finding a needle in a haystack. Basically impossible."

He shakes his head, making his hair fall into his eyes in a way that makes my fingers itch to smooth it back. "There are data-bases. Inventories. Especially for objects with some fame attached to them." He smiles at my dumbfounded expression. "Art history's sort of my thing, remember? Where'd your great-grandmother live?"

"Um, my mom's family is from Fujian Province."

"So just over the strait. Not far. That's good. We can start with the National Palace Museum here in Taipei. I worked with them for the display in the lobby, so I know their system. Tomorrow afternoon?" He smiles, pointing at the sky, which has lightened from black to dark gray. Dawn is coming. "Today, actually."

"Sure," I start to say, but remember I'm meeting Ethan for our date then. "I'm uh, actually have something. With someone. Sunday?"

I sound as deliberately vague as I am, but he doesn't press me. "Sure. I'll call them to see if they have anything in their archives.

If it's still around, we have a good shot at tracking it down." He's animated. Alive like in his pipa concerto, in a way I've never seen him in real life.

"This will be a big job," I say slowly. "Why do you want to help me?"

He gives me a sideways look, not quite meeting my eyes. "I made music tonight for the first time in almost two years," he says in a husky voice. "It was like—a lungful of air—after holding my breath for so long. You gave me that."

My skin tingles. I'm glad to hear it. Because he's doing something similar for me. I don't have the words to describe those feelings yet. Just a song in my heart.

I lead the way across the street. I still want to know if he's my devil in the dark. Even if that guy was Angry Kai without Music, finding another outlet to blow off steam. Maybe I'm just being stubborn, not letting that encounter go either. But I can't deny this charge between Kai and me. Strong feelings I've never felt with anyone. And I desperately want to know if the guy who made me feel new things in the dark is this same guy I'm starting to connect with in the light.

16

I'm still asleep when Ethan knocks on my door.

"Pearl? Are you in there?"

"Coming," I call groggily. My fading dream holds the memory of persistent knocking. The light through my shade is dim.

I open the door to Ethan in a navy suit, holding a bouquet of red roses as big as a laundry basket, and a box of chocolates.

"Oh!" The scent of roses tickles my nose. "Oh my God, what time is it?"

"It's just after dinner. The concert's in forty-five minutes."

"Oh no, I missed our dinner!" How could I have completely slept through? I was passed out for almost thirteen hours. Two weeks later, the jet lag has finally caught up with me, or maybe it was the all-nighter I pulled with Kai. "Did you come by then, too?"

"Yeah, I knocked, but—I thought maybe you were out."

"I fell asleep after class. I'm *so* sorry," I say. "Thank you for the flowers. They're beautiful."

He holds them out, but I hold up my hands, regretfully warding them off. "Sorry, I'm allergic."

His face falls. "Oh no. I should have thought to ask."

"It's okay. I like looking at them." I gesture across the hallway. "We could give them to Iris and Hollis?"

He knocks but the twins are out, so he writes them a note on a sheet of lilac stationary I bought in the markets, while I quickly change into Ever's blue duster dress, fastening the long row of decorative buttons down the front. Ethan's already left the flowers at their door.

He takes me in from head to foot. "You look great," he says.

I tug self-consciously at the skirt. "It's my sister's," I say, glad I had something after all. "I mostly have concert clothing, so all boring blacks. Although I still need to find an outfit for our performance." I grimace. "Such a pain."

"My manager gets all my clothes," he says. "But you'll look amazing in anything."

"How did you spend your afternoon?" I ask.

"Practicing." He smiles. "I'm pretty predictable."

I feel a stab of anxiety. Of course he's practicing on his own, not just with me. Our time is fun for him, not his serious practicing time. And I'm *only* practicing with him, which is way less than my baseline back home. I really need to keep honing my own skills, for the comeback performance and if Apollo makes me reaudition, which, I should have realized sooner, they probably will.

Ethan opens the box of chocolates. "Iridescent, right?" he says slyly, revealing nine delectable-looking bonbons, glazed like very large pearls.

"Wow, I've never seen truffles like these." I try to bring myself back to this date I've already desperately failed. "I can't believe you found them." I pop one into my mouth.

"Pearl," he teases, then leans in and kisses me, nibbling on my upper lip.

For a moment, I kiss him back. But then I pull away. Truth is, even in the auditorium, our practicing time has been getting shorter, too, and our making out time longer. Yet another distraction. And I'm still not sure what we are. We're music mates. We're kissing mates. I can't pretend it doesn't feel good to feel wanted. And we're going on a date now.

But what about this connection I'm feeling with Kai? I don't want to mess up a good friendship with Ethan and an important comeback performance, all because I don't know what I want. I smooth back my hair.

"Should we go down?" I suggest.

We pass one of the renovated student lounges, where I catch sight of Kai talking to his friends by the fireplace. Jon's shuffling a deck of cards. Basel's lifting small weights. Kai's more animated than usual, gesturing with his hands.

"Who are you looking at?" Ethan asks.

I glance at him, startled. "Kai," I admit. "I found out he used to be a concert pipa player."

"Yeah, his career's over from what I hear."

So Ethan knows about him. I don't like the dismissive tone in his voice. "He's got a lot of years left," I say. "We played a bit together. For music class." Not exactly as part of the class, but close enough.

"I'd be careful of him latching onto you." Ethan puts a hand on my shoulder. "I don't like to badmouth another musician, but guys like him will do anything to get back into the game."

Ethan's only trying to give me good advice. It's what a real musician friend does for you. Tells you their honest opinion in a world where it can be hard to know how to parcel out your limited time and energy. But is he right about Kai?

"I don't think he's latching onto me," I say. If anything, I've been chasing him.

Ethan doesn't answer, just opens the glass doors for me. The dusky sky is gray overhead. Ethan flags a black car, which pulls up to the sidewalk. It's not a regular cab car. He's ordered it specially.

"Aren't we taking the metro?" I ask.

"I figure we'd make it a night. It's not every day we get to meet players in a world-famous orchestra."

True, although it's on the tip of my tongue to mention we have one right here on campus. Kai was a guest performer with the Tokyo Philharmonic. Ethan must know that? But for him, maybe it's just in the past now.

"I'm looking forward to it," I say, smiling. Ethan holds the door open for me, and I gather my skirt and slip inside. The fabric tugs at my hand as a button snaps off the front and pings on the concrete.

"Oh, drat." I stoop to pick it up.

"Want me to hold onto it for you?" Ethan holds out a hand.

I don't have a single pocket on me, so I hand it over.

"Thank you," I say.

The Danish National Symphony Orchestra is wonderful and all 106 of them—strings, woodwinds, brass, and percussion—have traveled thousands of miles to be here. They carry us through a tapestry of sounds, a rousing rondo and passionate climax to a thunderous finale.

"Did you like it?" Ethan asks when the lights go back up.

My ears are full and so is my soul, the way I always feel after indulging in an amazing meal of music. "They were incredible. Loved their energy."

"Let's go meet them then. That lead cellist especially."

"He was a whole show to himself, wasn't he?" I'd enjoyed watching his straw-like hair whipping along with his bowing arm.

We funnel into the slowly moving line in the aisle, headed against traffic toward the stage. Ethan sets a hand on my waist and buffers me against the crowd, cutting smoothly through it like he's navigated them his whole life. If he really *was* once super shy, all that's gone now. Iris is right. Any girl would be so lucky to be with him. Especially a fellow musician like me.

So why am I hesitating?

Ethan reaches the stage and starts to climb the steps. But a Taiwanese man in a dark suit, a gold pin gleaming on his lapel, puts out a hand. Blocking us.

"No entry to the public," he says brusquely.

"I'm Ethan Kang," he says.

"Only orchestra staff and special guests are permitted backstage."

Ethan's ears turn pink, and he glances at me. "I was told I could come backstage afterward to meet the performers. I assumed there was a list."

"We don't do that." The man scowls at two local women approaching, waving them off. "Stage is closed," he says brusquely.

He's probably bounced a lot of groupies. I mean, Ethan's probably had his own share of superfans bounced without him knowing it.

But we aren't groupies.

Ethan's jaw clenches and I tug on his hand. "It's okay," I say. "I don't really mind."

"No, we were supposed to get in," he says forcefully, but the bouncer gestures to a security man in a uniform who starts toward us.

"Someone must have not gotten the memo," I say, trying to make light of it.

Ethan reluctantly follows me back into the aisle, then moves past me, taking the lead. His shoulders are set, and I can feel the heat of anger pouring off him. I glance back to see a blond couple not much older than us approach the bouncer. He lights up, bows, and ushers them through the door Ethan was trying to get us through. A completely changed person. But he's Asian, and so are we, and so were those women he wouldn't let through . . . did he just assume we couldn't possibly have backstage passes for the Danish National Symphony Orchestra? Ugh. I'm just glad Ethan doesn't notice them.

Outside the concert hall, Ethan turns to me. His cheeks are bright red. "One day, I'm going to play on that stage, and that will never happen again," he says.

I don't want him to feel embarrassed on my account. How often has that kind of thing happened to me and I just had to laugh it off? But I understand why he's upset. Kai might have said something snarky, too. Although more likely, Kai wouldn't have cared about meeting the Danish National Symphony Orchestra in the first place.

"I'm so sorry." Ethan takes my hand. "I don't mean to ruin the evening."

"No, no, I get it. That man was rude. And he didn't need to call security on us."

"Want to grab boba?" he asks. "We could get a blanket from my room and lie out on the rooftop back on campus. The door locks up there, so we can have some privacy."

A blanket. A rooftop. A locked door. The strangeness of Love-boat time is at work. Just two days ago, I would have said yes, and then who knows what might have happened up there? But tonight, I'm feeling all jumbled up inside. Not because of the backstage non-passes. More like I've been playing fragments of music all summer, and just realizing they don't belong to the same piece.

I can't just let things keep playing out with Ethan like this.

"I need to be up early," I say. "I'm going to the National Palace Museum in the morning."

"Oh?"

"It's an art history thing I need help with." It would take too long to get into the whole story about my great-grandma's pipa. "It's just a little research project," I conclude.

Ethan's ears burn even brighter. He releases my hand and flags a cab.

"All good," he says, opening the door for me. "Let's get you home."

As we settle into the back seat, I turn to him. "Ethan," I say, then pause.

He leans against his window and looks sideways at me. "Why do I get the feeling I won't like what comes next?"

This is hard. Much harder than I expected. "I had a great time with you tonight," I say painfully. "And I love what we're doing for our duo. I just think we should slow down, and get to know each other better. I'm afraid that if we keep going down this path, we won't be able to stay friends."

He sits with that while I hold my breath. Is he upset? Reconsidering our duo? The streetlights flash over his face as our cab eats down the kilometers toward campus.

"Please tell me this isn't because we just got bounced," he says.

"No, of course not," I say forcefully. "You have to believe me. It's just that, I've been thinking about us." Do I have the same feelings for him as he does for me? Maybe the problem is, I'm not sure what I feel yet. "We have our music. It's really important to both of us."

"And I'm still in for our performance, no matter what happens between us." He gives me a crooked smile. "You can't play a duo by yourself."

"Thank you." I let out a breath. He's a good guy. Maybe things will change as I get to know him better? Although I've spent more hours with him than anyone else on this program. All the more reason I don't want to hurt him while I'm figuring out what I want.

Back at my room, I'm too tired to do anything else but remove Ever's dress and peel off my NuBra, and crawl into bed in just my panties. Julie calls as I've tucked in, and I answer without video, letting my pillow hold the phone to my cheek.

"Hey, Julie."

"Pearl, how are things with Mr. Kang?" Yikes! Does she have a periscope that can see me around the edge of the world? I sit up, pushing my hair from my face.

"To be honest," I say slowly, "it's gotten a little complicated."

"Are you two dating?"

When she asks straight up like that, there's no hiding.

"Not exactly, but we—he invited me to the theater tonight and I went. It was nice. The Danish National Symphony Orchestra." *And we've been making out every day, but I'm connecting with another guy, too. Oh, and there's also this mysterious kisser from a party. Don't ask me who he is, the whole thing was in the dark.*

"This is fantastic, Pearl," she says, surprising me.

"Oh?" I ask weakly.

"I've always thought Ethan would be a great match for you. I just didn't want to interfere. But yes, your feelings of connection to him make complete sense. The rising star couple."

"Oh. I don't know, Julie." Was I wrong to pull away then?

"Take it slowly. No need to rush. But it would definitely add to the *Teen Vogue* splash if you two were an item."

"Right," I say. Don't rush, but definitely be a couple. Now I'm more confused than before she called.

After we hang up, my eyes fall on Kai's pipa case on Sophie's old bed. On impulse, I unlatch it and pull it out. I lift one foot onto the rung of my chair and prop the pipa against my bare thighs, cradling it with my arms. The wooden back is cool and smooth against my stomach as I softly pluck the strings. In my mirror, shadows form a hollow in my shoulders and the rest of my skin seems to glow. Is this what a summer of mysterious kissers and requited crushes does for you?

I imagine Kai's arms around his pipa, and I can't help wondering what he'd think of the nearly naked image in my mirror.

Then my door flies open, banging against the closet door. I shriek and hide behind Kai's pipa as Iris and Hollis burst through, Iris in a pink negligee and Hollis in cotton pajamas.

Hollis's eyes open wide. "We are here for all the goss!"

I yank on my nightgown. "Oh my God, you guys scared the bejesus out of me! What are you doing in here?"

"We heard your instrument and knew you were awake." Iris crosses her arms over her chest. "It's time to *tell all.*"

"Over chai?" Hollis holds up a mug. The scent of the hot spiced tea coaxes me out of bed. I really am wiped out, but I can't say no to these two. Guess bedtime will have to wait after all.

"Okay." I laugh. "But next time maybe be a little less dramatic with the entrance?"

I follow them into their room and sit on Iris's bed and accept a warm mug from Hollis.

Iris raises her brow at me. "Well? How did the date go?"

"It was fine," I say truthfully. I take a careful sip of chai so as not to burn my tongue.

"Fine? That's it?"

"That's it," I say.

Hollis leans forward. "So we're going to have to dig? Fine. What do you think is the sexiest thing about him?"

I reflect. "His tattoo. Hands down. Watching his bowing arm move up and down is mesmerizing. But honestly, I'm confused now."

"Confused about what?" Iris asks.

"Is it Kai?" Hollis asks knowingly.

I frown. "Is it that obvious?"

They smile. "Just a bit. I would be confused, too."

It's all too new and uncertain with Kai. He isn't the bane of my existence anymore, but Ethan's warning is in my ears. But Kai really has been through a lot. I deflect the attention back to the twins. "Tell me about *your* dates."

"Oh, don't even. It's like we hit a dead end," Iris says. "I had another blind date. *Negative* chemistry. I truly give up. Maybe I can only be with someone in the dark when they can't look into my eyes and there's no pressure to actually have a deep conversation."

"I chickened out meeting my person from the party," Hollis admits. "I'm still working up to it."

"Any luck with Wolf?" I ask. Though I don't feel the importance of figuring out our mysterious party planner so much anymore. If someone was going to out me, it would've happened by now.

"Nothing there either," Iris says. "We even tried sending incognito messages. Maybe that's the end of the trail. He named himself Wolf for a reason. He's a loner who doesn't want to be found."

"Bummer." I lean back against the wall. "I just have one lead left, and that's flat out asking Kai."

"Kai Ai," Iris says. "If he's your kisser, I can see why you're having trouble deciding."

I pinch a fold of their comforter with my toes. "My dad would have really liked Ethan," I admit. "He passed away a few years ago."

"Oh," Hollis says. "We didn't know."

"He was really into classical music. He would have swooned if Ethan presented him with tickets to see the Copenhagen Orchestra."

"Does that influence you liking Ethan?" Hollis asks.

"Maybe it does," I say wistfully.

"Our parents' approval matters to us, too," Iris says.

"It seems different for you, though. Maybe because they're the same culture as you?" I say wistfully. "I mean, it's different with my dad gone and me having to guess. But you guys don't seem to have the same hang-ups my sister and I do."

"Maybe. I don't really relate to stories where the kids hate their parents," Hollis says. "We like a lot of the same things our parents like, and we're okay with that. Don't feel a need to rebel for the sake of rebelling. At least I don't," they amend, with a glance at their sister.

"But *you* remind us of our parents," Iris says.

"You're like our mom," Hollis says. "Hungry."

"Hungry?"

"Us—not so much," Hollis says.

"I haven't heard that word used to describe me before. But it's not wrong."

"They faced a lot of pressures we don't. Our parents," Iris says.

Like making up for Mom trying so hard to be accepted. And now with Dad gone, wanting to live a life he'd be proud of.

"Our parents just want us to be happy," Iris says. "Do what we love. Find a wonderful person to love."

"As long as we don't starve on the streets," Hollis points out.

"But we also don't have the courage they do," Iris says. "I mean, their parents flew across the world to live in a foreign country. They had that as a model. They've taken a lot of risks."

"Maybe it's because we have more to lose, too?" Hollis muses. "They grew up poor, and they knew they had to take big risks to change things. Now Dad runs a travel podcast and Mom's a professor. We're not rich, but we're . . . fat and happy?"

"Fat and happy." I smile. Iris is strong and muscled and Hollis's pretty lean, but I get the picture.

I drain my chai and say good night, then head across the hallway. To my surprise, my door is slightly ajar, the light shining inside. I must have left it unlatched. A note is propped against it, pinned to the button of Ever's dress. I pick up the note.

>*Hey Pearl, I still had this in my pocket. Just getting it back to you. See you at practice tomorrow. I'll bring the iridescents. Ethan.*

It's a sweet, funny note, but I picture him coming upon the open door and poking his head inside, only to clock my empty bed, despite my begging off for the night. I set the button on my dresser. When I see him tomorrow, I'll let him know I was just across the hallway with Iris and Hollis.

A text chimes on my phone. It's a program text from Apollo. I must still be on an old thread. Everyone is reminded to arrive on time to the auditorium for a special private gathering with Howard Shore, the legendary composer of one of my favorite film scores, *The Lord of the Rings*. I feel a jolt of loss. By now, the students will have solidified their pieces. Built the intimacy and camaraderie that comes from working out incredible music together. For the first time, it occurs to me that one of them got in when I was kicked out. I don't ever want to know who.

Since I'm being reminded of what I blew, I steel myself and peek at my TikTok account. My followers are still decimated, but they're actually starting to rebuild organically. And my notifications are quiet. No more hat drama. It's died down, as Julie predicted it would. Come end of summer, I'll be rightfully on this Apollo texting thread soon enough.

A yawn threatens to crack my head in half, and I finally tumble into bed and fall into a dreamless sleep.

17

Sunday mornings are quieter on campus. I wait for Kai in the lobby by his zodiac display. We're beginning week three of the program, but he still has a small crowd of people admiring the golden horse. I can't help feeling impressed again how he arranged for all of this. I trace my finger over a little plaque displaying the National Palace Museum logo.

But ten minutes pass, and no Kai.

I find his number in the directory and text him. **Hey, just making sure I got the time right?**

I frown at my phone, waiting for him to answer. I'm sure I have the time right. He offered to help but then again, it was on a whim. He's so unpredictable: sometimes mad, moody, normal, exuberant. I understand why now, more so, but can I rely on him? Maybe I should I just go without him . . . but he's the one who called the National Palace Museum, and I wouldn't even know where to begin. This search could take months. I only have weeks left.

"Pearl, hey! Sorry I'm late."

He's coming from the elevators, dressed in a soft blue shirt over red-checkered shorts. My insides are so knotted up that my stomach actually, physically hurts. I'm surprised at myself. I don't want to be like this, all dependent on him. Seriously.

"Hey. There you are." I nod briefly and fall into place, moving toward the door. I pull out the pork buns I grabbed from the dining hall and offer him one, then bite into the other. He looks different somehow. Not just his funky shorts.

We pass through the electronic doors at the same time, brushing up against each other. His cheeks pink a bit, but this time he doesn't freak out.

"Your hair," I say, placing the difference. It's tidy. Still heavy but slicked back neatly behind his ears. Probably not easy to maintain.

He scowls. "You told me to comb it . . . so I did."

His voice warns me not to laugh, so I press my lips together. His clothes have a little extra sharpness to them today, like maybe they were ironed.

"Is your hair why you're late?" I blurt.

He opens his mouth like he's going to protest, but then he shuts it. "Sort of," he says sheepishly. And then I do laugh.

We start up the driveway. "I looked up your great-grandmother," Kai says. "I wanted to make sure we were on the right track. It's helpful she had some notoriety. So she has more of a paper trail."

Notoriety. So she had it, too, the benefits and pitfalls. But the language of the paper trail is all Chinese, more reason why I'm dependent on Kai.

"What did you find out?" I ask.

"Like your mom said, she was a rising star in Shanghai. She played pipa with the Shanghai Symphony Orchestra."

I glow. "Amazing. I wish we had recordings."

"One thing though," Kai says. "She was a Tan, and her husband, your great-grandfather, was a Lim, but I thought they were on your mom's side?"

"Right. I don't actually know his name myself," I confess.

"But if he's Lim, then your grandpa would be Lim, and then your dad—but she's on your mom's side of the family. Are both your parents Lims?"

Damn. Of course Kai has figured this out. I shove the rest of my pork bun into my mouth to hide the change in my expression.

"It's the most common last name for Chinese families," I say finally. "Across dialects. Lim. Lin. Lam. Lum. They're all the same."

"True," he says, but doesn't look convinced. I do want to come clean and tell him the truth about my real name and my blown-up summer. But his anti-Western stance makes me think he won't exactly *understand* about the Chinese hat and all the fallout that came from it.

"I guess back then it was more common for distant relatives to get married," he says.

"Right," I say, but I don't like misleading him. "What about Ai? I've never heard it as a last name before. And did someone name you Kai on purpose?"

"My parents liked the sound. Ai is the two hundred and fifteenth most common last name in Taiwan, which isn't that common. It means different things depending on which character is transliterated, but ours means love."

"Love that," I say, and he cracks a smile. "Sorry, couldn't resist."

"Not like I've never heard that one before," he says dryly.

He's funny, in an understated way. I can't help loving these glimpses of what must be the real Kai Ai, before he lost his music. *Thought* he lost it.

"It's actually part of my name, too," I say. "Ai-Zhu." I stop myself from including *Wong* at the last moment.

"Love-Pearl," he says, and even though of course I know what it means, hearing him say it makes my heart flip-flop as we ride the escalators into the subway.

Then I noticed he's massaging his hands.

"Do they hurt?" I ask. "Was it the other night?"

He's startled. "I'm always slightly feeling them. Some days are worse than others." He bites into his lower lip. "It's more an emotional burden, you know? Not knowing how it'll stop me. But Friday night was so great. I'm trying to book an appointment with my doctor ASAP."

"I'm glad," I say. I am, because like I told him, I care. But maybe I care too much. I head down the subway escalator ahead of him, putting some distance between us.

But at the bottom, Kai catches up to me. "I, uh, made you a playlist. Pipa songs you might like. They're not always on You-Tube."

"Oh my God," I say, stunned. Not what I was expecting at all. "Really?"

He ducks slightly. "Didn't mean to be presumptuous. I just thought maybe you'd like them."

"I do! No one's ever made me a playlist before. Except my piano teacher, for my practice."

He laughs. "Well, I guess I'm your pipa teacher until you get an upgrade."

He texts me a link and I put the earbud into my ear and give him the other, and we listen to the songs as we ride the train. They all have a distinctively Chinese flare, and the twang and cadences make my soul sing. I close my eyes and let their temperamental outbursts and intricately varied repetitions pulse deep in my chest. They're like Kai. But channeled this way, into music, it's a miracle.

As we reach our stop, I sigh, "I'm in love." I pull out my earbud and take Kai's back, realizing too late what I just said. Something about the crook to his lips makes me suspicious. "How many of these songs did you personally write?"

He gives me an innocent look back. "Why would you suspect me?"

"Two of them sound like you."

"*I* have a sound?"

"Yes. You do. Let me guess. The second and sixth songs." The sixth had been a MIDI rendition, not a live performance, but that wasn't the giveaway.

Kai holds up his hands, a sly smile on his face. "I only wrote the last one last night, so don't judge it too harshly."

"Just *last night*?"

"I have a software program I use to write down what's in my head. For the RSI."

"That's not why I'm amazed. It was perfect." Romantic and soft and yet still charged. My body heat. I'm not sure why.

And Kai keeps going. He leads us around a corner. "We're almost here," he says, and I come face-to-face with a massive, white five-panel gate topped by a yellow and green roof. Behind it, a sprawling Chinese-style palace rises into the mountains, with broad yellow walls and tiers of green pagoda roofs.

"It looks exactly like its name!" I say. "National Palace Museum. It is *definitely* a palace."

Kai smiles, like he'd set me up for my eyes to pop out. "Pretty amazing, huh?"

"Yeah. Do you think I'll find it here?"

"It's the best place to start. The director said to look around, and if we don't have any luck, go to the information desk. It's not *likely* to be here, but hopefully we'll find clues where to look next."

He's done all this work for my quest. Almost as if he wants to find this pipa as much as I do. More unexpected. My throat swells to aching.

"Thank you," I manage.

Red-carpeted stairs the width of an auditorium lead up to galleries of ancient Chinese exhibits. The museum doesn't have a section devoted to Chinese musical instruments. Instead, instruments are scattered in various halls, some with artifacts from their time periods, some for other thematic reasons. I spot an old zither and an erhu, their varnished surfaces lovingly worn. I take a breath, trying to find the balance between optimism and guarding my heart. But my hopes are already orbiting the moon. I'm questing after my musical heritage. A tie to family, which matters even more to me after losing Dad.

Kai moves just ahead, scanning the glass cabinets. The light catches the lines of his cheekbones, softening his expression. Or maybe it's being here. At the moment, surrounded by all these amazing works, I just feel grateful he's here lending me his knowledge of art history.

Mom calls as I step into a gallery of jade sculptures. "Hi, Pearl!" she says. "My aunty scanned more photos for me. I'm sending them to you now."

A black-and-white photo, faded to a pale tan, shows my great-grandma holding her pipa. I feel a jolt of excitement. It's exquisite—sleek and compact, with a face sprinkled with five cherry blossoms.

"It was made of wenge wood that rested for fifteen years after it was cut. And aged bamboo frets." She's reading from a slip of paper. "Silk strings instead of nylon-wrapped steel. The pipa is blue, although you can't tell from the photo."

"That's unusual," Kai says.

"Why blue?" I ask Mom.

"I don't know, but that must be why she wore a blue hairpiece. To match."

I've only seen one blue acoustic violin. A blue painted instrument, at least in the West, would be played by someone who wants to buck tradition a bit.

"Blue will make it easier to find." I study her pipa with new eyes. The standard pear shape. A deeper shade. "Who painted the blossoms? They're beautiful."

"I don't know. My aunty didn't say."

My great-grandma herself? An artist friend who wanted the outside to reflect the beauty of the music it could make?

"When was the last time she had it?"

"When she left to join her husband, she left it with family. But it was seized by soldiers during the war."

"I figured," Kai says.

I frown. "That's terrible. She was probably devastated to lose it. I guess from there, it made its way to a museum?"

"Seems so."

I save Mom's photos to my family album on my phone. I have photos going back as far as our Disneyland trip when I was four, eating cotton candy with my grandparents. I feel a stab of loss, looking at us all. My grandparents only spoke Chinese, so even though they could hug me, I couldn't talk to them. Beyond their generation, it's a blank. I don't even know anyone's names.

I shut off my phone. "Thanks, Mom. I'll keep you posted. I've got to go."

"Wait, Pearl?" Mom says.

"Yeah?"

"Talk to your sister," she says. "Talk sense into her about Rick."

I sigh. "If you keep bugging her, it will only make her dig in her heels more."

"That's why I'm asking you."

If this was about anyone but Rick, I'd feel annoyed. But it *is* Rick, so—

"I'll call her later," I promise.

"Your great-grandma's career ended pretty abruptly," Kai says as I hang up.

"You know more about my great-grandma than I do," I say grudgingly. "Can I see the articles you're reading?"

He pulls an old Chinese newspaper up on his phone, which I can't read, not even with my translation app, maybe because the script is old-fashioned. So frustrating. Like staring at a locked chest of family heirlooms that I don't have the keys for. But he points out the three characters of her name: 譚 美丽. "Tan Mei-Li."

"She was only twenty when she had to leave the country," Kai says.

"What? That young? I'd assumed she was older by then." That she'd had a long, illustrious life in music. I stare at the article, wishing I could will its secrets into my mind. "So she didn't just lose her pipa. She lost her entire musical career, thanks to a big bad thing outside her control. Everything was taken from her. Her home. Her *art*. Her pipa!"

"Sucks, doesn't it?" Kai says quietly.

I whirl to face him. "I'm sure she *loved* that pipa. So much. She'd have wanted it to be played by family, not drying out in some museum!"

"I'm sure she would have, too," he says. "It won't be easy, but we could definitely make a case to get it back."

"Right, for sure." My insides are buzzing. I need to make this right for her. I'm here a hundred years later, even if she couldn't have known I was coming. I'm going to bring her pipa back into the family and make sure it's played once again.

I tug on Kai's hand. "Come on," I say. "Let's keep looking."

We scour thousands of objects in what feels like hundreds of galleries: sculptures, paintings, vases, snuff bottles, and what feels like every other Asian instrument but the pipa. My legs start to cramp.

Finally, on the top floor, I spot two lutes on display in a glass case. Varnished wood. No blossoms. They might have been painted over, but they were so beautiful I can't imagine anyone wanting to cover them up. I take out my phone and compare them to the picture. These ones are the wrong shape. Slightly larger, less refined in workmanship. But I still aim my translation app at the Chinese inscription. One is from Beijing, 1945. The other from Guangzhou, 1800s.

Neither is my great-grandma's.

"Wow, these pipas are the real deal," Kai's breath brushes the back of my neck. He's reading the placard. "Playing them would be like getting anointed by an angel."

"It's not here," I say.

He looks at my face and grips my shoulder in a comforting way.

"Let's try the information desk," he says. He leads me to the counter, where a slim clerk calls in his director, an artsy, long-limbed woman in a suit printed with coffee cups, with a blue scarf tied around her snowy hair. She wheels toward us in an electric wheelchair and shakes our hands.

"You must be Kai," she says. "And Pearl—Kai says you're looking for a pipa." She smiles. "Such a lovely instrument. So spirited and graceful."

"My family believes my great-grandmother's instrument is in a museum," I say. "You guys are one of the closest to where she lived, so—" I gesture at the halls.

She taps her lips thoughtfully. "I don't know if we have such an instrument, but if we do, it might be in our archives. Would you like to take a look?"

"Yes, thank you!"

A text from Ethan pops up on my phone, but I pocket it. The

director introduces us to an elderly curator in a pea-green coat, with a face as wrinkled as a map of Taipei. Our guide hasn't heard of my great-grandmother, but he leads us through an interior door into a warehouse maze of shelves littered with every kind of artifact: old photographs from the Japanese occupation, gilded bowls, teakwood boxes carved into compartments, crinkly scrolls of an emperor's calligraphy, even a pair of pointy silk shoes made for bound feet.

"My great-great-aunt on my mom's side had bound feet," I say, picking one up with our guide's permission. I remember Mom's harrowing description of the bones breaking. "Thank God we are constantly evolving as a society."

"Makes you wonder what else we don't even realize we're putting up with. Like the fact that all this stuff is in here." Kai points at the shelves stocked with ancient ceramics, nude jade statues, and lustful paintings of kissing couples. "We take for granted museums have treasures from other countries, but how do they get them? Like the Gates of Babylon in Berlin."

"What?"

"The Ishtar Gate. A huge gate, a hundred and eighteen blue friezes with golden lions that used to line the Babylon Procession. German archaeologists took it, early 1900s. Iraq keeps asking for it back, but to this day, it's one of the biggest attractions in Berlin's Pergamon Museum. All they have in Babylon is a little replica."

I frown. "That seems wrong."

"It's really common. Don't even get me started on the British Museum."

"I don't know about their situation, but for us, it's complicated," says our guide. "We pay a fair price and do our best to ensure the property's chain of ownership. But it is not always easy to tell."

"Well, if my great-grandma's pipa is really in a museum, then I guess my family owes it a debt of gratitude. Her pipa could've been destroyed in a fire or bombing."

"That's what museums say to justify keeping all the stuff looted in wars," Kai says.

I hadn't thought of it that way. "But isn't it partly true?"

"Not in every case."

Our guide stops before a shelf loaded with wooden crates, each labeled in hand-scrawled Chinese. "These are from the time period you were describing." He hands us each a pair of soft gloves. "Please. Take a look."

He steps away and I look at Kai. "Is he really going to let us paw through these?"

"I've been in and out of their collections for a year now. They know me," he says.

I pull down a wooden box labeled "Chang Kai-shek Army, Amoy, China," grunting slightly under its weight. Dust wafts down. I sneeze as I pull out a stiff brown army jacket, a rusted, twelve-point star medallion, tin plates, yellowed Chinese newspaper clippings, a jade statue, and a chest carved from rosewood. The pieces are literally a hundred years old. They remind me of my friend's attic with the poodle skirts. But these could have belonged to my family. Maybe a soldier like my dad's grandpa had slept in a jacket like this. Maybe the medallion belonged to a general who didn't want to go to war . . . if I had had more time, I'd study them all, but I'm here for her pipa.

I work through the shelf of boxes, but they don't contain a single musical instrument.

"Is this all?" I ask.

"Everything from that place and time," answers our guide, returning with a vase that he adds to the shelf.

"It's not here," I say, disappointed.

"It's a start." With his hip, Kai nudges the last box back into place.

Still, I do feel more hopeful. Now that I've seen all these back rooms, I feel sure my great-grandmother's pipa must be somewhere, in another museum or in a music lover's collection. I just need to track it down.

"Pieces turn up everywhere," says our guide. "Don't be discouraged." He leads us back into the brightly lit lobby that smells of fresh cake from the adjacent café. The director rejoins us by the information desk.

"No luck, I hear?" She adjusts her blue scarf more securely over her cloud of hair.

"Do you know where else we can look?" I ask.

"I can search our database of museums. There are musical instruments museums all over the world. Brussels, Vienna. Even one in your home country. Phoenix." She types on a computer. "Let's see, I'm on the MIM Arizona website, searching for 'pipa'— they've got a performance by Wu Man coming up but no actual pipas in their collections."

"Okay." So no luck in Arizona, but this feels like a promising direction.

"One in Brussels, but it's a newer pipa. One in the Vienna Collection of Historic Musical Instruments, from Central Asia.

Looks like there are two in the British Museum in London. One secured at the end of the First Opium War in 1860, and a second one . . ." She flips her screen around, showing me the distinctive pear-shaped instrument. "Is this it?"

I lean in eagerly. The pipa on her screen was made in Hong Kong, 1900 to 1972, so it's the right range. *Acquired from a Miss Susan Walston in 1972. Not on display.*

I pull out my photo to compare. They're similar, but Great-Grandma's pipa is thicker in the body. Fewer frets.

"It's not it," I say, flipping my photo around.

"Have you tried sending your photo to other museums? With the internet, more and more museums are cataloging their inventories online."

"No, but that's a great idea!"

"Yes, I'd start there. The Hamamatsu Museum is just outside Tokyo. It's the only public musical instruments museum there."

"Public?" My smile fades. "Does that mean there are a bunch of private ones?"

She spreads her hands. "A pipa this pretty could easily be decorating someone's living room."

My heart sinks. "If it's in someone's home, how will I ever find it?"

"It's not as impossible as it might seem. Even if it's in a private collection, pipa enthusiasts might have heard of it. I'll try my counterpart in Tokyo for leads."

She places a call on her landline. *"Moshi moshi,"* she switches to Japanese effortlessly. *"Ichika onegai shimasu."* Her gestures all seem positive, but the only thing I recognize is Tan Mei-Li. She sets down her phone.

"They have pipas. Several that could fit your bill. Some are in storage, so they'll have to order them taken out." She hands me a note with an eight-digit phone number. "Call them in a few days. Ask to speak to Ichika. Tell her Mila sent you."

"I don't know how to thank you," I stammer.

"I understand why you're searching. I have my own eye on a Stradivarius in Tainan." She sighs gustily. "But the owner's hoarding every violin of significance he can get his hands on. Well, best of luck to you."

Outside, Kai and I head down the long, broad avenue toward the white five-arch gateway. My insides are buzzing with hope.

"That was promising," I say.

"It will show up somewhere. I'll ask my art teacher from school for leads, too."

"Thank you," I say. "Honestly, I wasn't sure what to expect, but now we're actually on a path."

"We sort of always were, you know." He's amused.

"Sorry, yes, you knew what you were doing! I'm really grateful."

"If you get it back, you should do a performance to commemorate it. A victory show."

"Yes! Like something she'd have done." And maybe Kai could play with me. If he's up for it. Beyond the gateway ahead of us, cars honk as they pass. "Everything out here feels so futuristic now," I observe. "I feel like we were just time traveling through imperial China from centuries ago."

"See? We have our royal families and ancient battles and even composers on this side of the ocean, too."

I frown at him. "What exactly do you have against Mozart and company?"

"My point is, there are other greats, in other civilizations. For some reason, people don't acknowledge them. It comes from a colonial mindset."

"As in the thirteen colonies?"

He laughs, although not unkindly. "That's what I mean. Your frame of reference is the United States. The American Revolutionary War. The thirteen colonies. Other countries had all those, too."

"So what's a colonial mindset?"

"Meaning you believe everything that came from the colonizer is better. Their music. Their fashion. Their belief system. It's why Americans are so into British accents and even here in Taiwan, so many of the fashion models are European."

"You can't just lump everyone together like that."

"But you can't argue against history. The Greek Empire spread their mythology throughout their territory. The Romans spread their roads and architecture. And the Austrian Empire spread their music. We still feel their influence. It's not random chance that their art forms are so dominant today."

He's like a firing squad of information. Can't be stopped. I dig in stubbornly. "Well maybe some things are dominant because they're just so amazing—like Mozart and Beethoven. Like," I try for a Chinese example, "Papermaking. Porcelain. Tea. Silk. Fireworks. Everyone loves them. So just because I like Mozart and even *piano* doesn't mean I'm colonized."

"What do you eat for breakfast back home?"

Ugh. I already know where this train will crash. "Eggs. Toast. Cereal and yogurt."

He crosses his arms over his chest. "Favorite book?"

"*Chronicles of Narnia.*"

"Religion?"

I grit my teeth. "Protestant. But three kings from the East were the first to meet baby Jesus. My pastor swears they were Chinese."

"So you're saying God intended the world to be ruled by white people?"

"Jesus was from the Middle East!" I throw my arms out, accidentally banging him on the chest. "I'm not *changing my religion* just to fit some narrow view of what it means to be Chinese."

"You don't even see it!" he says, throwing up his own arms. "This is exactly my point."

He stomps toward the gates. What the hell, seriously? Part of me wants to march off in the opposite direction. He and I just don't see the world the same way.

But I can't leave it like this. I run after him.

"Wait!" I'm out of breath by the time I catch up by the gates. "Look. I'm here learning Asian culture, right?"

He slows slightly. "Yes," he admits.

"I'm learning a lot," I say. "I'm learning a lot from *you.*"

"You don't need to learn it from me," he says.

"Well, I am. And we still have three weeks left." And it's not enough, I realize. I'm just getting to know Kai and the unique, frustrating, but also making-me-ponder ways he sees the world. I'm just discovering my great-grandmother's pipa and everything surrounding it. "So, like, just let me learn as much as I can. I'm trying, you know?"

He exhales a long breath. "I know."

I look back at the Palace Museum rising into the lush mountains. "I'd love a photo here," I say. Maybe for my eventual TikTok. But also just for me. Because, as Kai is trying to point out, this is part of my heritage. "Would you mind?"

"Sure." He takes my phone, and I stand under the archway looking straight at the camera.

"You have to make it more fun than that," he chides.

"It's not my fault you made me grumpy!" I put my hand on my hip and tilt back my head. He snaps a million and one photos.

"What do you think?" he asks. We meet in the middle, and he scrolls through the photos with me. They're good. Balanced. Good lighting.

"This one's the best. You're still mad." He points to the one with my hand in my hair and my face tipped toward the sun. And he's right. I *am* still mad in it. My nostrils are flared. My cheeks are red.

"You're still a jerk." I turn to him, and he's much closer than I expected. We've leaned into each other without realizing it, so close that our sides have pressed together. But instead of pulling away, his eyes travel down my face to my lips. And linger.

My body tingles. My heart is pounding so hard I'm sure he can hear it. His mouth moves toward mine, instinctively. Our noses bump.

Then he blinks and pulls back.

"I'm sorry I keep giving you a hard time." He looks away, at the museum. His throat moves with a hard swallow. "It's just that . . . I don't want you to walk around with blinders on."

I sway slightly on my feet. We almost kissed. And I wanted to.

And if we had, I'd know, I'd just *know* if he's the guy in the dark.

"Why do you care so much?" I ask in a shaky voice. "You could just let me wallow in my ignorance."

"It'd be a waste. You're so smart. You're talent. But at the end of the day, you've got to make your own choices. That's the real point. *You* make the choices. Not the dominant culture. And definitely not me."

I can feel his words, right here, in the center of my chest.

"Why did you bring your pipa to Loveboat?" I ask.

He lifts his chin, like he's daring me to laugh. "To lend to you."

It's what I suspected. After I understood he'd gone home for his old books for me.

"Why?" I ask.

"I told you. I'd rather it be played by someone good than not played at all."

"You *do* just say whatever's on your mind."

"How do you know I've said it all?"

We're silent a moment. A million possibilities hang in the air.

A cab pulls up and the driver calls, *"Nǐ xiǎng qù nǎlǐ?"* Asking if we need a ride. I've picked up that much.

Kai looks at the driver, then back at me. "How tired are you?"

"You mean other than the fact that we just walked for five hours through the museum?"

"Yeah."

"I could play an entire concert. What do you have in mind?"

He smiles. "I was thinking more of a farmers' market, but maybe we could squeeze a concert in somewhere along the way."

18

Kai's favorite farmers' market sells a variety of purple, prickly, and lumpy fruits I've never seen before. We split a dragon fruit, each scooping out spoonfuls of the purple flesh. We eat until I seriously could burst. Neither of us have brought up the almost-kiss, like we have an unspoken agreement to not cross any permanent lines that could damage this fragile and precious new friendship.

As we wander, I come across a vendor selling fabrics, including a wild, patchwork skirt on display. "Oh, I love it," I say.

"Nice colors," Kai says. The vendor is surprised I want to buy it—apparently, it was just for showing off his various cottons, silks, and batik. But he quotes me an affordable price and hands it to me in a bag. Kai buys a few more dragon fruit to share with his hallmates. As he lifts his bag, I automatically reach for it.

"I can carry it," I offer.

He looks embarrassed. "It's okay. I bought them."

"As long as you're not just being polite," I say. "I want to help, but you have to let me."

"This one's okay. Honestly, the hardest part is when someone asks me to do something I can't. Like the time an elderly woman boarded the train with a big bag of groceries, and this man kicked my foot, saying, 'Carry it for her.' Then rolled his eyes and said to his wife, 'Kids these days, no respect.'"

"Ouch," I say. "That's not fair."

"It's too much to explain. Too tiring."

I know how he feels. Having to explain yourself over and over is exhausting, whether it's on TikTok or a subway car. And it must only be harder when your first language is music. "You probably wanted to help."

He doesn't contradict me. Only gazes with thoughtful eyes around the market as we head out. "I used to come here with my family as a kid."

"I can see how it would have been fun to grow up here."

"The biggest benefit of my parents moving back here was I've spent more time with my extended family. Over time, I pick up the family stories."

I feel a twinge of wistfulness. "What have you learned about them?"

"One of my great-great-grandpas helped build the railroads in California. Then he came back to China, and then we went back again and ran a restaurant."

"So technically you're fifth-generation American, even though your parents were born here. You're more American than I am."

Kai laughs. "That's ironic!"

Across the street, a white stucco cathedral catches my eye. It's trimmed with brown beams, and the massive double doors are open wide to the public.

"I didn't realize there were cathedrals in Taipei," I say, slowing. I toured a few when I performed in London and love how they're built for glorious acoustics. "Want to look inside?" I ask, before I realize he might not be a fan.

"Sure," Kai says.

We climb the stone steps into a beautiful sanctuary. It's modest, with plain wooden pews and rectangular windows instead of stained-glass ones, and a high ceiling painted white and trimmed with brown buttresses. Silver organ pipes line the entire back and side walls. It's nearly empty, with a single woman kneeling in prayer in the front.

"Come on," I say, moving toward the organ built into the side. "Here's our concert."

"Do you play?" he asks.

"No, but I've seen people playing it. I've always liked organs. They look like pianos in a fun house," I say.

The organ is set up with two parallel keyboards for hands, and for feet, a pedalboard made of wood that looks like elongated keys. I gaze longingly at the keys.

"I've always wanted to try one," I say.

He glances around. Then makes a beeline for a man in a soft black suit folding silk cloths. A moment later, Kai returns.

"Go for it," he says. "I asked and he says it needs to be played more."

"What? Thanks for asking!" I climb onto the bench, then I look at Kai. "Play the foot pedals."

"I don't know how," he says, but scoots in beside me.

"Figure it out." I play "Battle Hymn of the Republic," because it feels appropriate. The notes from the pipes overhead fill the cathedral. My whole body vibrates with the sound.

I nudge Kai and his feet take over the pedals. As his foot depresses one, a deep note rings out, clashing with my melody.

"Maybe not that one!" he says, and we both laugh. He tests each foot pedal, running bass notes under my lighter ones. The bench is too small for the both of us. Our elbows tangle up and our hips press tightly together as we make a big mess of our song, then find a groove where he chops up my song with a bass beat, turning it into something syncopated and otherworldly. As the song ends, we both hold still, still wedged together, listening to the overtones ring on above us.

He traces a finger down the back of my right hand, and then the left. "You've been holding out on me," he says. "Although I'm not surprised you play like this, after seeing what you can do on an instrument you'd never even heard of."

My hands are tingling where he touched. I should come clean. He deserves that much. I open my mouth to finally tell him the truth, but my phone buzzes in my pocket. Ethan.

When are you back?

Practice tonight? I'm around.

"Have to go?" Kai asks.

"Yeah," I admit. "But thanks for today. For everything. I, uh—"

He slides off the bench, and a gust of cold air takes his place. I follow him outside and down the sidewalk, but he stays slightly ahead of me. Something about his stride, the set to his shoulders, clues me in.

"What's wrong?" I ask, catching up.

"Why are you always hanging around Ethan Kang?" he asks without looking at me.

So he saw the texts. But how does he know we've been hanging out? And how can I explain what I don't fully understand?

"We're doing a duet together," I say.

"He's a really big deal violinist," Kai says, sullen again.

"Yeah . . ." What does he mean by that? Is he surprised Ethan's willing to do a duet with me? I frown. "I'm playing piano with him. We're practicing a lot."

"In a locked auditorium?"

I give him a hard stare. "Were you following me?"

"I was looking for you once. Saw you go in with him. I tried to follow but—" He spreads his hands.

But the door was locked. And did he hear us playing or . . . ? My face warms, imagining Kai hearing us playing, or not playing, inside.

"That was nosy."

Kai's brows pull together. His lips turn downward. "You're right. It's none of my business."

His stride quickens. I follow him, frustrated.

Just a half block away, he stops abruptly outside an antique store. Large plastic bins on tables are full of vintage magazines and pamphlets. As I catch up, Kai pulls out an American magazine from the 1920s.

"This is terrible," he says, distressed. "I'm surprised they're selling it."

Kai drops the magazine and strides on into the subway entrance. It falls to the table, and I pick it up to reveal a cover with a grotesque caricature of a Chinese man with enormous buck teeth . . . under a conical straw hat.

It reminds me, disturbingly, of my TikTok photos. Which I had almost been about to confide in Kai, along with the truth of my life in music. Maybe the trolls were upset because they thought I was making one of these caricatures. Which would maybe make Kai like a troll, and make them not-trolls?

I shove the magazine back into place and scramble to catch up with Kai. I'm glad all over again that Kai has never seen my Tik-Tok video. If I'm going to keep him as my friend, not to mention how badly I need his help in my pipa search, I need to keep that tight under wraps.

It's a forty-minute ride back to campus, but Kai puts in his ear-buds and I'm left alone with my thoughts. I peek over at him a few times. He looks tired. Maybe I've just worn him out. He can't be *that* mad about Ethan.

I want to talk to him, but my instincts tell me giving him space is more important. So I pull out my phone and do a little research on Chinese caricatures. I pull up a set of images that makes me wince: cartoons with squinty eyes, fat cheeks, a wide mouth full of big teeth . . . and almost all of them are wearing the straw hat covering up half their faces. Some of them are even in big-name magazines.

I hate to admit it, but they *are* similar to my TikTok video. No wonder people reacted so strongly. I shut my phone off, feeling slightly sick. Even if I it wasn't my intention, I feel terrible that I caused pain to people who were reminded of these stereotypes. If I could do it over, I don't know that I could have done anything

223

differently, because I didn't know any better. But I hope I'd have apologized more meaningfully.

Kai's toes are tapping slightly, his eyes closed. I can't help comparing my jumbled up feelings for him with how I feel about Ethan. They're both star musicians in their own ways. Ethan is so smooth and says all the right things and knows what he wants and goes for it. Including me. It's flattering, it's easy, and Julie's so excited about him.

Meanwhile Kai riles me up with his bald statements and questions out of left field. But the touch of his fingers are lingering on the backs of my hands. *You've been holding out on me.* Like my musical abilities were a treasure. But he also hates everything he seems to think I stand for. And if he knew me, really knew me, Chinese hat and all, he might actually hate me, too.

Our train pulls to a stop and Kai opens his eyes, pulling out his earbuds. He catches my eye, then turns to the opening doors.

"Guess we're back," he says, and heads out without another glance.

On campus, a few dozen students are sprawled on the lawn under the stars, cozy with little electric lanterns shaped like bells. Some are folding paper stars. Others are weaving a giant friendship bracelet. Kai and I walk up the driveway together, and a few kids cast curious looks in our direction. Despite his coolness, two spots of color burn on Kai's cheeks. I shy from their gazes, too. Yes, this is Loveboat. Yes, I've been out all day with Kai. No, nothing's going on between us.

"See you in class tomorrow," Kai says,

"Wait," I say as he starts to slip off. I'm late to meet Ethan, but I don't want to part with this odd tension. "Are we still on for lessons?"

Kai meets my gaze. Then his lips turn up in a tentative smile. "Of course."

At least I have that to look forward to. He heads off and I hurry down the hallway toward the auditorium with a lighter step.

I missed a call from Mom earlier, so I call her back as I reach the auditorium foyer, where a few students are reading plaques on the wall. Her voice is pitched with excitement. "I got the whole story from my aunty! My grandfather, your great-grandfather, was arrested during the civil war."

"Civil war. A Chinese civil war." Kai's right. I've only learned about the American one, but it makes sense that there would be others—in China, and every country.

"Yes. His friends broke him out of jail, and he was forced to flee to Singapore. My great-grandmother didn't want to be apart from him, so the friends smuggled her out on a boat and she had to leave her pipa behind because it was too recognizable and would identify her. That was the last she played it."

"Oh my God, that's so romantic!" I say. Fleeing together in the dead of night, leaving everything you ever knew behind, and all for love. Who knew I had that in my DNA, too? And so does my sister, who seems to have lost her ability to believe in the power of pure love. "Does Ever know the story?"

"No, I just heard it myself. It wasn't something they wanted to dwell on. Jail. That must be why we've never heard it."

"Tell Ever," I say. "She needs to hear it. Thanks, Mom." I don't know if this story helps with my search. But it helps me understand more. My great-grandma gave up the stage and her pipa to be with my great-grandpa. Family mattered to her. And he must have been some guy.

Another call beeps. "It's Julie."

"Go ahead," Mom says. "We can talk more later." She signs off.

"Hey, Julie," I answer.

"Pearl, I just learned this program you're on has a rather unsavory reputation among some Asian American parents."

So. Word finally caught up with her. "Um, yeah. About that." I slip outside so we can talk privately.

"Apparently, there's quite a debaucherous group of kids every year," Julie continues.

"Not everyone's like that," I say guiltily. Meanwhile, *I* went to the Party in the Dark. *I've* been with Ethan behind locked doors, and *I've* snuck out past curfew with Kai . . . even after Ever's experience, I'd never have guessed I'd do any of these things.

"Well, I need you to remember why you're there, and stay out of trouble. And when you do your *Teen Vogue* interview, keep the specific program you're on vague."

"Won't that be a basic fact they'd have to cover?"

"Let's keep the spotlight on you guys. And on culture."

"Okay," I say.

But even as the word leaves my mouth, I feel a dig of resentment. Am I *supposed* to be ashamed of being on Loveboat now? My sister and her friends are all so accomplished. And the ones that came before them, they're like congresspeople and founders of tech companies and famous singers and authors.

What's the difference if, while they were here, they went out clubbing and kissed a few people? Not for the first time I find myself wondering, *Whose rules are these?*

"Everything else going well?" Julie asks. "Practice? Are we on track for the performance?"

"Yes, it's great. And I should be able to find a dress once I focus on it."

"Yes, something stunning for the cameras. Maybe one of those pretty silk dresses with those elegant collars and the slit on the side—a qipao?"

I wrinkle my nose, although she can't see. A qipao. I like the silk material, but every Chinese girl I see in films wears a qipao, even Cho Chang in Harry Potter. My mom has a few she hasn't worn in years. After the bamboo hat incident, it seems like the absolute worst choice.

Good thing I'll have Sophie's help.

"Actually, I wanted to tell you about something interesting that came up." I head back inside, pausing outside the double doors to the auditorium. Beyond them, I can hear the sound of Ethan's violin. "I found out my great-grandmother played pipa. She was a professional player in China when she was my age."

"A *pipa*? What's that?"

From her tone, I can picture Julie's carefully plucked brow rising in her forehead. I explain the instrument to her. "My great-grandma was famous in her day, but her pipa was lost during the war. I'm trying to find it."

"Sounds like a nice way to reconnect to your roots," Julie says. "Well, then. Keep me posted on Mr. Kang."

The article, the performance. They're all she's focused on. I set my hand to the auditorium door. That's her job, I suppose. I can't expect her to be as excited about the pipa as I am. It's personal for me, not her.

"I will," I promise, then push my way inside.

Ethan is playing his violin onstage for a small audience of Loveboaters in the front row. I recognize some of them from our night out clubbing.

Ethan catches my eye and gives me a gallant wave. "Bonjour, mademoiselle."

The other kids turn to look at me, and I start down the aisle. If he was mad at me for brushing him off last night, would I actually be able to tell?

"Your French accent is scarily authentic," I say.

"I spent a week in Paris for a photo shoot." He plays the "Wedding March" in time to my footsteps. A laugh bubbles from my lips. One of the guys whistles.

"Stop! Stop it!" I break stride, his rhythm, and pretend to charge him onstage. He dances out of reach, getting in all the last notes to complete the whole stanza. His gallery cheers.

"You are . . . *too much.*" I wipe tears from my eyes. Iris would say something pithier, but that's all I can manage. The crowd is laughing, too. It's warm and festive in here, and I can't help appreciating that Ethan's responsible for it.

"All right, ladies and gentlemen, the show is over," Ethan says to them. "This special lady and I have secret business to conduct."

I blush as the kids exchange knowing glances.

"Dinner at Din Tai Fung later?" says one of the guys.

"Sure, see you," Ethan says. They head out a side door, leaving us alone again. The box of pearl bonbons is sitting on the piano. Ethan glides his bow up and down his cake of rosin as a pregnant silence falls.

"Um, last night," I begin.

"You don't have to explain," he says.

So he *did* notice. "I was just across the hallway. With Iris and Hollis."

His shoulders relax. "Cool," he says. "They're so great."

"Yeah, well, they're having a blast with all the blind dates you've been setting up for them."

"It's my superpower. Matchmaking. I call them like they are." He crooks a brow at me. "I have a surprise for you," he continues. He pulls out a thick stack of glossy brochures and hands the whole pile to me. "I got the okay from Marc. He said he appreciated us helping to spread the word for the other students." I smooth my hand over the page on top.

CHIEN TAN TALENT SHOW

11 August, 4:00 o'clock in the afternoon
Featuring student talent along with
a duo by
Ethan Kang, violinist, and
Pearl Wong, pianist

W. A. Mozart   Piano and Violin Sonata in G Major,
1756–1791   K. 301

I. Stravinsky
1882–1971

Duo Concertante for Violin and Piano
   1. Cantilène
   4. Gigue
   5. Dithyrambe

L. van Beethoven
1770–1827

Piano and Violin Sonata no. 9 in E Major,
op. 14, no. 1

P. de Sarasate
1844–1908

Zigeunerweisen (Gypsy Airs), op. 20

"I figured you'd be using your real name by then, right?" Ethan says. "It's three weeks away. And a packed auditorium will look better for *Teen Vogue*." He tugs at his collar. He's sweating just a bit.

He's taking my comeback performance so seriously, and that means a lot to me. Although what am I going to do about my name? I meant to keep it on the downlow, only giving it to *Teen Vogue* for the article that few people here will read. I'll ask Julie, but if she says no, can I really ask him to scrap these? He's already printed them.

"Is the order okay? Ending on the Sarasate would be nice, but we could switch it."

"No, no, it's perfect," I reassure him. And then my eyes fall on his shoes.

Veja blue sneakers.

Wait, what?

"Should we warm up with Mozart now?" Ethan says.

He says something else, but I can't register his words. Are Veja shoes even more popular than I realized? Ethan said his manager buys all his clothes. Either way, these are the shoes of my devil in the dark! Could he be Ethan? After all this time?

"Pearl? You okay?"

"Yeah. Fine," I say, and sit heavily on the piano bench. I run a few scales to warm up my fingers. But my mind spins.

Ethan said he was going to bed that night. Could he have doubled back later? He knew what mask I was wearing, so it wouldn't even matter if he saw my face or not, as long as the light was bright enough for him to see the purple glitter. But that would mean he's been lying this whole time. He doesn't seem like that kind of guy. And what about Kai and *his* shoes?

"Pearl, you sure you're okay?" Ethan's brow is furrowed with concern. I've stopped playing, staring into the piano's soundboard. If it's Ethan, he's in hiding, and I can't exactly confront him, can I? If it's Ethan, then it's not Kai . . . but what if it is? And why am I getting *so distracted* by boys when I really need to focus on my comeback?

I bring my hands back to the keys and play the Stravinsky, trying to bring some of his order into the discord of my life. Ethan joins me and we make our way through the piece, repeating the difficult sections a few times.

"We're solid," he says.

Musically, maybe. But otherwise?

He reaches for the box of chocolates, but I can't possibly stomach one right now. Then a text chimes on my phone, and on Ethan's at the same time. Which can only mean it's from one person.

Wolf. And as it turns out, he has a very important announcement.

Your prayers have been answered. I hope you didn't lose those masks.

Party in the Dark II. Stay tuned for details.

19

"You *have* to come, Pearl," Iris says as we line up for a buffet dinner. "This is the only fighting chance we have to find our princes."

"I don't know," I say. "I want to figure out who he is"—more than ever now, I want to settle this Question once and for all—"but it seems like asking for trouble." But my mind immediately schemes my way around *that*. I won't let my mask slip this time. I could wear a larger mask and maybe a cape with a hood . . .

Wolf texts us more details. Next Saturday. Same time. Same place. Everyone is encouraged to bring name cards. You decide whether to give them out. And he's put a plan in place. The second half will be the usual no-holds-barred free-for-all. **Because anything can happen in the dark,** Iris reads aloud again. "This Wolf is too much."

But the interesting part is the first half of the night. It will be a Party in the Dark I reprise. All the same songs. If you can remember where you danced that special song with that special someone, you can try to find them in the same spot. Your choice whether to wear the same mask to be recognized, hide behind a new one, or a combination of both.

"I really can't remember my song," Iris says. "They all sounded the same to me."

"Mine was an Adele song," I say. "Then an indie pop."

"Oh, right. I remember Adele. Maybe I'll remember if I hear it."

"He's set it up like a dating app," Hollis says. "Swipe right. Only better. Maybe I'll get brave this time." I squeeze their hand.

"Our mom was just reminding us that she and our dad were a love match on Loveboat," Iris says. "Just think, Pearl. If you find your mystery kisser, he could be THE ONE!"

I shiver. It's absurd, of course. THE one? But a part of me still hopes settling the Question will bring clarity to the confusion of Ethan and Kai. And will he be there? Will he look for me? Will we find each other, and if we do, will we reveal our identities?

"There are so many ifs," I say. "And who's to say people won't pull stunts like passing along other people's names, instead of their own?"

"Yes, this could get messy," Iris says cheerfully, undaunted.

I shudder. "Well, you're not going to believe this, but I found another pair of Veja shoes," I say. "On Ethan's feet."

"What?" Hollis gasps.

"No way!" Iris grabs my arm. "He didn't come to the first party. He said he wasn't going."

"Yes, but maybe they're more common than I realized."

"But what if he was . . . fibbing?" Hollis asks.

"Too bad you can't DNA test his shoes to see if there's beer on the soles," Iris says.

I gasp. "Iris! You're a genius!"

She furrows her brow. "I am?"

Leaving the twins, I dash upstairs to my room, shove my clothes aside, and find my pumps kicked under my bed. I dash back to them, holding them out triumphantly.

"Look!" A speck of purple glitter remains on the toes, but when I flip one over to reveal its sole, the entire leather bottom glitters purple. "When my mask fell, a bunch of glitter must have shaken loose. It's possible it could be on the bottom of my mystery kisser's shoes, too."

"Glitter *is* really hard to get off entirely," Hollis says.

"There's a good chance at least one speck is still on his soles," Iris says. "IF he was at the party."

"So Kai versus Ethan. Who would you rather it be?" Hollis asks.

"Ethan, obviously," Iris says. "Kai was such an ass to you." Hollis shushes her.

"Honestly, Kai's sort of grown on me," I admit. "He's changing. He's pretty different from what I thought at first. But . . ." But he doesn't know the real me.

"So if he's *him*, would you think worse of him?"

I purse my lips. "Maybe I would. He just doesn't seem like the type, so it would seem hypocritical. But neither does Ethan. So I don't know," I admit. "Maybe I'm rooting for a third unknown. A dark horse candidate."

Iris laughs. "A Loveboat *quadrangle*. This one's going down in history."

I groan. "No thank you."

The twins stay up all night plotting and planning how to trap Wolf, but nothing seems feasible. Even if Wolf's there, he'll just be one of the crowd. There's no way to identify him unless he comes forward and confesses. But that's not likely to happen. He's gone to so much trouble to hide himself.

All week, between quizzes and extracurriculars, Party in the Dark II is the talk of the campus. Everyone's debating whether people will be able to find anyone or stay under wraps this time. There are so many ways for someone to get caught entering or leaving the club.

In Mandarin class, Ethan catches my eye. "Pretty funny how into it they are, huh?"

"Have you decided if you're going this time?" I eye him carefully, gauging his reaction. Unfortunately, he's wearing plain old Nikes today. No chance for a glitter check.

"Maybe," he says, smiling. "According to Iris, I'm a matchmaking failure, so maybe I need more real-world experience."

He sets a hand over mine briefly, then lets go. His brown-eyed gaze is so clear that I have to take a step back internally. He can't be him.

"Just make sure your disguise is extra secure," I say.

I'm excited for the party, but I'm more excited for the progress I'm making on my pipa quest, not to mention in my pipa lessons with Kai. We have two more. I'm learning so much—even Kai seems genuinely impressed by my progress. But we only talk about the pipa, and then he has to rush off for this or that meeting or class. We don't talk about Ethan or those charged moments between us at the museum and on the organ bench. Just lessons. Just what Kai committed to Maya he'd do. He's pulled away again. He was

236

generous going to the museum with me, and maybe he's not that interested in spending more time together. *I* can't expect more of his time. But that doesn't mean I don't want it.

Still, I keep going because that's what we have to do. I call the Tokyo museum and leave a message for the person the National Palace Museum named. I reach out to every musical museum I find online and scroll through thousands of photos of Asian artifacts in museums around Europe. I'm stunned by the sheer numbers. Kai is right—so much was taken during colonial periods or wars. And almost every single museum has one or two pipas. But what if the blossoms have been painted over? How will I prove it's the same one?

On Wednesday, I text Ever, who I've kept in the loop on my pipa quest. I can't possibly check them all out, I conclude.

Maybe you can tap the Loveboat alum for help. They live in cities all over the world.

I'm skeptical, but I post a request on the alumni channel. I wonder if anyone will even see it.

Thursday afternoon, Iris and Hollis find me sitting on the sofa with my phone. "We're going to scope out the PDII club tonight," Iris says. "Maybe people will be setting up . . . they'll have to at some point and maybe we'll see something. Want to come?"

"I would, but I'm meeting my sister's friend," I say, opening my text thread.

"Sophie Ha?" Hollis asks, reading over my shoulder. "The fashion designer? You know her?! Can I touch you?"

I smile and show them the photo of the two of us in my dorm. "She's like my big sister. Do you want to meet her?"

"I would die to meet her! But we're also meeting a family

friend for dinner. Another time?"

"Definitely." I smile. "You guys are practically family now, too."

Maya teaches us the erhu next—the Chinese version of the violin with the bow threaded through the strings instead of played on their outer surface. I imitate her arm as she draws the bow back and forth in clean, deft motions. This is what Ethan is the master of.

Kai leans in, head moving slightly to the beat. He's wearing his sandals today. I'm starting to think he can't be my devil either. With him, what you see is what you get. He's an open book, honest about what he's thinking and feeling to a fault. He catches my eye and gives me a tentative smile that warms me more than I wish it did, then he returns his attention to Maya.

During class, a few notes come in on the Loveboat thread. I read them as Maya breaks us to practice on our own while she moves around giving personal instructions

> Hi, Pearl, the MIM in Rome has two pipas but they're both too early for what you're looking for. One was played by a famous pipa player from Hong Kong.
>
> Here's a pipa in Australia. Donated by a local family that inherited it. Yours?
>
> I found a pipa in a private collection from Beijing, fifty years ago.

It's generous of the alumni to pitch in, and it's helpful to eliminate museums like this. But we could be a hundred pipas later and find that none are my great-grandmother's. This won't be easy.

As I'm putting away my erhu, my phone rings. It's the Tokyo Hamamatsu Museum, calling me back. Finally! I draw away from the other students to answer.

"Hello?" I say.

A woman behind a counter appears on my screen. Behind her, a sign reads, The Space of GOD, PRAYER, and BEAUTY. So fitting.

"Hello, Ms. Wong, is it? I'm Ich. You're the one looking for a pipa?"

My heartbeat quickens. "Yes."

"We had one that unfortunately broke a few years ago. Was this it?"

God, I hope not. Her phone shifts to show me a pipa narrower in the body.

"That's not it," I say with relief. But what if my great-grandmother's pipa *has* been destroyed? It came through a war, after all. "There's nothing linked to my great-grandmother's name?"

"No, but we had a pipa sold by a dealer in 1955 to an antique dealer here in Tokyo, who sold it to a collector in Taipei. No photo, but it's described as 'bird's egg blue.'"

My heart lurches. "How many other blue pipas could there be?"

She gives me the name of the antique dealer, and I furiously jot it onto my hand.

"It's a store around Yongkang Street," Kai says, startlingly close. Maya and the rest of the kids have left and I didn't even notice. But Kai stayed. I give him a questioning look.

He smiles and shows his phone to me. "I looked it up."

"Thank you," I say gratefully. So he's still in this with me. And I'd never have come this far without him. I dial the store's video chat number.

"*Wǒ kěyǐ bāng nǐ ma?*" An elderly man in a faded pinstriped shirt blooms on my phone.

"Um, hello, I'm looking for a blue pipa." I explain my quest and text him the photo. "I got a lead that you might have something like it."

"Pipa?" He puts spectacles on the bridge of his nose and studies it while I hold my breath. "I haven't sold a pipa in several years. I don't have any now."

"But you sold one?" I grip my phone tighter. "It *could* have been years ago."

"So I sold it?" His brow crinkles like he's trying to recall. "Did I now?" he muses, talking more to himself than me.

My trail hangs in the brink, dependent on his memory and willingness to help me.

"It's possible," I say.

He sets his phone down on his counter, where I get an enlarged view of a clay teacup and his shrinking slightly hunched back as he totters over to an ancient filing cabinet. He begins to page through files with arthritic hands. "Pipa. Pipa. Pipa." Kai holds up crossed fingers.

"Ah, yes," The man removes a sheet of paper and squints at it.

"An art adviser picked it up for her client. The Renmai Museum."

"Where's that? Please don't be in Fiji or somewhere unreachable, like the moon . . ."

"Tainan," Kai says. "It's two hours south of here by train." He gives me a tentative smile. "I can go with you, if you want."

I swallow hard. "Are you kidding?" I say. "Tomorrow? We'd have to miss a Friday of classes." I frown. "How much are train tickets? I doubt I have enough."

His smile deepens. "There's always playing on the streets again. Tonight?"

My own smile breaks out. "I'm meeting my sister's friend soon, but after—let's do it."

"See you then," he says, and heads off.

My eyes linger on his back. A road trip with Kai. And maybe with time to really talk, I can finally find the courage to ask him some hard questions, and share some truths of my own.

20

The moon is large and low in the night sky when I head out to meet Sophie. She picks me up in a BMW van driven by a driver in a navy cap. She's like a picture as usual in a peach cotton dress printed with navy sketches of famous buildings. A thirteen-year-old girl with short, spiky pink hair is snapping gum in the back seat.

"My cousin. She's in a punk phase," Sophie whispers.

"I'm Fannie, and I heard that." The girl sticks out a plump hand and shakes mine. "Nice to meet you, Pearl."

"Fannie's also my summer intern," Sophie says. "She's been applying since she was five. I finally gave in."

"You said you were *lucky to have me*," Fannie points out.

Sophie tousles her pink hair. "I am."

"Fun to meet you," I say. "I like your shoes." I point to her pink gels, and she cracks a half smile.

"Mango smoothie?" Sophie offers me a frosted bottle as we head off. "What Loveboat excursion am I making you miss?"

"Everyone's doing a fan dance class. Special world-famous instructor."

She smiles. "That was a girls-only elective when I was here. Marc's really shaking things up, isn't he?"

"We even have an app now!"

"Right? So should we talk about your performance outfit?"

"My manager suggested a qipao for me to emphasize the cultural part of my trip, but it feels like too much for me. I mean, if another girl *wanted* to wear one, I'd say go for it. And I want to show I'm proud of my heritage, but it feels—like I'm trying too hard? Ugh. Why are clothes so complicated? Shouldn't I be spending my time practicing?"

She laughs. "You won't believe how often I hear performers say that. They think it's all about the music, or the acting, the dancing, whatever. But the outfit matters—you've come to the right person! This won't be any old dress. It will be a *Sophie original*."

"Oh!" I sit up. "I wasn't complaining to get you to solve my problem. I was just . . . complaining."

"I've got your back, girl." She flutters a hand as we turn into a historic part of Taipei I haven't visited yet. "This is the Dadaocheng Wharf, where Xavier's family business has operated for hundreds of years." A note of pride rings in her voice. "I've set up my first shop in a store on the same block."

I take in the lush scenery. Ornate buildings of red bricks and white stones fill the block, with tidy second and third floors set with nine-paneled windows. A covered walkway fronted by Roman archways runs the length of a paved street. Large Chinese characters label each shop and strings of red lanterns crisscross the street. The part of me that loves old places and traditions falls in love all over again. We pull past an imposing brick building dominating the corner of an intersection. A huge black dragon encircles a tree-like Chinese character: 葉. It gleams as though it were just freshly inked with a very large calligraphy brush.

"Yeh headquarters." Sophie points it out.

"I remember you said a while back that Xavier and his dad don't get along. How are things now?"

"Much stronger. His dad's retired. His youngest sister runs the company with help from Xavier and his cousin, Victor. She's fantastic. I started working with her before Xavier and I even got together! And then I opened my shop last winter . . . just over here."

We stop before a pair of beautiful rosewood doors, with silver handles shaped like the two halves of one heart. The ceiling over the doorway is a single painting depicting an intertwined dragon and phoenix, gold-crested blues, greens, and reds.

"It's *gorgeous*," I say.

"Xavier painted it." Sophie blushes. "My Chinese name is Bao-Feng. Xavier's symbol is Dragon. So together, we're *Feng*-and-*Lung*." The words roll off her tongue in a rhyming cadence. "Phoenix and Dragon."

"So sweet." I can only hope I'll find a love like theirs one day. And that Ever and Rick will find their way back to their own.

I step into a well-lit space bursting with exquisite gowns of silks, gossamer, bold prints, and delicate tulle. Ladies' hats in every pastel shade top a shelf behind a counter with a modern sewing machine and long ruler to measure fabrics.

"Wow. You designed all these?" A waist-high robot, triangular in shape with a sweet face, wheels by. It selects a meticulously stitched dress off a rack and carries it toward the back.

Sophie smiles at my expression. "Everything you see. Robots

and all. We're showing off the best pieces in my fashion show at the end of summer. We'll have tons of press there." She fingers a furry orange stole. "I did all this on my own. That was really important to me."

"I feel like I've stepped into Willie Wonka's factory." I pause before a three-way mirror framed in intricately wrought copper. My black hair frames my smile and then my clothes blur on my body and swap out for a silver sequin one-shoulder dress I just saw hanging on her racks.

"Whoa, what just happened?" I cry.

Sophie smiles. "It's my Magic Mirror!"

"Oh my gosh, I remember Ever gushing about it!"

"I worked on it with Xavier's aunt. It's advanced over the years, and now we've set them up in boutiques all around Europe and Asia."

I twirl before the Mirror, letting purple silks and lacy brocades unfold over me. A wreath of flower buds adorns my head.

"Hey, Pearl!" To my surprise, Rick is coming toward us, dressed casually in a blue shirt over khaki shorts. His black hair is damp and slicked back, like he just came from a workout and shower. "How's Loveboat life going for my Girl Wonder?"

He swoops me into his signature bear hug, while Sophie scolds him for distracting the Mirror, which is now busy dressing him in a lumberjack plaid.

I laugh breathlessly as he releases me. "Other than you breaking my ribs just now, I'm hanging in there. What are you doing here?"

"A little bird told me you were coming by for a Sophie original."

I smile. "I am." But on closer look, Rick looks . . . terrible. His clothes are hanging loosely on his body, like they were bought for a larger version of himself. A small scar on his upper lip marks where he cut himself shaving.

"How are you doing?" I ask seriously.

"I feel like half a person," he admits.

"Pearl, can you join me?" On the other side of the room, Sophie is pulling dresses off her racks. I give Rick's arm a squeeze and hurry over. He tags along as Sophie piles glossy silk fabrics into my arms until I can barely see her over them.

"You're more pink than Ever," Sophie says. "Blue or teal would look amazing on you." She lifts the entire load out of my hands. "Come with me. I'll get you fitted. Fannie, grab the pins?"

I thank God for Sophie as Rick and I follow her to the back. Julie and even *Teen Vogue* will definitely approve of any of these dresses. Sophie has me model them all before a mirror.

"This mulberry silk is the ticket," she says after I've tried the last one. She adjusts the shoulders, then steps back to examine me. "Rick, what do you think?"

Rick shifts forward on a loveseat. "She looks beautiful."

"That's unhelpfully unspecific." Sophie smiles at me in the mirror and kneels to pin my skirt up around my ankles. "I keep telling Rick he needs to move back to the States to be with Ever," she says. "You know. Rocketship start-up versus the love of his life. How can it be a choice?"

"Seriously," Fannie says, popping in to remove the discarded dresses. "Ever is like a Porsche. Rick's like a . . ."

"Unicycle?" Sophie suggests.

"Trust my family to always have my back." Rick sinks into

246

his plush seat. "I've looked into jobs in New York, and the States. Ever insists I can't give up the job here for her. She doesn't want me to regret it. I told her I wouldn't, but it was always, 'Why can't we just hold out another year?' One year turned into two turned into six."

"Well, maybe you've got to figure out who has more to lose?" Sophie asks around a mouthful of pins.

"We've had that talk. From a career standpoint, it would be me at the moment. And she can't leave her mom and Pearl alone with Mr. Wong gone." He meets my eyes, and I feel another swell of love for both: Rick loved my dad as much as we did. Still do. "Bottom line is, we don't want to pit ourselves against each other."

"You're looking out for each other instead of yourselves. That's the most loving, mature thing I've ever heard."

Rick frowns. "Then why isn't it working out?"

It reminds me of my great-grandmother. Forced to leave her pipa career behind to keep her family together. But every story is different. I don't know how theirs will end.

"She's still working on your puzzle," I say. "It's really hard, but she's sticking with it. That's something." It means Ever hasn't given up entirely, despite her misguided openness to the Yawns in her life. I send Rick a heart with my fingers and thumb and he sends it back, all the while I'm keeping my body still as Sophie tugs the silk into place over different parts of me.

"How's the loveboat part of Loveboat going?" Sophie asks. "The twins? The musicians?"

I feel a twinge in my chest. So much has evolved since I had dinner with her and Xavier. "The twins are great. We're like best buds now. The musicians—"

"I didn't get to hear about musicians," Rick says.

A surge of emotions pulses through me. "I have no idea what happened!" I say. "I went from the girl who never went on a date to being in a semi-love triangle." Maybe quadrangle. I've definitely topped Ever's experience. Not that I'm competitive about it.

"Well, it's Loveboat," Sophie says, tying a luxurious sash around my waist.

"It's a lot of heartache," Rick says. Speaking from experience, clearly.

"Tell us more," Sophie says.

I gulp air. "Well, the violinist. I was a little starstruck when I met him."

"Got it," Sophie says knowingly.

"The other, Kai—"

"The grumpy beatboxer?"

"Xavier was right about him. He's . . . complicated. But he's teaching me this Chinese instrument that my great-grandma played, and we're trying to track it down and earn some money tonight to take the train to Tainan tomorrow. Also, there's another Party in the Dark late Saturday. It's masked." If I dare go.

Rick groans. "I'm glad I'm too old for Loveboat now. I'd be outclassed."

"How do you feel about them?" Sophie asks.

I turn her question over in my mind, wanting to give her a good answer. "When I'm with Ethan, I'm the person I was supposed to be this summer in New York. But even better. And we've, um, kissed, more than I've ever kissed anyone. Does *that* mean anything?"

"Measured against how much experience?" Sophie smiles. Touché. "And Kai?"

"I don't know him as well," I say, but then I'm not so sure that's true. I haven't spent as much *time* with him as I have Ethan, and yet for some reason, I *do* know him better. "But he's sort of hot and cold—I'm not even sure how much he likes me."

"But you like him?" Rick asks.

Honestly, at the core of his irritability, there's a purity of heart. "I guess the question is, do I like him *that way*? And does he like me back?"

"So let's be real. No false modesty. A lot of guys will fall for you over your lifetime. No, I'm serious," Sophie says when I start to protest. "And that means you need to be picky. They've made their choice, but you still need to decide for yourself what *you* want. Don't just fall into the first relationships that comes along."

This is all new for me. I cling to her words. Sophie knows what she's talking about.

"But you've got time to figure it out," she finishes. "I was hellbent on finding my guy on the program, but there's no rush to seal the deal."

Yes, anything can still happen. Rick found Ever on Loveboat, but now he's heartbroken. Sophie didn't land her man there, but she's been with Xavier for almost seven years. Ugh. I don't know where anything is going. But I do know that I'm anxious/eager for my trip with Kai.

Sophie gathers my hair into her capable hands and deftly clips the mass to the top of my head. Then she slides golden silk gloves—fingerless—up my arms. They caress my skin. I flex my hands experimentally and hold them to my cheeks.

"I can't wear them playing piano, but they're gorgeous."

"Oh." Her face falls. "I didn't realize."

"I'll wear them for the photos," I assure her.

"Nice work, both of you," Rick says.

Sophie takes me gently by the shoulders and turns me to face the mirror. I stare at myself. My hair is swept into an updo and a simple strand of pearls graces my neck. The blue teal silk wraps a wide collar around my shoulders and falls to my tapered waist and then the floor in a stunning cascade. It pays tribute to the qipao with the row of pearl buttons along my shoulder. Simple, not overdone.

"This is stunning," I stammer. "It's perfect. I just never knew it could exist."

"That's my job." Sophie's smug.

"It's not exactly a qipao like Julie wanted, but . . ."

"My personal view on the qipao is we should make it our own. But if you're really opposed to wearing one, you should just tell your manager no."

"Wise words," Rick says.

"It's not that easy. I mean, she's my manager. That's like, my boss." How often have I really, truly contradicted Julie? Never. "But there's no way she won't love this, right?" Wearing it makes the concert with Ethan so much more real, elegant even. I send Julie a photo of me in the new dress. I'm sure she'll approve. "It's the best possible comeback dress I could have imagined."

"One last gift I had in stock." Sophie sets a delicate Venetian mask in my hands. "For your party." She smiles.

It's a real mask of cream felt, not like the paper one I wore the first night. With a hawkish nose and green retro flowers made of cloth, and delicate branches spraying backward. It matches my patchwork skirt perfectly, actually, the one I found with Kai.

250

"Thank you," I breathe. Even if I decide not to go, it's an incredible gift. "I feel so daring. In all of these." I wrap my arms around her in a hug. "My manager was able to land the *Teen Vogue* interview," I say. "I'll be sure to let them know this is a Sophie Ha original."

She squeezes me back. "Love that."

"We're excited to hear you play in two weeks," Rick says.

"You're coming?" I turn to him, clasping my gloved hands. This is how it should be. The two of them are family. They *should* be family.

His eyes are understanding. "I'm keeping faith, Pearl. And no matter what, we're pals. Always. Okay?"

I hug him, too. But pals forever is not enough. I just hope Ever will finally realize there's no way around that truth.

21

I set Sophie's delicate mask in my dresser drawer beside my purple one. Then I take Kai's pipa case and head out to meet him. Iris and Hollis pounce as I close my door. I'm wearing an off-white tank top over the patchwork skirt.

"More playing on the streets?" Iris asks.

"I need the money," I say.

"You look like a forest sprite," Hollis compliments me. "You just need to kick off your shoes and go barefoot to finish the look."

"It's even better with my new Sophie Ha mask." I laugh. "I *feel* good. I'm even going out *before* curfew."

"We're coming," Iris says. "We can help drum up audience support, and it's a good excuse to lurk around the club."

"Wolf still has two nights to set up," I point out.

"Even more reason to go now!" Iris says. "He'll assume we'd scout tomorrow night."

I laugh. "Sure, come along," I say, and we head toward the third floor. Kai is in the lounge, in his striped blue shirt and bright-blue pants, deep in an argument with Jon and Basel. He's shaking his head, disagreeing with Basel. He holds up his hands as I get closer, in time to hear him say, "This is so petty. I'm washing my hands of it."

He catches sight of us and frowns. "Pearl, there you are. Let's go."

His voice is curt. He starts swiftly for the staircase, not introducing me. I fall into step beside him and the twins hurry after us.

"Everything okay?" I ask, glancing back at the guys bending their heads together.

"Just more dumb Loveboat stuff."

"How do you know them, anyway?" Now that I know Kai better, breaking into staff offices like those two did doesn't really seem like his thing.

"They've been in my tae kwon do class in town since fifth grade. Always up to something."

"There's a lot of scheming going on around here."

"That's putting it mildly." Kai gives me a sideways look. "Your hair looks nice."

From Kai, that's high praise. I touch a coil of my updo, my smile a bit giddy. "My friend Sophie did it. I was picking out an outfit with her for the end-of-summer performance."

"Pretty fancy for a Loveboat show," he says.

I can't get anything past him. I realize it's the first I've even mentioned the performance.

"There will be some . . . photos," I say. He'll find out anyway, so I add, "We're expecting press for the duets with Ethan."

"The duo you've been practicing? Mozart and Beethoven?" If the press surprises him, he doesn't show it.

"Yes." I brace for a critical comment, but he just rubs his chin thoughtfully.

"You really like that kind of music, huh?"

"It's part of my DNA." I lift his pipa case. "And so is this, as it turns out. I don't know what it all means, but I'm figuring it out."

He holds the door open for me. "Thanks for letting me be a part of it."

It's pretty touching how humbly he says it. As I step past him, my arm brushes his. I drop my gaze . . . to his blue Veja sneakers.

"I like your shoes," I say. It's a very belated compliment.

He flexes his right ankle, rotating the shoe. I don't see any glitter, but I'm also not getting an angle on his soles.

"I liked their mission," he says simply.

"It's totally okay for you to ignore us," Iris says, surprising us both. "We're spoken for already."

Trust Iris to spice things up. I groan but Kai just smiles rue-fully. "I'm Kai. You guys?"

"Iris."

"Hollis. We're here as your hype people tonight."

"And don't worry, Kai, they're not *hitting on you* like you thought I was," I tease.

Kai gives me a mock-growl. "That's because you *were*."

"I was not!" I say, before I realize he's teasing me back. Grumpy Kai. Teasing, maybe even flirting, with me. He gives me a lop-sided smile, which I return.

"Okay, lovebirds," Iris cuts in. "Are we doing this or not?"

We set up on a corner a block from FRANK Taipei, while Iris and Hollis head off to scope it out. The air sizzles with the scents of grilling meats. I settle in my chair and rearrange my skirt over my legs. Behind me, a man hoses down his fruit stand, misting water onto my hair.

My life feels like a dichotomy. By day, preparing for my comeback performance, designer dress and all. By night, sneaking out to play street music. I love it all, but I also feel like I'm flying down a mountain on skis with each prong pointed in opposite directions. Eventually, they'll glide too far apart.

But for now, I set my fingers to the pipa and I play.

Where does sound end and music begin? Kai tests all the contours of it as he cups his hands to his mouth and beatboxes a structure into my songs. He turns to the Theramin, and we lean into our dark duet theme, a minor key, devastated notes of untamed jealousy and tragic loss. And maybe it's the temple so close by and the spirits at work, but we collect a lot more blue bills this time. Kai asks me a question with his eyes and I nod, and he shifts into a counter rhythm against me holding fast to our main one. A crowd bursts into applause. Iris and Hollis are coming back toward us, clapping along.

Then I hear the sound of an accordion playing. Another street musician is moving in our direction. Wild curly black hair spills to his shoulders. Neon flowers glow on his hat and he's wearing so many stone necklaces it's a wonder he can stand up under them all. He joins his music to ours, stepping side to side to the beat in zebra-print shoes.

His lovely wails interweave with my somber harmonies, Kai's energetic backbeat. We chase each other round and round until we end the song with a flourish. Iris is holding out her hat, collecting bills, and Hollis is pointing their camera video at us.

More wild applause. My heart pounds so hard it could win its own beatboxing awards. Rising, I take Kai's hand and the man's in the other and we bow together. My cheeks ache from smiling. A part of me that was sleeping all these years is awakening. A part of me I didn't even know existed.

"Lan-Lan, how's it going, man?" Kai offers a fist bump, which the man returns. Lan-Lan wags his fingers, laughing so hard he can't speak yet.

"You know each other?" I ask.

"I used to volunteer teaching at a community center nearby," Kai says.

"Teach . . . pipa?"

"Music."

"Best teacher I've ever had," Lan-Lan says in Mandarin, but I get the gist.

I believe it. Kai has a way of translating the music in his head into actual steps for my fingers. I just hadn't pictured him teaching. There's so much more to Kai that I don't know about, and want to know.

"You play like magic," I say to Lan-Lan.

"I'm just happy to play with good people." His voice is ragged in a soothing way. "Nothing more lonely than playing music by yourself."

Kai translates for me. "I feel that," I say, setting the tips of my fingers over my heart.

"I always figured, when the world doesn't let you have what you need, then you gotta go after what you want," Lan-Lan says. He runs a loving hand down the edge of his accordion.

There's a lot to unpack in that statement. But it will take me a lifetime. For now, I gather up the bills from that last song and shove them into Lan-Lan's hands.

"Thank you." He blows out a long note on his accordion. Then he begins to play a Scottish folk song, and slowly meanders away through the crowds. I exhale, watching him go. Then turn to Kai.

"I didn't know you taught," I say.

"I did," he corrects me. "I forgot how much I liked it until I started working with you. It feels good to give music to people."

"Maybe you can pick it up again. You're really good at it."

"You think so?" he asks, pleased.

"Definitely."

Iris is counting our stack of cash. She catches my eye and gives me a thumbs-up. "Enough for the train fare *and* a snack or two along the way," she says.

"Awesome," I say. "How was your stakeout at the club?"

"No Wolf spotting, but we're not the only ones trying to nab him. There were some guys from Loveboat lurking around, too. We all got a look through a crack in the blinds, at people inside setting up refreshment tables. We're going to scout a bit more. Kai, you going to the Party in the Dark Saturday?"

"Wasn't invited." Kai shrugs.

"Really?" I say. "What about the first one?"

"Not that one either," he says easily.

The twins and I exchange a look.

"I'm sure you can crash if you want," Hollis says.

"Pearl, you heading back?" Iris asks.

"Yes, I'll go back with Kai."

This time, the twins flash identical smirks that make my face heat. "Don't stay out too late," Iris says slyly, and they head off, leaving us alone.

A slightly awkward pause descends. Kai catches my eye, then we both glance away. I could ask him about Party II. Whether he's thinking about crashing it. But it doesn't seem to matter right now.

"Want to see something cool?" Kai asks then.

"Um, sure," I say, and he takes hold of my arms, surprising me, and positions me at a curved archway built of bricks so my nose is nearly touching the brick.

"Wait here and don't look, okay?" He slips away and I laugh. There's a long pause, which I finally break.

"What am I waiting for?" I ask.

"Why are you standing all alone over there?" Kai's voice is suddenly in my ear, but he's not near at all—he's standing almost a block away, waving at me. "It's an echo chamber," he says in my ear. "Try it."

I open my mouth and belt out the most recent Taylor Swift song straight at the bricks. His laughter bubbles back at me. A minute later, he touches my back.

"Like it?" He's all boyish. "My cousins and I used to play with it."

"You could pass secret messages to each other right out in the open and no one would be able to hear you."

"Right?" He seems like he wants to say something more, and then he takes a few bills from our can. "Want a drink?"

"Good call—let's do it."

He heads for a tea shop, and I finish packing up for the both of us. As I set the pipa case upright, I spot Kai coming, a cup of bubble tea swinging gently from a holder. It's opened to the air, not sealed with a film of plastic as usual.

"That's not for my head, is it?" I ask warily, thinking of our first meeting. "Forgiveness is a virtue."

He smirks just like the twins, which might be the first time I've seen that expression on him. But then he passes me the cup. "Just thought you could use a refresher."

I take a long pull of tea. It's got just the right amount of ice and sweetening. "Mmm," I say. I glance up and he's looking down on me with this sort of amused, bemused expression, and suddenly I'm reminded of what he looked like with the tea streaming down his hair and I laugh.

And manage to spill my tea all over my shirt.

"Oh no," I say, dismayed.

Kai laughs. "I will consider your debt paid. But this was not my revenge, I promise."

"I know it's just me being clumsy with anything that's not an instrument." I pluck at my damp tank top. Note to self, never spill liquids on a white shirt. My pink bra is like a siren screaming through. I hold my arms over my chest, trying to cover up.

"Here, take this." Kai pulls his striped shirt over his head and hands it to me.

"Oh no," I refuse, but a passing man does a double take, and the look in his eyes is enough to send me scrambling into Kai's shirt. It's big and warm from his body and smells so good. Like detergent and a scent that's just him.

When my head emerges, I get a glimpse of his bare arms. He's wearing a sleeveless undershirt, but it doesn't conceal his leanly

259

muscled biceps and the scoop of tan flesh at his chest.

I yank my eyes back up to his, and now there's a darker expression in them. One that makes those goose bumps break out all over me. He's never looked at me this way before.

"My shirt looks good on you," he says a bit shakily.

I smile, equally shaky. "It's supposed to be the other way around, dork. The shirt's supposed to make me look—never mind."

I lean into Kai to brush a white fluffy seed that's landed on the corner of his lips. His skin is warm under my fingers. Without thinking, I rise onto my toes and brush my lips against his.

After a startled moment, he kisses me back.

And I feel it in the warmth of his mouth. He's not the mystery kisser. This is Kai, who would never do something in the dark. Only scowl in the light and let the chips fall where they may. I take a step back.

"Thank you for caring," I say, and then I duck away and hurry into a cab, scoot to the far end of the back seat and fasten my seat belt. "*Chien Tan Xiàoyuán, xièxiè,*" I say.

It feels like an eternity before Kai appears in the open doorway. As he joins me on the seat, I look steadily out my window so he can't see my face.

"Pearl." His voice is strained. "I'm not—"

"Don't say anything. Please." I don't want him to end the dream of tonight with his grumpy reminder he's not on Loveboat for Loveboat or pointing out that I was definitely hitting on him, because I definitely was. "Please don't say anything," I say. "Not yet." Maybe not ever.

He falls silent. The cab lurches forward.

My feelings for Kai are scary. They go way beyond liking. But he doesn't even know my real last name or anything about my life as a concert pianist or the TikTok hat that maybe symbolizes all the ignorant colonialism that he hates. I need to come clean with him. I want to. I'm just afraid of complicating things between us more than they already are.

Kai's hand rests briefly on mine. His thumb brushes over the back of my wrist. I close my eyes, savoring his touch. But then his hand is gone, leaving its tingling imprint behind.

22

Ethan texts me in the morning. **Do you have a half hour right now? Sorry for last minute, but my manager booked a PR agency to prep us for Teen Vogue. I figured it'd be useful.**

A PR agency. It's a kick in the pants that I need, getting me back on track after a confusing night. I have to admit, it feels pretty glamorous to put on blush, mascara, and lipstick and head over to Ethan's room. I'm already at his doorstep before I realize how neatly he's convinced me to come over. His door is ajar. I rap my knuckles, rat-a-tat-tat, and he turns from his laptop.

His face lights up. "Hey, Pearl." His comforter is thrown back. His dresser is completely covered with skin care products, from face masks to rows of white bottles to little red glass jars. No wonder his skin glows.

A man and woman in chic suits appear on his screen. The mock interview is kind of fun, rolling through questions like: How long have you been playing your violin/piano? Is this your first trip to Asia? What's been the most fun? The most surprising?

"Break a leg," the man concludes. "You two will rock this."

After he and the woman sign off, Ethan flashes me a smile. "What do you think? Helpful?"

"*So* helpful. I'm amazed people will actually care to read our answers," I admit. Maybe with the actual interview with *Teen Vogue*, I'll have a chance to explain myself more in depth. Who I am. Not the TikTok blown-up girl, but someone three-dimensional. Julie really knew what she was doing, securing this interview. She's already given me talking points if any questions come up about the video: *It was a misunderstanding. I'm here in Taipei now, reconnecting with my roots.* Although after doing my own research, I want to modify the comments a bit: *I understand why people were upset. There's a long history that people might not be aware of.*

Ethan shuts his laptop and stretches his arms. "Want to grab breakfast? I know a good Taiwanese breakfast place. Great soy milk."

"Oh, um. I'd love to, but I'm meeting Kai for the day."

His eyes flicker. Is another warning coming?

"Okay," he says. "Have fun."

The Taipei Main Station is set inside a palatial building with a wide red Chinese roof and walls of round columns. Kai and I pass a few Japanese and Taiwanese food counters and buy tickets, Taiwanese fried chicken, and a boba drink.

We're shyly quiet, that kiss from last night still hovering between us. Kai's wearing his usual bright clothing: a jade-green pair of pants and a complementary violet-and-green paisley shirt.

I was right that his clothes had come from a former life, and I'm glad now that he seems more comfortable inside them.

He breaks the silence first. "When I was a kid, I'd beg my mom to bring me here to watch the trains come in. I liked the noises and vibrations. Still do."

"I get that," I say. "Sound is our jam."

On cue, the ground vibrates under our feet as our train arrives with a wail of wheels on steel. I follow him on board and down the aisle. He glances back at me. "I was thinking about your great-grandmother this morning. She didn't exactly have a choice whether she could pursue her dreams after the war broke out, right?"

"That's exactly what I thought." My gaze falls to his hand. "And you didn't have a choice about stopping the pipa. For now."

"Life throws curveballs sometimes, doesn't it?" he says wistfully.

"Our ancestors knew that more than we did," I say. "The question is, what do we do then?"

"Right." He finds our seats. "Window?"

"I prefer it, but happy to take either."

"Perfect, because I prefer aisle. Easier to make my escape and leave you in the dust."

"Ha." I smack him on the arm. He grins as we take our seats.

"Nǐ chīle ma?" A woman in a powder-blue uniform pushes a steel cart toward us, sounding like Mom offering me food. Her cart is loaded with more kinds of snacks than I've ever seen: seaweed, meats and fruits on sticks, shrimp chips. With my mouth full of savory to-die-fors, I take photos of everything and text them to Hollis and Iris.

Iris sends back videos of our street performance yesterday: Kai swaying with his hands cupped over his mouth, me bent over his pipa, and Lan-Lan pulling at his accordion. I like how Kai plays with his entire body and soul, and how Lan-Lan closes his eyes to relish the music, and how my fingers dance on the strings.

The videos are great, but they're exactly what Julie wouldn't want out in the world.

Please don't share with anyone, I text them, and they text back, **Of course not.**

I'm going on my fourth blind date, Iris texts. **Wish me luck!**

Good luck! I write back. I smile at Kai. "Loveboat at work. My friends are going on blind dates. Have you ever gone on one?"

"Never dated period. Kids didn't date much in my high school, and if they did, it was usually serious. I've just had crushes and heartbreaks."

"Aw, who broke your heart?" I tease.

He smiles ruefully. "Issa Lee. She was the tallest girl in first grade and could outrun everyone."

"Did she know you had a crush on her?"

"Nope, never. She moved to London, and I never had the chance to tell her."

"Coward."

"I promise you I've never pretended to be a hero."

"So you're an innocent."

"That's me." He's not embarrassed, which I find endearing. My lunch mates at school used to say "sixteen and never been kissed," as though it was a bad thing, but there's something sweet about his innocence.

"Your turn," he says. "Start at the beginning."

265

"Wait," I say slowly. "Last night . . . was that your first kiss?"

He lifts his jaw. "It's your turn."

I am Kai's first kiss. I can't get over that. Am I gloating? Yeah, a little. Okay, a lot. But he's glaring at me, waiting for an answer.

"I dated a few guys at summer camp," I say.

"That's it?"

"That's it. I guess I'm a camp dater. Maybe it's safer? If it doesn't work out, you can always not come back the next summer."

He cocks his head. "You're holding out on me."

Yeah, there's Ethan. And the devil in the dark. But I don't even know who that guy is, and what I'm feeling with Kai—this means so much more.

I reach over to help myself to one of his shrimp chips. "If I tell you all my secrets, I won't be a mystery anymore, will I?"

He smiles. "You are really something, Pearl."

I smile back. "I know."

"But one thing I'm still confused by," Kai says. "I looked up Pearl Lim online, but she doesn't exist anywhere. Most kids our age have at least some internet presence, even if it's just a mention of a school or town." He holds my gaze, trying to read me. "Is Pearl Lim not your real name?"

I should have expected him to look me up at some point. That he cared enough to say something, but I wish I'd been the one to clue him in first. I look down at my clasped hands. "I'm sorry I kept it from you," I say. "Pearl's my real name, but I'm going by my mother's maiden name."

His brow furrows. "Why?"

"I needed to lay low for the summer. My other name—if you

266

looked that up, you'd see all sorts of stuff I didn't really want people here reading."

"Laying low—meaning acting like you're not a music prodigy? That's what you've been hiding, right?"

I flush.

"What's your real last name?" he asks.

Am I ready for him to know everything just yet? TikTok? Apollo? "So I'm actually a concert pianist," I begin.

His eyes dawn with understanding. "Of course you are."

"I study at the Cleveland Institute of Music." I stop, unsure whether to continue.

After a long beat, he says, "I haven't told anyone here about my RSI. But I told you."

I feel a stab of guilt. "It's not that I didn't trust you. I wanted to tell you."

"Did something happen?"

"It's not like RSI for me." He's had it far worse than I have. "I'm still playing piano. It's still my life. My dad was a huge part of it. Piano keeps me connected to him, I mean, because he passed away a few years ago."

He sucks in a breath. "I'm sorry. My parents passed away when I was fourteen."

"Really? *Both* of them? I'm so sorry." All this time, I had no idea he was an orphan. He never said. He's even talked about them, though never in the present tense, I realize. Then again, I never said anything about Dad either. "Who do you live with now?"

"My grandma took me in. She's in her seventies, so it's helpful I'm around. My aunt and uncle are with her this summer. That's partly why Maya suggested I come here. Maya's sort of like my adopted mother," he adds.

"What were your parents like?" I ask.

"Good people," he says. "Both software engineers. They didn't always get my music, but they were supportive."

"We just can't know how long we'll have them with us, do we?" I say wistfully. One of the reasons Ever can't leave Mom behind in the States. It's real. "One day, they're gone, and you can never know for sure how they'd feel about the latest in your life."

"Yeah. I'm glad they never knew I had to stop pipa."

"Would they have been . . . disappointed, of course?"

"On my behalf," he says. "But they faced life head on. Maybe they'd be more disappointed how I've reacted." He frowns.

Then we both fall silent. I gaze out my window at the lush green mountains rolling by. How would Dad feel about me practicing piano so much less now, and instead, traveling miles to chase down a pipa? Disappointed? Or would he be as intrigued as I am? I wish I could know, too.

The gentle screech of rails wakes me. We're pulling into the Tainan station. To my embarrassment, I've fallen asleep with my head on Kai's shoulder.

"Sorry," I mumble, lifting my head. But Kai has fallen asleep, too, his face relaxed, young and vulnerable. He's a surprise to me, like the pipa. I came to Taipei to escape and renew. I didn't expect this person to show up and shake the foundations of my world.

Kai's eyes flutter open. His gaze is soft and unfocused.

"I've never wanted to kiss a girl before you," he mumbles.

Then he sits up and runs his hands over his face.

"What did you say?" I ask. Heat spreads across my cheeks.

"Hmm? What? Sorry. I, uh, think I was dreaming."

Dreaming . . . about me? If his cheeks got any redder, he'd be stopping traffic all over town. He looks like he's trying to melt into his seat. Then the train stops with a hiss of breaks, and we both lurch gently forward. Relief crosses his face as everyone gets up and haul suitcases off the overhead bins. I want to say something back, though not in so many words.

But he's already slipped past me and out the doors.

We follow a crowd along a pathway between fragrant camphor trees. The foliage hides the Renmai Museum from view until we round a corner. I stop short. A wide pathway flanked by two long rows of Greek statues leads to a Capitol-like building of white stones, complete with a row of Greek temple columns.

"It's . . . a castle," I say, frowning.

A gorgeous European castle, right smack in the middle of a Taiwanese city.

I glance at Kai, who shakes his head. "I can just see the guy who built this thinking, 'I'm the man now!' This can't get any more lame."

But inside, it does get worse. A reception desk sits before a re-creation of a Victorian period living room behind glass. That part's normal enough. We get our tickets, and I follow Kai into a sun-bathed space filled with paintings. French paintings. Italian paintings. Russian paintings.

Then I pass by a sign on the wall. It divides the exhibit into the "European Gallery" from the next one, labeled the "Non-European Gallery."

I have to read the sign twice to make sure I'm not making it up. Ahead of us, I see pieces from Asia, Africa, Latin America.

"I think this must be what you mean by being colonized," I say slowly.

Kai's reading it, getting grumpier by the word. "They wrote themselves out of their own exhibit." He leads the way to another gallery, and I follow.

"Well, maybe there wasn't anything else like the Renaissance in the art world?" I ask.

"There were renaissances here in Asia, too. One in Taipei during the pandemic. Taipei was doing so well managing Covid that the best and brightest came from all over the world to find refuge here. Even Yo-Yo Ma came through. They had a chance to meet each other, and now they're back in the world doing their thing."

For me, the Western canon was all I knew until Loveboat. Because I was born in the States. But could that be why I love Mozart and Beethoven? It bothers me.

But then we enter a space full of special musical instruments that drives everything else from my mind. These are instruments I didn't even know existed. A trombone with three bells. A horn with seven heads shaped like snakes. This collection restores some of my respect for whoever created this museum. There's so much to look at. Scores of brass-horned gramophones, accordions, electronic pianos, jukeboxes, an entire wing set up exactly like the floor of an orchestra with all its instruments represented.

A sign labels the whole exhibit as the largest Western collection of musical instruments in the world. I hope that means there's a non-Western collection of any size around. And better yet, that it isn't labeled that way.

The next room houses a dozen violins from a wide range of time periods behind a glass wall. Opposite it, a reconstructed violin maker's workshop is laid out with cut wooden frames in the distinctive oblong shape, with two f-shaped holes.

"They have a Stradivarius violin—*wow*," Kai says. He peers into the glass box that houses it solo. "Even I'll admit that's impressive. I'd kill to pluck those strings."

I laugh. "Isn't that the one the National Palace Museum director mentioned she was after?" I'm encouraged. This is a collection focused on unusual and famous instruments, so maybe there's a chance my grandmother's pipa is among them.

We finally enter a room full of familiar Asian instruments— all the ones we're covering in our Loveboat class. Hallelujah! I spot at least a dozen pipas on display: pear-shaped instruments hanging from hooks on the walls and sitting on stands behind glass. A surge of hope fills my chest. I hurry between the exhibits, pausing to study a large pipa, a smaller one, one of dark wood, one unfinished. An entire row of pipas! . . . and none of them are my great-grandmother's.

When I reach the last pipa, the disappointment whales me in my gut. I sit heavily on a bench.

"I was so sure we'd find it here. They have every other instrument under the sun. But maybe I'm just on a wild-goose chase."

"We haven't seen the rest of the museum," Kai says. He's become the optimist between us.

But I shake my head. "I'm sorry, Kai. I dragged you all the way down here."

"Are you kidding?" He holds out a hand, which I accept, and he tugs me to my feet. "Let me buy you a cup of tea, and we'll go from there."

At the museum café, our waiter brings us the most artistic tea kettle I've ever seen: turquoise, kiln-fired, angular instead of round. I wrap my hands around my warm cup and inhale the steaming jasmine. Then I look at Kai.

"My name is Pearl Wong," I say.

"I know. I looked you up online while you were sleeping on the train."

"You did? Now who's nosy?"

"Pearl, age seventeen, concert pianist, Cleveland Institute of Music. Wasn't hard to find you with that info, Pearl Wong."

So he's seen everything about me—my pianist website, the articles about my performances . . . and me in the Chinese straw hat.

"And?" I say.

"And what?"

I grate my teeth. "You're driving me bonkers."

He shrugs. "So we're even."

"You!" I bat him on the side of his head. Gently, since I believe in nonviolent protest.

"I already knew you were an A-list musician, and it just confirmed it. I saw your performance at Carnegie Hall."

"But what?" I ask warily.

"Does there have to be a but?"

"It feels like yes, with you."

"What are you worried about?"

"Did you see the thing on TikTok?"

"Yeah. It looked like a clusterfuck. I read the comments. All two billion or so. Shitty to have the world pile onto you."

Two billion feels about right. I haven't even seen a fraction of them myself.

"I messed up." I let out a shaky breath. "Now I'm paying for it."

"Did you though?" Kai asks. "Mess up?"

"What do you mean? I posted that stupid video! Just like that magazine we saw outside the subway. It was my fault."

"Different symbols mean different things in different contexts." He gently turns the ring of moisture left by his cup into a spiral. "The hat to an Asian American girl in Ohio probably means something very different to the Asian reading the *New Yorker*, and something entirely different to a kid like me who grew up in Asia. The haters misunderstood you. It was complicated."

He's not mad at me at all. The opposite, actually. And of all people, I hadn't expected *him* to understand what I still don't understand myself.

"Is that really how you see it?"

"Asian caricatures *were* a problem for a lot of years. Some people have devoted their lives to fighting those sorts of hurtful stereotypes. Like my dad," Kai says. "He told me about signs on a bridge in Shanghai, No Dogs and Chinamen Allowed. A hat like that, maybe it pointed back to demeaning attitudes like that."

"It was probably really triggering." I envision people like Kai's family scrolling through their feeds and getting punched in the eye. By me. I poured salt into open wounds without even realizing I was doing it. "But how can I keep people from misunderstanding?"

"I'm not sure you can on social media. It's the worst place to try to solve centuries of misunderstanding. A bunch of posturing-making statements for clicks, and people talking past each other. All this history to unpack—on social media? It's like using a mole whacker for a delicate surgery."

"I feel that, for sure," I say. "Do *you* think I was wrong for wearing that hat? We're not on social media now. I want to hear what you really think."

He takes his time, considering. Which I appreciate. "You weren't wrong. But the people who were upset weren't wrong to be upset."

I turn his words over in my mind. Maybe he's right. Maybe it's not an either/or. I'm not entirely right, and others aren't entirely wrong. There's room for a lot of perspectives.

"I never meant to hurt anyone," I say.

"I know."

"And I never should have responded online. I only fanned the flames."

"Well, live and learn. You'll make different choices next time." Something my dad would have said.

"I hope there won't be a next time," I say fervently. "If this ever happens to me again, I'll just hide forever."

He gives me a look. "That's not an option. Hiding forever is giving up."

"*You've* been hiding," I say, accusatory.

"And I was wrong to. Who else knows about it here?"

"Ethan's known from the first day," I admit.

I catch the flash of hurt in his eyes. "Were you ever going to tell me?"

"I was afraid you'd hate me for it," I say.

274

He gives a rueful smile. "Judge you, you mean."

"Yes," I admit.

"I deserve that. I'm sorry."

It's a huge weight off. I meet his gaze. "Ethan knows because—he's helping me. We're going to have a performance together. It's supposed to be my comeback."

"Comeback? From what?"

"I was supposed to be a part of the Apollo music program in New York this summer. After the whole blowup, they withdrew my invitation." I fill him in on the call from Julie and the decision to come here.

Kai is quiet a beat. "The bigger problem, it seems to me, is Apollo."

"Apollo?" Now I'm genuinely stumped.

"Yes. How could they let a TikTok incident sway them like that? You're a kid new to the entire industry," he says. "They're supposed to be helping *you*. They have the power. They could have stood by you. Dug deeper to understand what actually happened. They could have helped you explain your post and people would have listened to them."

Kai being Kai, coming at me from left field. It clashes with my reality. Apollo is the golden prize. They let me in. I blew it.

"My manager said they were already facing accusations of reverse discrimination."

He frowns. "Meaning they're under fire for not letting enough *white* musicians in?"

I bite my lip. "I hadn't thought through it."

"So they took away your spot because you're racist against Asians, and gave it to a white person because you only had the spot . . . because you're Asian? Apollo is trash. You should find some other—"

"No, no, no. Wait. It's not like that!" God, he's so frustrating. "Apollo picked me. I put them in a tough position. They did what they had to do."

"But who are they protecting?" he presses. "Shouldn't it be the girl who has to fight against so much misunderstanding and stereotyping already?"

"Kai, just *stop*!" I yell, and he does. I know I'm overreacting. But I can't bear to hear another word against Apollo. It's not that they *didn't* want to protect me, right?

I gulp down another breath. "Look. I'm caught in the crossfire of a bigger storm. You said it yourself. I can't single-handedly stop racism, especially when people don't even realize they might be acting on it. I can't stay out of it either. The world won't let me. So what I can do is carve out my little piece of existence. And the best way I can is to get myself back in to Apollo and building from there. Not to mention it was my dad's dream for me."

"I didn't mean to upset you."

I bite my lip so it hurts. "You're not afraid to say what you think, that's for sure."

"Maybe I should be. I'm just angry that you're buried away here. Like, why? Your music shouldn't be hidden. Why do they get to say whether you matter or not? Why is your manager okay with this?"

I breathe deeply. He means well.

"It's just for now," I say. "While things blow over."

He doesn't buy it. I can see that in his face, and I don't know how to convince him, and I'm not sure I'm convinced myself.

"I read your dad's obituary," he says. "He seemed like a really wonderful human being."

I choke a bit. He read about Dad. It means a lot to me, since I can't share him in person with anyone anymore.

"He was," I say.

We sit for a beat while a small crowd of visitors moves by us. Then after a moment, he collects our teacups and moves them to a tray in the corner.

"Come on. Let's go ask about their inventory," he says.

The reception desk sits in the atrium under a beam of sunlight. The hall is beautiful, with a vaulted ceiling and bright landscape paintings on the wall. But my feet drag. If my great-grandmother's pipa were here, it would not be gathering dust on a warehouse shelf. It would be out on display for the world to admire: its elegant neck, striking blue shade, and five beautiful painted blossoms.

It's so real in my mind that when I see it with my eyes, I don't believe it.

The blue pipa.

It's here!

Not in a display of Asian instruments in a far-off wing, but behind the glass panel that fills the entire entranceway. We both breezed right by it on our way in. I stare at the Victorian-style tableau it's a part of. There's a silk sofa. Portraits of elegant ladies with parasols hang on the wall. A Persian rug covers the floor. The room is European in style, with Asian accents.

And on display on a stand beside the sofa, another Asian

accent with a familiar paddle face: the blossom-painted pipa.

I run to it and press myself against the glass. I count the flowers. Five.

"Kai, look!"

He comes up behind me. "No way! We found it!"

I rub my eyes to make sure I'm not dreaming. The blue paint is fading. There's a worn patch at the base of its neck where her hand must have rested. But the strings look like they were replaced in the past ten years.

I was right. Her pipa *was* meant to be on display, and it is. Out here in the most trafficked area of the museum, for every visitor to admire. The pipa she gave up to be with my great-grandpa. A real heirloom connecting me to a greater family history.

I catch Kai's arm, throwing us both off balance. I laugh giddily. "Let's go find someone in charge."

23

"Do you have proof of your relationship to Ms. Lim?" The curator's silvery hair is pulled taut into a bun as severe as her expression. We found her preparing a special traveling exhibit on Impressionist paintings from the 1800s.

Her question stumps me, though I should have expected it. "She's my mom's grandmother." I'd been so focus on *finding* her pipa, that I hadn't really thought about what came next.

"You can understand my position." The curator tucked a tablet under the arm of her cotton blouse. "I cannot engage with everyone who comes in claiming a connection to our displays."

"I can't be the first person who's found their family heirloom in a museum," I say.

"We've never had anyone make a claim that wasn't fraudulent."

Her nose is high and sniffing. She reminds me of the man who blocked Ethan and me from the Copenhagen Orchestra. *Ragamuffins! Begone.*

"It's not fraudulent. Look." I pull up the photo of my great-grandmother. "It's black and white, but it's the same pipa. Five custom-painted blossoms."

She gives it a cursory glance. "That piece is under contract to be sold to a museum in London."

"London!" That feels like a planet away. "No, it belongs to my family! I can prove it. I'll bring proof. You can't sell it."

She removes a protective layer of plastic from a framed painting, going about her work.

"Look, the pipa didn't even have the right caption," I say desperately. "It's mislabeled as coming from Tokyo. Once you have the real story, it will be so much more valuable." Proving it's Tan Mei-Li's won't be an issue, thanks to her notoriety. There are undeniable public pictures of her holding it.

"You can't sell it with someone telling you it's stolen," Kai says.

"Please don't sell it," I beg. "Give me a week. I'll bring proof and come back."

She removes a second plastic layer. "You will have to speak to the owner, not to me."

I call Mom as soon as Kai and I burst back outside. She blooms on my screen, her black hair damp from a shower and her blue floral towel draped around her neck.

"Pearl? Where are you?"

"Mom, I found the pipa! It's in a museum here in Tainan. Do we have proof I'm descended from Great-Grandma? Like, a birth certificate for Grandpa? Plus yours, plus mine?"

"Slow down, Pearl. You're talking too fast."

I heave a breath. "I need to show the pipa is ours in a week or they'll sell it again." My stomach knots. I sit on a marble bench to steady myself. There's no assurance the pipa won't be sold *tomorrow.* I have to move as fast as I can.

Mom frowns. "I don't know if your grandpa had a birth certificate. And since your great-grandpa wasn't supposed to leave the country, he had to change his name, so his last name is different from your grandpa's."

I groan. "He *changed his name?*" My eyes meet Kai's. "But how can I prove great-grandmother is really my relative?"

"Let me call my aunty and see if she has ideas," Mom says.

I hang up and give Kai a stricken look. "This will be harder than I thought."

"Anyone else you can ask for help?"

The words have barely left his lips and I'm dialing.

Ever answers hands free, juggling Rick's puzzle box. "Hold on, Pearl, I think I've cracked it!" She's seated at her desk in her apartment near NYU. She slides a wooden lid aside to reveal an inner compartment, then lifts out a crisp fortune cookie, twice the normal size.

"Oh my gosh. This looks like he baked it himself," she says. She holds one of the side holes to her eye, peering inside.

"Is there a fortune?" I ask.

"Yes." She's trying not to smile. She breaks it open and removes the hidden slip of paper, flipping it over to reveal: B4GA89.

"Another puzzle." Ever taps her finger against her lips. "Not a combination lock number. Not a pin code. Wait, is this . . ."

She types frantically. "I knew it."

"What?"

"Flight confirmation code. He got me a ticket to Taipei. No change fee." She shoves her chair back and stomps around her room, her dress swishing around her.

"It's just one trip. You owe it to yourself to figure this out."

She purses her lips. "Wait, you called me. What do you need, Pearl?"

"I found the pipa!" I explain the conundrum with verifying my relationship to Great-Grandma. "Too bad we can't use one of those ancestry DNA web services."

"Yeah, I doubt they'll have anything about our family. What about the family shrine?" Ever asks.

I blink. Family shrine? I picture the shrine at my favorite Chinese restaurant in Cleveland, which always has a bowl of oranges before an image of what I assumed were gods.

"I have never once heard of that."

"It should have a registry of family from even before Great-Grandma's time. It might not have everything you're looking for, but it could be a start."

"*We* have a family shrine? Why did no one ever tell me about this?"

"Mom and Dad are Christian. Maybe that's why you've never heard of it?" Ever says. "But lots of families have something back in China. Ours is in Fukien Province, right across the strait from Taipei. Tell Mom to ask her family about it."

"So a registry—like a list of names?"

"Yes, I think so."

"That's what I need—I knew you'd solve my problem!" Kai pulls open a cab door for me. I squeeze his arm in thanks and pop inside. "Use Rick's ticket. Come to Taipei. We can go over and visit together!"

Nestled into the back seat with Kai, I call Mom and leave a long voice mail. I leave another for Julie with the pipa update. A pang hits my stomach, and I realize we haven't eaten a proper meal all day.

"I'm so hungry," I say to Kai, who smiles.

"Good, because I'm taking you to the local Night Markets."

"Cool, are they different than in Taipei?"

"You'll see."

They *are* different. In Taipei, the Night Markets are jammed inside alleys between blocks. But in Tainan, this one has ample room to spread out. Small booths form dozens of rows, filling an entire block with the scents and sizzles of frying meats and the clatter of pans. We walk up and down the aisles, and Kai points out all his favorites and we try them all. I scarf down oyster omelets and a spider-like fried squid bigger than my hand. I get us a bottle of gleaming white soy milk. The space is packed with locals, with very few foreigners like me.

"You know, my mom's family went through something similar to yours," Kai says, as we share a candy tomato kebab between us. "Chinese civil war. One brother stayed in China. One brother came to Taiwan—my grandpa. He never saw his parents again. And he didn't see his brother until they were both grown up and strangers to each other."

"They went through *so much*, didn't they?" I say. "Puts things in perspective." I hold my hands in balance. "Fleeing civil war," I let one hand sink. "Reputation tanking." I lift the other.

"Well, in your case, reputation also meant your whole career," Kai points out. "It's not that simple. Nothing is." He looks out over the Night Market. "Honestly, when I see those displays in the museums, all those people who've done great things with their lives . . ." He sighs. "I wanted to be great, too. Make great music. It's burning inside me, but . . ." He examines his palms with a helpless expression that tugs at my heart.

"You can write. You can compose. You can still make great music."

He lowers his hands. "And I can say the same thing back at you. Apollo or no Apollo."

Mom calls then. "Pearl, I spoke with my aunty." Her voice is pitched with excitement. "You can visit my family's village in Fujian Province. It's not far for you. Just a ferry ride."

"I didn't even know we *had* a family village. Why didn't you tell me?"

"My family left before I was born. Apparently, three million Lims scattered all over Southeast Asia and around the world have their roots in that area."

"Three million Lims!"

From us four in Ohio to three million relatives! That's more than the population of some states.

"It's possible we can find my father's birth certificate there. It would have your great-grandmother's name. And Dad would have wanted you to go. He always thought it would be a valuable experience for you to meet your extended family."

A family village. The stories Mom has are so sketchy. I want more—all of it. What was Great-Grandma's childhood like? How did she rise to fame? How did she feel when it was taken from her?

And most of all, what happened to her afterward?

"You should come with me," I say impulsively. "It's your family. Besides, my Chinese is terrible. I'll need your help."

"Oh, we will find people to meet you."

"Just like that?"

"Yes, my aunty can arrange it. They're all family, after all."

Family I've never set eyes on. The ones who didn't leave. But Mom is my bridge. And they're Ever's family, too.

"*Come*, Mom. It will be a really special family time. And Ever has a ticket out here that shouldn't go to waste. The three of us can go to the village together, and then she and Rick can reconnect in Taipei. But you'll have to convince her. I'll buy you my favorite pineapple cakes from Taipei 101," I promise.

Mom smiles. "I miss the desserts." So she's considering.

"Actually, can my friend Kai come along, too?" I ask, glancing at him. He gives me a thumbs-up.

"Sure, I'll feel more comfortable if you have an escort from Taipei anyways," she says. Not even a single *is-he-your-boyfriend*? Amazing.

We hang up and my phone rings again almost immediately. This time, it's Julie. "It's my manager," I apologize to Kai. "I left her a voice mail about the pipa earlier."

"Take it," Kai says, smiling. He finishes off our soy milk.

"Julie! I'm in Tainan right now, and I'm going to my great-grandma's village!" My words tumble over each other. "If I can claim the pipa, maybe I can play it as part of my comeback. I've been taking lessons here." I smile back at Kai. "I was thinking—"

"Pearl, what are you doing?" Julie's sharp tone cuts across the miles.

I fall quiet.

"Successful musicians are successful because they're *focused*. But ever since you went to Taipei, you've been running from one distraction to another."

"I—" I want to argue with her, but she's not truly wrong.

"I've been distracted from the piano," I admit, "but I'm not so sure that's a bad thing."

"You still have all your talent. All your hard work. None of that went away because of that TikTok video. Pearl, you're afraid of failing—of not being able to meet this difficulty head-on and overcome it. But you will overcome it. You don't have to run away."

I frown. "I'm not running away. And I'm not giving up the piano. I just want to add to my repertoire. There are *so many* pianists, Julie. You've said so yourself. It's why I have to work so hard to stand out. If I can master this instrument, standing out would feel . . . effortless."

The clack of keys on her end tells me she's at her laptop. "You're not getting back onto Lincoln Center's stage with a pipa."

I pause. At the start of summer, I'd have completely agreed with her. Now, I still think she's right. But that doesn't mean that's the way it should be.

"Writing off an entire instrument because it isn't Western seems really shortsighted," I say.

"Pearl, I'm giving you my best advice. This is why you hired me," she shoots back, her voice cool. "And I am telling you, now is not the time to color outside the lines."

A beat of silence ticks by. Then another. "Honestly, Julie," I say. "I'm tired of living inside a sketch I didn't draw."

Then I do something I've never done before, to anyone, and especially not to Julie.

I hang up.

Then I panic. I turn to meet Kai's gaze. Wordlessly, he wraps his arms around me and pulls me into a hug. My entire body fits just under his chin, and I hold on to him.

"What did I just do?" My voice is hoarse.

"Looked to me like you followed your instincts." His hand runs down my arm, warm and comforting. His chin slides slower on my hair, and his voice by my ear is warm and comforting. "Want to watch the sunset? That always makes me feel better."

We find a spot on the sand on the edge of the ocean. The soft crash of waves beats a rhythm on the beach, and the sun slowly slides down like an egg yolk toward the gray edge where air and water seem to meet. I do feel a little better, but my call with Julie is still weighing heavily on me.

Kai unconsciously massages his hands. "Do you see it yet?" he asks. "The pink glow?"

I squint at the sky. Am I imagining one? "No . . ." I admit.

"That's because it hasn't started yet."

I whack him on the arm. "You cannot pretend picking on me is for my benefit."

"No, it's just so fun. You get so mad. Then your face gets red and your voice gets deep and strong like a bull's—"

"I DO NOT SOUND LIKE A BULL!"

I pretend to throttle him. We wrestle on the sand and I pin him down, my knee on his hip, then he rises up and suddenly I'm on my back under him. I can't stop laughing, especially because his face is right above mine, looking right into my eyes.

I reach up and touch his cheek. He brushes my hair from my cheek. His chest rises and falls with long breaths as we hold each other's gazes. Then he rolls off me, landing on his rear. I sit up and we shake sand off our clothes, laughing a bit more shyly.

A space has opened again between us. But I take his hand in my lap and intertwine our fingers, and we sit in a cozy silence as the pink finally does tint the sky. The darkening dome above us feels achingly empty without sun, moon, clouds, or stars, and maybe that's what prompts me to ask him, "Is it true what they say? It's lonely at the top?" Because he was there. At the very top.

"It can be, but it wasn't for me. My family was supportive. I have music friends who play different instruments, so we weren't competing. We cheered each other on. That's the part I miss most. All my friends."

"Where are they this summer?"

"Traveling and performing. Summer festivals. Salzburg. Berlin. London."

Places I've been to, too. "And here you are, still at home."

"Still at home."

"Everyone's at Apollo this summer," I say wistfully. And I am here. Hanging up on my manager.

He shifts to face me and traces a single finger down my nose. I feel his touch all the way into my toes.

"If I *wasn't* here," he says simply. "I'd never have met you."

I feel *that* even more than his touch. The sky has lightened up like a rose petal. And then a curtain of darkness slowly comes down over the whole world.

"Good night, world," Kai says softly.

"No wonder so many songs have been written about sunsets," I say.

"It's practically a song in itself," he agrees.

"This must be your favorite view on the whole island."

"Second favorite," he says. He gives me a shy smile that makes my heart hiccup.

And then the corners of my mouth turn up in answer.

24

We sleep on an overnight train ride home, with my head pillowed on Kai's shoulder the entire three-hour ride. Morning sunlight finally tickles my eyes through my lids. I open them as we pull into Taipei's Main Station. I lift my head and check the time on my phone. Mom texted me several hours ago. **I'm coming! I got our visas. We will see you in two days!**

We. That means Ever, too! I eagerly read the rest of her notes detailing the plan: they'll fly to Fujian directly, arriving Monday afternoon. I'll take the ferry over with Kai. A driver arranged by the family will meet us at the ferry terminal.

"The Wongs are descending on Asia!" I say. "I'm actually so excited to check out this family shrine. You're coming for sure, right?"

He laughs. "Meeting the whole Lim clan. How can I resist?"

I smile. Photos from Iris and Hollis come in, showing a game of charades in the student lounge that, apparently, lasted all night and is only now wrapping up. Thank goodness for Saturdays. It's nine o'clock and I'm itching to get back to campus, but I have an errand to run.

"Okay if we stop by Taipei 101?" I ask Kai. "I want to buy the twins' special pineapple cakes for Mom and Ever."

"And for us, too, I hope," Kai says, smiling.

We take the subway to the World Trade Center stop, exiting to a view of the pale-green pagoda-like building. As we near its massive entrance, I remember what Rick told me to do, so I make my way past a few early-rising shoppers to the glassy wall and pling my finger against its surface. It returns a dull *thwack*.

Kai is watching me, amused. "Does it meet your every expectation?"

"Not the reverberations I was hoping for," I admit. "But hey, we don't always get everything we want, right?"

My phone chimes again. I put out my tongue and moisten my lips as I check my phone. Sure enough. It's from Wolf: **REMINDER: PD2 TONIGHT.**

Kai's phone didn't ring. "Did you get the text from Wolf?" I ask.

He pulls out his phone. "No . . ." I show him mine. "That party is ridiculous." He snorts. "You're not going, are you?"

I bristle at the look he's giving me. "And what if I am?"

"It's asking for trouble. They already had one party with everyone acting like masks kept them hidden, and then word started leaking like an oil spill."

He's not saying anything the twins and I haven't thought ourselves, but he knows more about the Party in the Dark than I expected. And does he know *I* was there?

I start to pocket my phone, but he grabs my hand. "Pearl, I'm serious. Don't go to that party. You won't like what you find."

"Like what?" I fold my arms and raise my brows at him. Is

he about to admit he was there after all? Kissing a certain Pearl Wong, maybe? He didn't *exactly* admit that our kiss was his first.

"Just trust me," he says, and heads inside.

I exhale. So what happens in the dark stays in the dark? Fine. If he wants to keep his secret, I'll let him. For now.

We wander the mall for a half hour, searching for the pineapple cakes. I find a shop selling the most adorable miniatures, and pick out a Night Market stand the size of a matchbook for Mom's collection. The food court on the basement level is full of amazing smells—Korean barbecue, Japanese ramen, Singaporean rice noodles. I find Iris's favorite pineapple cakes and the vendor wraps my box in festive blue tissue.

"Let's go to the top before we go back," Kai suggests. "It's a great view of Taipei."

"I'm game," I say.

We reach the elevator. To my surprise, Marc steps in with us, dressed more formally than usual in a white collared shirt and black pants.

"Hey, Marc." I haven't actually spoken to him since he busted Ethan and me and propped open the auditorium door. Now he's seeing me with another guy.

"Hey, Pearl. Kai. Getting some shopping in?" Marc smiles knowingly, like maybe this is the Loveboat he wants to see.

"For Ever and my mom, actually." I hold up my package. "They're visiting."

"Sweet. Can't wait to see her again."

"Where are you going?" I ask.

Marc presses the button for the fifty-second floor. "My friends invited me to a church here. I've been meaning to check it out while I'm in town."

"In Taipei 101?" My stomach dips as the elevator begins its rapid ascent. "Must be some church."

"Right?" He smiles. "They said it's a little closer to heaven. Want to come along?" As the elevator doors part on fifty-two, beautiful piano music pours in, along with the clear notes of a talented soprano. And I'm hooked. I exchange a glance with Kai, who gives a tiny shrug okay.

"Sorry it's more Western music," I whisper to Kai.

He steps through the door after Marc, his arm brushing mine. "Music created to worship a power greater than ourselves is in another category." He smiles. "We're both evolving this summer, huh?"

The service is beautiful: with purple drapes and vivid flower arrangements, gorgeous choral music, and a message from a pastor in jeans about identity. Judging from the rapt attention around the room, it's resonating with everyone. Even Kai's listening hard. At one point, we both shift slightly and my left leg presses against his right one. It's electrifying. Kai's ears redden, and I'm not sure if Marc notices, but neither of us pull back.

We stay that way the whole service.

Afterward, we stand up with everyone else and slowly move toward the doors. Kai and I take the sermon apart. I'm the skeptic, he's the defense. We've reversed roles and I don't even know what we're talking about—except that we're very carefully not talking about what it meant to sit touching for the past hour.

"I'm going to chat with some friends," Marc says. "See you back on campus."

He joins a group of people up front, and Kai and I return to the elevators.

"Up or down?" I ask lightly.

"We still need to see the top," he says, pressing the up button.

We get on, and a large guy in a black suit steps in between us, on his cell phone, obliviously knocking us apart. Kai leans back slightly and puts his hand to his brow, pretending to search for me from a great distance off. I put my hand over my mouth to keep from laughing. Then the elevator opens on fifty-three, and the third passenger steps off.

I punch the elevator doors closed again. We're alone. And as it ascends rapidly, Kai and I step into each other, and our mouths meet.

His mouth on mine is warm and hungry. His lips, despite the pressure, are soft. He tastes like pineapple. His hand slides into my hair, cradling the back of my head, pulling me to him with a ferociousness that throws me off-balance. His heart beats rapidly against mine, threatening to burst from his chest.

Our kiss feels both thrilling and familiar. In the way our rhythms and counter rhythms meld in our songs, so do our mouths and bodies. My lips part, wanting more. And receiving. This would be the part in the opera where the soprano hits the high notes with her overtones ringing all around us. Or maybe I'd just crow like a rooster. Even when the elevator begins to slow and my stomach dips, our mouths keep exploring, and only when we come to a stop do we finally, reluctantly pull apart.

There's a smile hovering on his now-puffy lips. The kisses on my mouth feel like a promise. He's not my mystery kisser. That stranger was exciting *because* he was in the dark, but he definitely was not Kai. And I'm glad. Kai is so honest, brutally honest. He would never be hating on Loveboat in the light and taking advantage of its debauchery in the dark.

"Woof," Kai says, and a goofy smile breaks over my face.

"How was your second kiss in your whole life?" I ask archly.

"Even better than my first," he says. Still holding hands, we turn to face a startled guy waiting to enter.

"Pearl?" says Ethan.

25

Ethan's sapphire-blue shirt ripples in a blast of AC over his white tennis shorts. My hand is still in Kai's. I yank free instinctively, and then immediately regret it. A couple arrives for the elevator, so Kai and I step out to let them pass. The doors close.

"Can I . . . talk to you?" Ethan asks stiffly. I feel Kai shift beside me.

I step from the elevator, but I'm obviously not moving fast enough because Ethan grabs my arm and tugs me over to the window.

"Pearl, I saw the videos of you and Kai playing on the streets. You can't do that! What if your manager found out? *Teen Vogue*?"

"It was fun," I say defensively. I'm not mad at Iris and Hollis for sharing them. They would have considered Ethan safe. "Isn't that the point of music? To have fun."

"It's like eating Doritos when you could have steak. One day, people will pay hundreds of dollars to hear you. Don't sell yourself short. Only musicians who can't"—his eyes slide to Kai, who is scuffing his foot on the floor, looking over a pile of pamphlets—"play on a real stage do things like that. Don't taint your brand."

I bite my lip. No matter what, I'm always doing the wrong thing. Posting the wrong photos. Liking the wrong composers. Liking the wrong *boy*.

But I let out a breath. He's only trying to help. "We're done playing on the streets anyway," I say. "I needed to raise money for a trip to find my great-grandma's pipa. That's all."

But as soon as the words are out, I can't help feeling a pang of loss. Am I really willing to commit to never having that much fun again? And why should I?

Ethan frowns. "Is this why you've been spending so much time with him? Because of that pipa?" Kai is studying the plaque of a large antique vase. Hopefully out of earshot. I try to move farther away, but Ethan doesn't budge. "You can't seriously be thinking about getting involved with him. He's always brooding in some corner."

Is he right? I don't know. Everything is still so early with Kai. But I like how he pushes me. Challenges me.

"Pearl." Ethan's hand rises, like he wants to touch me. Then it falls to his side again. "I know you wanted to take your time and explore, but I know we have something really special. We could have an amazing time in music together." This time, his finger-tips do run down my cheek.

I swallow hard. Ethan-and-me is everything Julie wants for me. What I thought *I* wanted at the start of summer. But now, everything in me tells me this is just another way to stay inside the lines.

"Ethan, I love playing together. We make a good music team. And you're a great fr—"

"A great *friend*." He purses his lips. His eyes are pained, resigned. But also pleading. "It's not like I haven't heard that before. But, Pearl—"

Wait, Kai has vanished. Where did he go? Ethan's talking but I crane my neck, searching among the guests. I realize what Ethan and I must look like to Kai, standing so close together with his fingers brushing my face. A woman enters an elevator heading down.

"I'm sorry, Ethan," I blurt. "I have to go."

Then I duck into the elevator and let the doors close behind me.

The elevator descends at a speed twice as slow as I ascended kissing Kai. I hit bottom with a dip in my stomach and race outside in time to spot Kai disappearing down the escalators to the metro station.

"Kai!" I break into a run. I power down the stairs into the station. Air scrapes in and out of my lungs, but when I reach the platform, it's jammed with travelers and commuters. No Kai.

I text him: hey, where are you?

There's no answer. Stumped, I board the next train back to campus. We were only gone a day, but it feels like an eternity. In the dorms, I knock on his door and poke my head into the music room, but he's not in our usual haunts. Then through a third-floor window, I finally spot him sitting outside on the grass, looking out over the Keelung River. He's throwing stones into the water.

I race back downstairs and approach him cautiously. "Kai?"

He doesn't turn around. "If you're looking for a virtuoso, sorry, none here."

I sit on the grass beside him. He refuses to meet my eyes. "I've been looking for *you*."

Another stone plops into the waters. "Look. I never asked to teach you the pipa or to play with you. I don't even need to go to Fujian with you if that'll *taint your brand*."

Damn. He heard Ethan. "I don't care about all that."

He hunches so his back is toward me and wraps his arms around his knees. "Of course you do. You have to. You've got a fancy magazine all over you. Your big comeback concert. I don't need those frills to be a musician."

"They're not *frills*. They're opportunities." Now it's my turn to be frustrated. "I'm a musician. I'm fighting to get my place back. What's so wrong about that?"

"I thought you were serious about learning the pipa."

"I am! We've been to Tainan and everything. Xiamen's next."

"No one gives up a music life like you have."

Kai did. He had to, and he knows what that means. But that can't be why he's upset with me now, is it? I scoot over the grass so he's forced to look me in the face.

"Is this because you found out I was Pearl Wong?"

He shoves one of Ethan's and my flyers into my hand. I hadn't known Ethan had distributed them already. "Ethan Kang is a big deal. So go forth and duo. I'm not standing in your way."

"But you want to." My fists clench around the flyer.

"He's as big as they get in the Western canon." It's not a compliment. "I know what the rules are, and I know you've got to play by them."

"Because you used to play by them yourself?"

He flushes but doesn't answer.

"Ethan was right about you," I say, frustrated. "It's not enough to be talented. Look at you, you're incredibly talented. But what do you want? Because it seems to me that you don't really want anything anymore. All you do is point your middle finger at the establishment. Because if they're the ones who are wrong, you can't be blamed for giving up."

"*I'm* giving up?" His dark eyes snap. "What about you? You're spending all your energy creating the image of you that *Apollo* wants. It *kills* me that you let those people tell you what parts of you matter or not. You told Hollis and Iris to hide our videos on the street. But what we did out there? What we did on the organ? The kind of music we made, that Ethan who's a total *sellout* wants you to stop—it was—"

"It's not the same!" I yell, cutting him off. "Playing at Apollo is *real*!"

His face goes white. Damn.

"Kai, I'm sorry. That's not what I meant to say."

"Maybe not. But it's what you really feel."

He climbs to his feet. I grab his arm. "Kai, don't shut me out. Talk to me."

But he wrenches free and stalks off.

I lie on my bed and stare at a tear-shaped patch on my ceiling. The roof must have leaked at some point. Before Ever slept under it, or after? She never mentioned a leak. She never mentioned a lot of things about Loveboat. Like how confusing and heart-wrenching less than six short weeks could turn out to be.

Iris pops her head into my room. "Pearl, you coming?"

"Coming?" I stare at them blankly.

"Party in the Dark II, baby! We be hunting wolves. Or one at least."

What's the point? Everything's ruined. What does it matter? I'm regretting what I said to Kai, but it was true. Playing on the streets was for fun. That was the whole point of it.

"I need to leave for Fujian Monday morning. I should get ready for it. It's important." Kai was supposed to go, and now I'm going alone. My eyes fall on Kai's Tokyo Philharmonic tote bag. Damn. I still have his books *and* his pipa. Which I obviously have to return ASAP. "I—"

I stop as Hollis comes in behind Iris and lays their head on her shoulder. They level twin stares at me, identical faces silently mock pleading. Iris holds up several blank slips the size of fortune cookie fortunes. For our names.

I laugh. Truth is, I want to go. I want to find my devil in the dark. I want to finally let go of this weird obsession I have with him. Or maybe, after my two strikes with Ethan and Kai, the third time will be the charm.

"Fuck it," I say, taking the slips from Iris. I print PEARL on one—one is enough. Then I open my drawer and lift out Sophie's Venetian mask, leaving the glittery purple one behind. "Let's go."

26

Hollis, Iris, and I tuck our hair into big top hats and wear our masks all the way from the metro stop to the club. I've curled my name label into a tiny cylinder in my sweaty hand.

"Are you two going to give out your names?" I ask.

"I'm willing to try," Iris says. "But it's like any other blind date. Once the blinders come off, maybe you won't like each other after all."

I shudder. But maybe it will be different with my devil. Or maybe, depending on what happens tonight, I'll still never know.

The Dark Club sign gleams on the door. The bouncers let us through. I try to get a peek at their guest list, but it's like they're waiting for that because they back off.

Hollis grabs my hand and Iris my other and the three of us enter the darkened room, making a pit stop by the mouthwash stand. As I swish the minty liquid through my teeth, a cool mist spills over our feet, along with rock music. I recognize the third song that was playing the first night.

Iris giggles nervously. "It's not as dark this time," she yells over the music.

"Maybe because the lights outside are stronger?" I say.

"No, it must be on purpose so we can find each other," Hollis says.

We dance. The second time doesn't feel like the first. We're old hats now, and I know what to expect. And *I'm* different. The stakes are different. I'm not here for curiosity's sake or random hookups. I want to confirm who my devil in the dark really is and maybe it's a matter of getting his slip without giving mine away. Maybe I should have asked Iris for a few blank ones after all. Anticipation curls in my middle, and I study the moving shapes and shadows all around me. Could he already be here?

And what if he *is* Kai?

A tall guy touches Iris on the arm. She turns and their heads bent close together, mouths to ears, holding a conversation through the music.

"Who's that?" I ask Hollis.

"I don't know."

Iris turns back to us, eyes glowing in the dim light. "He found me!" she cries over the music. "My prince is *Randolph* from cooking class—can you believe it? He felt my bracelet while we were dancing and recognized it just now." She holds out the plastic friendship bracelet on her hand. "His hands are *so cold*." She laughs.

"Way to go," I hug her. Not even ten minutes in and she's already found her prince. It bodes well for the night, although there's an unfamiliar scent to the air that I don't love. Like burning grass. Slightly sweet and cloying. I sniff at it.

"Randolph got a clue about Wolf," Iris yells. "The bouncer let slip that he cut his arm during setup tonight, right *here*." She squeezes my left forearm, just below my elbow. "So if you see a Band-Aid on someone, that's him!"

It's too dark to make out much more than the silhouettes of waving arms, so it's a good clue. "I'll be sure to squeeze a lot of arms!" I yell back. It's still early, but the crowd is already going wild, singing madly along with the song. I join in, belting out the lyrics until my throat aches. I luxuriate in sheer freedom. I can be anyone without judgment. I can even be myself.

A Taylor Swift song begins to play. I remember the progression of music. The next will be a 1970s song, then an Adele song. Our song. I squeeze past a dancing body, moving toward the windows where we met. A hand grabs my waist, too familiar, and I slap the person away and move on. Warding off overtures in the dark only underscores that it's infinitely better to be touched by someone I like. Duh.

That cloying scent in the air is making me lightheaded. Then I spot the devil horns silhouetted against the shades. In the darkness, I can't tell if he's Kai or not. The horns distort the shape of his head and although he looks broader in the shoulder than Kai, his clothing could be bulking him up.

I move closer to him. What the hell. He's kissing someone. A girl taller than me, wearing reindeer antlers. Judging from the way they're leaning into it, it's a really good kiss. I feel a surge of disappointment. Whoever he is, he's had a lot of practice. I ball up my name slip and tuck it into my bra.

The music changes. Adele's rich voice rings out, bringing me back to that first night. And now's my chance.

I move to the spot where we met . . . and so does he. Reindeer girl melts away.

"Hi," he says as he reaches me.

"Hi," I answer. "We meet again." My heart is pounding, but I'm not the same shy girl I was here on the first night. "We danced right here, didn't we?"

"So let's dance again." He puts his hands on my waist, and I put my hand on his shoulder—padded—and we move to the music.

"Do you know who I am?" I ask.

"Do you know who *I* am?" he answers.

He speaks like he's American-born, but other than that, all the inflections and qualities that make a human voice distinctive are muddled by the music. His hands slide down my sides and over my hips. My hands glide up his light sleeves, searching for features I can use without giving away who I am. His arms are smooth, muscled, slightly hairy. And then I feel a Band-Aid right over his left forearm. Just below his elbow.

Wolf.

My Mr. Kisser, who apparently likes to kiss a lot of girls in the dark, is Wolf. My heartbeat quickens. I need to get his name but in case he won't give it to me, my fingers keep exploring. I skim my palm up his sweat-damp neck to cup his jaw, and my fingers find a second scar just under his right jaw. Same place as the left. Exactly parallel.

He takes my hand and pulls it to his chest, and his mouth comes down hard on mine. Before I can pull away—he was JUST kissing reindeer girl—he chews on my upper lip, pulling my mouth open with skilled teeth. His tongue slips through.

The kiss is shockingly familiar. And not just because of Party in the Dark I. I have experienced this playbook multiple times. I just wasn't experienced enough myself to realize it was one.

As I yank myself free, bright white lights stab into my eyes. The room is a large warehouse with unfinished ceilings and a dozen naked lightbulbs hanging on wires. It's jammed with people in fantastical theater masks, top hats, glittery stoles, and wigs in every color. Everyone's stopping dancing, lowering their arms, and detaching from embraces. Someone yanks my hat off my hair, ripping out bobby pins, and other hats and masks go flying around the room.

Right in front of me, in a wide-striped suit, a red devil's horn mask over his face, is Ethan Kang.

"Pearl?" he says, thunderstruck.

In the five seconds I see him in the light, everything changes. Maybe it's the yellowish lights, but his face looks plasticky. Purple lipstick—not mine—smudges his neck. Two thoughts click in my mind. One, that he lied. He claimed he wasn't going, but he was Wolf all along. He doubled back to kiss a ton of people.

And the second: *He's not Kai.*

I *knew* that. I told myself that over and over. But the disappointment that whales me in the gut tells me how much I still, so stupidly, hoped the guy I thought I had so much chemistry with was him, and that this moment would be our way back together.

"Did you know I was me this whole time?" I ask.

Ethan's eyes are like a deer in headlights. "No," he says hoarsely. "Pearl, I—"

"It's a raid!" someone shouts.

Oh my God. Two guys in oversized wolf masks run in wielding iPhones, snapping a million photos. Screams go up around the room. About fifty people in tight-fitting outfits and summery slacks and shirts make a break for the doors.

"Woof, woof, come out and play!" the wolves yell.

I duck behind a large guy in a sequin tuxedo, avoiding their camera lenses. I catch a glimpse of a familiar bluish birthmark on the back of one of their necks. Kai's friends.

"They're after Wolf," someone says, laughing.

Ethan swears. "Let's get out of here." He turns and melts into the crowd, but I need to find Iris and Hollis. I run in the opposite direction, toward the place I last left them, but sweaty, laughing masked people are jamming the place. It's impossible to find anyone.

"Who turned on the lights?" people keep asking. "Was it Wolf?"

"Did you see her face?" someone says.

"Oh my God, I can't believe it was Parker all along!"

Everyone's finding out truths, and the reactions are a mix of horror, joy, and disappointment.

"Hey, baby, hot mask," says a Hulk.

I dodge him and squeeze my way out a side door with a few people disguised as gray-haired hags.

The air outside is a welcomed blast of freshness. I round the corner and jerk to a stop at the sight of masked Loveboaters boiling out the front door. More cameras are flashing. Behind me, someone squeezes by.

"Pearl!" It's Kai. No mask. And he's not surprised to see me here. He did warn me not to come, after all. Basel and Jon. Puzzle pieces are clicking into place.

"Did you know this would happen?" I seethe.

"I came to make sure you were okay," he says. "The cabs and

Ubers are booked for hours. I can walk you home."

"Those guys are your *friends*," I seethe. "Were you involved?"

"I tried to warn you. This whole thing's a clusterfuck. I hoped you wouldn't come—"

"Warn me? You didn't say anything about a raid when you know I can't afford any kind of blowup this summer." It's a betrayal. A burst of anger wells in my chest. "I'm so sick of you passing judgment on us. We all could be working at orphanages and all you'd see is a bunch of rich, spoiled Americans that needed to be taught a lesson. Better yet, get a good hard spanking."

I start across the street, but he grabs my hand. "Pearl. They're not my friends. Not anymore. I'd never do anything to hurt you."

I wrench free. "That doesn't change the fact that you have, does it?"

I stalk away, opening my phone to text Hollis and Iris. Several texts have come in. The first is from Ethan: **I can explain.**

Explain what? That he's been a controlling hypocrite about everything? I want to delete our entire thread and never talk to him again. Except that *Teen Vogue* is still coming and we still need to do the performance. But the girl on the keys will be Angry Seething Pearl, so I don't know how that's going to go down.

Two other texts have come in from Kai. They're from earlier this evening, even before the party started. I've texted him, but he's never actually texted me before, but I'd have recognized his icon anyway: a blue heart encircling the Ai character: 爱

I ignore them. Probably more of what he said tonight.

You okay? I text Hollis and Iris.

I got a name! Hollis texts back. **Lux Wu. They tell the best jokes. I didn't know that would matter to me!**

We're down the street with Randolph, Iris texts. **All good but it's packed! See you back at the dorms?**

So they're okay. And finally met their matches.

Happy for you! I text back. **See you there.**

I'm tempted to tell them I've found Wolf. But even though I'm furious with Ethan, I can't just expose him. Someone knocks me sideways into the wall, scraping my arm. I need to get out of here. But the streets are jammed with masked kids fighting over a single cab. I dial a number. It's almost four in the morning.

Answer. Please. Answer.

"Hello, Pearl?" His warm, familiar voice makes me choke at last. "Everything okay?"

"Rick." I sob with relief. "I need you to pick me up."

Rick is an enormous teddy bear in a navy Cleveland Guardians shirt. Outside a café called Boba Guys, he folds me into a warm hug, then buys me a jasmine cloud bubble tea. We scoot into a booth for two, and Rick hands me a tissue and I blow my nose.

"I was so *stupid*," I say for the tenth time. "I was dumb enough to hope it was Kai. Turns out I was in a love triangle with Ethan and *Ethan*!"

Rick passes me a fat plastic straw and gestures with his at our unopened boba. "Ready? One, two, three!"

We both puncture the plastic film that seals our drink tops.

"That's always so satisfying," Rick says. "It makes everything a little better." He smiles, holding his cup out for a toast. I bump him back, then take a long, sweet pull.

"Yum." I sigh. I swirl my cup against the ring of condensation on the table. "I mean, what did I expect from a guy who was into making out incognito? Even if it was good. If you kiss someone who doesn't know how to kiss yet, all that means is they've kissed fewer people. Sign me up for that guy."

"I'm just here to listen. You're going to get to the right decision on your own."

I moan. "No, I've made such *bad* decisions, Rick. No wonder I have a manager. I can't be trusted to make my own."

"Look, dork. From what you've told me, this party wasn't that big a deal. Some kids hooking up. I get that it's a big deal in an Asian family. But it's not like you were doing heavy drugs or getting into a full on—you know."

"No, I don't," I say. "Full on what?"

"I'm not telling you anything Ever wouldn't tell you."

I cross my arms and glare at him over our straws. "You're just like her in so many ways. It's super annoying. I'm seventeen!"

He gives me a small smile. "There's a reason she and I came together."

My arms press into the edge of the table as I lean in. "You know what the worst part is? It wasn't even Ethan in the dark that I liked. I liked ME in the dark. I liked how I became free. More free than I ever feel in the light. But I don't want to live like that. I can't."

"Then don't," Rick says. "But don't beat yourself up about it either. Just work toward it. Work toward being yourself in the light."

I squeeze his big hand. So thankful. And yet, still so hurt. I feel betrayed by Ethan. I feel betrayed by myself.

"So you like Kai way more than Ethan," Rick says.

310

"Kai isn't an option," I say stubbornly. "And I'm *furious* with him."

He smiles. "Funny enough, as you get older, being mad at someone ends up not being a reason you can't live without them. Are *you* interested in him? That's what matters as a first step."

"Like you and Ever?" I ask.

"In my heart, I know she's the one. But I can't force her to make a choice."

"Well, maybe you should take your own advice and go after *her* instead of moping from afar."

He frowns. I've hit home, although it doesn't feel good to. I stir my fat straw through my bubbles, sending the dark balls spiraling through the milky liquid. "I've never liked calling this pearl milk tea, you know? It's like I'm drinking myself."

He laughs, which I need right now. To feel appreciated despite the mess. That's Rick. His understated superpower is making people around him feel good. And he's right. I'm feeling a tiny bit better already, about everything.

"What's the worst that can happen?" I ask. "A tweet about a busted party of dumb overseas kids. I've already survived one social media debacle."

"Things will blow over. And if they don't, I know you, Pearl Wong. You'll keep standing."

I smile. "I'm going to Fujian Monday," I say. "I'm trying to prove my relationship to my great-grandmother so I can claim her pipa."

"Sounds like a fun quest," Rick says. "It can be your escape for a few days."

I give a short laugh. "I can't keep retreating. But my mom and Ever are meeting me there."

"Ever's coming out? Why didn't you say so?" His face has lit up to a wattage that could keep the lights on throughout Taipei.

"Saving the best for last. I worked hard to convince her to come on your ticket. We've got each other's backs, right?"

A determined look has come into his eyes. It's his turn to squeeze my hand. "Always, Pearl."

I sleep in most of Sunday, avoiding the world. I can't bring myself to check my texts or social media to see the frenzy of the Party in the Dark bust. At some point in the evening, I hear a faint knocking on my door, but I keep my eyes closed and the knocking eventually stops. I sate my hunger with cakes from Sophie's cornucopia, and crawl back into bed again.

At least Julie hasn't called. Which means word hasn't gotten back to her. Not yet.

My alarm clock rings at 6:30 on Monday morning. I rub the sleep from my eyes, opening them to find I've flipped upside down in bed and have a view of Kai's red pipa case beside my chair. A row of cute Asian food stickers lines the bottom—a *bāozi*, a dumpling, a boba tea, all with smiling faces. I've never noticed them before.

A pang hits my chest. He's been the biggest part of my pipa search, and now, I don't even know if I'll ever speak to him again. Even after sleeping on it almost twenty-five hours, I'm still angry. I believe him that he wasn't directly responsible for the raid, but he was in the know.

I've packed an overnight bag for the village trip. Now, I dress carefully in a pale green dress I bought here in Taipei, sturdy for traveling but nice enough that I hope it will show respect to my family. I put on a jade necklace I found with the twins, and gaze anxiously at my reflection. Is the jade cliché, too? I vaguely remember green hats and white headbands symbolized cuckolded husbands and death, and hope I haven't worn anything offensive. Mom and Ever are on a plane, so I can't ask them. Kai would know—but I can't think about him right now.

I feel strangely alone as I leave the sleeping campus, ride the subway full of strangers commuting to work, and then board the two-hour ferry across the Taiwan Strait to Xiamen. On the deck, I lean against the railing and listen to the waters lap against the boat. They're an impossibly bright shade of greenish blue. The breeze in my hair is balmy. As we draw closer to the lush green shoreline, the Loveboat disaster shrinks behind me. But I meant what I said to Rick. I can't keep retreating. I will need to return and, as they say, face the music.

Xiamen turns out to be a quaint working port, with large red cranes, piles of colorful boxcars, and ships moving in and out. A pleasantly salty tang is in the balmy air. I read up on the city as I slowly disembark in a line. It's the capital of Fujian Province, made up of a bit of the mainland plus two islands. Mom said it was a popular honeymoon destination in China, like Florida in the States. I can see why and I like that detail. It makes this place real and specific, instead of just a single block on a puzzle map of the world.

And for me, it holds a key to my quest.

Just beyond the ferry terminal, a driver with a leathery face under a cabbie's cap waves a sign with my Chinese name. *"Lái, lái, Wong Xiao-Jie,"* he greets me with a handshake. Miss Wong. *"Wo shi Koh."* I am Koh. He was arranged by our family to pick us up, but a nervousness rises in me. I've been so focused on my quest, but I'm about to meet real people. *Family.* When the Wongs have been our lonely four—then three—unconnected notes in Ohio for so many years. Will my family here like me? Will I connect with them, even if I can't speak the language?

"Your mother and sister's flight is delayed," he says, leading me to a navy blue van. "I'll take you to Gulangyu while you wait. It's the most famous site in all of Fujian. Your great-grandfather worked there as a young man."

A plan for while I wait, when a performer's life is mostly waiting. It's so considerate. And thank God Mom will be here to help translate. Some of my nervousness eases.

"I'm game," I say.

Mr. Koh drops me off at a pedestrian-only island. No cars or bikes. I walk the peaceful streets between redbrick archways and stone buildings that remind me of London. Or the Renmai Museum. I frown, looking up at the high brick walls. It's nice, but why is it their most famous site?

I look up the island on my phone. It's a UNESCO World Cultural Heritage site, known for its beaches, winding streets, and architecture—that's pretty big. After China lost the First Opium War in 1842, it came under international control. Eventually, thirteen countries had land privileges here, including Great Britain, France, and Japan.

Stories are clicking together in my head. This was where my great-grandpa became a Christian through Baptist missionaries. I sort of always imagined the missionaries living among the Chinese with their hair in a long braid like in photos I've seen at church. But Gulangyu is a European city.

Kai's voice is in my ear, and I'm troubled as I make my way down a winding brick pathway. I try to imagine my great-grandfather working here as a young man. I don't know what his trade was. Just that he wasn't one of the rich homeowners, clearly. Was becoming Christian a genuine choice for him, or did he have to convert when he joined this community? Why is the most famous site in Fujian a town built by Westerners after a war? It's beautiful, yes. But it came from ugly roots. Can we still appreciate it?

I wish Kai were here so I could talk to him about it. I can't actually imagine what he'd say, because he always surprises me.

I came to make sure you were okay.

Did he really come for me . . . even after our fight?

I give in and pull up his pipa playlist, which couldn't be more fitting as Pearl Wong wanders China. The harmonies give me an outlet for the churning inside me. The rhythms are moody, maybe the way he gets when he's feeling trapped by his own body, like he can't do the thing he feels born to do or make the music that makes his soul sing. I wonder what he's doing right now. If his fingers are aching to play, or if that stormy look is back in his eyes . . . and if he's thinking about me at all.

When it's time, Mr. Koh drives to the Xiamen Gaoqi International Airport. I gaze out the window at the glittering city. By now, social media must be wild over the Party in the Dark bust. I'm afraid to check, but I pull out my phone and . . . nothing.

Nothing hashtag-Loveboat. Nothing on the Loveboat app or alumni chat.

Any word on the raid? I text Iris and Hollis.

Crickets, Iris replies. **No one's getting sent home or anything.**

After all that effort and drama to get those photos? Maybe the paparazzi don't want to reveal their own identities by posting publicly. Or maybe Wolf—Ethan—intercepted them. It sounds like his secret's still safe as well.

Guess we're in the clear? I write.

Iris marks my note with a thumbs-up. **Hope so!**

Kai's unread texts are still burning in my inbox. He sent them after our fight by the river, but before our fight at the Party in the Dark. And then he came for me. I open his text: **My doctor messaged me back today. He's skeptical about the Theramin. I felt like my music was taken away all over again.**

Oh no. No wonder. It was too cruel, holding out his music and then snatching it back. And then what I said to him to drive the stake deep into his heart. I owe him my own apology.

I'm sorry, I text him. **Let's please talk when I'm back?**

I want to write more, but I spot Ever and Mom stepping out of the airport. Ever raises her hand to her eyes, squinting against the bright sunlight.

"Ever! Mom!" I yell, waving.

"Pearl!" Ever squeals. We all rush headlong into a fierce three-way hug. All we can do is laugh and talk at the same time.

Mom holds me out at arm's length. "Are you *taller*?"

"Fatter for sure! I've had a *bing* something or bao every day."

"Bing something? You mean bread?" Ever asks.

"Yes, that's what I said!" I give her an extra hard squeeze. I want to ask whether she's seeing Rick, but she looks so tired. Not a good sign.

"Where's your friend?" Mom asks, looking toward our van. My heart squeezes painfully.

"He couldn't make it after all," I say, playing it down. "But I brought you pineapple cakes!" I hold out the box Kai and I bought together, another painful reminder that he's not here. But my family *is*, and we get to take this special trip together. "How was your flight?"

"Oh, wonderful. The flight attendant was so friendly." Mom's looking around with wide, awed eyes, Kai forgotten. "It's been so many years since my parents left here! I can't wait to meet everyone!" She heads for the van.

"Everything okay?" Ever asks as we fall in behind her.

"I'm figuring it out," I admit, and she gives my arm a quick squeeze.

Mom overflows with excitement as we load their bags into the van and squeeze into the front row just behind Mr. Goh. As our van merges onto a highway, Mom removes a handful of brownish photos protected by a plastic bag.

"My aunty mailed me all these," she explains. "Here's my grandma, your great-grandma. She was born in the village we're visiting but spent her young adult years in Shanghai. Then she and Great-Grandpa went to Singapore for ten years, but eventually they came back here. Your grandfather was born on Easter, and then he and your grandma went back to Singapore where I was born and met your father before we moved to the US."

Ever and I share a smile. My quest has ignited a new passion in Mom. I let her stories wash over me as we leave the city behind for green farmlands. The stories are comforting and grounding. A line of men and women I know so little about, but whose choices shaped the course of my life.

The farmlands give way to square earthen fields, sprouted with pale leafy greens. Farmers stand ankle deep in the waters, gleaning.

"What are they growing?" I ask.

"Rice. These are rice paddies," Mom says.

I study them. Farmers to me have always felt so all-American, like Laura Ingalls Wilder on the frontier. Which is silly. There are farmers in every civilization. A few wave and Mom waves back, but I twist in my seat to stare after them.

They're all wearing the conical straw hat.

It's the first time I've seen it anywhere besides our hallway closet. And on my TikTok.

"We're probably related to at least some of them," Mom notes.

"Rick said it was a one in a million chance that he became a Yale grad working in tech," Ever says. "By rights, based on his family, he should have been a farmer himself."

"Most of our family were farmers for generations, too," Mom says.

"Their hats," I blurt, nudging Ever in ribs.

She takes a second look. "You got blasted for wearing a hat that some of our relatives wear."

It's like a final piece in a puzzle I thought was solved. To them, that hat is just what it is—a tool to keep off the sun.

I squeeze my sister's hand tightly. It feels as though all the events of the recent past have led to this moment. The conical straw hat. Now me here in the land of my ancestors, to get their help recovering a musical instrument taken from our family, and in the process, finding out so much more about where I come from. My story doesn't end with my blowup. It's just beginning.

"We're here!" Mom says, and I sit up taller.

Our car rumbles past squat, one-story bungalows with ancient Chinese rooftops, and over a gravelly road that runs between a row of two-story buildings covered in square tiles. Those bungalows and this one road seem to be the entire village. It's a humble place. Nothing like the small town of brick homes and green lawns that I grew up in or anything I've seen on TV or on my trips to Europe. The buildings are plain and rectangular, uniform, covered in inexpensive tiles. The first floor of each building, from here to the end of the road, is like a mall—featuring one-room restaurants and small, garage-like shops selling cookware and bolts of cloth. Above them, rectangular windows lead to what I assume are living quarters. Mopeds are parked literally everywhere.

Mr. Koh pulls to a stop in front of a cobbler's store. A man with a feathery head of white hair limps rapidly toward us. His dark-brown eyes are bright in his tan face, and his light cotton shirt swims with pale-blue patterns.

"I know your face," Mom says as he reaches us.

"Ah, li ho! Li ho bo!" he cries, pumping Mom's hand up and down. She gushes back in the Hokkien dialect she uses with her sister and they have a rapid-fire exchange. Then she turns to us, her face glowing in a way I've never seen.

"He says my grandmother used to babysit him! He's her third cousin. You can call him, ah, Great-Uncle."

The miracle who is Great-Uncle shakes my hand, then Ever's,

his wrinkled face beaming. A few black-haired women approach shyly on delicate steps, of similar petite height as us, wearing soft blouses and bamboo slippers. Mom turns from one to another to another, overwhelmed and delighted, and tries to introduce us: "Ah, this is your grandpa's third cousin once removed, your second, no third cousin three times removed? No, I have that all wrong!" She laughs, as confused as we are. *"Piao yee ma,"* she says.

"Grand-cousin-aunt?" Ever suggests.

"On your mom's side. And first born. So *Piao tuayee ma.* Chinese is very precise about family," Mom gushes. "Not like English. In English, everyone is a cousin, aunt, or uncle, but here, it's very specific. Do they come from your mom's side or dad's side, what birth order?"

"That's a *lot* more vocabulary to learn," I say. And I love it. It gives family an extra-special place. As it should have.

More friendly faces descend on us. Mom tries to introduce us to each one, finding just the right family term. "This entire village is related to us!"

"It's unbelievable!" Ever says. "In Ohio, our nearest relative is a six-hour drive away."

"I see the resemblance!" I say. I have friends with long faces shaped like kernels of corn and friends with square faces, and others who are oval. Everyone here is somewhat in between. Petite, but sturdy. I'm the tallest girl around at five feet four inches.

They have to feed us first thing. That same food-as-love language that my mom speaks. We have lunch in a room weakly cooled by an AC. The tablecloth paper tears easily under my fingers. The plates are a plain beige. The floor is covered by interlocked spongy tiles.

"We come from humble roots, girls," Mom whispers, a little embarrassed toward us, her American daughters. But she doesn't need to be. Not one bit.

"We're with family," I say firmly. And the bounty of dishes could feed a royal household. "That's what matters."

We dig into the meal: a savory beef, eggs, and tomato dish, stir-fried noodles Mom often makes, and lots of green vegetables. I'm scarfing down desserts of red bean soup and golden coconut cakes when a group of young girls and guys my age peer curiously in. They're dressed in slightly more modern shirts, shorts, and skirts. Mom springs up and chatters with them, then grabs a few hands and brings them to us.

"Meet your aunties and uncles." Mom laughs. "They're younger than you, but you have to call them aunty and uncle. It's respectful."

Ever and I smile and repeat their titles after Mom. *"Piao Diyee. Piao Diku."* Our newfound aunties and uncles laugh—we can't talk to each other, but the fun of meeting doesn't need words.

"Need help translating?" Mom offers.

"Yes, please!" I say. Our relatives are as fascinated by us as we are them.

"Do you have self-driving cars in America yet?"

"What music do you listen to?"

"Do you see Keanu Reeves when you walk around?"

"I got a photo with him once!" Mom takes that one for the team. "Years ago when I was visiting LA. I spotted him on the street. He was so kind."

"Americans are *so* lucky," sighs my younger-than-me aunt.

"You're lucky, too," Ever says. "You get to live with your entire extended family. Every day. All of you together." Her eyes are shadowed as she looks around the cousins teasing and even pounding on each other. "It's funny," she says softly to me. "Mom and Dad left Asia so we could have a better life. But they have something really special here. And we've all missed out on it."

"Are you thinking of Rick and moving out here?" I ask. "Like what you might be missing out on, with him?"

"A bit," she admits.

"If you came, it wouldn't have to be forever," I say. "We could Zoom a lot among us, like I did this summer. You could live in Taipei for a few years. Then New York, then who knows after that?"

"Loveboat's already made a convert of you." Ever smiles wistfully.

"We can have all this, too!" I wrap my arm around her, snuggling my head on her shoulder. "We just have to work a little harder at it."

After lunch, Great-Uncle takes us on a tour of the local school: a small campus of rectangular buildings, simply surfaced with white tiles and trimmed with pink bricks. A group of kids runs laps around an Astroturf track. Another group is flying kites—blue, purple, green—high in the sky.

"It's summer holidays," Great-Uncle says. "The classes are enrichment."

"This school was funded by Lim relatives in the States," Mom says. "I don't know them myself."

"Can we ask about Grandpa's birth certificate?" I ask Mom.

She chats with Great-Uncle. "They don't have birth certificates from that time. If he had one, it was lost or destroyed. It was a different time. They didn't need to prove their identity the way we do today."

I feel a stab of disappointment. But Great-Uncle beckons us to follow him down the road, hands down the fittest octogenarian I've ever met. I'm winded trying to keep up as his legs pump powerfully up a hilly roadway to a long, low brick house with a sloping roof and sliding double doors of dark painted wood. Red paper banners flutter on either side of the doorway, and before it, a woman with short gray hair sweeps its porch with a twig broom.

Inside, the rooms form a square cross pattern, each one sectioned off from a central courtyard by sliding doors of wood and paper panels. A few shirts sway from a laundry line. The back room is open, and its walls are filled entirely with black-and-white photos featuring oval faces like the ones here. Faces that aren't very different from mine or Ever's or Mom's.

With a jolt, I recognize a photo high up. "Look, it's Grandma and Grandpa!" They are standing before a boat named with three Chinese characters that I know means *Lucky*. It's a story I've heard, of the day they left for Singapore. The sight of them is like a friendly wave.

"The folks here try to keep up with all the Lims," Mom says. "But there are so many of us now."

And I didn't even know they were here.

Mom points to another photo. "That's my oldest cousin."

A thought strikes. I feel a new burst of excitement. "I just need something that proves I'm related to Great-Grandma to show the Renmai Museum. It's got to be here. A wall of photos that includes all of us, or something."

"It's not enough to be on the same wall," Ever says dubiously.

"Is there anything else?" I ask Mom, who checks in with Great-Uncle.

"Ah, *lái, lái, lái*," he says, gesturing passionately for us to follow him.

He leads us down another curved roadway, to a temple surrounded by a stone wall. The temple is a long, low building of red bricks and green stones, topped by three tiers of swallowtail rooflines. A red lantern with a fat yellow tassel hangs over the wooden doorway and two larger ones flank it.

"This is the Lim family temple," he says.

"There's an entire *temple*? Just for us?" So much for the little shrine I imagined. Ever looks just as awed. Mom is already peering inside through slits in the wall. "Does Dad's family have something like this, too?"

"I think so," Mom says. "We will have to take another trip to visit his family one of these days!"

"Yes, for sure!" It's another connection to family, to Mom and to Dad, that I didn't even know existed. I hover impatiently behind Great-Uncle as he unlocks a padlock and slides the doors apart. Inside, the sun shines into another open courtyard. The back half, sheltered by the roof, is an altar, with gold calligraphy running down four posts. A table before it holds an incense stand and bowls of fruit. Flowers overflow from porcelain vases to either side—this place is well cared for. The walls are covered in large-tiled mosaics of yellow, blue, green, and pink, depicting phoenixes, mountains, and rivers.

And the centerpiece of the whole shrine: white stone slabs side by side, filled with a very long list of names in golden Chinese characters—three, sometimes four—printed column after column. I scan the rows. The Lim character 林 is repeated across the top of each row, over and over.

"Two trees. It means 'forest,'" Mom says.

Great-Uncle sets lit incense sticks in a bowl of sand. Their sweet fragrance reaches my nose. He bows respectfully toward the slabs, holding his pose for a full ten seconds.

I nudge Ever and whisper, "Should we do it, too? Is this ancestor worship?" It's one of the customs I've only heard about through Chinese American friends of the family or seen in movies like *Mulan*.

"I don't know. Mom?"

I'm here to show respect, no question. But if I'm honest, Kai-style, I don't actually believe our ancestors need the bowls of fruit laid out for them. Is my not-believing disrespectful?

"Great-Uncle says this shrine is for worship," Mom confirms. "But we can think of it as a way of honoring our family."

It's a relief to have Mom's direction. I bow my head along with Mom and Ever. Maybe this is also a way forward with this struggle of how to navigate my different cultures. We can evolve. We can build upon. We can do it all with a posture of honoring.

Great-Uncle takes a feathery duster to the glass covering the slab, although there's not a speck of dust in sight. Mom moves closer. "Each generation shares the same middle character." She points out clusters in the list of names. "That's why you and Ever are both 'Ai.' 'Ai-Mei' and 'Ai-Zhu.'"

"Love-Pearl." I smile, thinking of my conversation with Kai.

"In Rick's family, everyone's middle character comes from a poem, with each generation taking the next word," Ever says.

"What if your generation got stuck with 'a' or 'the'?" I ask.

"Maybe if it's a poem, there aren't extra words?" She frowns. "I'll have to ask him."

"Your great-grandmother is here." Great-Uncle runs his finger down a column on the last slab. He stops near the bottom. "Tan Ch-you. 'Autumn.' And here's her son, 'Lim An-Pai. 'Peace.'"

"My grandpa." I feel a rush of excitement. "So those last two names are—"

"Mine and my sister's," Mom gushes. "My parents gave them our names. So now it falls to me. We will have this updated to include you and Ever."

"That's amazing, Mom," Ever says. "I didn't even know there was a list to be added to, but it means so much."

"It does," I say.

"And someday you can include your own kids!" Mom says.

A small smile touches Ever's lips.

I snap a photo of each of the slabs. On my phone, they look like sheets of paper. You'd never know they were carved into a stone tablet like the Ten Commandments. But I go ahead and take a wide angle, a close-up, a video of the entire place.

"Is this all I'll need?" I wonder aloud.

"It may be the best we can do," Mom says.

"What about family photos?" Ever asks. "Someone here must have some."

Great-Uncle answers, his arms opening expansively.

"We can visit Old Aunty's home," Mom translates. "She's the

unofficial village historian. She has the largest collection of Lim family photos. She's your—" She looks to Great-Uncle for help, which he provides at length. She laughs. "Your dad would have been better with these titles." She smiles at me, and I'm glad Dad's with us in memory and more. "She's your great-grandfather's second cousin's daughter-in-law."

I link arms with Mom, smiling back. "I love her already."

Old Aunty's house sits at the top of a hill. It's Chinese architecture, but something about it reminds me of our home in Chagrin Falls. Maybe it's just homey. Three kids in cotton shirts and shorts are running barefoot in front of it. We pause for about ten minutes figuring out how exactly we're related, something like fourth cousins twice removed.

Then we head inside. The blue-and-white tile floor is laid in an eight-point star pattern. A circular doorway leads to a room of black lacquered Asian furniture and embroidered blue cushions. Threadbare and well loved, as if generations of Lims have nestled themselves in these chairs after a day's work.

Old Aunty's silvery hair is held back by a plastic headband. Her soft linen dress swishes gently and she smells faintly of Tiger Balm, a menthol ointment I associate with my dad. She pours tea from a metal kettle. Just plain and round, with simple sky-blue cups, nothing like the fancy tea set at the Renmai Museum. And yet her pouring me tea means everything to me.

We pull up plastic stools around a low plastic table. My eyes are everywhere, taking in the details. My family's taste, a preference for the color blue, their interest in collecting miniatures—scales, cash register, grandfather clock—it's all here, too.

And music. A violin case sits beside the coffee table. Not tucked out of the way gathering dust, but left carelessly there after practice. An upright piano sits in the corner, keys exposed, its velvet runner curled on the floor. A red Chinese drum lies on its side.

Old Aunty brings out stacks of leather-bound albums. Their covers are crinkled with age, but inside is a treasure chest. Side by side with Mom and Ever, I flip through the photos.

"Everyone looks so young!" Mom says. "This is my great-aunt who had the bound feet. She was the strongest woman I've ever met. There's your great-grandma at her wedding." I catch my breath, studying her closely. She's my age, smiling beside a handsome man in a military uniform. My great-grandfather, thin and stern and black-haired, has Mom's eyes and Ever's nose.

"Great-Grandma looks just like you, Pearl," Ever remarks.

It's true. I didn't notice it as much in her stage photo, with her hair styled and her face made up. But the shape of our jaws. The placement of our noses. These could be pictures of me in period costume.

"These are me, when I was a kid," Mom says. "I've never seen these." She flips through colored photos of her growing up with her own parents. "Apparently, my parents sent them. This is how they've known us all these years." Her eyes are moist.

She often comes across as so tough, but she had to survive on her own. She had no community like this around her. She worked hard to make friends in Ohio, assembling platters of deviled eggs and endless green bean casseroles. Food people there loved and appreciated when she came to potlucks to find friends. Not her food, but theirs, and because of her efforts, those foods became mine, too.

Old Aunty is telling Mom a story. Her softly wrinkled face is animated. Sharing these stories, I can tell, means so much to her. I hear it in the cadence of her words.

"After the war, Great-Grandma and Great-Grandpa were eventually able to return to this village," Mom translates. "They went on to have six children. The youngest was my grandpa."

I turn the leaves of the album carefully, and Great-Grandma gets older and older. A child appears. More children until my grandpa. They grow older until at the very back, I reach the last photo of her with my great-grandpa and six grown kids. My grandpa is about thirty and my great-grandma sixty.

"That was taken the last time my father saw her. He left for Singapore for a business trip. She caught a flu, and he wasn't able to return before she passed away."

"How sad," I murmur. I trade a glance with Ever, then close the album with a sense of awe and reverence. Those stories are our life.

"Do you have a photo of Grandpa and you together?" Ever asks me. "To finish the family tree."

I flash her a grateful smile. "Good thought." I scroll my album on my phone until I find the one of us with Grandpa and Grandma at Disneyland. He's in his sixties, but he still has a full head of graying hair. I compare it to the one of him at thirty. There's no questioning it. They're the same man.

Three photos, an album, a family tree. This is what I came for. But this visit has already given me so much more. I come from a village of people who have lived here for centuries. Most of them have never been out of the province, let alone traveled the world like I have. But we share a common ancestry and blood. We share music.

Ever's sitting very still, like only a ballerina can do, studying the open albums.

"It makes me feel like I'm not alone in the world," she says, summing up everything I'm feeling.

I hug her tight. "You never were. We were four notes on the page. Then three. But now, there is a whole symphony."

Ever and Mom ask a million questions. But there's only one more from me.

"After she gave up her pipa to find her husband, did she ever play again?" I ask.

Old Aunty and Great-Uncle look at each other across the table. And they smile.

28

I hear the pipa music long before I see the instruments. Familiar twangs not quite in time together, but trying. Inside a classroom at the school, about two dozen kids in light cotton clothing are plucking the strings of pear-shaped pipas on their laps.

"Lessons!" I say.

There aren't enough pipas to go around, so the kids take turns, two or three to a wooden one. They're playing "Colored Clouds Chasing the Moon," practicing the tremolo, with the non-playing ones eagerly waiting their turns in a way that hits me hard. And they're *good*.

"After the war, your great-grandfather was pardoned," Great-Uncle says through Mom. "Your great-grandma had a chance to return to the stage in Shanghai, but she would have had to leave her family behind. Her husband's work was here. So she chose to come back and found this program. She asked her musician friends to donate five pipas at the time. I was one of her first students."

"You play the pipa!"

Dear Great-Uncle. He gives a modest bow of his head. Which

tells me he must be smashingly good.

"She taught so many of the town's children to play. Few of them stuck with it, but she believed music education is never wasted."

"So she *did* keep playing," I say.

"For the rest of her life," Ever says.

"She would perform for the village from time to time. Just over there in the outdoor auditorium." He leads us toward it.

"Did she have another pipa then?"

"Yes. It was a serviceable instrument. Nothing like her stage pipa. Your mother told us that you found it in a museum. How remarkable. I'm sure she never imagined it would end up in such a place."

"Yes, and it's still blue. Still with five flowers painted on it."

"Ah, your great-grandfather painted those."

"*He* did?! We wondered."

"She shared the story. He wasn't an artist, but he was determined to make them beautiful. So he practiced for hours with a local artisan until he could do them himself. He painted five for each kiss they stole before they were married."

"No, that can't be true," Mom protests. "They wouldn't have kissed before they got married."

Ever laughs. "Go, Great-Grandpa!"

"She let him paint on her *pipa*," I say. "That's true love." He knew her heart. And he made sure he was right in its center. A grand romantic gesture. And it worked. She chose this life with him. Teaching kids to play. Growing old with her husband and six children between them.

"She must have been so sad to lose it," I say.

"When you have lived a long time, loss is part of the cycle. But she would have been thrilled to know she would one day have a strong descendant who would pick it up again."

"I hope so," I say fervently. The war had taken her instrument from her. She didn't know how her story would end. None of us know how our stories will play out after we are gone. She just kept on going, making music in many different ways.

And so can I.

The students have shifted to another song, this one borrowed from Mozart. Now playing in this small Chinese village. Kai might say it's a sign of the reach of colonization, that Mozart is even being featured here. Or maybe, together, we could come to a different conclusion.

I don't know. And I'm not sure it's my job to find the answer that fits everyone. I can only find the answer that fits Pearl Wong.

I step back outside with Ever and take a seat on the humble fountain in the school's courtyard. "I'm glad you suggested I come." My sister gestures expansively with both arms at the village. "They're ours. And we're theirs."

"Great-Grandma's story is amazing, isn't it?" I say.

"Yes, when you marry someone, you're taking on whatever their life brings with them," Ever says. "If they're sick, you care for them. If they have to flee the country because of war, you'll yearn for them and worry for their safety, or you go after them and leave all you have. So who you marry, *if* you marry, should be someone you're willing to give everything up for. Otherwise, what's the point?"

"He loves you that way. You know he does."

Ever plucks a violet flower by her feet and twirls it between her fingers. "You've always been so fearless," she says wistfully.

"So sure about everything you feel. I've always envied that about you."

"Maybe." I glance back at the school. "Do you think Dad would have enjoyed the pipa?" I ask. Something I've been trying not to think about. "I mean, he loved piano so much."

Ever squeezes my hand. "He loved piano because *you* played it."

It's a relief to hear her say it. Freeing in a way I didn't expect. I give a soft laugh. "Turns out I needed this summer to figure out a lot of things after all," I say. "And now, I'm ready."

"I'm getting there, too," Ever admits. "I want to stay here another week. To spend time with our cousins my age. I didn't know they existed until this trip."

"You're not avoiding Rick?"

She smooths back my hair. "No. He called me and we spoke a bit. I agreed to meet him at your performance on the eleventh."

"Good," I say. Rick isn't going to let my sister leave Asia without a fight of his own. "Maybe coming back to Loveboat will be good for you guys, too."

A smile touches her lips. "We got ourselves in plenty of trouble on that program. But looking back now, all that sneaking out, escaping, rebellion was actually good for us. It made us better leaders, in a weird way."

I hear the sound of a pipa then. Not the steady, lively strum under practiced fingers. But wild twangs. A small child, not more than three years old, has gotten hold of Great-Uncle's pipa. He's playing loudly and awfully, but his joy is palpable. Ever and I share a smile. The sounds he's making—that's real music, too, and I wouldn't take that pipa away from him for a million dollars. I was so wrong about what real music is. It's so much bigger than I can know. And I need to tell Kai that as soon as I'm back.

"Pearl?" Mom says. My family is approaching. Great-Uncle is speaking with a woman who gives me a deep curtsy from the eighteenth century.

"The village mayor asked if you'd be willing to perform tonight," Mom says. "On the stage where your great-grand-mother played."

A lump thickens in my throat. I came here for a pipa.

"I would be so honored," I say. "But there is one condition . . ."

I play on a school pipa at sunset, as the sky bleeds into an orangey-red. This outdoor arena is a small clearing in the woods behind the school, with a semicircle of logs for benches. My condition: we're joined by Great-Uncle, the pipa teacher and a few of her students, and two other old-timers of the Lim village. I play a well-named song Kai taught me from the pipa canon, "The Moon is High in the Sky."

Music is a language everyone can understand. And it's fitting that my debut in Asia, the land of my ancestors, is on my family's stage. Surrounded by two hundred relatives, my young aunts and uncles, my old cousins, my sister and Mom, and, inside me, Kai's killer beat to buoy the music on, I put on the best performance I've ever given. Not with a bunch of movers and shakers at the Lincoln Center, but with people inextricably connected to me in a permanent symphony.

Something opens up inside me. My story. Not the girl barely clinging to the Apollo program or the one trampled by TikTok. But the girl from humble farming roots. Who had the chance to grow up in the States and learn to play the piano. Who is made up of so many different parts as a result. Chinese. American. Christian. Female. Mozart. Pipa. And who found, in her travels, the music that was her own family.

29

Old Aunty's son and daughter-in-law give up their rooms for us for the night. In the morning, we hug Ever a temporary goodbye and bid the rest of the family farewell, with promises to return soon. I feel the heart of the village beating in my chest as I ride the ferry ride back to Taiwan. Mom takes a seat in the shade on deck, and I stand at the railing, letting the wind sweep through my hair and listening to the music of the water.

New plans are stirring inside me.

On the other side of the world, in just a few days, the Apollo musicians will perform at Lincoln Center. It will be a smashing success. Featuring the music of great composers whose works have lived on for centuries. I do love Mozart. I've been playing him since I was four, just like he was when he started, and his compositions are permanently carved into my musical soul. But I'm also itching to do more. Because the classics can share the spotlight.

I text Julie: I want to add a few more songs and people to my performance for Teen Vogue. I can still do the duo pieces with Ethan, but I'd also love to do a pipa song with performers from my family, and maybe a contemporary one with my friend Kai, who's a beatboxer.

If Kai's willing to do it with me. He texted another apology for the Party in the Dark, and I tell him it was my choice to go. The rest will have to wait until I see him in person.

I send Julie the recordings from the village performance along with the video Hollis took of Kai and my street show with Lan-Lan. Funny how when we took that video, I didn't want it getting out, and now I realize it's one of the more interesting performances I've ever done.

Ethan's **I can explain** text is still in my inbox. **Let's talk later today,** I write back. Then I send a similar message as I just sent to Julie.

Ethan texts back immediately: **Thanks, Pearl. I'll check with my manager.**

Two trains and five hours later, our cab drops Mom and me off at the Renmai Museum in Tainan, at the beginning of the broad walkway lined with those Greek stone statues. We've arranged to meet with the director. But Mom falters when she catches sight of the museum's castle-like facade.

"Oh, Pearl, you didn't tell me it was like this," she says. "It's— so big. I don't want to fight." I get it. After a lifetime of fighting for fairness—and usually losing—she's tired. But I'm not giving up.

"It's our pipa, Mom. They asked me to bring evidence. That's what I'm doing."

I take her hand and move ahead with a firmer step. The receptionist at the front desk escorts us to an English rose garden café in a side atrium. Window curtains, printed with French paintings, flutter in the breeze and look out onto trimmed garden hedges. The table is black steel wicker. This space is charming, but I'm too nervous to appreciate it.

A broad-chested man arrives. He looks exactly like this museum in a sleek black Prada suit, sporting a tie made of a playful Monet print. A heavy gold watch gleams on his wrist as he shakes Mom's hand, then mine.

"Hello, I'm Mr. Chi. Pleasure." He removes a handkerchief from his pocket and wipes off our table. He takes a seat across from us.

"Tea?" he offers, and a girl brings us a blue-and-white porcelain kettle with matching cups. He pours three steaming cups and arranges them before us. "I understand you are making a claim to a pipa in our collection," he says pleasantly.

"Yes." He's already in the know. So far so good. "The pipa belonged to my great-grandmother. My mom's grandma." I take a warm sip, but the tea is weak.

Mom clasps her hands in her lap. She dressed up for this meeting, wearing the floral print midi dress she wore for last night's concert. "We've just come from our family village to gather the proof your staff asked for."

My own hands shake as I remove my evidence from my purse, the plastic bag protecting the precious photos inside. I spread them carefully before him.

"This is my great-grandma with her pipa—the one with the blossoms in your collection. And here's a photo of her with her son, my grandfather." It's undeniably her, ten years later. "And them again, growing up over the next ten years. And this is me and my grandpa." Finally, I show him the new photos on my iPhone: the list of names from the family tree.

I sit back hard in my metal wicker chair, scraping its legs over the ground. Here it all is. All the evidence linking my great-grandmother to me.

"You look like her." Mr. Chi picks up the photo of her with the pipa.

"That's what people say."

He leans back in his own seat, mirroring me. "Why do you think we have pieces in our museums?" he asks kindly.

"So people can see them. Learn about them."

"Yes. A pipa in the British Museum is there to represent an aspect of Chinese culture."

"Unless it was stolen," I say, thinking of Kai.

"It can get complicated, I agree," he says. "Traveling exhibits like our new Impressionist paintings represent their cultures to others around the world."

"Yes, they're . . . ambassadors."

"Exactly. We have many ambassadors in this museum," he says. "All by nature come from somewhere else. Museums in Europe, China, Japan, Australia. Private collections. Antique dealers. We do our utmost best to ensure the provenance of every item. The place of origins. Everything is paid for. We paid over ten million NT for the pipa in question."

Ten million NT! People don't just give up millions of dollars. Even if it's the right thing to do.

"The prior owner bought it for almost the same amount," he adds. "It passed through several hands on its way to him."

My teacup has grown lukewarm. "I understand you spent money to get her pipa. But my family never sold it. It was taken

341

from her during the war."

"We have thousands of visitors a year. Every year, multiple people assert a relationship to our pieces. We are glad when they find themselves here, as you seem to have done." He opens his hands. "I can ask my staff if the previous owner would be willing to meet with you. Perhaps he might be willing to offer your family a settlement fee."

"This isn't about the money!"

Mom touches the crook of my arm. She wants me to give up. But she's wrong about this.

"I'm not any claimant," I say. "This pipa belongs to my family. I brought in the evidence you asked for!"

"Ms. Wong, what precedent would we be starting if we gave our collections away, especially when they will sit in private family living rooms, never to be appreciated? It wouldn't be good stewardship."

"Her pipa won't be sitting in a living room," I say. "It will be played on the world stage."

His brow rises in his forehead. "You're a professional pipa player?"

"I'm a professional *musician*," I say. "I've played on stages in San Francisco, London, Berlin, Paris, and Vienna." I've never named them like this, but now the experience rolls off my tongue. Because I've had a lot of it. "I'm doing a performance being featured by *Teen Vogue* later this week. This is just the beginning." It's the first time I've ever spoken so boldly about my own career. But I stand behind what I've said a hundred percent. "Your pipa will be on much better display in my hands than moldering in your case here. These instruments were meant to be *played*."

Mr. Chi checks his watch and stands. "I'm afraid we are at an impasse. Please enjoy your tea and take a stroll through our gardens."

My eyes sting. He's only behaving just like every other museum has. How many countries have asked world-renowned museums for their national treasures back . . . and how often do they get them?

But as a museum head here in Taiwan, he should know better.

"Wait," I say as he turns to go. "So many national museums have artifacts from other countries, treasures taken during colonialism or war." Kai would be proud. "So many of them still need to give them back or at least pay for them. What if the Renmai was an example of doing the right thing? Aren't museums here to show people the truth?"

His face hardens. "We are done here," he says, and vanishes inside.

Just like that, my quest has ended. I hadn't expected the pipa to be handed over on the spot, but even with all the proof I've gathered, he's not even willing to consider it. The wrong done to my great-grandma won't be made right.

My body has turned to stone, joining the statues in this garden. Finally, Mom takes my hand, and I let her hold it as we drift back out to the walkway.

"I'm sorry, Pearl," Mom says. "I know how much you wanted this to work."

My eyes brim with tears. Her pipa really truly belongs to me in so many ways. It should be ours. But I lift my chin. "If I hadn't found it, I never would have gone all the way to our family's village. I'll still do the concert with Ethan. I'll still work toward getting the pipa. Maybe I can bring it up in the *Teen Vogue* interview."

Mom's phone chimes. "It's my friend Suzy." An old high school mate who happens to be in town, who she hasn't seen in almost thirty years. She'll be visiting with her for a few days here in Tainan while I return to the Loveboat campus.

"I'm glad this trip to Tainan wasn't a complete waste for you," I say.

"Of course not. You've grown up so much in just a summer, Pearl." Mom tucks a strand of my hair behind my ear. "I'm glad I got to be a part of it."

I help her flag a cab and give her a hug. She takes off, and I'm flagging a second cab when my phone chimes with a text. I reach for it eagerly. Kai? Recognizing by telepathy that I've been channeling him for the past twenty-four hours and now desperately need to talk to him?

It's Julie. She texts me a link to an article in the *Daily Post* and the words: **CALL ME ASAP.**

Which can only mean bad news. My stomach tightens. I stare at the two colored photos that topline the article: a picture of younger me at my piano debut in Carnegie Hall, side by side with a photo of me in my elegant Venetian mask, shell-shocked and exposed at the Party in the Dark II.

Ever, Rick, and Sophie text me almost identical messages: **Pearl, are you okay? Do you need help?** More texts arrive from Iris, Hollis, and Kai. Just like that, I'm thrust back into the real world. I touch the *Daily Post* link. Its headline takes over my entire screen.

Loveboat Unmasked: Prodigies Meet Debauchery in the Dark.

30

"Pearl, where is your head?" Julie's voice crackles with fury over my phone. Even though she's seven thousand miles away, I can feel my natural tendency to cower before her folding my shoulders inward and shrinking me down to my core. "First this *orgy*—"

"Julie, please listen to me. It was not an orgy—"

"Drugs! Sex on the dance floor! Then you send me a picture of you playing with a *homeless man*."

What is she talking about? "That man has a name, Lan-Lan, and he's not homeless as far as I know, and he's also a really good musician," I say. A taxi honks, and I wave it by and frantically text my family back. I'm fine. On a call with Julie.

"This piece is a disaster," Julie says. "Your name is right up top. Big neon letters. 'Pearl Wong, an American piano prodigy, and summer student at Chien Tan, was seen entering a Loveboat party in Taipei featuring heavy drinking, drug use, and sexual encounters in the dark.'"

My mouth feels numb as I scroll through the article. *I'm* the headline. Pearl Wong. How did they know I was here? Only Marc, Ethan, and Kai knew the truth. They wouldn't leak it. I think.

It's a terrible piece, blasting the spoiled entitled kids who've come through the place. They make a veiled reference to the LBTGQ+ director, in what feels like a weird way to mention Marc. And either this article has overblown the truth of the party, or there was a whole lot more going on in the dark than I knew about.

But none of the photos captured by the paparazzi guys even make it. Just *my* photo. And near the bottom, they take on my blowup on TikTok: *The musical socialite came under fire earlier this summer when she posted photos of herself in a racist caricature* . . .

Oh my God, they're making me sound like a nightmare. There's even a mention that I was supposed to attend Apollo . . . and didn't.

"Julie, I can explain—"

"Apollo called. They've asked you not to apply again in the fall."

I sit heavily on the curb. "They canceled me . . . again?"

And this time, I have no one to blame but myself. My mask slipped the first time. I knew the risk, and I still went to the second party. No matter how safe I might have felt behind my mom's maiden name, I still went.

"I can't reach *Teen Vogue*," Julie continues. "I honestly don't even know what I'd say to them."

If they haven't dropped me yet, they will.

"Well, we can still videotape our performances," I say. "With Ethan, with Kai and the pipa—"

"NO, Pearl! I don't know how else to impress this on you. *So much is riding on this performance!* Your comeback. Your college application. Your *reputation*. And you seem hell-bent on throwing it all away! Nothing less than a stellar, spotless, pristine performance can save you now. Which means calling off this circus of obscure instruments you're planning while I—"

"It isn't a circus! It's an exploration of the music of my culture! If you could just hear me for once—"

"Pearl, this is ridiculous." Her voice sharpens. "You are not an established musician. If you get on a stage with a bunch of—"

"A bunch of what? *Real* people? Not perfect people but real ones. Because my reputation is so fragile, my hold on my place in the music world is so tenuous, that I cannot afford to get a splotch of dirt on my shoes?"

"We've invested too much to allow you to taint your brand," she says.

"I am not a brand!" I fight back the tears that threaten to spill. All those years of playing what everyone else wanted me to play to get on this or that stage or please this or that critic. "I'm a person."

"Pearl, I am simply asking you not to cut off your own nose. Do you realize how many other musicians are out there trying to break in? Even if Apollo is off the table, no reputable arts organization will want one of their ambassadors performing like a common street musician."

"Then I don't want to be one of their ambassadors," I say.

"What?" she splutters. "Are you quitting?"

"No, I'll never quit." I pull a deep breath. "Not when there's obviously so much work to do. I never should have had to justify myself to Apollo in the first place. And you never even questioned that. I'm sorry, Julie, but I need a new manager."

For the first time since I met her, she's at loss for words.

My lips tremble. "Goodbye, Julie," I say, and hang up. I blink at the long stone walkway before me. I'm sitting all alone on a curb outside a museum that won't give me back my family's heirloom. My text messages are still blowing up. More people from Loveboat asking if I'm okay. One asking if I want a do-over with him, wink.

I burst into tears. What have I done? And what will I tell Mom?

31

The wind blows a familiar flyer onto my leg as I reach Chien Tan. I grab it before it blows away. It's my flyer for the performance with Ethan. But now, bold red marker spells over our faces: CANCELED.

My stomach clenches. My sides ache from running here.

"Pearl!" Iris catches up with me, followed by a gangly guy with his black hair in cornrow braids. Judging by the way he's sending her puppy-dog eyes through his hip-nerdy glasses, he must be Randolph. Hollis is right behind them, holding hands with a pixie-haired person who must be Lux.

Iris's eyes widen when she sees the brochure.

"Because of the article?" she asks.

"This is Ethan's handwriting," I grate. He moved even faster than Apollo did, distancing himself from my taint. Probably so no one would dig deeper and figure out his own secret. That he was the hypocrite using all of Loveboat.

Iris gulps a huge breath of air. "Pearl Wong. That's why you looked so familiar. You were in the *World Journal* a few years ago.

The piano prodigy. You were like, my grandma's heroine. She's always wanted me to play a musical instrument well."

"I'm sorry," I say. "And I'm sorry I didn't tell you who I was sooner."

"We get it," Hollis says. "You're allowed to be who you want to be. Even if that's a different person than who you were before."

"I just wish you'd felt like you could have trusted us sooner," Iris says. "Not for our sake, but yours, if that doesn't sound patronizing. I hope not."

I don't have any words. I just pull them both into a hug that I desperately need right now. I couldn't have asked for kinder, better friends. I'm a little teary as I pull back from them.

"The program's investigating the party," Randolph says. "Looking into who was there. They're going after Wolf's list."

"Do they know who Wolf is?" I ask.

Hollis's sober. "I don't know, but we all may get sent home. Getting kicked out was the one bright line our parents didn't want us to cross."

"We're not getting sent home." I crumple the canceled brochure and toss it into the trash. "We need to talk to Marc."

Iris, Hollis, and I crash Marc's office as he's setting his desk phone down in its receiver. He looks very official with his huge desk, large monitor, and award plaques with gold emblems hanging on the walls. But his blue polo shirt is rumpled, and his long hair is tied hastily back in a low ponytail. His face has a shadow of stubble, like he was routed out of bed this morning before he had a chance to shave. His eyes are lost. Stunned. They come into focus only when he spots me coming through his door.

"Pearl." He rises, turning his screen around. It's the article with my photo. "I didn't realize you had a brush with the media earlier this summer." A mug of tea sits on his desk, forgotten.

"I'm sorry, Marc. I should have told you. But I was afraid you'd pull the plug on me, like the Apollo program did."

"I wouldn't have pulled the plug. I'm a journalist, and I see this all the time. Girls and minorities come under fire in the media way more than others."

"Really?" So weird to hear myself as part of a statistic. There's an injustice being done. I wish Julie and Apollo had understood this context. But it's comforting that Marc does—I'm not alone.

"The bigger problem is they tend to self-cancel and withdraw," Marc says. "But I hope you don't. I want you to know I have your back."

"Thank you, Marc," I say thickly. Words aren't enough to capture how much his support and understanding means. I lift my chin. "I'm not retreating anymore. We have to issue a statement countering that article, everything it's saying about Loveboat."

"I'm afraid it's out of our hands. The board has stepped in."

"The board?" I exchange a glance with the twins. Loveboat has always just been Loveboat. The kids. The teachers. The director. Never had I imagined a governing board overseeing the whole place, but of course there would be one.

Marc runs his hands down his face. He looks like he's aged about twenty years. "The board's been concerned for many years now about the overall reputation of the program." He takes a deep breath. "They're considering shutting it down."

"Shutting down Loveboat?" I'm stunned.

"But it's an institution," Iris says.

"Iconic," Hollis says.

"What reputation exactly?" I ask.

"The hookup culture. Disrespecting the locals, although fortunately, most of that is in the distant past."

"And doesn't represent all of Loveboat. Not by half," I say.

Marc doesn't answer. I wipe my sweaty palms on my thighs. This is my fault. If I weren't here, that juicy piece probably wouldn't have even been written—my notoriety and my choices brought negative attention to the program, the same way I did to Apollo. And it's about time I acknowledge that notoriety so I don't do any more damage.

"I'm so sorry, Marc," I say. "I've messed things up for so many people."

"It's not just you." Marc sits on the edge of his desk and looks out the window. "If you read the comments on that article"—he purses his lips—"some people are unhappy that the head of the program is queer," he says. "They think that's why there's been so much debauchery this summer."

"What the hell?" I sputter. "You had nothing to do with the party. You've probably been the first program head to manage to keep people from sneaking out."

"I hate to admit it felt like a punch out of nowhere," Marc says. "Taiwan was one of the earliest in Asia to legalize gay marriage. But there are still a lot of misconceptions out there."

"There were way worse summers than ours," Iris says. "Girls came back pregnant. Eighty guys broke into a shop."

"A kid drowned one year," Hollis says with a shudder.

"I appreciate your vote of confidence, but those headlines

don't really make a strong case for continuing the program," Marc says mildly.

"You modernized everything," I say. "You improved the curriculum so we actually learned. A lot. They're so lucky to have you." Julie didn't stand up to Apollo for me, and no way am I letting that happen to Marc. "We'll tell them. All of us."

"Count us in," Iris says, and Hollis nods vigorously.

"Thank you," Marc says. "But I can't ask you to defend me. The board won't listen to a bunch of teenagers anyway. Especially ones caught at that party."

He stands. "And I'm afraid this party's coming to an end. If you guys will excuse me, I have to meet with the staff now."

"Wait." I grab his arm as he moves past me. "You just said yourself we can't withdraw when the world comes after us."

He pauses, his gaze on the floorboards. "This is a different situation."

"It's not," I say stubbornly. "We're not letting Loveboat go down on our watch."

He smiles, but it doesn't reach his eyes. "That's awesome, Pearl. Thanks." Then he leaves.

The board won't listen to a bunch of teenagers. But we have to try. Because not engaging is just quitting, and I am not a quitter. I search for Ethan and Kai. I find Ethan first, playing billiards with a group of guys. He straightens warily from the pool table, cue stick in hand. His face is like a young god's. Perfection, that's Ethan. But it's only a veneer. Strictly on the surface.

"Wolf." I hold up a CANCELED flyer. "We need to talk."

The other players cast curious glances at us. Ethan drops his cue stick and makes a beeline for the doors, taking us outside into a side courtyard. A group of kids are leaving a smores firepit, taking a bag of marshmallows with them. I step toward it, gazing into the flickering orange flames.

"You're a freaking hypocrite," I say.

"How did you know?" He looks terrified. Probably that I'm going to leak it.

I hold up the flyer. "You couldn't wait until we could talk before defacing a thousand brochures?"

"I tried calling," he says. A trickle of sweat rolls down the side of his face. "I couldn't get through."

"Possibly true. I was in China for a day."

"My manager warned me not to do the duo with you in the first place," he blurts.

That's a surprise. All this time we were making music, he had a devil on his shoulder, whispering. It shouldn't hurt, but it does. I was honest and up front with Ethan about everything. He was anything but.

"Why did you agree to perform with me then?"

He looks away, his mouth working. "I like you, Pearl. I've liked you for a long time, maybe even since Carnegie Hall. My manager was never happy about me performing with you because of your TikTok blowup. But I did try. I did want to play with you."

"So you were almost brave."

He winces. He runs his hands through his hedgehog hair. "Pearl, people like you and me are barely clinging to the ledge. We don't have the luxury of making mistakes."

"*You* made the mistake that got to me! *You* threw that party!"

"And you attended," he shot back. "Look. Reputation matters. I'm sorry you've wrecked yours. I can't let you wreck mine, too."

In him, I see the me I'd have been if the TikTok debacle didn't force me to reconsider my entire life. And I'd still be stuck in that world—on probation, if not condemned—if I never met Kai or played on the street or found out my great-grandmother's story and her pipa. And I don't want it. Any of it. I've seen truth and courage, and Ethan and Julie and Apollo are not that.

"I refuse to believe we have that little power," I say. "We have power when we band together. And that's what we need to do if we're going to get anywhere."

He doesn't answer.

"Why did you come on Loveboat, Ethan? Was it really just to blow off steam? Or did you have this niggling doubt about whether the life you were living before really leads to happiness?"

"I came because I was on the brink of burnout. And your blowups. I see them and they make me tired all over again. I've worked so hard to make sure that never happens to me. And you just—" He gestures. "Kaboom, Pearl." He's almost pleading. "It's exhausting to play defense all the time."

"So maybe we should play offense for a change. Like, did it ever occur to you that I went 'kaboom' because they expected an angelic, hardworking Asian American girl, and instead, got an actual human being? Because that's what Loveboat has been for me. Learning how to be human."

"Are we finished?" he asks stiffly.

I'm angry, but I mostly feel pity for him. He's hiding all his own imperfections, the things that make *him* human, behind a mask he can never take off. "You know, maybe the reason you're always the matchmaker and never the love interest is because you don't actually let yourself be you. No one knows the real you. Just the airbrushed Ethan Kang."

His cheeks grow pink. "I did let myself be myself—with you!"

"And then as soon as it got hard, you undid it." I set our crumpled flyer in the flames and watch it char into ashes. "I'm not going to out you. I'm not the threat. I get that Ethan Kang can't be seen at parties in the dark, let alone be the mastermind behind it all. But it was pretty convenient *I* got nailed and you didn't. Just saying."

As the last glowing ember fades, I turn and walk away.

"Pearl?" Ethan calls. He's watching me, his beautiful brown eyes tormented. "If I was braver, would we have worked out?"

"But you're not," I say, and take the stairs two at a time into Chien Tan.

Mom texted, so I call her back. Her bright-eyed face blooms on my phone. She's at her hotel in Tainan, looking more relaxed than I've seen her in years. Her visit with her high school friend must have gone really well and I'm glad.

"Hi, Pearl," Mom says. "I hope it's not too hot in Taipei."

"It's good here," I say. "I'm in some trouble, but I'm getting myself out of it."

"What trouble?" Mom says, alarmed. "From that museum?"

I wish I could reach out and give her a reassuring hug, but I do the next best I can.

"No, it's more negative press. It comes with the territory of being a little famous. I know I can't make you not worry, but

356

please try to trust me. Everything will be okay. Oh, and I've split with Julie. I can't update you at the moment, but I'll fill you in later. Okay?"

Mom sucks her cheeks in a moment. "I want you to be happy, Pearl," she says. "So whatever you think is right, we will support you." She pauses. "Your father would feel the same way. We love you."

"I know. I love you, too." I hang up with her, feeling something stirring inside me. Maybe love isn't that rush of adrenaline I felt with Ethan in the dark and in the light, but something deeper.

More like what I feel with Kai.

The thought surprises me. Deeper is what Kai is. He makes me dig into every part of myself. What music is and what it means to me. My career. My family. And even my place in the world. It's not smooth and easy, and there's definitely room to put on padded gloves when we duke it out. But I come out a better person on the other side.

I text him next. **I still have your music bag and pipa. Can we meet?**

I wait. Three moving dots appear. Then his answer. **Yes, of course.**

I wait for Kai in the lobby, studying the jade dragon's exquisite scales in his display. The convenience store is overflowing with kids pumping boiling water into bowls of instant noodles. I realize I haven't eaten all day, but the thought of food only makes my stomach constrict.

"Pearl." A low voice right behind me sends a shiver up my spine. Kai.

Somehow, even when he's not moving, I still feel a deep pulse within him. Like he's connected by his feet on the ground to the heartbeat of the earth. That's Kai, too. He IS rhythm.

But right now, he looks like he's slept as well as I have, which is not at all. He comes over and takes my hands, holding them gently. I squeeze them back, and we just stand there, holding hands, letting the hurt of the past few conversations slowly ebb away.

"Did you meet with your doctor yet?" I finally say.

"Not yet." He looks down at his hands in mine. "Tomorrow. How was your trip?"

"I didn't get my great-grandma's pipa. But I found something better," I say. I fill him in on the village visit. The school of pipa that my great-grandma founded. The music of the village that is still ringing in my ears. And then I share a story from my younger days.

"When I was eleven, my music progressed to the level of complexity where it was hard for me to read it. Partly because of my dyslexia. It was a challenge for me. All I wanted was to make the music as beautiful as I knew it was meant to be. And when I did it, my dad and mom and I would celebrate with a cup of hot chocolate—and don't tell me hot chocolate is for the colonized, because I'm never giving that up."

"I'll never ask you to give up anything, ever. I never should have. No one should tell you what to play. Not your manager. Not fucking Apollo. Not me."

My heart swells painfully. Of course that's all true. But I

needed to hear him say it. "Everyone else has told me what to play," I say. "Even my brand was dictating what I had to play—a brand for a person I wasn't even sure I wanted to be.

"And along the way, I lost sight of the most important part. But you brought me back to it. The music."

"My problem was I wanted everything. And when I couldn't have it, I decided I should have nothing. But the truth is, I want so much. I want to play again. I want you to be the big star you deserve to be and take over the world, which includes the East and West, last I checked. And get to play the music that you want." He pauses. "And I'm arrogant enough . . . to want you."

I swallow hard. "That's not arrogant."

"Life's like a beast coming after us. And there are some people who make you want to stare it in the face and fight back with everything you have in you. You are that to me."

I squeeze his hands. I'm glad. Too glad for the words to come at first. "I want to see you back on a stage again," I say finally.

"I'd be lying to say I wasn't jealous of Ethan at first for having it all. Music, the stage, *you*—"

"He doesn't have me," I say firmly.

"Okay," Kai says. He's so obviously trying not to smile that I want to smack him. Then he releases my hands and sets his fingertips to his dragon display. "But honestly, now? I realize, I don't need to be on a stage. I'm never going to be a star on a Theramin. But that's okay with me. I'm liking where I'm at. Still figuring it out but moving in the right direction. You, though. You *should* be on a stage."

"I don't *need* to be on a stage either. What I love about

performing is knowing the sounds I'm making have the power to make people less alone, or heal some of their hurt, or make their joys bigger. Make people *feel*."

"I still don't love how people go gaga for Western over Eastern culture," he adds.

"I know, but that's not me." I smile. "We don't always see the world the same way . . . but I want to keep trying to see it from your point of view."

A text chimes on my phone. **Ms. Wong, this is Cathy Yeh from Teen Vogue Asia. I know things must be rough with the recent press and I understand from Mr. Kang's manager that he's no longer participating in your show, but my preference is to decide for myself what the story is. I want to confirm I'm still planning to meet with you after your show, assuming it is still on.**

My mouth falls open. Bless Cathy Yeh, whom I've never met but now can't wait to.

Yes, I reply. **It's still on.**

Not everyone is a troll. Or Apollo. *Teen Vogue* is still in. And I'm going to try to tell my story, in my own words, and to be transparent about who I am.

"What's that?" Kai asks.

"My interview with *Teen Vogue*. I know that might seem like I'm doing it to get another Western stamp of approval, but I actually love them. If I was profiled by an Asian magazine with as big a reach and with pages as gorgeous, I'd be just as happy."

"Would you?"

"Yes," I say firmly.

"Good," he says. And that's that.

And then I realize what I need to do to help save Chien Tan.

"Come on," I say, grabbing his hand. "I need to talk to Marc again."

I find Marc coming out of a meeting, shoulders slumped in defeat. I'm out of breath as I hurl myself at him.

"Marc. We need to rehabilitate the Loveboat reputation," I say.

"What do you have in mind?" Marc asks.

"The board won't listen to a bunch of teenagers, but maybe they will to a bunch of superstars. The Loveboat alumni are *incredible*. You know it yourself. They're doctors, lawyers, singers, members of Parliament. We can do a Loveboat performance with as many of the alumni who want to join us. Have them share what this program has meant to them." I smile. "Ever told me that all the rebelling that goes on at Loveboat made everyone better leaders. The proof's in the pudding."

"I like where you're going," Marc says. "Loveboat should be a safe place to make mistakes."

"And that's the Loveboat story to share with the world," I say. "We've got *Teen Vogue*, and even if they don't help us, we've got social media."

"I thought you were off it for good," Marc says.

"I'm going to use it on my own terms," I say. "We'll tell our story. We'll ask the alumni to spread the word. I'm done with laying low."

Apollo pulling the rug out from under me caused even more damage than I realized. They made me insecure about my own judgment and power. *That* was the biggest cost.

And now I know better. I have privilege, and this is what it's for. Not to cling to my fragile spot in a program created by other people. But to blaze my own path.

I sweep my arms wide, embracing all of them, all of Chien Tan, all of the world.

"I want to bring in *everyone*," I say.

Marc bows with a flourish of his hand. "Ms. Wong, our stage is all yours."

32

CALLING ALL ALUMNI! You may have seen the recent press damaging Loveboat's reputation. For those who are local or able to fly into Taipei, we are inviting all alumni and friends to join us for a celebration on Saturday, August 11— and to show the world the truth.

Over the next few days, comments flood into the open invitation I post on the Loveboat alumni chat group. People take sides, ranging from: I'm embarrassed to be associated with that program. Please remove me from this list. To: Loveboat transformed my life. How can I help? Even among the alumni there's a range of perspectives. And that's okay. We're not all the same.

I send a mass invitation to the whole campus—including Ethan: Come one, come all. I email the alumni I know personally through Ever, and I text Sophie a very special invitation:

Sophie, I want to show the board how amazing the alumni are. Will you consider holding your fashion show on campus for our celebration? I understand if you can't, if it's risky to your business. And short notice.

Just a bit over two weeks away. But Sophie answers lightning fast. **Count me in**.

The next week and a half literally fly by. In Mandarin classes, we wrap up with common phrases for special occasions and—sniff—saying goodbye. Kai and I show Maya pictures of the seven-headed horn and other unique instruments we saw at the Renmai Museum, and we end up spending a few days exploring them, finally returning to our music series to finish off with the flute-like dizi.

On a Wednesday, our last day of class, we bring out all the instruments Maya has in storage for a no-holds-barred jam festival. At the end, I strike the gong with the padded mallet, letting its reverberations echo in my bones and through the room. As I lower the mallet, Kai gives me an amused look.

I beam at him. "It actually takes very little to make me happy."

Iris and Hollis are deep in a huge argument when I return to our hallway. Huge for them means sitting face-to-face, serious as they talk it through, instead of flitting around their stove.

"I've always wanted to model," Hollis is saying. "But nothing was ever the right vibe."

"I'm just worried about you," Iris says.

"I *am* careful where I need to be. And this celebration isn't it."

Iris folds her fingers together in her lap. "All right," she says. "I'm not standing in your way."

I realize I'm eavesdropping, so I knock on their door frame.

"Everything okay?" I ask.

"Yes, of course," Iris says. She looks to Hollis, who smiles.

"I'm in Sophie Ha's fashion show! Thanks so much for introducing me."

"Amazing," I say, and give them both a hug.

We devote the last few days of the program to setting up our show. Iris and Hollis have gotten a small budget from Marc to set up an international food festival. Another dream come true for them. We talk nonstop as we work to transform the campus courtyard. Iris and a few volleyball players remove the net. They build wooden booths out of scrap lumber.

"Kai, bro, can you give me a hand with this table?" asks a guy.

Kai instinctively looks down at his hands, and I swiftly intervene. "I actually need Kai's help with the program. Would you mind asking Randolph?" I hand Kai the clipboard. "Can you organize all the performers in a lineup that makes sense?"

He smiles with relief. "Happy to," he says.

I work next with Marc and the campus facilities manager, Tai, to figure out seating and online streaming. We decide on two parts to the program, starting outdoors and moving indoors to the auditorium. Hollis designs our new pamphlets and folds them into a zillion paper cranes. I unfold one, smiling at the medley of images of campus life, including Hollis and Iris nerding out over their stove:

LOVEBOAT, TAIPEI
join us for a fashion show, concert, and
international food festival
Chien Tan Campus
11 August
4:00 in the afternoon

Over the next few days, RSVPs roll in from all six—seven!—continents, including a very cool alum from 1990 stationed in McMurdo Station in Antarctica. I write up my statement responding to the article and beg Ever and Sophie, Iris, Hollis, and Kai to read it. They make very few changes.

"It's authentic," Ever says. "That's what matters." She hugs me. "I'm proud of you. This isn't easy."

Kai's doctor appointment goes down as well as we could have hoped. After he showed his doctor how the Theramin worked, his doctor gave the okay to play, as long as they monitored his hands carefully. "I'm sort of glad for the excuse not to practice so intensely," Kai tells me. "I think it makes the music better, to have breaks. From any instrument."

"That's a huge insight," I say. "You should share it more. Share more in general."

"Me?"

"You have a lot in you besides the music," I say.

The day before the performance, Hollis and Iris bake a cake shaped like a G-clef, frosted in inky black with white sprinkles. It's the sweetest thing I've ever seen. They take about ten thousand photos of it from every angle.

In the courtyard, Kai and I set up arrow signs pointing to the auditorium. He grins at me. "If you told me a year ago that I'd be working my butt off to save Loveboat, I'd have thought you were high on something."

I smile back, then catch sight of Ethan coming up the driveway.

Of course, he's deceptively angelic in his white tennis shorts and polo shirt, holding a Shiseido shopping bag in hand. He averts his eyes when he catches sight of me and Kai.

"Wait a moment, okay?" I say to Kai.

I walk over to Ethan and hand him one of Hollis's flyers. "You sure you won't change your mind about joining us?"

He looks longingly at the crowds of kids setting up booths. "I can't."

"Fine," I say, and I mean it. I start back toward Kai.

"Something happened," Ethan blurts.

He holds out his iPhone, opened to Instagram. It's two photos of him, side by side, one gorgeous, the other an overexposed, bad hair day photo from maybe six months ago. Posted not by him, but by Anonymous, about an hour ago.

Just another pretty face.

The post has gone viral. Thousands of barbs and hate.

Faker.
Pretty boy.
Must have been a really ugly baby to need that much plastic surgery.

A few threads click for me. Those scars under both sides of his jawline. That he's gotten such a glowup beyond what I'd remembered. Ethan had plastic surgery. And even though it's not anyone's business but his—Anonymous has made it everyone's.

"Oh no," I say. I wouldn't wish this on him or anyone. "I'm so sorry, Ethan."

The before photo isn't bad, actually. Considering Anonymous the Coward must have found the worst possible one out there. Ethan just looks like a different boy. And now he meets my gaze with those gorgeous eyes that, I realize, couldn't look sad if he wanted them to.

"I was tired of people making fun of the slant of my eyes. And my flat nose. My manager said Asian guys couldn't become stars because they didn't have the right look. He wouldn't represent me unless I got my eyes enlarged. My nose done. So." He gestures at his face. "It sounds . . . immature. But it's what I've had to deal with. And it's helped. I have more confidence now than I've ever had."

"This is why you came on Loveboat," I say. "You were hiding out, too."

"I've been off the grid since January. I needed time to heal. And I wanted some time to pass before people saw me again."

I can't help feeling sad for him. How he's felt he's had to conform—to the point where even his face isn't his own—to what his manager thinks the establishment wants of him. When really, what I've learned this summer is that there is a power in being ourselves that no one can take from us.

But reality is so much more complex than what can be served up on social media. Hollywood is full of performers who've gotten plastic surgery. And how much better have I been? I put on a mask so I could do what I wanted in the dark, instead of being brave enough to be myself in the light.

"We're all afraid that something that's not the way we want it will keep us from our dreams," I say. "Not just being Asian American. But like, I wish I was taller. My sister wishes she'd started dancing seriously sooner. But those things can't stop us. Because no one and no situation are perfect. And there's not just one path forward."

He hastily sweeps a tear from his cheek. "I've never been allowed to *not* be perfect. When I had a stomach bug as a kid, I vomited before I reached the toilet. My mom made me clean it up until the bathroom was spotless, even though I felt like I was dying. I felt so much shame, but in retrospect, throwing up was normal for a sick little kid."

I'm glad he's starting to open up, letting the real Ethan out. I hope he continues. There's nothing more I can say, but I squeeze his hand.

On his phone, Instagram has a prompt for me: **Add a comment**.

"There's more," Ethan says. "After our talk, I confronted my manager. You were right to be suspicious. He all but admitted he leaked the Party in the Dark story to the press, along with your photo. Word was leaking about me being there, and he wanted to drown that out."

I narrow my eyes at him. "How did he find out I was there?"

Ethan hangs his head. "I mentioned it. I'm so sorry. I didn't know he would weaponize the information against you. If I had, I never would have told him. Pearl." He gives me a pleading look. "I just wanted to be someone different this summer."

It's yet another betrayal, even if he wasn't the one who threw me under the bus. But I'm glad he came clean about this. He could have kept it under wraps.

I close out of the Instagram account, declining to comment.

"You're still invited to perform with us tomorrow," I say. "Maybe try something new and different—and messy. Why not? You pay your manager, not the other way around. Just come backstage and add yourself to the roster if you change your mind."

33

Bang! Paper confetti explodes over the campus as the alumni pour in on foot and by car. They range in age from college kids to an elderly couple with silvery hair, holding hands, one of the spotlight features in our show. They are everywhere: touring Kai's art exhibit, checking out their old dorm rooms, and marveling over the updated cafeteria, which is serving steaming bamboo baskets of everything delectably sweet and savory.

It's a sweltering Taipei afternoon. Thank God for Sophie's mulberry silk dress, which is pleated in all the right places and keeping me cool. At the top of the entrance steps, I nervously tug on my silk gloves. As it turns out, they're even better with the pipa than the piano, where half the show is watching your hands dance over the strings.

"Have any of the board shown up?" I ask Marc, who has stepped up beside me. They are one of our key targets. But with or without them, our show will go on.

"Two so far." He points out a gray-haired man shaking hands with a woman, both sweating slightly in their navy suits. I'm tempted to suggest they take their blazers off, but we have bigger fish to fry today. "I'm expecting all twelve to be here."

"Great. Getting them to show up is half the battle," I say. "Can you introduce them to some of the alumni? Maybe Mr. Carey Lai. He just got here." A venture capitalist who'd flown in from Silicon Valley for work here and came by to show support. "The more amazing Loveboat alumni they meet before we begin, the better."

I head toward Iris and Hollis and their food festival, featuring seven booths of snacks: Korean hot dogs, musubi, crispy shrimp burgers donated by Cé La Vi, salted egg chips, giant fortune cookies courtesy of the recipe from Rick, and even fresh coconut milk in their shells. The twins struck a compromise on their ongoing menu debate—try all their favorites at this event and see which ones were most popular.

"Welcome to Street Snacks of the World," Hollis says, handing me a tiny cup of boba tea. "Lactose-free, so you can try it all!"

"You've brought in enough food for the continent," I say. Iris takes a pen from between her lips and jots a note on a pad of paper. "Hey, Iris, I just realized I haven't seen you smoke in ages."

"Oh, I quit," she says breezily. "I've got a new addiction." She clinks her tiny boba teacup against mine.

Then Sophie Ha breezes up the driveway, arm in arm with Xavier Yeh, like a royal couple. She's decked out in a stunning red gown, her waist marked by a wide black belt with an oblong gold buckle and the skirt cut at an asymmetrical angle. Gems catch the light, setting her on fire. Xavier's dressed all in black, down to a smudge of charcoal on his fingers. A crowd of alumni squeal and fall into their arms.

Just behind them is Rick in a crisp white button-down over

army-green pants, shredding a bouquet of magnolia blossoms with nervous thumbs. He spots me, and his eyes go devastated. "I shouldn't have brought flowers." He waves them helplessly. "They're so cliché, and she's not really into them . . ." He drops the heavy bundle into a trash bin with a thump.

"I didn't say anything," I protest, giving him a hug. "Those were beautiful."

"Is she here yet?"

"Soon. She got back from Fujian this morning and is coming with my mom from their hotel."

His face is greenish with nervous anticipation, and he looks toward the flowers like maybe he's reconsidering.

I shake him gently. "I'm keeping faith, Rick. You guys will figure this out."

He squeezes my hand. Then Sophie swoops me into a hug. "*Love* being back with everyone! Why haven't we done this sooner?"

"I've never actually set foot on campus since we left," says Xavier. "Even when we picked up Pearl."

"That's because you two don't need Loveboat anymore," says their friend Debra, with a mock tragic air. A group of Ever's and their friends are crowding around us. "Six years later, we're all still single."

"This might be the last chance for people like me," Benji says.

"Then some matchmaking is in order tonight." Sophie winks at me and makes a beeline for Xavier's cousin, Victor, who is walking in with Sophie's friend, Emma Shin.

Just beyond them, a white van is slowly navigating the people-crowded driveway.

"Who are they?" Debra asks.

"The board?" I ask, pressing forward.

The passenger door slides open and a group of people with cameras and leather bags press through. At the same time, a reporter with a press badge moves toward me from the lobby.

"Pearl?" she says. "Cathy Yeh from *Teen Vogue*." She straightens a pair of designer sunglasses perched on her short purple hair. She takes in the new crowd with surprised eyes. They're all wearing official badges: NBC. *Cosmopolitan. Vogue Asia. South China Morning Post.*

"Is Pearl Wong here?" asks an elegantly manicured woman, adjusting a gold choker around her throat. *HerWorld*, says her badge.

"Um, that's me," I answer, dazed. "How—?"

Sophie slings an arm around my shoulders, laughing at my expression. "I told you I'd have tons of press for my first fashion show, didn't I? Gang, meet Pearl Wong, our star. You'll be hearing from her later in the program, but maybe you can squeeze in some questions now."

I find myself shaking a few dozen hands, blinded by a lightning storm of cameras. Cathy Yeh from *Teen Vogue* looks dazzled.

"Well, looks like I made the right call," she says.

"How are you feeling?" asks the NBC reporter.

I already know who gets the first shout-out. "This might be the most important performance of my life yet." I smooth the silk of my dress with one gloved hand. "And I couldn't be more thrilled to be wearing a Sophie Ha original."

"How many viewers have dialed in already?" asks another.

"We're still a half hour from the performance," I say.

"Almost four thousand," says Marc, coming up beside me.

"And the numbers keep going."

"You're joking," I say. He's not.

As the reporters head toward the press section, I spot Mom coming around the sidewalk in a stunning green qipao, another Sophie original. Just behind her walks my beautiful big sister. Her hair is shorter—she must have gotten it cut while she was with the family in the village. Her red-and-cream toile dress accentuates the clean lines of her dancer figure. A spotlight seems to shine on her.

Rick sees her at the same time she does him. All the tension pours out of him as their gazes lock and six years between them condense into one split second. He crosses to her and takes her hand. She looks up at him, her eyes full and luminous.

"Ever, I know you didn't want me to quit my job for you, so I didn't. I've quit for myself. I'm moving to New York City for myself. To go after a girl who matters more to me than anything I could possibly do in this lifetime."

Her eyes widen. "I gave notice today. I told my artistic director I'm moving to Taipei."

"But what about your mom living in Ohio?"

"We had a long talk in Fujian. She reminded me she's stronger than I give her credit for. She survived immigrating to a foreign country and losing her husband. And with Pearl about to go to college in a year, she'll be able to visit us here for longer periods and spend time with our family. We both want to get to know them better. And visit my dad's family. There's so much I want to do out here."

He runs his hands through his hair. "Well, we're both jobless. Now what?"

They stare at each other, lost. Then both burst out laughing.

I smile at Kai, who has joined me. "Well, that went well," I say.

He's accompanied by an elegant Chinese woman in a powdery blue qipao that couldn't suit her more.

"This is my nai-nai," he introduces us. Her face wrinkles in lovely folds and she speaks Chinese to me. I answer in English. Somehow, with smiles on both our faces, it works.

I take his hand and bring them over. "Mom, Ever, Rick, this is Kai and his grandma."

Mom's eyes are a little wide as she shakes their hands. Rick pumps Kai's hand up and down. Ever's eyes are cautious, sizing him up.

"I'm so honored to meet Pearl's family," Kai says, and the nice thing about a guy who never bullshits is I know he's completely sincere.

As for me, I'm just happy to have my favorite people within hug's length.

We kick off our show with the fabulous Loveboat alumni.

Sophie's fashion runway takes over the curved driveway, as one gorgeous model after another struts between a divided crowd of guests. Her models are all different heights and body shapes and sizes. Their luxury hats and lush, daring, cozy, and comfy-chic clothes flatter each one in a unique way. Hollis sashays down in a stunning gold tuxedo dress, accompanied by Lux in a flowing black chiffon gown.

"That's my friend, Hollis!" I tell Mom as I whoop and cheer.

"She's very beautiful," she says supportively.

"They go by they/them pronouns," I say. "And yes—gorgeous."

"Oh," she says, looking confused. "They/Them. I'll try to remember."

Iris is cheering beside me, snapping photos. "For my parents," she says. "They'll be so proud."

A surge of applause. Sophie waves from the top of the wide steps just before the entrance to the main building, which is serving as our outdoor stage. A blue silk loveseat has been set up beside her.

"Thank you to our fabulous models!" she says. "Sophie is a fashion boutique with branches in Los Angeles, Manhattan, Paris, and Taipei, and growing. If you're in town, please stop by!"

She passes the microphone to Ever, who takes her place. "Thank you to the board, the alumni, the campus leadership, and my sister, Pearl, who asked me to be here today. I attended Loveboat six years ago. I have fond memories of sneaking out clubbing and even climbing over that big blue water pipe over the Keelung River. We were not the best and brightest, for sure."

Chuckles from the Loveboat audience.

"But as it turns out, the rebelling was good for us," Ever continues. "A lot of us grew up in a culture where we were taught to respect the hierarchy and rules. But coming on Loveboat, learning to rebel in a safe place—those were valuable skills. We learned the consequences of our choices. Sometimes it was disaster, but more important, usually it wasn't. In fact, in the States, as Rick Woo has said to me, it's the disruptor who turns industries upside down for the better. It's the challenger who gets everyone to the best answers. Turns out Loveboat isn't just a cultural program or a summer free-for-all. It's in the business of creating leaders. In every industry. All around the world.

"So let me introduce a few of the amazing alumni who represent the decades of Loveboat from the late 1960s, when the program first began."

A gray-haired couple from Paris, hand in hand, takes the love-seat for a fireside chat. They speak of how they met on the last day of the program and have been together ever since. Then a former counselor who is now a Taiwanese legislator gives a short talk on how his friendships with international students helped him become a leader. Dave Lu, who raised tens of millions of dollars to fight anti-Asian hate, talks about how Loveboat helped reconnect him to his Taiwanese roots and heritage.

Then Ever opens the mic, inviting all the alumni to introduce themselves. They line the stage. They are entrepreneurs, figure skaters, Emmy-nominated artists, Sabrina Ellis, a leader at Google, *New York Times* bestselling author Stacey Lee and her Loveboat husband, and the studio exec and publicist, Emmy Chang.

Then Hollis and Iris join her onstage, accompanied by a crowd of fifty kids ages two to forty. Ever hands Hollis the mic. "We're the kids of a Loveboat couple," they say. "Without Loveboat, *we literally wouldn't exist!*"

The kids wave, and the answering cheers are heartwarming. A guy begins to sing a Hong Kong pop song from the 1990s, and people throughout the crowd join in. Sophie's journalists madly take notes and shoot footage. *Cosmopolitan*'s reporter dictates into her phone, "Perhaps most surprising is that the so-called Loveboat in Taipei turns out to have been around for over sixty years . . ."

I smile. The best part of Loveboat is all right here. Friendships and kickass talent. And music. The ultimate indulgence. You can never have too much of it.

And so, I lean back in my chair and let the music wash over me.

For the second half of our program, we move the guests to the auditorium. After spending so many hours practicing here alone with Ethan, my heart feels full to see the space completely packed, with people standing in the back and seated in the aisles.

My speech is being live streamed on all the major social media channels. My backdrop is an old grand piano graciously lent to me by a local piano store. It was ready to be taken out for kindling, but I have better plans for its last laugh. I had the back leg removed so the entire piano lies at an angle, then I removed the black lacquered top and made a slide with it. Deconstructed, it's dramatic and eye-catching. And making a point. That there are many ways to come at a piano.

It's possible this speech won't change anything. It could spark more negative press and fallout. But I'm ready for it. Bring. It. On. So as the cameras begin to roll, I slide down the piano to the floor. In my arms, I'm holding Kai's pipa.

"I'm Pearl Wong, classical pianist and sometimes pipa player." Some laughter. "Earlier this summer, I posted a photo of myself on TikTok in a Chinese straw hat that my sister picked up here in Taipei on her own Loveboat trip. It's a hat that, it turns out, is worn by some of my own farming relatives in Fujian Province. It sparked an uproar from over a hundred thousand commentators, and as a result, my spot to play a piano concerto with a prestigious summer music program was rescinded.

"It was a very painful time for me. And I'm here to say social media wants to blow things up that don't deserve our attention, and ignore the things that do. But I understand now why some of the people commenting took the stance that they did. Some of you have really been wounded by harmful stereotypes. And to all of you, I'm sorry. I'm sorry I hurt you by triggering memories of racism. I know it can be so damn tiring to have to fight and explain all the time. And that we're dealing with a lot of pain. One day, I hope we live in a world where a hat really can just be a hat.

"After that incident, I found myself without summer plans. I was advised to lay low and let it blow over, so I came to Taipei for a cultural immersion. But another confession—I didn't really come here for that. I was supposed to focus on rehabilitating my piano career. But what I found instead was a pipa." Chuckles. I hold it up. "My great-grandmother played it. She faced her own trials in a civil war that chased her and her husband out of the country for years."

I don't speak about my family's village. That time was sacred and just for my family. Social media and the world doesn't have any right to it. But I do speak about what it meant to come to Loveboat. Ever had her own journey. Sophie had her own journey. And I had mine.

"I came to Loveboat with one identity. Musician. I am leaving with another. Ambassador. Because I realized that's my job as a professional musician. To build bridges across divides. Whether that's between generations who don't share the same taste in music or between cultures who don't share the same instruments. Music shows us that there's something of all of us in everyone else. And my job is to help bring that out."

I also don't address the Party in the Dark article. Because that's also my choice, and I've learned to honor that. My ability to stand up here before the world speaks for itself.

"And now for the fun part," I say, as the applause fades. "Introducing our performers."

The next hour is pure magic. A trio from our Traditional Chinese Music class plays erhu and dizi, with Maya on her zither. Zao the counselor plays a searing French horn solo. One after another, Loveboat alumni take the stage, from a professional cellist with the Singapore Symphony Orchestra to an a cappella chorus to one of Ever's friends, Spencer, on drums to a trio of counselors singing karaoke.

Kai moves onstage to a foot drum with a double-necked bass and his laptop on a stand beside it. He rolls up a sleeve of his black button-down shirt, untucked over skinny mauve pants with daring chartreuse polka dots and a matching pair of Veja shoes. We talked it over, and decided his Theramin world premiere and comeback would be stronger played solo. Now I listen with pride as his hand gestures naturally shape its eerie wails, making us all wonder where the human ends and the instrument begins.

As he takes his bow to applause, his eyes find me. I rub my

fingers together. *How are your hands?* He flashes me a thumbs-up.

And then to my surprise, Ethan walks on next, in a fitted black leather jacket covering a red shirt. A second guy takes the drum set, another the keyboard, and two amp up their electronic guitar and bass. They're all in printed black, with a splash of red per person—a scarf, a pair of shoes. I lean forward eagerly. What's he doing?

Ethan lifts his violin onto his shoulder and plays the sweet opening notes of the theme song from *Phantom of the Opera*. But then the keyboardist's fingers crash down on her keyboard, pounding out the rhythm at a frantic pace and twice the normal volume. Ethan turns his back as the others leap into an electronic rock remix, and then suddenly Ethan is back with a purple electric violin. He picks up the melody—not the straight-up line, but dark and frenetic at triple speed, twisted up with unbelievable runs and cadences. His bow whips madly over his strings as his entire body, hair flying, bends into the song.

I cheer along with Iris and Hollis and the crowd.

"I had no idea he had this in him!" I say as the band bows to thunderous applause.

We are down to the last three performances. As the Lim village pipa class assembles onstage, I take the microphone.

"This summer, I fell in love on Loveboat . . . with a lute." The audience chuckles. "And that is what you are about to hear next. Those of you not from Asia may not be familiar with the pipa. I'd never heard of it until this program. It's been a staple of Chinese music for two thousand years, originally coming from Central Asia through trade on the Silk Road. Other cultures have their own lutes: the Arab oud, the Indian sitar, the Persian barbat.

Some famous players include Apollo the Greek god, King David in the Bible, musicians in medieval courts in Europe, and Wu Man in the present day. As an ambassador, I couldn't be more thrilled to play an instrument that is played all over the world, no matter what it's called."

I introduce my great-grandmother's pipa class, and they fill the auditorium with the thrum and twang of two dozen pipa voices. Great-Uncle plays next, a solo from an expert that gives me a taste of what my great-grandma's playing must have been like.

When he finishes, the musicians don't leave the stage. Instead, they all look at me, just off stage. Great-Uncle beckons me to join them. I walk uncertainly on with Kai's pipa in my arms.

To my surprise, the two oldest musicians present me with a cloth-covered pipa case. Great-Uncle opens it to reveal a worn pipa. Its varnish is scratched in places and one of the frets has been so worn down it can barely be called one. But the strings, when I pluck them, ring sweet and true.

"This pipa belonged to your great-grandma," Old Uncle says. "We heard from your sister and Mr. Ai that the museum wasn't able to return the blue one, so we tracked this one down in the village. It was her pipa until the day she passed away. It's not as fancy as her performance one, but it's seen many years of love and use and is quite serviceable."

Kai is at my side, grinning, ready to take his pipa back. I had no idea this was in the works, but he obviously did. I hand his pipa over and reverently take my great-grandma's into my arms.

"I tuned it for you," Old Uncle says.

When I pluck the first notes of my song, I feel their timbre deep in my chest. Her pipa feels exactly as I'd hoped—like coming home. I play the song Kai helped me prepare: "Ambush from All Sides." It's so fitting. We *were* ambushed, but we prevailed. Not with a concerto and an orchestra behind us. But by playing as ourselves.

I play a modified Mozart sonata next, another of Dad's favorites.

When I finish, the applause shakes the floor beneath my feet. I take a bow, several bows, but the applause keeps going. It moves from scattered to structured, everyone clapping to a steady beat.

"Encore! Encore!" Iris yells, and the audience picks up the chant. But I'm not playing on my own this time. Reaching out to both sides of the stage, I invite the performers to join me. Then I strike the opening notes, Kai chimes in with his beatboxing, and everyone plays. It's a messy, muddled free-for-all. And a smashing success.

We are attacked by bouquets of flowers that make me sneeze. We spill outside onto the lawn and a whole crew of us line up our forearms under the sun: almost a hundred arms, all different shades from milky white to chai to chocolate to ebony. Another hundred photos are taken.

"Pearl, your social media is blowing up," Ever says.

"It doesn't matter," I say. "I'll shut down my account in a few months. I just want to let our message stand for a while."

"It's blowing up in a good way. Take a look."

She shows me her phone screen. My follower count has shot into the hundreds of thousands. #SaveLoveboat. But there's more.

"Lute lovers around the world are following me!" I can barely believe it, but there they are, excited by my little performance and offering to help me get our pipa back. Between them and *Teen Vogue*, who has the exclusive full story, Renmai can rest assured they haven't heard the last from us.

"And people say a pipa's obscure," Ever says.

I smile at her. "You could argue it's one of the most widely played instruments in the world."

"Amazing," Ever says.

Sophie gives her own interview to reporters and the BBC interviews the twins. "Our menu runoff was inconclusive," Iris reports. "We realized there isn't one perfect menu. People's tastes are always evolving. Ours included."

"So we're going to keep evolving, too," Hollis finishes.

An international music manager I met earlier takes my arm. "Pearl, a word, please?" Another manager finds me, then another, and another. I didn't know they'd be here. "We heard you'd be performing something unique," one man says. "And you did indeed. I would love to represent you. You on the pipa, you on the piano, it's a powerful combination."

I'm dazed as, one by one, they offer representation. One even addressed the TikTok blowup as something to lean into. "Let's take the trope back," says a hard-charging gal Ever's age. "If I'd been representing you, it wouldn't have gone down that way." They make offers to Ethan, too, for a new brand, a new image.

"I hope you're considering," I say to him. "Because that was one amazing offensive if I ever saw one."

"I want to be myself," he says. "Tonight was the first step."

Invitations to play at concerts in Moscow, Dubai, Lima pile

on. I understand why Julie has always said it's important to meet other people. You find out who wants to do the same things. You find your tribemates.

"What does it feel like to be famous?" asks a young girl.

"Like a responsibility," I say truthfully. "A big one. I'm honored to carry it for as long as I have it." As my great-grandmother must have done as well.

The girl skips off to hug her mom. "She answered me!" I hear her say.

Kai and Great-Uncle have taken a seat on a stone bench deep in conversation. To my surprise, Great-Uncle wraps Kai in a hug.

Mid-hug, Kai catches my eye and joins me. "What are you smirking at?" I ask.

"Your face."

"*My* face?" I point to it.

"You wear all your feelings on it. It's sort of priceless right now."

I try to frown, but I can't. "Like how?"

"Like—" He opens his eyes wide and lets his mouth fall open like a kid coming face-to-face with a candy shop. *"I'm in love."*

I punch his shoulder. Not so gently. "I have never looked like that."

"Yeah, all the time!"

"I give up. What were you and Great-Uncle talking about?"

"My hands." Kai spreads them, palms up. "He knows a Traditional Chinese Medicine doctor who specializes in repetitive stress injury. He'll put us in touch."

"That's wonderful, Kai!" I fling my arms around his neck, earning an *oof*, forgetting I'd just punched him.

He smiles as I pull back. "In the meantime, I'll lean in on teaching at the community center. I sort of seem to have a knack for it."

"*Definitely.*" I twirl my fingers against his chest, the pipa technique he's helped me perfect, pretending to pluck his heart strings.

He covers my hand with his, smiling. Letting me feel the steady rhythm of his heartbeat.

"I saw you getting mobbed by managers," he says. "Make sure I introduce you to mine before you make a decision. She's had my back for years, not just through my RSI, and she knows the pipa world."

"Thank you," I say. "I hope she won't mind that my Chinese is still terrible."

He laughs. "You have a long career ahead. Plenty of time to keep learning."

Hollis and Lux join us, sharing a pineapple cake between them. "Hey, gang, don't look now," Hollis says. "Moment of truth."

Across the courtyard, Marc is deep in conversation with the Loveboat board. We slip closer. Marc's hands are clasped respectfully behind his back. The mood is focused. Serious. Then Marc shakes everyone's hands with both of his. They clap him on the back.

"What just happened?" Iris asks.

I smile. "We just saved Loveboat."

"Pearl!" Mom calls, hurrying toward me. She looks like she's about to faint. "Your sister and Rick are over by that rock over there. Come with me."

34

Ever leans against the iconic rock with Rick gazing down at her. They're cocooned in their own world, oblivious to our crowd quietly gathering around them. I slip between elbows toward them until I'm within earshot.

"... both been so afraid of the other making a sacrifice and regretting it one day, we didn't give ourselves a chance to *not* regret it," Rick is saying.

"So I have something very important to ask you." She gets down on one knee, holding his hand in both of hers. Rick's eyes widen, and an impish smile touches her lips. "Will you change your last name to Wong?"

With his free hand, Rick opens his little blue box to reveal the diamond set between two sapphires. "My last name is cooler." He slips the ring onto her fourth finger, his voice rough with emotion. "Objectively."

"True." She admires the ring, letting it catch the light. "So we could be Woo-Wong."

"I'm in for it all. Come here, you." He reaches for her, then stops, concerned. "Did you say yes?" he asks. "Just confirming."

She laughs. "Yes-Rick-Woo-I-will-marry-you!"

Her black hair flies out as he scoops her into his arms and spins them both. By the time her feet reach the ground again, they're locked in a fierce kiss.

Beside me, Sophie sighs gustily. "To each their own happy ending." She tucks my hand securely through the crook of her arm. "Xavier once asked me how he could let me know he was here for me. And I asked him to just show me. It's what he's done for the past six years. I told him I didn't need anything more than that."

"Watch out for the seven-year itch," Debra warns.

Sophie smiles. "We're good." She holds out her finger, displaying a stunning two-carat diamond. Then lays a gentle hand on her stomach. "We're expecting, actually."

Hours pass before I get to spend a few minutes with Ever. Kai and I and all our friends have cleaned the campus into better shape than when we first arrived. Ever walks into the lobby with her new ring sparkling on her finger and her dress mussed. Her slightly disheveled hair frames a sly smile.

I hug her. "Everything's perfect now," I say.

"No, it's imperfect," she corrects me. Like Sophie, she threads my arm through hers and we walk to the lily pond. "Something else I needed to realize. Relationships aren't a ballet routine. We won't ever have a perfectly executed one with never a hurt feeling or regret. And that's why it will be wonderful."

"I'll miss you," I say. She and Rick will be here in Taipei and I . . . will be everywhere.

Her eyes are damp. "We'll chat, we'll visit."

I smile. "Life doesn't stand still. Like music. You have to hear it in the moment or you miss it. It makes for a good way to live. Always listening."

She ruffles my hair. "There's my wise little sister."

From behind, Sophie flings her arms around our shoulders. "We're going over to Cé La Vi. Drinks on us. You two coming? Friends invited."

"Rick and I are in." Ever gives Sophie an affectionate hip bump.

I catch Kai's eye as he signs the cover of someone's journal. "Thanks," I say. "But I have plans. Rain check?"

"Of course." Sophie gives me a citrus-scented hug and heads off with Ever.

I rejoin Kai, waiting patiently for him to finish signing flyers.

"I came up with a name for your song," I say when he turns to me.

"Oh yeah? I'm nervous. Lay it on me."

"Something dramatic, like the other pipa songs we've been playing. 'Ai Dazzles the Canon.' It's fitting, right?"

He cocks his head, considering. "Not feeling it."

"Ah well," I say. "I'll keep trying."

I smile and pull my purple beret onto my head, and we walk up the driveway toward the street. The moon is full and bright and the night alive with the rumble of cars and motors and, in the distance, the wail of an accordion. I feel at peace, like a lullaby is playing inside me.

"We've come a long way this summer," I say. "I'm glad we're friends."

"We can't be friends," he says firmly.

"Why not?"

"I like you too much, and that will always get in the way of a platonic friendship."

"Oh," I say. We can't be platonic friends.

I could get on board with that.

"I have a confession." Kai's hand finds mine. "On the train ride to Tainan . . ."

My heart. "You said you were dreaming."

"I *was* dreaming. About a moment like this one."

The accordian playing in the distance is incredible. We stop under a banyan tree to listen. A cool breeze passes between us and I turn to Kai. The streetlamp highlights the edge of his jaw, and I lift my hand to his cheek and he lays his own warm hand over it.

"You said you fell in love with a lute on Loveboat." His voice is suspiciously husky. "Did you find anything else to love?"

I tip my head back to gaze into his warm brown eyes. "You said I get a *look* on my face when I'm just . . . happy. Is that why you thought I was hitting on you when we first met?!"

He smiles. "I'm still sorry about that. The truth is, you were just so . . . beautiful and just *there* all of a sudden. And geeking out over a pipa with that LOOK. So yeah, I was thrown."

"Well, just to set the record straight, I'm definitely hitting on you now."

I rise up on my toes, and he bends his head. His mouth is warm and gentle, but my hand tightens around a fistful of his thick hair, pulling him deeper into me. The lullaby is over, shoved aside by a firestorm. Kai's lips travel down my neck and skim my collarbone, and I feel his kisses all the way down into my toes. He comes back up to find my mouth, and we kiss as the moon waxes and wanes and the seasons roll from winter to spring to the heat of a Taipei summer night.

We both want more than we can give under this tree with traffic passing us by. But at last, he pulls back. His palm glides down my cheek, and I press myself into its warmth. We hold each other, catching our breath, feeling the uneven rhythm of our hearts beating together. His fingertips skim down my back, tracing my spine to my tailbone and back up again.

"Boba? Or hot chocolate?" he asks finally. "I know a place that has both."

I smile up at him. "Then that's the one."

Joining hands, we round the corner into the Shi Lin Night Market, into the conversations and the sizzling of meats and clinking of coins, and lose ourselves in the music of Taipei.

Acknowledgments

I wrote this novel on three continents: Asia, Europe, and North America, including California, where I make my home, on a book tour through Ohio, Pennsylvania, and Chicago, in Taipei during quarantine and on set for the film during downtimes, and wrapping up in Vienna, Austria. I am deeply grateful for how my times abroad have given nuance to and informed the way I look at identity and life in America.

All mistakes in this work are mine. This Loveboat book, and the series, would not be what they are without these key people. My heartfelt thanks:

To my incomparable agent, Joanna Volpe, and her team at New Leaf Literary. You are truly a modern example of leadership, not only as a woman-owned business leader but through the thought leadership you bring to the world, author by author, book by book, film by film.

To Kristen Pettit, my brilliant editor. The Loveboat series would not be what it is without your unfailingly keen insights. Thank you for championing these books and launching them in such a big way into the world.

To Tara Weikum for taking on the Loveboat world, and to the teams at Harper—marketing, publicity, copy editors, administrators, assistants, sales teams, graphic designers; my cover illustrator, Janice Sung, and letterer, Jennet Liaw, and art designer Corina Lupp; and to all who've worked on translating these books into different languages. So much work and love goes into bringing a book into the world, and these books would not exist without you.

To all who have brought the *Loveboat, Taipei* story to life on-screen. To the film cast and crew, for our own Loveboat experience together while we shot in Taipei. To Ashley Liao, Ross Butler, Nico Hiraga, and Chelsea Zhang, thank you for taking on these characters, and for knowing them as well as I do. Ashley, you told me on set you wanted Ever to have a ring on her finger by the end. Well, here it is. To Janet Hsieh, Cindy Cheung, and Julie Liao, I'm thankful for you.

To my beta readers and story sounding boards, who have all left their mark on this novel: Sabaa Tahir, Anne Ursu, Judy Liang, Cathy Yardley, I. W. Gregorio, Trinity Liang, Jenny Duan, and Eileen Tucci. A. M. Jenkins, my fairy godmother. Joan/Hungry in Taipei for the food recs. To Jay Xu, executive director of the Asian Art Museum in San Francisco, for our conversation on provenance and your example of integrity. To my composer kiddo for your thoughtful musical insights throughout the writing of this novel, and for taking me to Vienna, Austria.

To my family, for every precious moment of our shared lives.

And to the One who transcends all cultures.